In Gathering Shade

In Gathering Shade

Shades and Shadows Book 2

Natalie J. Case

For all of those who suffer from discrimination and the systematic belittlement of the other *among us, whether that other is skin color, gender, faith, sexual orientation or some other factor beyond their control, with the hope that we can find a way to fully embrace all of our kin as one.*

Chapter One

"I am told that a Shade has no soul and cannot be saved, however, my superiors have instructed me to extract information from you, so that more of your kind can be hunted and killed before they can corrupt those whom God loves."

The colonel liked to hear himself talk, Mason had learned, but when he was talking, Mason was less likely to be beaten, forced to swallow salt, or any of the other torments they had laid on him in the days he'd been their prisoner. Mason was once again in the center of the cell and under artificial UV light, his arms up over his head so that he was swinging from his chained wrists.

"Today we are going to explore your healing more." He held up a knife and Mason swallowed. Up until now his injuries were largely superficial, at least the external ones were. Internally, he wasn't as sure. The prisoner called Alaric had used his fingers to make him to throw up the salt each time that Shallon forced it into him, but his stomach was starting to feel like it was ripped to shreds. His ribs were painful and the little bit of self-assessment he'd managed in the dark between torture sessions told him that it wouldn't take much to make the cracked ribs into true breaks.

His shoulders screamed and his wrists were bloody, and the amount of water he'd been given was barely enough to keep him alive, even if Alaric had tried to supplement it with his own water and, at least once, blood. It was probably wrong to wish the bastard tormenting him would just cut him too much, too deep, and spill all the precious blood in his body into the dirt and let him slide into the dark.

Instead, the cut was shallow along his collarbone, just enough to make him bleed. Mason hissed, closing his eyes against the new stinging pain. "There now, that seems a simple enough matter. Show me this healing."

His blood was thick and slow, hot against his skin. Mason licked dry lips with a drier tongue. "Can't."

"Come now, I'm told–"

"Colonel."

Shallon turned away from Mason to the soldier in Battalion blues at the door, dipping his head to listen as the man whispered in his ear. He looked up sharply, snapping at his men, and they all left the cell without another word.

Alaric was at his side instantly, hands sliding up Mason's arms and fumbling with the bindings that held his hands.

"Leave him." Bryan said, pushing past them to the door. He pushed on it, but it didn't budge. "Riley will be here any minute."

Alaric pulled on the chains holding him without responding. Mason closed his eyes and tried not to move.

"Alaric, we have to go *now*."

Mason opened his eyes. Alaric's blond hair was tickling his cheek and suddenly his hands fell free and his body crashed to the ground. The door was open and for a long moment, Mason couldn't understand why.

Being deprived of darkness and liquids had taken a toll on him, and his brain was sluggish, slow to realize what was going on. Unless he got some darkness and some water soon, he would not be able to recover.

"Can you stand?" Alaric's voice was strained, and he could hear the fear and the tension in his tone. In the hall beyond Mason could hear men moving and Bryan was gone, leaving the cell was empty now but for the two of them.

"I… maybe." He offered his hand for help up and Alaric took it, hefting as Mason pushed off the floor.

"Lean on me. I'll get you some cover soon, but we have to move." Alaric's arm slid around his waist, tugging Mason's body close as Mason managed to make his feet move.

Mason tried to focus as they went, but everything was moving very quickly around him. They followed Bryan's back and after a few minutes, Alaric ducked them into a blessedly dark room.

"Stay here. I'll be right back." Alaric pushed Mason up against a wall and was gone.

In the distance thunder rumbled… or maybe it was an explosion. Men were shouting, and there was a spattering of gunfire before Alaric was back. "Here, put these on." He shoved clothes at Mason, peeking out the door. "It's daylight outside. You need to cover up."

Alaric helped him figure his way into the clothes, belting the too-big pants tight and shoving his feet into boots that weren't too bad, if a little tight. "We have to hurry. Bryan and Riley are making sure our path out is clear. Take this." He shoved a canteen into his hands. "It isn't much. I'll try to get us more before we're outside."

Mason tilted back his head and poured the water into his mouth as Alaric checked the hallway again. "Okay, come on."

Mason stumbled as they hit a set of stairs, but Alaric hauled him back to his feet. Bryan was above them, telling them to hurry. "Out the door, to your right, Riley's holding the fence. East and then north."

Bryan shoved another canteen at him and Alaric tugged Mason out the door. They made the fence, where a grinning young man with spiky white-blond hair was holding open a cutaway piece of the fence and a big automatic gun. "Let's move, Cassandra's illusions aren't going to keep them busy for much longer."

Alaric pushed Mason through the fence first, then followed. They started running once they were out, or as close to running as Mason was capable of. Bryan and Riley caught up, and Mason thought there were other people around them as well. The sun beat down on them without mercy and the ground was baked sand and rock, radiating the heat and light back up at him. Mason guzzled water from the first canteen, dropping it when it was empty and he tried to keep from falling.

He didn't know how or why, but it was pretty clear that this was an escape orchestrated with outside help, and for whatever reason Alaric had inexplicably chosen to take Mason with them. He wasn't about to complain. Even dying all dry and burnt out in the desert was a better way to go than in the hands of a man like Shallon.

They ran across the barren landscape with little for cover, and he was sure they would be recaptured. He stumbled as he tried to look back over his shoulder, nearly going down before Alaric's hand fisted in the loose fabric of his stolen shirt and hauled him up again. "Don't worry about behind us," Alaric said. "Just focus on moving."

Mason clung to Alaric, fairly certain he wouldn't survive this mad race from captivity, but not quite ready to let go of the hope that he might. The desert sun was no place for Mason, and he knew Alaric felt guilty for dragging him through the daylight, could feel the guilt in the air around them, but Mason wouldn't have survived had he been left behind.

So, they ran. Alaric pulled him down into a ditch of some kind, offering him the meager shade cast by the opposite wall. Mason couldn't slow his breathing and his skin was hot and dry.

Alaric leaned in, his hand on Mason's face. "You still with me?"

Mason nodded, lifting the last canteen with shaking hands. "Need liquid, dark."

"I know. Catch your breath. I'll be right back."

Alaric disappeared and for a long moment, Mason wondered if he would bother coming back. He gulped at the water, but it wasn't enough to make a big difference. He dropped the canteen from numb fingers when it was empty, closing his eyes and leaning back against the wall of the ditch.

His breathing was slowing down, his racing heart calming some. Alaric reappeared, ducking down so that his blond head wasn't visible over the top of the ditch. He held up another canteen, pouring its contents over Mason's head and shoulders in an attempt to cool his already burning skin, which absorbed the water almost immediately.

"You have to keep moving." Alaric said. Mason nodded, though for the life of him he didn't think he could. "The others have bought us some time, but eventually those guards will figure it out and head back this way." Alaric tugged on his arm and got him standing again, but Mason's knees buckled and he went down again. Alaric went one knee beside him. "We aren't far from a series of caves where we can rest out of the sun."

Mason's skin was red and had that clammy feeling that comes of too much light and not enough water. But they were out of water. He couldn't figure out why Alaric was still with him. Mason made a show of trying to push him away. "Go with your friends."

He shook his head with a sad sort of smile. "I could help you." Alaric offered tentatively, holding up a knife he must have stolen in their escape.

Mason's hand stopped him. "No." He shook his head. His mouth was dry and his hands were trembling. He squinted up at the sun. He knew he was well over half way to sun-shock, and soon, he would no longer be able to move.

"You need fluid." Alaric insisted, the knife in his hands, the blade on his skin. "And blood is all the fluid that I have to offer."

Mason closed his eyes and fell back against the hot sand wall. "Save yourself." No matter what help blood would be, it wouldn't be enough, not without darkness and water.

Alaric only responded by slicing into the meat of his palm and holding his hand to Mason's mouth.

Mason couldn't, he pulled away, shaking his head. He'd never taken blood that way, never tasted any but his own, but his body craved sustenance and the blood was wet on his lips. He licked his lips and when Alaric pushed the hand back to his lips he couldn't stop himself. He raised a hand to cradle Alaric's and held it still as Mason sat up, his eyes fluttering open to meet Alaric's, vulnerable and ashamed as he drank.

The taste of it was familiar and he flushed with memory of blood in his mouth in the dark cell. Alaric had done this before. Mason closed his eyes and pushed his hand away. It wasn't enough, but he wouldn't take more.

Mason's breathing was rapid, echoing the sped-up beat of Alaric's heart. "Let's get you to shelter." Alaric said, standing. He helped Mason up, let him lean into his side.

"You shouldn't have done that." Mason whispered, his voice ravaged and raw.

Alaric smiled and brushed dirty hair out of his face. "I know. But my grandmother told me it was bad luck to let a Shade die in the sun. She'd skin me alive if I left you here just to save my own skin."

Mason looked up at him, his eyes an impossibly blue reflection of the sky above them. He forced himself to smile, remembering his own Nana. She'd never abide him leaving someone behind to die either. "Can't have none of that then." Mason's head dropped onto Alaric's shoulder, letting his concentration fall on keeping his feet moving toward the shelter Alaric told him was ahead of them.

It seemed to take forever, the dry ground and glaring sun making it difficult for him to judge distances, but then Alaric turned them and set Mason's hand against a rock while he ducked in under an overhang to make sure it was safe. Mason groaned with relief as Alaric guided him in, bending him and holding him to get into the shallow cave made by large boulders that seemed to make a wall.

With the dark, his body began to cool almost immediately. The cave was just enough to get them out of the sun, to let the dark sooth his skin, and with that something of the pain would start to drain away, or so he hoped. He'd never been in this kind of dry before. It was bad, and he knew it.

His lips were cracked open and his flesh was red. There wasn't a spot on his body that didn't hurt. Mason closed his eyes and willed the pain to subside. He didn't dare expend the energy to attempt to heal. As his breathing calmed and his skin cooled, he could sense beyond himself. There was water nearby. It called to him and he knew he only had to wait for the sun to go down before he could search it out and let it restore him to something closer to himself.

Alaric's body blocked more of the sun near the entrance to their hiding place. Mason hadn't even realized that he hadn't come inside with him. "Bryan and Riley sent a signal. They made it into the car, they should be safe enough to make it the rest of the way."

Mason didn't ask how they signaled or what car, just nodded, fighting back the grimace of pain as his ribs shifted and his sun-burnt skin cracked. He swallowed around the dry, raw feeling in his throat and told himself it would only be a few hours at most.

A deeper shadow fell across him and he looked up to see Alaric sliding to his knees beside him. Alaric held up his hand with its barely scabbed over cut, and the knife.

"No." Mason pushed his hand away and tried to sit up more. "Save your strength." His voice was a rasp of heated sand on stone.

"Let me help you," Alaric said almost urgently.

"You should go be with your friends. I'll be fine. Just got to make it to dark."

Alaric looked at him like he didn't believe him, like he knew that it was mostly false bravado talking. "You'll die if you don't get some more fluid. What you took before was nowhere near enough."

He sliced over the old wound and there was sand in the bright crimson of the blood, but Mason almost couldn't help the way he licked his lips. He could almost feel the ease of pain that would come with the blood, nutrient rich and wet. "No." He shook his head. "I swore...never..." It was a promise he'd made to himself, made to his Nana. A Shade could live richly on the blood of others, and the old lore told stories of a time when Shades did just that, surviving on blood and water. It was what his body needed.

He closed his eyes and turned his head away, but the smell of the blood followed him and there was a warm wetness on his lips. "Please let me help you." Alaric whispered.

He couldn't breathe for the scent of it, his body seizing with the need for it and though he was sure he meant not to, Mason opened his mouth and took it in. Alaric's heartbeat roared into his head, his life, his breath filled his senses. Mason was aware of all of him. He could sense worry and taste pain... from the cut, from being manhandled by the men who captured him and... something more, something... Mason forced himself to pull back, licking his lips and thanking Alaric with a nod of his head.

Alaric smiled at him and moved to sit beside him. It was too close in the small space, but Mason just closed his eyes, determined to get what rest he could because he knew the dark would mean more running.

He slept fitfully through the afternoon, chasing and being chased through dreams of people he couldn't fully see, and he woke with a start, unsure of where he was for a moment. His head was on Alaric's shoulder, Alaric's arm around him, holding him, his body protecting Mason's from the mouth of the cave.

Over Alaric's arm, Mason could see that the sun was well on its way to down. He could feel the pull of the water even more strongly. He stirred, tried to figure out how to get up without waking Alaric, but before he'd moved more than an inch or two, Alaric's blue eyes were staring at him. "Going somewhere?"

"Sun's down." Mason rasped. "Water."

Alaric nodded. "You know where it is?"

"North." Mason pointed as Alaric sat up.

"You were going to go without me." It wasn't a question. Alaric pushed himself up, keeping his head bent as he moved to the mouth of the cave.

"Don't need me slowing you down." Mason followed him out of the cave.

"In the dark, I'm going to be the one slowing you down." Alaric said. He slipped his arm around Mason's shoulders to support him and started them walking in the direction Mason pointed.

The night was cloudy, blocking out the soothing touch of the moon, but Mason followed the pull of water. They kept the wall of boulders between them and the facility they had escaped from. By the time they had reached a dirt road that ran alongside a hill, it was little more than dark spots on the horizon.

Even with the sun down, Mason's skin was uncomfortably warm. He had no idea where they were, or where they were headed, aside from the fact that there was water within reach.

He pointed into the trees and Alaric helped him climb the incline, pausing to rest when Mason's body screamed at him. "Any idea how far this water is?" Alaric asked, holding up the canteen he had apparently kept.

Mason pointed and pushed off the tree. He stumbled a little and Alaric was right there, keeping him upright and moving. Eventually, they found a small stream. It wasn't much, but Mason was tugging at his clothes and wading in as quickly as he could.

It was only knee deep, but cold, and running at a decent current. He went to his knees, then lowered as much of himself as he could into the water. Alaric picked up the clothes Mason had dropped, folding them and setting them near the stream on a rock. "I'm going to have a look around."

Mason nodded, not actually caring beyond the pull of the water, the cooling and energy it offered. He breathed in deep and dunked his head, blessed cool surrounding him, caressing him.

He needed to heal the ribs before they caused more damage, but this wasn't the optimal situation for that. Maybe he could find something to wrap them with instead, at least for now.

As he surfaced, Alaric was returning, a decided purpose in his steps. He squatted beside the stream. "If you can, we need to move. There's a patrol headed our way."

"How far?" Mason asked, already standing and stepping out of the water. Mason felt Alaric's eyes on his naked body and blushed, turning away. There was something in that look he couldn't place, couldn't help but feel on display. His skin absorbed the water quickly, leaving him damp, but able to dress.

"I figure twenty minutes, they'll be here." Alaric handed him his pants, then held his shirt. "We can find you more water."

Mason shoved his feet into the boots and nodded, still pulling on his shirt as they headed up stream. They followed it part way, then crossed it to continue west. "I take it you have someplace in particular in mind?" Mason asked when Alaric stopped to look up at the stars, then squinted at the landscape around them.

"Into the mountains. We have a camp."

The sound of men talking startled them both and they ducked behind rocks. Two men moved along the far side of the stream, calling back to others that were further away, then splashing, and they were moving again, back downstream.

They waited until they couldn't hear the men, then a little longer before they came out of hiding and headed out again. "I've never hiked it from this direction." Alaric said. "But, if we keep going that way," he pointed northwest, "we should get to a little town called Brettles close to morning."

"It's going to get cold." Mason said.

"Yeah, we'll get snow soon." Alaric agreed.

"So, what then, after we get to this small town?" Mason asked.

Alaric sort of shrugged. "You have somewhere else you need to be?"

"I have obligations."

Alaric nodded. "Your job?"

"You could say that." The night air was definitely cooler than the hot sun they'd escaped into and would get downright cold as they got higher into the mountains. It was refreshing at the moment, helping to draw the heat from his skin, but his wounds were wearing him down and his steps slowed. "You know, I need to say thank you for getting me out of there, but I'm not sure–"

"I am." Alaric said, smiling at him. "I'm sure." He pushed his hair back behind his ears, his smile fading a little as he looked around them. "I should probably tell you that even though we escaped, it isn't likely they'll stop looking, even after we get back to camp."

"Which still doesn't tell me why you were prisoners back there, or why you're hiding in the woods."

"Let's just say that the 8th Battalion doesn't like us very much, and leave it at that for now."

Mason was sweating already, his heart racing. He needed time to soak and heal. "I'm just going to slow you down," he said, stopping. "You should point me toward the nearest water and get moving."

"And leave you to get recaptured?" Alaric smiled and Mason's stomach tightened, feeling his face flush with heat he didn't understand. Alaric's hand was warm on Mason's shoulder. "Come on, we should keep moving."

Chapter Two

Bryan was grateful to reach the turnoff to the camp. They hadn't heard from Alaric, but he was counting that as a good sign. Had Alaric been recaptured, he would have sent out a distress call.

The last Bryan knew, Alaric was laying a glamor over the cave where he'd hidden the Shade, protecting them from anyone that might come snooping. Bryan had argued that they needed to keep moving, but Alaric had just sent Bryan and Riley on without them.

Bryan and Riley had fled on foot down the dirt road to the car Riley had hidden, making better time than Alaric would with a wounded Shade in tow. They had planned to wait there, then get in as close to Alaric's position as they could and get the two of them into the car. But he was close to exhaustion, and Riley was done before they reached the car. He'd outdone himself in the effort to coordinate the "attack" on the facility, stretching his abilities to the breaking point.

Bryan had taken over as soon as he was capable, and he had to admit he was impressed. The younger man had never shown much in the way of what Bryan would consider useful gifts, but he'd managed remarkably well. Bryan tracked Cassandra and her team until they gave the all clear.

It wouldn't take long after that for the men chasing them to realize they'd been tricked and circle back to the facility to find the trail of their escaped prisoners. They figured it out a lot faster than Bryan had hoped, and with his energy shot, once he'd hidden them from the second snooping patrol, he knew he needed to get them out of there, leaving Alaric on his own with a burned-out Shade.

Alaric was wounded too, though he'd pushed Bryan away when he'd tried to get a look. It was obvious as they ran though. Alaric had banged himself up pretty good when he'd fallen on the tracks, and the less than gentle handling by the 8th Battalion hadn't helped any.

Bryan left Riley sleeping in the car and back tracked to a spot where he could see the long, low line of boulders that eventually ended up against a cliff. He'd reached out to let Alaric know they were leaving and that they would try to send back men to help. Instead, Alaric told him they'd get back on their own through Brettles. Bryan didn't bother trying to argue. He used the last of his strength to bolster Alaric's glamor and erase the tracks that led to their hideaway, making it seem as though the footsteps carried on south.

He'd been able to hold the illusion for a few hours, until he was too far away and stretched too thin, but by then any patrols would have followed the false trail.

Beside him, Riley stirred as they pulled off the paved road. "We good?"

"For now." Bryan opened the wards and drove up the rutted path, stopping when they reached the inner gate. Riley got out and opened it, letting Bryan drive through before closing it again. The wards went back up behind them, and Bryan eased them up the road.

The night was frigid this far up the mountain and their breath plumed on the air as they got out of the car. Emily waited for them on the porch of the bunkhouse, a blanket pulled tight around her.

Sahara was with her, those sharp eyes watching his every move. He wasn't sure if it was flattering or irritating. He stepped up beside them and silently they all turned to go inside. There was a fire burning in the fireplace, pushing back the chill, and Cassandra, Matthew and Jacob were waiting there.

Bryan turned to Emily. "Everything good?"

She nodded. "Sahara was the first back, but Mila and Matthew weren't far behind. Where's Alaric?"

Riley stepped closer to the fire, warming his hands. Bryan sighed. Emily wouldn't like the fact that they had left her son behind. "He's somewhere behind us. He's got an injured Shade with him, had to stop to wait for nightfall. Said he'd come through Brettles."

There was a ruffle of unease through the group at the mention of the Shade, and Bryan was not inclined to disagree with them, but it wasn't his place at the moment. That would wait until Alaric was back in charge of his people. "We should double the sentries. Keep an eye out. Not sure how bad the injuries are. They might need help."

Jacob nodded and set off to set up the watch, the group scattering at the same time.

He held up a hand and brushed his mind to Emily's shields, letting her know everything was fine. "Alaric was fine last I saw. He's got a little bit of bruising from a fall, but other than that, he's fine. They never even got around to questioning us."

"You were there for nearly a week." Emily said, her face clouding.

"Yeah, day after they caught us, they got their hands on a Shade."

She glanced past him at the others still milling about. "Is that what has you bothered?"

"They've never been nothing but trouble." Bryan said with a sigh. He didn't have Riley's ability to see into the future, but he didn't need it to see that Alaric wasn't thinking with his upstairs brain. Bryan had seen it in his eyes. "Alaric insisted we bring him with us when we escaped. He's pretty banged up."

"And Alaric wouldn't leave him behind." She nodded. She knew her son better than most. "Thank you, Bryan."

"There's a lot to do, I should go update the map, and—" Her hand on his arm stopped him.

"That can wait. You and Riley both need some sleep."

"I don't need a mother, Emily," Bryan said.

She smiled at him. "Apparently, you do, Bryan." She reached for Riley, taking his arm and walking the two of them toward the back door. "I can hold down the fort a few more hours. You two get some sleep."

Bryan couldn't hide his yawn, and so grudgingly agreed, trudging out to the spot where the trail broke. Riley kept moving off to the right at the fork, lifting a hand in farewell as he trudged uphill toward the cabin that he shared with Emily and Alaric.

Yawning wider now, Bryan headed down the trail that led to the cabin he had claimed as his own. It was smaller than most of the others, little more than a single room, but it suited him and no one expected him to share it with anyone. The dark deepened as he headed lower into the valley, and his steps slowed. The skies above him were brilliant with stars, and it was quiet so far from civilization.

Ahead of him the shadows moved and he stopped, his eyes working to figure out who or what was waiting for him in the dark. The silhouette of a large cat, something like a lioness, separated from the brush, moving toward him slowly. Gold eyes met his. The cat looked at him like it wanted something.

Bryan shook his head and resumed his walk. He could feel her behind him, even as he climbed the stairs to his cabin door. "Come on if you're coming. I'm tired and I'm cold."

He held the door and watched the cat bound up the last two stairs and into the cabin. He stepped in behind her, pulling the door closed. He kept his eyes averted and crossed to the wood burning stove, building up a small fire. By the time he'd finished, Sahara was a woman again, wrapped in the quilt from his bed.

The room was dark but for the light of the small fire in the open stove. "Did you want something?"

She tossed dark hair over her shoulder, her eyes still mostly gold as she moved closer. "You were a prisoner for a week."

He raised an eyebrow and crossed his arms. "And?"

"And, I know what they do to prisoners, especially ones that they think can help them."

Bryan moved across the room to the table to light the lantern sitting on it. "They didn't even try. That freak adept didn't even travel with us, just drugged us so we couldn't whammy our way out."

Her eyes sparkled and the corner of her mouth tugged upward. "Is that the technical word for what you do?"

Bryan shrugged. "Wasn't my word. One of our guards used it." He turned to lean back against the table.

"And I'm just supposed to take your word for it that they didn't break you and turn you into a killer?" Sahara asked.

Bryan knew she had every right to suspect him. She had been a prisoner longer and had been subjected to untold amounts of torture as they tried to find a way to break her psyche and reprogram her to work for them. Bryan knew the highlights. After Emily had read Sahara and the girls she'd shared the information with Alaric and him.

"I guess you have a point." He met her intense stare. "What did you plan to do about it?"

She took a step closer. "I have my own ways of reading people."

"Is that so?" Bryan asked, slightly nervous as she came closer.

Her eyes caught his, brown and gold and fierce. Before he could respond, her hand shot out and grabbed his groin, claws making themselves very obvious. If he tried to move, she could unman him without much effort.

He swallowed and held up both hands as a sign of surrender. "Take it easy. Like you, I'm not easy to break. And they didn't even try. They got the Shade and forgot we were even there."

Her hand tightened almost imperceptibly and her eyes searched his. To his surprise, he could almost *feel* her pressing into his shields. He had appreciated her mind the few times he'd had reason to read the surface of it. For someone who wasn't a part of his tribe, her mind was ordered and strong. He held his shields against her for a moment, then rolled them open, curious if she was conscious of what she was doing.

Her surprising mind surged, but she didn't cross the barrier into his. The cat was strong, instinct and fire. The heat seeped into him and for a moment he thought she would devour him. The claws withdrew, but her hand didn't, and her eyes never strayed from his as she leaned in closer. Her teeth caught his lower lip and tugged lightly.

Bryan knew that what they were both thinking was a bad idea, but that didn't stop him from sliding a hand into her hair, pulling her in to return the favor, nipping at her lip until they crashed into a possessive kiss. His hand on her hip brought them flush against one another, then her hands on his hips turned them, sending a chair crashing. The quilt fell to the floor, leaving her naked in his arms.

Sahara lifted one hip to sit on the table before she grabbed Bryan by his shirt, dragging him in to kiss again. He licked her lips open, then nipped at her chin, kissing and licking down her neck. Her fingers were in his hair, her hands guiding him lower.

He paused, glancing up at her. "You know this is probably a bad idea?"

Her grin was fierce. "All the best ideas are," she responded. "I just hope you can keep up."

* * *

"You're not even trying, Alexis."

She closed her eyes and tried to ignore the voice. It wasn't so much that she wasn't trying; it was more that she was trying something different than what he had demanded. Wriggling against her restraints, she re-focused and tried again.

The problem, as she saw it, was that it was impossible to concentrate with him and the doctor, not to mention the goons in the observation room watching her like she might suddenly explode. Considering the experimentation they'd done on her, it was at least as possible as anything else.

The fact that he didn't react to any of those thoughts meant that at least she'd been successful in building a wall he couldn't get around, and it was well enough camouflaged that he didn't even seem to know it was there.

Which meant she could finally start planning her escape. She bit down on her sense of victory and turned her mind to the task he wanted her to complete. Her skin slicked with sweat as she reached out for the four elements set on the table.

As usual, fire came the easiest, the candle flaring to life, the flame dancing. Water responded next, sloshing against the side of the glass. The stone that represented earth shook a little, but nothing she had could make the feather lift on the air. She gasped and let it all go, panting as she opened her eyes.

"That's it. I'm done with her. If she isn't even going to try, and we're only halfway through the procedures..." He sighed and turned his back on her. "It isn't worth my time."

"Sir, we did only complete the cycle yesterday. Give her body time too—"

"No. It's time to move on to a new subject." The Doctor removed her restraints and she shifted to sit up. "Take my daughter back to her room."

The doctor helped her from the procedure chair into a wheelchair and took her from the room. "I told him you'd need to complete the initiations to master them."

"As usual, he only listens to himself," she responded. They stopped outside the door to her room and she stood.

"Get some rest, Zero."

"Yeah, I'll do that, Doc." She let herself into the room that had been her home since her mother's death a few years before. The stark white of the walls was offset by splashes of neon orange and a verdant green that she'd painted against her father's wishes.

Collapsing on the small bed, she reached under it for a bag, pulling it up onto her lap. She rummaged through it without pulling anything out, keeping the contents hidden from the cameras. She was almost ready.

She'd need to move fast once she was. If her father kept to his regular schedule, he'd leave in the morning for his trip west. She would make her move when he was gone and security was lighter. She wasn't worried about getting out of the compound, she'd done that enough times in the past. No, her concern was not letting them catch up with her once she was out. She needed time to complete her initiation, before her father buried her memory of what he had done to her, before she forgot she was ready for it.

* * *

Raven ducked the punch meant for her head and moved to her left, reaching both hands out to grab her opponent and use the momentum of his jab to throw him to the ground. She pivoted fast, straddling over him and dropping to her knees, pinning him and getting her hands on his neck.

He tapped on the mat and she patted his shoulder. The instructor reached down to help the man up as Raven backed off. "And if your opponent is a Shade as Raven here is, that could be your death. Not just yours, but possibly hundreds of others."

She looked at the line of new recruits. They were young, handpicked by Adam Darvin out of the FBI academy: three men who clearly didn't like getting beaten at hand to hand combat by a woman, and two women who were looking at her like they wanted to tear her apart on the mat. At least this group was more competent than the last, and so far, she hadn't found any of them harboring resentments that they hid to get the position.

The door to the gym opened and she looked up to see Darvin waving her over. She jogged past the class and rounded the heavy bag. "I need you."

She nodded. "Where?"

"Atlanta. We have a problem."

"Another Shade?" The number of rogue Shades seemed to be growing in direct response to the growing anti-Shade sentiment. There had been attacks in at least three cities since she'd gotten back to D.C.

Darvin gestured into the hall and she followed. "Probably not, unless they've all gone crazy like Darchel."

"So more bloodless bodies?"

"Yeah, three so far." He led the way to the elevator. She could feel the stress in his body without even touching him.

"Have you heard from Jerah?" Raven asked as they stepped into the elevator.

"No." He rubbed his hands over his face and into his hair, ruffling the normally neat style.

"I told you California was hot."

"I know you did. You know what I'm up against." She did know. The agency didn't officially exist, and their mandate was hidden under the strictest clearance levels with their funding allocated from certain dark slush funds that fewer than fifty people knew existed.

They were quiet then until they were in his office. Darvin handed her a folder. "Here's what we have."

"What's the weather in Atlanta?" she asked as she opened the file and glanced through it.

"They are holding without National Guard troops. Police are on high alert though, and if any more bodies drop, there will be riots."

She nodded. "And I'm going there to... what, exactly?"

"Confirm that it is not actually a Shade, see if you can get any information on who is really doing the killing."

"So standard recon then. Tell me who I'm working with."

"Who do you want?"

That made her look up. The agency had been small when she started, with a limited number of agents from the scattered tribes. They had seen their fair share of losses in the last six months. "Someone I can trust." She put the folder down on his desk. "The Shifter."

Darvin scrubbed his face and for a minute she was sure he would tell her no. "Okay. He's dealing with a family matter right now. I'll have him meet you in Atlanta."

She left his office then, aiming for the residential level of the secret government facility. Raven let herself into the small room she lived out of when she was in DC, pulling the elastic out of her tightly braided hair and running her fingers through it to loosen it. She was worried about Jerah. He was too green to be thrown into the thick of this mess, and she got the sense that his inexperience went beyond the job Darvin had him doing. He was young and sheltered, not exactly the best material for an operative.

The last word they had gotten was that the caravan taking Jerah and his handler to their next assignment was hit. The charred out remains of their vehicles had been found with very little sign of the people once in them. It was presumed they had all died, but both she and Darvin knew that the 8th Battalion was under orders to try to get a Shade alive.

Her last handler had confirmed that for them before she had disappeared into a small, dark hole reserved for traitors. She had also confirmed Raven's fear that the military had been infiltrated at multiple levels, and entire squads were serving a cause other than the will of the government.

The country was headed for civil war; she could see it and couldn't understand why the people higher up in the government couldn't. The war that was coming would be messy and rip the fabric of the country. There were no neat and orderly lines to be drawn. The people were divided everywhere.

Decisive action from the President now might prevent all-out war, but he was bound up in his re-election efforts and trying to placate both sides. No one wanted to be the person who advocated for actual war against US citizens.

Which put her in the position she was in.

Raven sighed and tried to put her thoughts to the coming mission instead. The only thing worse than a rogue Shade was someone pretending to be a rogue Shade to stir up trouble. Even with the Shifter at her back, she needed to be on her toes.

Chapter Three

The night was still, quiet and cold, and a little surreal. They hiked in near silence, working their way up the mountain toward this camp Alaric had said was waiting for them.

It had been hours since they had climbed out of the tiny cave in the boulders. At least twice, Mason had tried to give his rescuer an easy out, but Alaric never took them.

Mason was unsure why, and he couldn't seem to think straight when Alaric smiled at him. It was like his brain just stopped while his heart raced. He told himself it was just because he was woozy... too much light, not enough water. He'd be fine once he got a chance to soak and work on healing himself.

Alaric changed their direction, pointing at something Mason didn't see. They had fallen into an easy sort of silence that gave him time to analyze the damage to his body, even if he didn't have the energy to attempt healing.

Two of the ribs were broken, and a third was cracked. He knew his entire ribcage was a mass of bruises, and his back probably was as well. His wrists were raw from the ropes and chains, and he had to worry about infection, at least until he could get the open places closed up. His head was better than it had been, though he imagined his face was bruised.

Mason glanced aside at his rescuer. Alaric seemed to be in his own thoughts, his eyes dark as they picked out their path. He was taller than Mason by a couple of inches, and lean. There was an air about him; he was a leader of some kind, and the others had listened to him even when it was clear Bryan would rather have left Mason behind.

His gait was a little uneven, his step a little shorter on the right side. Mason frowned, and might have tried to sense the reason, but Alaric looked at him and derailed him. "Need a break?"

Mason nodded, following Alaric to a fallen tree to sit for a bit. He hurt all over and he really wasn't sure how much longer he could keep moving without getting some water.

"Won't be long now," Alaric said, as if sensing his thought.

Mason looked up and Alaric gestured around them. "Water. There are all kinds of ponds and creeks through these woods. We should find some soon."

Mason nodded. "Yeah, I can tell." He licked his lips and figured he should maybe try once more to extricate himself from the man's care. "I'll be okay, if you wanted to—"

"In a hurry to get rid of me?" Alaric asked, grinning.

"No, I just…you don't have to…" He stuttered to a stop and shook his head. "I'll be fine." Alaric didn't respond, and they sat in awkward silence for a long time before Mason inhaled and nodded. "If I sit any longer I might not get started again."

"Onward then." Alaric pointed north, and they set out. Like before they settled into a silence that let him focus on keeping himself moving. He was slowing down, his injuries draining him, when he sensed water near enough that he wouldn't completely send them off course to get to it. He grabbed Alaric's arm and gestured to the west. "Water."

Alaric nodded and altered course, moving them through denser tree growth and up a ridge. "I don't see it."

Mason held on to Alaric's shoulder, closing his eyes and reaching out to find it. "There." He pointed down the other side of the hill. "Behind those trees." He didn't wait for Alaric, just set out down the hill. Whether or not Alaric followed didn't matter. He needed to get into the water.

In a small valley was a pond, fed by a slow-moving stream from further up in the mountains. Mason started to strip, dumping his clothes on a fallen tree near the water. He paused only long enough to lay his hand flat on the surface to make sure it was clean, then he was wading in, dunking himself quickly and letting himself sink deep.

The pond was dark and cold and Mason relaxed almost immediately as the heat drained from his body. He surfaced long enough to get a lungful of air, then went under again, his hands stirring the water around him as he focused energy toward his ribcage.

There was no way he'd heal the ribs completely in one go, but he could start the process of getting the bones to start knitting back together and lessen the pain. He kept himself submerged until he needed air, then rose and sank again. He lost track of how long he'd soaked in the cold quiet. He knew they needed to keep moving. Even though they hadn't heard pursuit in a long time, that didn't mean it wasn't still out there.

Slowly he rose to the surface, drinking as much as he could on his way up and floating for a long moment before opening his eyes.

He was half surprised to find Alaric perched on the fallen tree, watching the water with a sort of smile on his face. "What?" Mason asked as he swam toward the shore.

"Nothing, just... I... nothing."

Mason climbed out of the water, and he didn't miss the way Alaric looked him over before Alaric's face pinked up and he turned his eyes away. The water absorbed slower than it had earlier, but he still wouldn't need to dry himself before getting dressed.

"You could soak longer," Alaric said as Mason started pulling his pants up.

Truth was, he wanted to, but he knew that staying still for too long wasn't a good idea. "We should probably keep moving. I get the impression that Colonel What's-his-name isn't particularly going to like that I got away."

"You're not wrong. I got a pretty good read on him while he was distracted with you. He's a true fanatic, that one." Alaric stood as Mason bent to tie his stolen boots.

"So, let's not wait around for his men to find us." Mason said. He was starting to feel a little bit better for the water. It was going to take time to heal properly, but his head was clearer as they set out in the dark, working their way back up the hill and continuing in a northern sort of route.

Mason was just starting to feel the distant sun start rising when he paused to catch his breath, feeling Alaric's concern as he turned back to look at him.

"Town starts just a little way up. Not the friendliest folk, but we've bartered with them before. Don't like outsiders. You probably should let me do the talking."

"You trust them?" Mason asked, rolling his stiff neck until it popped. He was sweating, which wasn't good. The trees offered a fair amount of shelter, but he was over sensitive, his skin red from the exposure. It wouldn't take much direct sunlight to cause blisters and lesions.

Alaric shrugged. "They're the kind of people those men holding us would consider evil, which I realize doesn't say much."

"It's something I guess." Mason exhaled slowly and nodded. "I'm right behind you."

Alaric started walking again. The sun was almost fully up when they reached the dirt road that led into the town. Mason kept inside the tree cover as Alaric walked along the edge of the road.

Once they reached the town proper, Mason had to abandon the cover and Alaric moved them quickly to a wooden sidewalk shaded by an overhang. "Stay here. I'll poke my head in at the general store."

Mason eased himself into a chair outside what he thought was probably a tavern of some sort, breathing through the rush of pain that had come with the brief exposure. Obviously, he still had a lot of healing to do.

The town was still waking up. The single paved road was devoid of vehicles. In fact, the only vehicle he saw was parked outside what looked like a garage. There was a gas pump out front and as he watched, a man in overalls came out of the door to tug the rolling garage door upward, wiping his hands on a dirty rag.

From where he sat he could see the door of the store where Alaric had disappeared, the garage, and a few wooden houses that looked like something out of an old western. Sitting still had his body wanting to shut down and sleep. He let his eyes drift closed.

It was a few minutes before Alaric was back, his step on the wooden sidewalk enough to pull Mason up from his stupor. A sleepy looking teenage girl came with him, keys in her hand. She walked past Mason and unlocked the doors, gesturing for them to follow. Mason sighed in relief as the cool air and darkness embraced him. Like the town, the tavern was something out of an Old West movie, housing a handful of tables, a player piano with a small stage, and a long bar that looked older than most buildings in DC.

The girl led them to a flight of stairs in the back, then up to a door that she also unlocked, dropping the key in Alaric's hand. "I'll bring some food over once Mom's done with Joey."

"Thank you, Chelsea." Alaric smiled at her, his face bright.

"Pop just went to sleep, but I'll leave him a note telling him you're here."

Alaric held the door and Mason slipped inside while Alaric flirted with the girl, his eyes scanning over two twin beds with a nightstand between them. There was little else in the room, but two doors, one of which he found held a closet, and the other led into a bathroom with an old-fashioned claw foot tub.

He didn't even wait until Alaric had shut the door before he was filling the tub with cool water and pulling his clothes off. He sank into the water before the tub was close to full, closing his eyes and immediately pulling inside himself to get a better idea of how badly he was injured.

The ribs were starting to heal and he urged more energy to them, though he had little energy to spare. He was going to need to sleep before he could give it more effort. He drifted toward sleep as he soaked, knowing he shouldn't sleep in the tub, it was too deep and he could drown.

There was a knock on the door and Alaric poked his head in. "You hungry? Chelsea brought up some food."

Mason's stomach growled and he grunted. "Yeah, give me a minute."

"Take your time. She said she'd see if she could find some clothes in your size."

Alaric closed the door again and Mason eased himself to a more upright position. The water was starting to warm as it siphoned off the heat from his burnt skin. He sat a while longer with the reddest of his skin in the water.

When he finally climbed out of the tub he knew he was well on his way to healing. He wrapped a towel around his waist, and turned his attention to the mirror over the sink.

He desperately needed a shave. The swelling and bruising from the fists of his tormentors was starting to retreat but the red of the sunburn made it look worse than it actually was. His talisman lay against his chest. He still didn't know why they had let him keep it. His fingers closed around it and he inhaled deeply.

So much had happened. The 8th Battalion had killed the only man he had come to consider a friend. Bracker had been a good man. Darvin and Washington might as well be a million miles away. He was on the run with a man he barely knew, with no idea where they were going or why he wasn't trying to head out on his own.

With a sigh, Mason opened the bathroom door. Alaric was sitting on one of the two beds, eating a sandwich. Mason's stomach rumbled again. Alaric pointed at the nightstand where a pitcher of water and a glass sat beside a second sandwich. Mason sat on the bed and poured water into the glass, downing the whole glass before he picked up the sandwich. They ate in silence and by the time he was done with the sandwich and had drained the pitcher, Mason could barely keep his eyes open.

He slipped into the sheets and even though Alaric was talking, he sank quickly into sleep.

* * *

Mason woke shortly before the sun was setting, feeling a whole lot better for the hours of sleep. Alaric was still asleep on the other bed, but there was a pile of clothes on the end of Mason's bed and the water pitcher on the nightstand had been refilled.

He started with the water, drinking most of it quickly. He set the pitcher down and stretched, taking stock of the improvement in his body. The ribs were better, not a hundred percent, but he wasn't worried about them anymore. His skin was much better, still pink and tender, but at least it wasn't red and blotchy anymore. The open wounds at his wrists had closed and scabbed over, making them less likely to get infected.

His stomach rumbled as he swung his feet down to the floor and reached for the clothes. Alaric had said something to him the night before about Chelsea bringing him clean clothes.

He had to admit, even if they didn't fit any better, he'd be happy to be rid of the blue uniform pants. He pulled the new pants on and was just buttoning them when there was a knock on the door.

Chelsea was outside it, smiling up at him. "Alaric's not awake yet." Mason said.

"I just wanted to tell you the sun's almost down and Pop's got food on, if y'all are hungry."

"Thanks."

She peeked around him and bit her lip. "Just come downstairs when you're ready."

Mason got the briefest impression of another Shade as she walked away, enough to make him lean out into the hall and look around. There was no one there but Chelsea and he shook his head.

Alaric was sitting up as he came back into the room. "Sun's almost down." Mason said, gesturing out the door.

Alaric stretched, though he stopped in the middle and seemed to be favoring his right side. Mason frowned and moved closer. "Are you hurt?"

"It's nothing compared to what you had to deal with. I'll be fine."

Mason frowned harder as he crossed the room. "You should have said something." He pulled Alaric's t-shirt up, still frowning. The skin was bruised in a rough oval, deep dark black and red and blue just up from his waistband. "What did this?"

Alaric pushed his hand away and pulled his shirt down. "I took a bit of a fall just before we got caught. In fact, it was why we got caught." He rolled his eyes. "I'm fine."

"That doesn't look fine."

"It will heal. You need more water time before we get moving?"

"No, I'm better."

"Good, let's get moving. We still have a long way to go."

Mason finished dressing and pulled his boots on while Alaric used the bathroom. They didn't speak as they headed downstairs. The bar was obviously open – an old man was wiping down tables. He looked up with a grunt and ambled toward a door near the stage. "Get out here."

Alaric smirked and gestured to a table. A few minutes later Chelsea was coming out with a tray loaded with bowls and glasses and a basket of bread that she brought to them. She blushed when Alaric thanked her and Mason could almost feel her heart racing when Alaric's hand brushed hers as she handed him silverware.

"You know, I could probably make my way to Sacramento." Mason said after Chelsea had left them. He stirred his bowl of rich looking beef stew.

"You probably could, but then I'd be forced to hike all the way back home on my own." Alaric said, his voice warm. "You don't want me to get lonely, do you?"

Mason wasn't sure what to make of the man. He ate for a few minutes before looking back up at him. "Okay, give me a reason." Mason said. "One reason."

"I like you." Alaric responded, turning his attention to his own food. "And I did just save your ass back there, so you owe me one."

Mason snorted, "One what? You saying that if I come with you, that wipes out the debt?"

Alaric looked him in the eye, and for a moment, Mason wasn't sure he remembered how to breathe. The blue in Alaric's eyes was stormy and darker than he remembered and Mason felt as though Alaric could see through him, see into him. Alaric blinked and looked away. "I think trying to get out of Battalion territory is dangerous right now, and laying low until they've turned their attention elsewhere is probably safer for you."

Mason licked his lips and nodded, going back to his food because he wasn't sure how to respond. He was getting a string of mixed messages, leaving him uncertain of Alaric's motives in helping him. Though there were times when Mason thought maybe the man was flirting – sidelong glances and the stolen looks at his naked ass when Alaric apparently thought he wouldn't notice would seem to confirm that – when Mason left him the opening, Alaric backpedaled. Not that Mason was sure how he'd react if it was flirting.

Mason's experience was pretty limited, and honestly it was pretty much Liza. He'd spent his teenage years in a house in the woods with his Nana, which wasn't exactly conducive to experiencing love and intimacy. But Mason couldn't ignore the chilling words Alaric's friend had said, *"I'm just saying, don't get too attached, Alaric. He won't live long enough to be of use to us."*

Yet, Alaric could have left him to die, could have left him in the hands of their captors to face an even more uncertain fate than this. So, for the moment, Mason decided to stay with Alaric through the night, up the side of a mountain, deep into the shadows of trees older than both of them combined.

He was starting to feel a little stronger. His voice was no longer the sound of shattered glass, and while his stomach was not quite free of the salt problem, it was better with the more water he drank. He drained the glass on the table, and Chelsea appeared to refill it, her smile bright, her face blushing when Alaric thanked her.

Somehow it irked him, watching Alaric smile and make small talk with her. Mason shook his head and turned his attention to the room around him. The old man behind the bar met his gaze, and Mason was suddenly struck with the realization that he was the Shade Mason had thought he sensed earlier.

The old man seemed to be warning him off though, so Mason turned back to Alaric who was apparently talking to him. "What?"

"You ready?"

"I guess." He stood, draining his glass again before following Alaric to the door. Chelsea met them just before they stepped off the covered wooden sidewalk, handing Alaric a small bag.

Alaric smiled and thanked her, before pointing into the trees. They set out at a better pace than Mason had been capable of the day before. It was restive, kind of like coming home, a reminder of the woods and hills he played in as a child.

They each kept to themselves for the bulk of the night, stopping long after midnight as they came upon a stream. Mason stripped down and waded in, relishing the cold and the energy of a fast-moving current. Alaric scouted around the area before coming back to squat by the shore.

"Hungry?" Alaric asked as Mason came up for air.

"Yeah, I could eat."

"Take your time. We seem to be all alone out here." He backed off a bit and put the bag down, pulling out sandwiches and bottles of water. Mason dunked himself under again, letting the water help him direct the energy where he needed it most before he rose and dressed.

He sat damply across from Alaric, taking the sandwich Alaric left him. It was quiet, peaceful.

"We start climbing from here," Alaric said quietly as Mason finished his sandwich, pointing into the trees.

"How long?" Mason asked, climbing to his feet.

"Depends, we may need to find shelter again."

They walked side by side as they started up a hill, arms brushing together. The heat of Alaric's skin brought a sudden memory crashing back; the taste of Alaric's blood on his tongue, and the rush of sensations that came with it.

Mason swallowed around a sudden desire to taste him again, and he couldn't help but wonder if the pull he felt, the desire, for lack of a better word, had more to do with the blood inside him than it did with any of the niceties Alaric had bestowed on him in the short time since he'd been thrust into Alaric's cell.

But then, Alaric's first touch had been pretty intense. It was making Mason's head spin trying to figure it out, so he decided to stop trying and do like his Nana had told him, be direct.

"You gonna explain why?" Mason asked as they paused again in their long trek. Somewhere in the canyon below them their destination was laid out, near the bottom where a creek cut through, or so Alaric had told him. Mason didn't look at Alaric, but he could see him out the corner of his eye as they both looked down at the trees spread out under them.

The hills had swallowed them hours before, the trees and mountains hiding them from the sky. Even though the sun was starting to creep up from the horizon, they kept to the deep shadows, and he almost wouldn't know.

Alaric opened his mouth, then closed it again. He seemed to consider his answer for a time, and when he turned to Mason, his eyes sparkled. "I'm going to be honest with you, even though you're going to think I'm crazy."

Mason crossed his arms and waited, turning now to face him, watching his face.

"The moment I first saw you, I knew I was going to need you," Alaric said. Mason raised an eyebrow, but didn't say anything. "I knew when they caught us that I would find you there." Alaric turned away, walked to the edge of the long fall. "I'm... I can't do this without you."

"Do what, exactly?" Mason asked, moving to squint down into the shadowed valley from beside Alaric. He could pick out movement from there, small shadows among the trees at the bottom.

Alaric sighed. "Those people down there... They're my family, my... but when I saw you I knew."

"Knew?" Mason looked at him, and Alaric nodded slowly.

"I can't explain it." Alaric lifted a hand to cup his cheek and it was warm on Mason's cold skin. "I saw us when I looked into your eyes."

Mason licked his lips and lifted his eyes to meet Alaric's. The light was back in them, blue like morning skies, deep, beautiful... and he swore he could see into the man's soul. Mason was holding his breath as their lips met and was still holding it when they parted.

His face flushed and the taste of Alaric's tongue was sweeter somehow than that of water. Mason's blood roared, desire flaring, and he slid a hand into Alaric's hair to pull him back, opening his lips to the touch of his mouth, the memory of the taste of his blood singing to life inside him until he was lost inside the sensation.

It was only Alaric's need to breathe that saved them from toppling over the side of the mountain. He pulled back, gasping and they both realized how close they'd been. Mason exhaled and stepped back, pulling Alaric with him. "You okay?"

Alaric nodded and wiped his mouth on the back of one hand. "Maybe we should save that for when we're a little safer."

Mason had never felt anything like that, and okay, his experience was almost nonexistent, but his heart thundered and his face was hot and he wanted more. Mason smiled as Alaric bit his lip and blushed himself. "You let me know when that is."

Alaric grinned, sliding a hand into his and tugging him to start them walking again. "I will."

Chapter Four

Raven put one knee on the damp grass and held her bare hand over the dark stain that was all that was left after the cops had dealt with the crime scene. Behind her, Lieutenant Evan Chayton stood watching the area around him. He was uncomfortable with them this far out in the open.

The body of a kindergarten teacher was the latest in a string of deaths attributed to retaliatory killings by a Shade or Shades, purportedly protesting the increasingly violent propaganda and scattered physical attacks that were sweeping the country.

Raven put everything out of her mind but the slick stain of blood. She focused her attention on a single spot, slowly lowering her hand until she was touching the not-quite-dry, sticky blood.

There wasn't much left of either the woman the blood had belonged to or how she died, but one thing was clear. No Shade had been involved. She stood, pulling a folded piece of cloth from her pocket to wipe at the traces blood on her hand. Her eyes scanned around them, then came to rest on her escort.

"Did you get what you need?"

She shoved the cloth back in her pocket and ducked under the crime scene tape. "Well, just like the last one, this wasn't a Shade."

"Is that the good answer or the bad?" he asked, one eyebrow lifting.

"I wish I knew." Raven breathed, shaking her head. "If he is the same guy that was in Raleigh and Charlotte, he should hit again tomorrow night, before he disappears and heads to another city."

Evan looked over his shoulder at the spot she had just been kneeling over. "They said she was hung by her feet and bled out. You'd think there'd be more blood left behind."

"Not if the guy who did this wanted everyone to think he drank it. My guess is he killed her somewhere else and left just enough blood behind to make a mess here."

"Remind me again why we're doing this? I thought we were meant to be gathering intelligence to convince the president to send real troops to clean up the 8th battalion."

"I'm here because I was ordered here," Raven replied, checking her watch. It was close to midnight. They had plenty of time before morning; she just wasn't sure what more they would find.

The public park bordered on some woods. She could sense water somewhere nearby. "Okay, look, I'm going to go investigate some nearby waterways. If there are Shades around, I should be able to pick up a trail."

Evan nodded. "Need me to watch your back?"

"No, I need you to see if you can get the police to help us out. Uniform to uniform." He looked down at his decided lack of uniform and she rolled her eyes. "You know what I mean."

"I'll see what I can do. I'll check in with Darvin, relay what information we have."

Raven nodded, already heading for the trees. While having a Shifter for a partner was better than the traitor she'd had before, he was still a buttoned up, by-the book guy, and it was starting to really get on her nerves.

He was a good man, and his First Nations heritage had prepared him well for the role he now served. Very few knew him as anything other than an army lieutenant. She'd only known he was a Shifter because she'd accidentally seen his file.

Raven made her way through trees hung with Spanish moss, stretching her senses out. Eventually, she found a stream and squatted beside it to put one hand into the cool water. It teemed with life, but no sense of a Shade. She set out to follow it, hoping it would lead her to a bigger body of water.

The stream had other plans though, disappearing underground a half a mile later. She sighed and turned around to get a sense of where she was. The night was darker here in the woods and she knew it would be easy to get turned around and lost.

There was more water, but she couldn't tell if she was just feeling the underground stream running off into the distance, or if there was something else.

Raven stretched her arms up and out, trying to loosen the knot between her shoulders while she contemplated her next move. Out of the corner of her eye she spotted something in the woods to her right. She wasn't sure what it was, but she headed that way slowly, rounding an ancient oak tree.

There was a small bit of light ahead of her. Raven slowed her steps further, keeping trees between her and the light as she worked her way closer. There was a small clearing, barely ten feet across. In the mossy space between trees someone had marked out a small circle, set with stones and candles. In the center a small, a hooded figure was kneeling. Raven inched closer and she could hear words being whispered.

There was a feeling in the air like she was intruding on something private. She licked her lips and glanced past the circle into the trees beyond.

The hooded figure stood suddenly, both hands outstretched, head tipped back. Memory sparked and Raven realized what she was seeing. This was a Sage initiation ceremony, a coming of age. She pulled back instinctively. The ceremony was meant to be private, unwitnessed.

All around her the wind was picking up and light flared in the clearing, drawing her eyes back. The hooded figure was lifted off the ground, fire dancing on one outstretched hand, a water spout on the other.

Raven could see now that it was a young woman as the hood fell back from her face. There was pain etched across her features as energy arced up from the candles and stones, and the wind whipped around her, pounding the energy into her.

For the longest moment, she was suspended while her body was pummeled, then everything went still and dark and she fell to the ground. Raven was torn between going to her aid and slipping away unseen, but voices coming from the other side of the clearing, off in the trees pushed her to move.

While Sages were mostly well integrated into modern society, tolerated as part of the modern Pagan movement, Raven was pretty damn sure that anyone who found the girl would not have her best interests at heart, and she could end up in serious kinds of trouble.

Raven pushed through the underbrush, pausing at the edge of the circle, but the energy was gone and there was no barrier in place. She crouched next to the girl, reaching her hand to her face. There was nothing seriously wrong, and she would rouse on her own eventually, but Raven wasn't sure they had time for that.

She reached into the girl, pressing against the nerve centers that would wake her. Dark gray eyes fluttered open and Raven put a finger to her lips, warning her against making noise.

The voices were coming closer and alarm filled those eyes.

"Can you stand?" Raven asked as softly as she could. The girl nodded. Together they got to their feet and Raven pointed into the trees. Their movement was slow, but they got into the cover of the trees before they heard the voices again.

"She was here. The wax is still soft. Spread out and find her."

The young woman grimaced a little as they increased their pace and Raven could tell that she was hurting. No one absorbed that much power without feeling it for a few days.

"I can help take the edge off." Raven offered, lifting her hand.

"I'm fine," she responded, pulling away. "You should go. They don't even know you're here."

Raven had considered that, but the girl was young. If she was sticking to tradition for her initiation, she was seventeen, maybe a little younger. She couldn't very well leave the girl on her own to face whoever was looking for her.

"Who are they?"

The girl shrugged, then changed directions abruptly. "No one you want to know about." She pointed to the edge of a ravine where water tumbled from under a pile of rocks, down over rocks and into a pool below.

"Where are we going?" Raven asked as she followed her to what looked like a dead end.

"Somewhere they won't be able to find us."

Raven wasn't sure what she meant, but as she made another sharp turn, Raven could feel something in the air beside them.

"Watch where you step."

The trail was steep and slick with mist from the waterfall and Raven had to focus her energy on not falling. She couldn't hear the voices now over the sound of the water. They were getting awfully close to the water and then suddenly a rock wall was in front of them. The girl raised a hand and an opening appeared. Raven followed her in, feeling the opening close behind her.

"Careful, I can't light our way until we're around the bend." Her hand reached back, taking Raven's wrist and guiding her deeper into the black. When they had turned twice, she let go. Light sprang up, red and flickering, first near Raven, then around what she found to be a cavern. Torches and candles sprang to life, showing the place to be fairly cozy looking.

"It isn't much, but they won't find us here. Between the glamor and the hiding spells, we can hide here until they've given up the search."

"You live here?" Raven asked, moving away from the tunnel that had brought them in, her hand running over the carefully smooth rock walls. It wasn't huge, but it had all anyone would need. There was a makeshift bed in one corner, made from evergreen branches and a sleeping bag. The table in the center held a lantern and several books.

"Sometimes." She dropped the hooded cloak on the bed, revealing tight, black jeans with torn knees that ended in black combat boots. On top, she wore a close-fitting, black long-sleeved T-shirt. Her head was bald, and not like it had been shaved. It was smooth and clean. Judging by her features, the girl was at least partially Chinese, though her accent made it clear she'd been born and raised right there in Atlanta. "So, you going to tell me who you are?"

Raven turned to look at her, trying to determine how much to give away. "I'm Raven Ivany. I was looking for someone. Instead I found you."

"Cop?"

Raven moved past the table to a shelf that held a handful of wigs. "No. Well, not really." She turned from the wigs. "Are you going to tell me your name?"

The girl rolled her eyes and stuck her hands in her pockets. "You can call me Zero."

"Zero? That's an odd name for a young woman."

"So is Raven."

She conceded that. "My father chose it. I was born with a full head of raven-black hair. It was unexpected. Most of my family are redheads."

"Well, I won't use the name my father gave me." Zero said. She opened a foot locker near the shelf of wigs. "I don't have much in the way of food, but if you're hungry, I've got this stuff." She pulled a bag of microwave popcorn and a couple bars of chocolate from the trunk.

Raven looked at the popcorn then up at her. She smirked and put the bag down on the table, then held her hand over it. After a couple of seconds, it started popping and filling the bag.

"Neat trick."

"Comes in handy." Zero agreed, pulling one of the mismatched chairs out from the table and dropping into it. "So not a cop. What are you then, Raven Ivany?"

She came to the table, sitting in the chair opposite Zero. "I work for the federal government. I help them with… particular problems."

"You're here looking for that Shade that's killing people," Zero said, her eyes narrowing.

"Yes and no. I'm looking into it, but so far there's no evidence it's a Shade."

Zero pulled the popcorn open, spilling some of it out onto the table. "No, it really isn't."

Something about the girl's tone told Raven that she knew something about who was really behind it.

"I don't *know* know." Zero said, as if she'd said the words out loud. "But I suspect it's someone trying to goad the normals into a war with the rest of us."

"Normals?" Raven asked, crossing her arms as she sat back, taking a new look at Zero. She was a Sage, that much was obvious, but there was something more.

"The people who aren't us."

Which seemed to indicate that Zero had already accepted that Raven was something else. "Us?"

Zero rolled her eyes again. "You're a Shade, right?"

"What makes you think that?"

She laughed and rubbed at her forehead. "Anyone ever tell you that you think loud?"

"Do I?" Raven pulled herself back internally, raising up shields she seldom used unless she was dealing with a Shadow. "Oh."

Zero got up to pace. "Yeah, so there's that. Shadow on my father's side. My mother was the Sage."

"And that was your initiation?"

She rubbed a hand over her bald head. "Yeah. It kicked my ass harder than I expected."

"I meant what I said, I can help take the edge off the pain."

She shook her head. "I'm good. It's part of the process." She stopped suddenly, whipping around toward the entrance. "Shit."

"What?" Raven asked, standing.

"We need to go."

"Why?"

"They brought in a tracker. He's found the start of the maze." She grabbed a black wig and pulled it onto her head, then grabbed a worn looking messenger bag. With the wave of a hand, the torches and candles went out and Raven was frozen in the dark.

"Zero?"

"Yeah, I've got you." A hand closed on Raven's wrist and she let Zero lead her, not back out the tunnel, but toward the sound of the waterfall. "It isn't far, but we have to go down and we'll come out near the pool."

The dark was nearly absolute and under normal circumstance, Raven would have relished it, but not when she had no idea of the footing and a sense of urgency brought on by not knowing how close the enemy was.

Her foot slipped, but she caught herself. The descent was steep and Zero was moving fast. Raven imagined she could hear their pursuit, but she knew it was unlikely. The roar of the water crashing against rocks was louder and the patch of dark ahead of them wasn't nearly as black.

Zero slowed them as they approached the exit of the tunnel, crouching down to see out into the night. She closed her eyes, and Raven could almost *feel* her searching around them.

"If you follow the valley floor, it will bring you to a hiking trail, take it east, and it should bring you back to something like civilization," Zero said, pointing.

Raven could just see where she meant, following the water that flowed out from the pool at the base of the falls. "What about you?"

Zero pointed up their side of the ravine. "I'm going that way. They should follow me, so you should be safe."

Raven shook her head. "I can't accept that. You're a kid."

"Maybe, but I have experience with this guy, and now that I've finished my initiation, I have extra juice."

"But you're also still reeling from that initiation," Raven said. "I don't have to be a Shade to read the exhaustion on your face. Come with me. We can use the water to hide our path."

Zero frowned at her. "How do you mean?"

Raven smiled. "We can use the energy of the water to scatter our own. Hope you don't mind getting wet."

She eased out of the small opening, catching Zero's hand as she passed. Edging along the side of the pool, she kept them low until she could see where the pool shallowed and funneled into a wide stream of water. Raven stepped into the water, relishing the sudden rush of power. Zero followed her, still looking more than a little skeptical. Up near the top of the waterfall she could just make out movement.

Raven stuck her hands into the water, pulling energy to her, before she changed its pattern and spread it back into the water, throwing up a mist that would mask their movements.

Beside her, Zero nodded in understanding before she too stuck her hands in the water, augmenting the effect and weaving in a good dose of confusion.

Smiling, Raven nodded and started them down the stream. They could keep to the water for some ways before getting out of the woods and back to the motel where she and Evan were staying.

She wasn't sure what their next move was, but for the moment, Raven just focused on getting there.

Chapter Five

The woods were deep, old growth, and Alaric and Mason followed a path that seemed to mark a boundary of sorts. Mason could still feel a barrier that they had passed through shortly after their last stop. Alaric hadn't said anything more about what he knew or didn't know. In fact, they'd hardly spoken at all.

The path they followed was shaded and cool, but Mason was starting to feel the effects of daylight and he reached out for Alaric's shoulder. "Break."

Alaric nodded and stopped, then pointed to the shade of a large tree. Mason moved off the path and leaned into the tree, willing his lungs to stop protesting and his body to cool down.

"There's water in the valley." Alaric said quietly, his hand on Mason's. "We can wait for nightfall if you need."

Mason shook his head. "Just need a break."

"You're very warm."

Mason nodded but smiled. "I'll be fine. At least we have shade." His ribs ached and he needed the time to do a more thorough job of healing the many other pains as well. He swallowed and looked up at Alaric. "What about you?"

"I'm fine," Alaric responded, though Mason didn't miss the way his hand went to his side and pressed in. He wasn't really worried about the bruise itself, but deep bruising could signal a deeper problem. Part of him wanted to do what he could to heal it, even though he knew he was in no shape yet to be trying to heal anyone but himself. "We aren't far now; we'll get you into the water and something to eat."

"And then what?" Mason asked, standing upright again and looking at him.

"I don't know," Alaric admitted. "I haven't thought that far ahead."

"Fair enough." Mason nodded and gestured onward. Alaric took up the lead again, taking them through the trees and ever downward. Mason could feel the pull of the water more strongly as the sun inched toward setting. He focused on Alaric's back and the knowledge that relief was only a short way away.

"I was beginning to think you got grabbed again," a familiar voice said, bringing them up short.

"Just taking our time." Alaric replied, reaching back for Mason. "Had to make sure we weren't being followed."

Bryan stepped out of the trees and crossed his arms, looking Mason up and down. "Your mother is going crazy, especially after I told her about him."

"He has a name, Bryan. And we're both fine."

Mason was starting to notice that there were more people around than Bryan. They were quiet, but it was unsettling to think they could get that close without him noticing. "Just tell me we got what we needed," Alaric said.

"Yeah, Jordan and Riley got through just like they said."

"Jordan still here?"

Bryan shook his head. "No, already headed east again. Said he needed to get back to his family."

"Okay, let me get Mason settled and I'll come take a look." Alaric turned to him and inhaled. "We've got about an hour before the sun's down enough for you to get to the water. I'll show you where I sleep, introduce you to some people."

Mason nodded because there really wasn't anything else he could do, and he followed when Alaric walked away. The path widened as it turned past a clearing and started downward. The opposite hill cast a shadow across most of the valley that kept him safe enough for the time being, and the grove of trees before they reached the water helped even more.

They crossed the creek on an old wooden bridge, and Alaric gestured to a trail that led off to where Mason was starting to notice cabins. "My mother and I have that cabin there, but she's probably at the bunkhouse." He altered their path then, leading him past a garden that was turned under for winter, and up to a larger building where he could smell something cooking.

Mason could feel the sun, even if he was in the shade. It made him want to move faster. Alaric climbed the steps to the door, opening it and ushering Mason into a warm room, lit by the fire in the big fireplace.

A woman appeared from a door, wiping her hands on a towel. She rushed forward, pulling Alaric into a hug that lasted for more than a minute.

When Alaric pulled back, he was smiling. "Mason, this is my mother, Emily. Mom, Mason."

She was younger than he'd imagined, with red-gold hair that was streaked through with honey and white in equal measure, and sparkling green eyes that moved over him slowly. He felt as though he was some store display, being judged for the value he might bring her family. "You're the Shade Bryan told me about?"

He nodded and she inhaled, then looked to Alaric. "You may have a hard time convincing the others." Alaric leaned in and pressed his forehead to hers, a smile tugging at his lips. Her eyes closed and she sighed. "Of course, I see it, Alaric. I have a bed made up the second bed in your room and there's food ready."

"Here, sit down. I'll get you some food and water." Alaric took his hand and drew him toward a table, then disappeared through the same door Emily had emerged from. He reappeared with a bowl and a glass and brought them to the table where Mason waited.

He could feel Emily watching him, and Bryan was still at the door. It was uncomfortable, and he somehow imagined that they were talking about him, though no one said a word. He felt as though he was clearly missing something important, even as Alaric urged him to sit and handed him the bowl. "I promise, I'll tell you everything once I've dealt with a few things. Eat. I'll be back soon." He pressed a kiss to Mason's forehead, then blushed before he walked away, taking Bryan with him and leaving Mason alone with Emily for the moment.

"He doesn't trust people easily." Mason looked up as Alaric's mother joined him. "He's never brought someone home to me before." Mason could feel the color rising in his cheeks as she came to him. "I see what he sees though."

He didn't know what to say or how to respond. The way she looked at him made him nervous. "I don't know anything about that," Mason said finally. "I just..." He shook his head. "He saved my life. I'm not sure why."

"My late husband knew a few Shades. His mother married one, after her first husband died, though even Alaric doesn't know that." She turned to look at the fire. "She taught Alaric to be tolerant of those who are different, to care for those that others would throw away. I am grateful she did."

He drained his cup of water before tasting the stew in the bowl. It was rich and thick, made of venison along with potatoes and carrots and peas.

Emily stood and crossed to another table, bringing back a pitcher of water and refilling his glass. "The sun should be down soon. Until then, here."

He took the glass, setting the bowl of stew on the table. "Thank you. Not many are willing to share their shelter with one of my kind anymore."

"Nor mine," she responded. "Now, if you'll excuse me, I have to finish a few things."

He wasn't sure what she meant by that, but he didn't ask, didn't follow her. Instead, he lifted his stew and ate. It was a good stew, and it reminded him it had been a long while since food was easy to come by.

He was a long way from anything and everything he knew. His Nana and their little house in the woods, the government that had recruited him, the world where he could pretend to be something other than he was.

Mason could feel the sun fading and stood, setting the empty bowl aside and going to the door of the bunkhouse. He stood for a long time and watched the night come. The dark that settled into this valley was among the deepest he had ever felt.

He let it cover him, soothe him. It cooled the last of the remaining burns on his skin. He wandered back the way they'd come, then followed the stream to a spot where it deepened.

He pulled at his clothes as he neared the water, leaving them in a trail down to the creek that ran through the valley.

The water beckoned him, promising healing and strength. He was aware of the others in the area, but ignored them for the moment. It had been far too long since he had felt the kind of freedom that let him seek out the dark or the water so alone, back before he had seen the chaos of a coming war and found himself working for a government he didn't entirely trust and which didn't entirely trust him.

He slid into the water, remembering what it had been like those years alone with his Nana and the freedom he'd felt when his only obligation had been to take care of her. It seemed a lifetime ago.

Then had come his time with Paul, learning how little he actually knew about himself, before he'd seen firsthand what hatred could do to someone like him. Paul had taught him a lot, and then came his time in the hospital, where he'd learned so much more about himself, about his gifts and what it was to be a Shade. They were things he should have learned from family, if he'd had any family left to teach him.

Mason walked into the water, bare feet finding purchase on smooth stones and silt as the water deepened, coming nearly to his chest. He sank slowly, letting the icy-cold water flow over and around him.

On his missions, he at least usually got enough water, but it was seldom as easy as soaking. There was always a purpose, a job.

And then came the last one. It was another job trying to get intel on the 8th Battalion, only he'd learned more about them in the week or more he'd been their prisoner than in all his months of spying combined. Part of him knew he needed to get that information back to his handlers in DC.

Of course, it was known that they were rooted in the ideology of a religious background, but he was pretty sure most of Washington thought of them as just another alt-right organization using morality to win simple minds. They were scarier than that, though. It was the scariest sort of enemy – the kind that believed their own rhetoric, the kind that would kill over ideas, over belief. At least, the men he'd had contact with were like that.

And then there was Alaric.

Mason soaked in the water, sensing Alaric move through the camp... not that he could actually see him, but Mason could feel where he was. He didn't know how he felt about that. His lips burned with the memory of their kiss, with the taste of Alaric's mouth, his blood. Before his Nana had died, he'd never really kissed anyone. Not like that. He'd been homeschooled since his mother's death, since he'd taken her last breath and started manifesting his heritage early.

Liza had been his first, in more ways than just kissing. But he hadn't even thought about her in weeks. Alaric... Mason wasn't sure how he knew, but this was different, deeper somehow.

Alaric was coming toward him now, sliding through the trees in the dark almost as confidently as Mason could. He smiled as he appeared, Mason's clothes in his hands. "You left a trail."

Mason offered a smile of his own, tentative. He wasn't sure of himself with Alaric, and that made him nervous. But there was something he could do now that they were in relative safety and he had the water to do it in. He stood slowly, moving toward the shore with water running off his naked body as the moon peeked out over the nearest mountain.

The cool touch of the moon's light bathed him in a soft glow, tingled against his wet skin as he stepped from the water. "Maybe I wanted you to find me," Mason said softly, taking the clothes from his hand and tossing them to the side.

"Here I am," Alaric responded, licking his lips.

Mason nodded, his hands lifting to Alaric's shirt. "I never thanked you... For bringing me with you, for saving my life..."

Alaric seemed nervous now, too, as Mason undressed him, more so when his hand found the wound Alaric had been hiding for days now. "Let me."

Mason tugged on his hand, bringing him toward the water. Alaric came slowly, pausing on the rocks to take off his shoes and pants, and Mason stepped into the water, holding out his hand, drawing Alaric to him. "Let me thank you," Mason murmured as he walked Alaric out to a deeper spot in the water and pushed him down so that the wound was in the water.

He submerged himself, felt the water flow over his skin. He brought his face close to the wound and remembered the lessons Dr. Anthony had given him. It was easier in the water, easier when he could see the wound. His fingers brushed over the skin, washing away the dirt and sand, urging healing into the bruised tissue. The damage went deep, all the way down the kidney. The bruise was more than half way to healed when he lifted himself from the water.

"Once we were coveted for this, not feared for our other gifts," Mason said, smiling.

Alaric's hand covered the bruise, pressing against it. "That's... amazing."

Mason blushed and stepped away, suddenly very conscious that they were both naked and it hadn't been but a day since that kiss. Alaric's hand slid down his arm and their fingers tangled together, pulling him back. His other hand lifted to cup Mason's cheek, caressing over the skin before moving to his neck and drawing him even closer.

The touch of his lips was tentative, a light brushing over Mason's own. It was soft and sweet and more a question than Mason had expected. "Is this okay?" Alaric asked, his voice breathless as his eyes opened.

The moon reflected in the blue of those eyes and Mason couldn't look away. He sort of nodded, though he wasn't really sure anything was okay. "I... I've never..." His heart raced ahead of him and he had to remind himself to breathe. No one had ever affected him so much with so little before. It was only a kiss.

Only a kiss.

Except for how they were both standing naked in a river in a valley after escaping certain death. Except for how Mason scarcely knew the man, yet owed him his life... and already couldn't imagine what came next.

Alaric seemed to sense his distress and stepped back, running a hand over his face. "So, I thought you could spend a few days getting your strength back. My mother has made up a place for you to sleep. You have the creek. Whatever food we have, we share."

Mason nodded, watching Alaric climb out of the water, the moon glistening on his naked, wet skin. "And then what?"

Alaric turned to look at him, holding his pants. "Then I thought maybe you might help us, actually."

Mason stepped onto the shore, crossing to his own pile of clothing. "How exactly?"

"Well, we have wounded that could use your help, and there are always more. Our only trained healer is a midwife, a Sage."

Which only reminded him that he had questions. He pulled his borrowed pants up before he turned back to Alaric. "We probably should talk before I agree to anything," Mason replied. "I mean, all the lifesaving and kissing aside, I don't know who you are or why you're here. And there are obligations I have."

Alaric nodded. "Of course. I'm sure you have questions." He finished zipping up his jeans and turned to sit on a rock, looking up at Mason.

Mason nodded and pulled his shirt on, trying to figure out where to start. "Okay... I... The 8th Battalion, why were you there?"

"Bryan and I and a few others, we were a diversion for an important mission. We got caught."

"What sort of mission?"

Alaric offered a tight smile and crossed his arms. "There was something we needed to recover from Sacramento. An heirloom, a piece of our heritage. We left it behind when we fled because the violence got bad."

"And you fled here, to the woods?" Mason looked around them, then back at Alaric.

"We don't mind living rustic. Our ancestors generally lived outside the cities."

Mason narrowed his eyes and took a step closer. "And who were your ancestors?"

Alaric nodded. "I suppose it's only fair. I know your secret. I should tell you mine." He sighed, then bit his lip and seemed to search about for where to start. "I come from a long line of people known by various names depending on where we lived. My mother's side of the family was called the Dachte Lichte."

Mason frowned as memory not his own bubbled up. "Psychics?"

Alaric stood and shook his head. "Not like people think of psychics, no. Some of us can read the future, sure. But it's a gift that is rare, even among us."

"Shadows." Mason said, bubbling memory from some far-off ancestor coming to the surface. She had known an enclave of Shadows in Europe, hidden with them for a time. "But you can read minds, influence and manipulate them."

"Again, not all of us, and not every mind. There are many who are immune to our gifts." Alaric was clearly worried about how he was going to react. He looked at Mason from under long lashes, waiting.

"Have you read my mind?" Mason asked.

Alaric shook his head. "No. Nor has anyone with me. Well, except maybe my mother. But you have to understand she's protective. We have rules about how and when and who. It's complicated."

Suddenly Mason wondered if his own ability to communicate with other Shades mentally was similar. "You can talk to one another without talking, right?"

Alaric nodded, his worry clearly lessening. "Yes, it comes in handy sometimes. When I've worked with someone a lot, I can reach them across great distances. For others, I need to touch them."

Mason inhaled and made an impulsive decision. "*Can you hear me?*" Alaric didn't react, so he took a step closer, reaching out his hand to touch Alaric's hand. He focused and lifted his eyes to Alaric's. "*Can you hear me?*"

Alaric blinked, his eyes going wide as he nodded. "*You... how?*"

Mason let go of him and shrugged. "It's a Shade thing. I've never done it with anyone who isn't one." He pulled his hand through wet hair and sighed. "So... is everyone here... like you?"

"No, though they mostly come from families like mine. The gifts are dying out. And we have some others here as well, people who were also fleeing the violence."

"Okay, so why are you here?"

"My family, My father was the leader of our clan. We lived in Sacramento." Alaric shook his head and went to retrieve his shoes. "But then came the hate crimes against people who were... different, they killed people they claimed were Shades or witches, people who were Muslim or black. It didn't seem to matter if any of their claims were true or not."

He gestured up the path. Together the two of them headed for the cabin he called home. "My cousin was killed because she was known to predict the future. She was an amazing woman, and she hid her true nature behind reading tarot and tea leaves and the like. They burned her alive, burned her whole house down. That was when we decided it was time to leave."

He led Mason up the hill to a small group of people gathered around a small fire. "You know Bryan. This is Riley; the two of you didn't exactly meet. Next to him is Colin, Sahara, and Mila. Everyone, this is Mason."

Sahara stood, her eyes raking over him. "Shade." Her eyes flicked to Alaric. "You should have asked before bringing him here." Sahara said, standing and looking Mason over. She was his height with thick hair and brown eyes. He could guess she was in her early thirties and she had the aura of a woman who could handle herself.

Bryan snorted. "Cool your ass, Sahara. We ain't in the business of turning folks away because they're different, or your furry felines wouldn't be here either."

"That's my point." Sahara said, turning her eyes on Bryan. "He doesn't make all the decisions anymore. He's got others to think about."

"I'm sorry that you feel that way." Alaric said. "We can trust him."

Mason looked from Sahara to Alaric and back again. "I promise you ma'am, I got nothing but respect for y'all."

She spit on the ground at his feet, her eyes glowing a strange yellow in the light of the fire. "Respect isn't anything that can't be betrayed." She seemed to be sizing Mason up. "I know you want to unite the tribes, but you still should have brought it to us before you brought him here."

"Sahara, I'm sure it's fine," Mila said, joining her.

Sahara didn't respond, just turned on her heel and left with Mila in tow.

"Well. That went well." Alaric said, shaking his head. "She'll get used to you. She's just... well, she's been through a lot."

Mason watched her back, then turned to Bryan when she was gone. "What did you mean?"

Bryan poked at the fire with a long stick. "That there is Sahara Katan, one of the last surviving members of a clan of Shifters. Like Shades, they're misunderstood and worth a lot of money to the right people."

Riley slapped him across the back of the head. "You're an ass." He shook his head. "Don't mind Bryan. Or Sahara for that matter. She'll warm up to you eventually."

"If he's here that long," Bryan countered. He stood. "No offense, just don't expect a camp full of sun folk is any place for a Shade. I have early morning sentry duty, so, if you'll excuse me..."

Riley shook his head as he looked at Alaric. "He's never been the best at subtle."

"He could aim for polite," Alaric responded, then yawned.

"Never really been that either." Riley stood too. "I should get up to relieve Jacob. I promised him he could get home to Marcy early."

"How's she doing?"

"Any day now," Riley said, stepping around them. "That little one is ready."

Alaric watched him go, then sighed.

"Little one?"

"Baby." Alaric explained. "Marcy was due a week ago."

He moved to sit by the fire while Mason circled around it, just outside of the reach of its warmth. "So... You take in strays." Mason asked when the silence had grown long.

"Sahara and her girls... They were prisoners at some lab that is associated with the 8th Battalion. They were being treated like they were animals." Alaric traced some pattern in the dirt with his toe.

"Shifters? I thought they were all myth and legend, like bigfoot or something," Mason said softly.

"Yeah, Shifters," Alaric responded, smiling when Mason's face showed his disbelief. "I know; I wouldn't have believed it either if I hadn't seen it. From what I gather, there are even fewer of them in the world than Shades."

Mason wasn't sure he believed him, but somewhere deep inside him a memory stirred. Not cats, but shifters of a variety, that someone way back in his line had known. He shook off the distraction and looked at Alaric. "And the uniting the tribes comment?"

Alaric sort of shrugged. "It's something we've been talking about. For now, we're just trying to hold a space that's ours, you know? Safe. Where no one has to take sides, just be who we are." He looked up at Mason. "Is that someplace you can see yourself finding a home?"

Mason didn't answer, just turned his face up to the night sky. "You should probably sleep. You'll feel better."

Suddenly Alaric was beside him. "I know I don't have any right to ask it of you, and I'm not trying to push you, but these people are all I have." His fingers tangled with Mason's. *"Stay, at least for a while."*

Mason turned, brushing their lips together. *"For a while."*

It wasn't really a promise, but it was all he had to offer. Alaric seemed to accept it with a nod, and then he tugged on Mason's hand. "Let me show you where you'll sleep." He led Mason away from the warm circle of the fire, up an inclined path to a small cabin.

Alaric held the door for him, and Mason stepped through, his eyes scanning the cozy living room. Alaric pointed toward the back. "Riley's room is back there. We're upstairs." He led the way up and pointed to a door. "That's my mom. We're back here." He opened a door into a room with two twin beds.

"It isn't much," Alaric said, his face dark in the lightless room.

"It's fine." Mason insisted.

Alaric yawned and apologized. He pointed to the small dresser. "Most of what I have should fit you. Help yourself."

Mason watched him strip out of his jeans before he pulled back the blankets on the bed closest to the door. Truth was, Mason should probably consider sleeping too. It had been a long couple of days, and the week before that hadn't been a picnic either.

He crossed to the window, turning his face to the light of the moon for a long moment before he pulled the shade and closed the heavy curtains so that he wouldn't have a problem with the daylight in a few hours.

Mason took a deep breath and let it out, sinking onto the bed to pull the boots off. Like Alaric, he stripped out of his pants and crawled under the blankets. He closed his eyes and centered himself, feeling the solid mass of the earth under him and the heartbeats of the two closest to him. The water's presence was strong, the quiet of this place a balm for all that had gone wrong in the last few months.

He maybe wasn't sure what it was Alaric needed him for, but he could feel the need of the people here. He could see himself making a home in this kind of solitude, enough so that he was thinking that if he could rest up, find his way back to DC to get his things and relay his information, even though by the time he got there it would be old, he might consider finding his way back to this place.

He smiled to himself. What he meant, of course, was to Alaric. He just wasn't completely ready to admit that, even to himself.

Chapter Six

Raven and Zero squatted at the edge of the woods, eyes scanning around them. It was daylight, which would make the rest of the journey uncomfortable, but they had lost their pursuers in the small hours of the night.

"How far is it?" Zero asked.

"I'm not sure." She didn't know the city well enough to figure the distance to the hotel where she was sure her handler was cursing her out. She pulled a plastic bag from her pocket and took her phone out, smiling at the question she could see in Zero's eyes. "I get wet a lot."

She thumbed it on and waited for it to show it was ready. She'd learned the hard way not to keep it on when she was working. When the screen indicated that it was ready, she dialed the Lieutenant and put the phone to her ear. As expected, his first words were angry. "Where the hell have you been?"

"Busy," Raven responded. "I need a pick up."

Evan sighed and she could hear him pick up his keys. "Where?"

Raven squinted at the nearest street sign, but Zero touched her hand and pointed to a coffee shop. "There's a coffee shop called The One Brew, on Piedmont. We'll be there."

"We?" Evan asked.

"I'll explain later," Raven responded. "Just get here." She hung up and put the phone back in its bag and into her pocket. "You ready?" She stood, eyeing the distance from the shade of the trees to the shade offered by the coffee shop's awning. Zero stood beside her, nodding. "Okay, let's do this."

Raven pulled the hood of her jacket up and led the way out of the trees to the road, jogging a little to minimize her sun exposure. They crossed the road and ducked into the shop easy enough. The place was busy, but there was an open table near the front window. Raven took the seat closest to the door, where she could see out the window and the whole room at the same time.

Zero straddled the seat opposite her, gray eyes sweeping over the place before coming back to Raven's. "We should order something."

Raven nodded. "Just coffee." She reached for the pocket where she kept her wallet, but Zero waved her off.

"I've got this." She stood and headed for the counter.

Raven watched for a moment, before turning her eyes back to the window. It was a normal Monday morning in Atlanta, the traffic average. They seemed safe enough for the moment. She looked back just in time to see Zero slip the barista a piece of paper with a grin, her hand lingering on his for a moment, before she grabbed their drinks and returned to the table. Raven's eyebrow arched as she took her coffee. "What was that?"

Zero rolled her eyes. "Just a tiny glamor, nothing more."

"I have cash."

Zero sipped at her cup. "So do I."

"So, you'd rather just steal, even when you don't have to?"

She sighed and set her cup down. "I don't need a mother."

Raven held up both hands. "Not trying to be your mother. But you should be aware of the dangers you invite when you overuse your talents. Don't draw attention unnecessarily."

"Fine." Zero went back to her coffee, fiddling with the lid on her cup. Her energy was jangled and Raven could feel the girl's exhaustion.

"We need to talk about those men who were looking for you," Raven said after a few minutes of silence.

Zero looked up at her, then shrugged. "Not much to tell. They work for my father."

Of all the things Raven had considered, that wasn't one of them. "Why would your father send men like that looking for you?"

Zero's fingers began to pick apart a napkin, but she didn't look up. "Technically, he didn't. He isn't even here right now. I slipped through a crack in the security. They're just trying to get me back inside before he gets home."

"Back inside where, exactly?" Raven asked gently.

Zero's face screwed up in distaste. "This facility south of the city center. He keeps me locked in there whenever he's gone." She shook her head and pushed the remains of the napkin away. "He's an asshole like that."

Raven wasn't quite sure what to make of her story. Zero didn't seem to be any more willing to share details, so Raven shifted gears. "Okay, let's talk about something else. What do you know about the killings?"

Again, Zero shrugged, biting her lower lip. "I got a pretty good idea who it is."

That was not what Raven was expecting to hear either. "What?"

"There's this guy. He works for my father." Zero turned to look out the window, her eyes dark. "He knows a lot of stuff about Shades and Shifters. He has this library of books." She drank from her coffee and her knee started bouncing under the table. "I followed him one night. Lost him right around the park where the second body was found."

"Why would he want it to look like it was a Shade?" Raven asked, keeping her voice lowered.

"That's what my father wanted. He's all about spreading rumor and creating fear."

Raven started to ask who the girl's father was, but she saw Evan pull up in their rental. "This is our ride." She stood, but Zero didn't. "We can keep you safe."

"I doubt it." Zero stood and took a long swallow of her coffee.

"Do you have somewhere else to go?"

Zero looked up at her. "Not so much. A couple hiding places, but if they found the waterfall, they've already found them. I'm probably best just getting out of town."

Raven nodded and held out her hand. "We can help you with that."

For a long moment, Raven didn't think she'd come, then she rolled her eyes and stepped toward her. Raven grinned and led the way to the SUV. She opened the back door and held it, letting Zero slide in first before she climbed in out of the sun. She could feel Evan's eyes staring at her from the rear-view mirror. "Lieutenant Chayton, this is Zero. Drive. We should get out of the area."

Evan got them moving, but his eyes kept dancing from the road in front of them to the rear-view mirror. Raven sighed. "She might be able to help us find our killer."

"Is that so?"

"Just drive. We slipped the pursuit, but they had a tracker with them." Zero said. "We need to clear the area before he figures out where he lost the trail."

Evan was quiet then, and Raven settled back, patting Zero's shoulder. "How's the blowback from that initiation?" she asked softly.

"I'll live." Zero responded, folding her arms. "I'm exhausted though. Not sure how long until I'm gonna crash."

"We'll be able to get some sleep soon."

"And then what?"

Raven inhaled and let it out slowly. "And then, we figure out what comes next."

* * *

Sahara was ready with a blanket when Maddie shifted back to her human form, draping it over her and rubbing over her arms. "It's okay." Sahara said softly.

Maddie shifted, sitting up and pulling the blanket around her. "It happened again."

Sahara nodded and moved to sit on the couch in the main room of their cabin. It was big enough to not feel crowded when all three of them were there, but it wasn't large. A fireplace dominated the west wall, rising up through the second level to heat the whole cabin. "Stress makes the transition worse." Sahara commented as Maddie moved closer to the fire.

"Just tell me I didn't hurt anyone."

"You didn't," Mila said as she joined them. She'd returned at the same time as Maddie and had gone to get dressed while Sahara took care of her struggling sister.

Mila dropped into the chair, yawning. "I got you out into the forest before you started swinging."

"I'm sorry." Maddie stared into the flame, her face shining in the red glow.

"My transition was a nightmare." Sahara said, drawing both of their eyes. "I started when I was ten and it took forever. I think the last time I changed uncontrollably, I was in my twenties."

Maddie sagged visibly. "I can't..." Her voice trailed off and she pulled further into herself. Sahara sighed, pinching the bridge of her nose and wondering how she'd ended up in her current position. She'd never really been someone who had friends, not even among her own clan. Her parents had been secretive and withdrawn for the most part, attempting to pass as normal after they had come to the States.

Her mother was Indian, ostracized from her family for her "condition" as the first in two generations to present the Shifter traits as she entered puberty. Her father came from a family that was proud of their heritage. When he'd come home to Mexico from extensive traveling with her mother, she'd been accepted and welcomed, even if she never fully trusted their affection. Eventually, Sahara's parents had moved north, settling in a quiet neighborhood in Southern California where they helped a cousin of her father's run a restaurant.

Outside of her parents, she had known others from her clan as distant relatives who sent letters and occasional gifts, but it had been years since she had met one. Her mother had been friends with a woman from Clan Avek, a hawk if memory served. But aside from her, Sahara had only ever known of other feline Shifters, and there were fewer of them than ever. She was the last of her family. Mila and Maddie the last of theirs.

All of her instincts told her to run, to hide away in the mountains, to not get involved. Preserve what remained. And yet, she stayed.

Her knowledge of the other tribes was limited to the whispers she'd overheard when she was young and some books she'd been sent by her grandmother. Her parents had always warned her away from the other tribes. There was bad blood between them that went back centuries.

Everything she knew about the other tribes was hearsay and legends. Unless she counted the rest of humanity, those not of the tribes. They had dominated each of the tribes at one time or another through history, persecuting Shifters, Shades, Shadows and Sages alike. She knew enough about them to never want to be a part of their world again.

Still, these Shadows had come for her, rescued her... them. Sahara looked at Maddie, all huddled into herself by the fire. For all Sahara knew, they could be the last of the Fele clan of Shifters. Just the three of them.

Mila came to sit beside Sahara on the couch, concern in her eyes. Sahara smiled and patted her shoulder. "Just thinking, kitty."

Mila smiled, her face flushing a little. "Our dad used to call me that."

"Mine too," Sahara said.

They were quiet for a minute before Mila shifted and turned to look at Sahara. "So, what's the plan?"

Sahara raised an eyebrow. "Plan?"

Mila nodded. "What comes next?"

Sahara forced a laugh and stood, moving toward the only window in the little cabin. "What makes you think I know?"

"Somebody should, don't you think?"

She had a point. "I don't know, Mila. Probably."

"Are you counting on the Shadow to do it?"

Sahara sighed and turned. "He seems to be doing a good job of it so far. We're alive. And I think he may be right about us needing to work together in this." She shook her head, feeling the pressure of a position she had never wanted. "We only got a taste of what's coming. They seem to have more information."

"There's strength in numbers, Mila." Maddie said, standing. She clutched the blanket around her as she shuffled over to the couch.

"We seem to be greatly outnumbered." Mila countered.

"I'm convinced that they are only trying to help," Sahara said.

"Would that be because you're sleeping with one of them?" There was no malice in Mila's voice, only a need to let Sahara know that she wasn't ignorant of what was going on around her. "I'm not a child, Sahara. And even if I hadn't seen you slinking out of his cabin before dawn, you still smelled of him hours later when you came to breakfast."

Sahara bristled, letting some of her inner lion show. "I'm a grown woman. I'll sleep with whomever I chose. You'd do well to remember where you'd be if these people hadn't come to our aid."

Mila stared at her for a long moment before she nodded her head. "I mean no disrespect. To you or them." She reached for her sister's hand. "But I'm all Maddie has now, and I have to look out for her. And that means I have to stand up and make decisions for the both of us. I went along with the whole trip into Sacramento thing because we owed them at least that. But we're clear now. If we stay, it's because we choose to, not because anyone tells us to."

Sahara crossed to the couch, sitting on the wooden coffee table. "I respect that. I'm not your mother; I have no interest in being your mother. I have only taken responsibility for you because you are kin."

"And we thank you for that." Maddie said, leaning forward to touch Sahara's hand. "It means more to us than you know."

Sahara nodded, patting her hand. "I suggest that you take this up with Alaric then. Let him know that you speak for you and your sister, Mila. I think he assumes that because I am older, I will lead and you will follow."

"I'm not saying we won't," Mila said. "I'm saying I need to be included in the decision making."

Sahara nodded. "Of course, I'll do my best to make sure you're included." With the arrival of the Shade, they had at least one from each of the tribes in the camp, plus the others, those not from the tribes. Not that anyone other than Alaric Lambrecht was a leader of any of those tribes, but maybe they could start to at least live peacefully with each other.

She stood, determined to at least give it a try. She'd start with the Sage midwife. "You should get dressed, go have breakfast." She smiled. "Make friends."

"Where are you going?" Maddie asked as she headed for the door.

"To do the same."

Sahara left them and headed down into the camp. The sun was still climbing over the ridge, casting long shadowy fingers over the camp. She headed down the trail that led to the showers and bunkhouse. Just past the cabin where Alaric and his mother lived, she was surprised to find the Shade on his way up the trail. "Little late for you, isn't it?" Sahara asked, hoping it didn't sound confrontational.

He nodded a little, stopping to smile at her. "Yes, ma'am. I've been soaking and lost track of time."

"You look a little better than the last time I saw you. The water must be helping." She didn't know a lot about Shades, aside from the need for water and the need to avoid the sun.

"It is." Mason looked her over. "I'll admit, ma'am, I don't know a lot about Shifters, but I thought y'all were night people too."

She shrugged. "For the most part, but not like you. We can move around just fine in the daylight. We just prefer the moonlight." She glanced up at the sky. "You best be getting inside. Sun will be lighting this place up soon."

He nodded politely. "You have a good day."

Sahara watched him go. Her father, in particular, hadn't cared for Shades, but he'd never told her why. She'd always assumed that it was due to the mottled history between the tribes. She was going to have to put aside her preconceived ideas if she was going to get along here. And despite the rocky relationship she had started with Bryan, she knew that without this place, without these people, the three of them might not survive.

Chapter Seven

Alaric sipped at the coffee his mother gave him and watched Riley sort through the package that Jordan had brought from back east. In a modern world where most of them were used to standard mail delivery and cell phones, it was frustrating to live the way they were, with no phone service, no internet, and no mail service.

They were lucky to get anything at all, really. Getting in and out of the area was getting more difficult all the time. Once the snow started, it would be largely impossible.

The box contained letters for various people in the camp along with a few mementos and other little packages, plus news from outside their secluded little valley. There were stacks and stacks of newspapers from the last few weeks, with headlines that ranged from wild speculation to alarmist anti-Shade rhetoric. Alaric sorted through them, hoping to find something closer to actual news than the rest.

Riley lifted an envelope from the box and held it out to Alaric. His name was on the outside of the envelope. Alaric took it and set down the stack of newspapers in his hand. He could tell it was from Jordan by the handwriting. The envelope was heavy, and he frowned as he opened it carefully. There was a note inside in Jordan's tight, close style. It was a recap of the news, distilled down to the things Jordan figured to be important. His eyes scanned the words before he realized that Riley and the others were looking at him, waiting for news. "He says he got through with no trouble, though the southern states are getting more difficult to navigate as major cities follow the example of Salt Lake and close down access. You can still get around them with some extra miles, but he isn't sure how long that will last. There's talk of a coalition of states withdrawing from the U.S. since the federal government has responded to outside pressure from Canada and England to curb the violence against minorities."

"It's about time someone spoke up." Riley said. "What is the president waiting for?"

"Judging from what Jordan says, he's convinced that the National Guard is handling it, and he's laying the blame at Douglas' feet for whipping up the right with his rhetoric."

"Yeah, because laying blame is always the best way to fix a problem," Riley said, returning his attention to sorting through the mail in the box.

"It will get worse." Alaric warned. He dumped the other contents of the envelope into his hand. Cool metal filled his palm, a chain and pendant. Alaric turned the pendant face up to find a moonstone, smooth and polished. It was made for a Shade. There was an energy that clung to it that reminded him of Mason. He shook his head as he shoved the pendant into his pocket. Jordan never ceased to surprise him. For someone who denied his gifts, the kid was talented.

"What's that?" Riley asked, looking up at him as he finished emptying the box of letters.

"A gift for Mason." He stood, eyeing the sun. It would probably be another hour or two before Mason was up and about. "Distribute the rest. I'm going to take this information into the office. Maybe if I lay it out on a map I'll see something... more."

The office was small, cramped with old wood furniture the original owner of the place had left behind. One wall overlooked a trail up into the woods. On the opposite wall was a big map of the United States.

Alaric moved to the map. Already, he had spent time making sense of the things they knew or suspected, using pushpins to mark the cities that seemed to be held by 8th Battalion friendly troops. He pulled a box of pushpins from the cabinet and marked off the states that Jordan seemed to think might cede from the union, using red string to draw a nearly straight line from the top of Texas across to the Atlantic Ocean.

The blue dots marking 8th Battalion strongholds was growing. They didn't have a clear picture, but with the information Mason had given him, it wasn't looking good. The entire state of Utah was blue. Idaho, Wyoming and Montana were largely blue. Oregon and Washington were well on their way, and in his own experience California seemed ready to follow suit, though the generally liberal southern cities were not currently occupied by the National Guard.

Technically, their hidden valley was smack in the middle of 8th Battalion territory, and maybe they should have run east when they had the chance. But so far, they'd been fortunate. The remote location was hard to navigate, difficult to find, and with the lack of satellite coverage making communication difficult, they had not yet seen any signs that they had been discovered.

Alaric sighed and examined the map. He knew from Jordan's intelligence that the underhanded morality campaigns were already starting in the rest of California, spreading into Arizona and Nevada. The race for the Republican party's nomination for president was amping up the rhetoric and fanning the flames of bigotry that Alaric had never realized burned so hotly underneath the veneer of civilized society.

"Maybe it's time to consider moving," Alaric murmured to himself, his finger tracing through their valley.

"You see something I don't?" Bryan asked, filling the doorway and making Alaric jump.

Alaric shook his head. "Just uneasy. Their numbers keep growing. Eventually they're going to find us."

"Only if we give them reason to look," Bryan said, a hand on his shoulder. "We keep our heads down and our noses out of their business."

Alaric moved away, agitated. "Stick our heads in the sand and never mind that they're killing innocent people?"

"They're focused on Shades and the immoral," Bryan countered. "Not us. They've forgotten us for now. We should keep it that way."

"Their definition of immoral is a moving target." Alaric exhaled and shook his head. "The only reason they didn't question us was because Mason fell into their lap, distracting them. Made it easier for you to manipulate them into leaving us be. Besides, it's easier to prove someone's a Shade than to prove they can read minds." He made a face, disgusted by the practices he'd seen up close. "Jordan says that the first thing they do when they take a city is empty the jails and prisons."

Bryan nodded. "Yeah, and they execute anyone convicted of murder, rape or child molestation, which we should have been doing all along."

"They sterilize anyone with mental illness, force conversion, torture their enemies." Alaric shivered, looking away. Memory of watching what they had done to Mason was still far too fresh in his mind.

"I'm not saying I'm ready to sign up or anything." Bryan said. "Hell, they'd kill me as soon as look at me, I'm sure. I'm just saying that we should let them be, because so far they haven't come hunting us."

"And when they do?" Alaric asked. He knew they would. He knew it with every fiber of his being. If they stayed here, eventually the 8th Battalion would come and everyone would die.

Bryan inhaled and stood up straight, his good eye focusing on Alaric. "And when they do, we fight."

That was a conversation Alaric didn't want to have. He sighed and shook his head. "We're safe for now."

Bryan sensed his mood and changed the topic. "Jacob and I brought in a bunch of fish. Your mother and Cassie are cleaning them for dinner."

Alaric nodded. "Save me some." He left Bryan there as the sun was setting, casting the eastern slope in gold light while it dusted the western slope in shadows. He wandered over the bridge and up to the point that jutted out over the camp, the rocks still warm from the sun.

Bryan spoke for a fair share of the people and Alaric knew it. They didn't want to get involved, didn't want to be singled out yet again. Witch hunts of previous centuries were not easily forgotten in a clan with a long memory, and so many were so used to hiding.

Alaric was tired of hiding. He felt as though he'd been hiding his whole life. He also knew that a fight would only lead to ugly deaths for all of them.

He breathed in deep of the cooling air, wishing it would clear his head of the emotion and swirling memory of his cousin's death. He'd felt Abigail die just as sure as if he'd been there when it happened, unable to stop it. He rubbed his hands over his face. He'd been hiding then too. Hiding in plain sight.

It flushed through him again, the pain, the terror… he'd been trapped there inside her, not just watching. He had felt every single flame, Abi's fear and pain as real to him as if he was the one being burned to death while a mob outside shouted at her to burn.

The 8th Battalion hadn't even officially taken over. They were quietly moving into power, preying on people's fears and religious sympathy. It was how they worked.

The city council of the small suburb near Sacramento had been infiltrated by several people that led the fight, though he'd never discerned if they were 8th Battalion plants or just locals that they had riled up. They wore the mantle of public respectability – one of them was even a local minister – and they had started so subtly that no one had seen them coming.

Alaric had served as his father's aide, trying to stem the tide of so called morality statutes that were anything but moral. It started small with regulations on businesses they didn't like, such as tattoo parlors and bars, occult shops and fortune tellers. Then came the regulations on bars and making alcohol permits harder and harder to come by. They forced clinics that specifically served women to close, and drove out abortion providers with stricter and stricter ordinances, using zoning and other rules to hide the truth.

Then came the violence. It was isolated incidents to begin with, random beatings of someone who looked different, firebombing an LGBT nightclub, then a Mosque. More pointed violence followed with videos sent to television stations of men and women burned to death.

Alaric sat on the cooling rock and breathed in deep, pushing the memories away. The only reason the 8th Battalion wasn't actively hunting them was because they'd fled. As soon as they were done securing the ones that didn't or couldn't run, when they had secured the big cities and the small towns, they would come hunting. He knew it deep inside him.

He inhaled again and centered himself. He was no use to anyone when he was lost in the past. Another deep breath and he pushed all the memories back behind their doors, leaving order in his mind and a certain amount of peace.

Alaric rose and headed back down into the camp, pausing at a small cabin near the canyon floor to check on Marcy. He'd felt her contractions start earlier in the day, and wanted to be sure she was okay. He knocked on the door and was greeted by Jacob's grinning face. Alaric stepped inside, surprised to find Mason there.

Mason had his head bent over her extended stomach, one hand resting lightly on top of it. His mouth moved though no sound emerged. If he closed his eyes, Alaric could feel the energy Mason directed over and through her.

He lifted his head and opened his eyes, smiling at her. "Very soon, Marcy. He's strong, and the way is ready. How are the contractions?"

"Getting stronger now."

Mason nodded. "I'll be nearby if you or the baby need me, but everything looks good. Get some rest now, in a few hours you're going to be working hard." He turned, his smile widening at Alaric. "Hey."

Alaric lifted a hand to Marcy, then ducked back out the door, drawing Mason with him. "Hey yourself. You're up early."

Mason bit his lip, a habit Alaric found made him want to kiss him. "I was restless. She's really close."

"You do know we have a midwife, right?"

Mason ducked his head and blushed. "Yeah... just... I feel useless."

"You're not useless." Alaric countered, taking his hand. "You've done so much in just a few days." In the days since they'd made it back, Mason had worked his way through most of the camp, using his gifts to help with anything more than a stubbed toe, earning a begrudging respect.

He made a face and shrugged. "It wasn't anything. A few scrapes and bruises, a broken leg. It's not like it all wouldn't have healed without me, you know?"

"You've been moving around since you left home." Alaric murmured, his eyes searching Mason's. "Right?"

"You reading me?" Mason asked, his face tight.

"Maybe a little...but it's all there, on the surface. You're itching to keep moving." Alaric tried not to let his emotional need for Mason color his voice. It wasn't like either one of them had made a commitment. And Mason was young and inexperienced, and really, romance in times like these probably was not the wisest course of action. "I can't blame you, really."

He'd seen it, clear as day the minute he'd looked in those green eyes, Mason was the one the fates had tied into his life line. Not that it was going to be an easy road, and not that he could see any of it clearly, but the lines were obvious, and even his mother had seen it.

"It ain't you, or even them." He gestured at the camp. "I just find it easier to keep moving... and I have obligations."

Alaric nodded. "I know you do. I just... hoped you'd stay."

Mason tugged on his hand. "I ain't leaving yet."

Alaric grinned despite himself. "No?"

"No, I promised Marcy. And your mother."

"My mother?" Alaric crossed his arms and glanced up toward their cabin. "What does she have to do with you staying?"

Mason blushed again and turned away, heading for the water. "Nothing."

"You're a lousy liar." Alaric observed, following him.

Mason pulled off his shirt as they neared the deep pool that formed at a bend in the creek's path. He kicked off his shoes. "She just... wanted me to make sure I was a hundred percent before I tried to get back to DC."

"Right." Alaric knew his mother well enough to know that would be the least of her meddling.

Mason rolled his eyes. "Okay, she may have said something about you needing me and giving you a chance, and I'm going to get in the water now." There was a wake of embarrassment and uncertainty rolling off the man as Alaric followed.

Mason dropped his jeans and headed for the water's edge in his boxers. He waded out to his knees before glancing over his shoulder. "You could join me. If you wanted."

It was as close an invitation as he was likely to get, and Alaric wanted to, more than wanted to. He tugged his shirt off, and as he was undoing his pants he remembered the pendant from Jordan. He pulled it out of his pocket before dropping his pants and heading for the water. "I have something..." Alaric said, stopping Mason just before he might have sunk into the cold water.

"What kind of something?" Mason asked, watching Alaric pick his way over the rocky bottom to get to him.

"Just... something." Alaric held out the pendant, letting it swing in the air between them, suddenly feeling foolish about the whole thing. "Jordan sent it."

Mason raised an eyebrow as he reached for the chain. "I don't know Jordan."

Alaric nodded. "Yeah, well, the kid must have known we had a Shade here now." He watched Mason lift the pendant, and the other eyebrow joined the first.

"I haven't seen one of these in years." Mason brought the heavy oval stone up to rest in his hand, his thumb rubbing over it before his eyes lifted to Alaric's. "How... I mean... why?"

Alaric rolled his eyes. "I don't know... Jordan, he doesn't have much in the way of active gifts. Or he buries them. But he's perceptive. He probably saw it and something sparked to make him send it to me."

There was a light in Mason's eyes as he looked up, making the green look almost eerie. "You know what this is?" Mason asked.

Alaric shook his head. "Just knew it was for you."

Mason smiled. "See the stone?" It was moonstone, milky white and smooth, held in the center of a silver oval. "It is said that the stone can store up the healing energy of the moon, of good clean water, so that the Shade who wears it carries it with him or her."

"So, a good thing to have," Alaric said.

Mason moved a little closer, close enough to kiss him. Alaric held still, let him guide the kiss. It was soft and over quickly. Alaric had picked up the uneasiness with the whole physical side of things early on, and knew that while Mason was interested and attracted, he was inexperienced and uncertain. Mason pressed the pendant into his hands. "Traditionally, it was a gift given as a sort of promise."

Alaric licked his lips and let his thumb caress the stone as Mason's had. "What kind of promise?"

Mason's grin widened. "It was generally given as an engagement gift. The Shade who offered it would have set it out under the moon, from the night of fullness to the night of dark, and each night he or she would focus their power onto the stone for an hour, melding their intent with the stone's past, with all the Shades who had given or worn it before them. They were handed down through generations, each giver and each wearer leaving something of themselves behind." He bit his lip and narrowed his eyes. "I don't know if... maybe... Close your eyes."

Alaric did, though he could feel Mason more than just physically with his eyes open just fine. "*Hear me?*" Alaric nodded. Mason closed Alaric's hands over the pendant, then his hands around Alaric's. "*Can you feel it?*"

At first, he couldn't because all he could feel was Mason vibrating around him. Alaric took a breath and focused, bringing his attention down to their hands, then to the silver, and then the stone.

Far beyond feeling, voices lifted in his mind, whispered words of passion, of love, of promise, lives as vibrant as if they were there with them in the water, powerful and amazing. He watched as they grew still, their energy settling. As one they turned to him as clear as if they spoke in his ear. "*You are not one of us,*" they said together.

"*But he is.*" One tiny voice turned them all again, pointing toward Mason now. The silver thread that tied them together, the one Alaric had seen when he first laid eyes on Mason shimmered and expanded.

"*So he is,*" they agreed.

They withdrew then, leaving only the small voice, a woman and Alaric got the sense of her whispering something before she kissed his forehead like he was a child. "*On the next full moon, put the stone upon your skin. When midnight comes, if you would have him as your mate, bleed into the stone. If he accepts the offer, you will be bound by both your ways and ours.*"

Alaric opened his eyes, blinking at Mason who was watching him closely. "You...obviously got more out of that then I did."

Alaric nodded and cleared his throat. "You could say that. I'm... gonna hold onto it for a little while, if you don't mind."

"Not quite ready for marriage?" Mason teased.

Alaric managed a smile before he waded back to shore to tuck it into his pocket. "Something like that."

Chapter Eight

"Are you going to explain?" Evan asked, his face tight and guarded.

Raven pulled her eyes off of Zero, who was sitting on the end of one of the double beds in their hotel room. She was skittish, and Raven kept expecting her to run. They'd been in the hotel less than an hour, and Raven was fairly sure the only thing that kept the girl from disappearing was her exhaustion.

"She's a Sage. I found her in the woods," Raven said quietly. "She was finishing her initiation, and there were men coming for her."

"So, you brought her with you?"

"What was I supposed to do, leave her out there?" Raven shook her head. "Besides, she might know who our killer is."

There was a knock on the door and Zero stood abruptly, holding her bag tightly to her. "It's just pizza," Raven said, crossing the room and touching her shoulder. "I promised you food and a safe place to sleep."

Evan paid for the pizza and brought it to the table. Zero put her bag on the bed, blinking a little and nodding once. "Sorry, this is the longest I've managed to avoid them. If they don't get me back before my father gets back..." She shook her head and moved across the room, dropping into the only chair, with one leg up over the arm.

"Who is your father?" Evan asked, leaning back against the door.

"No one you've ever heard of," Zero responded as she grabbed a slice of pizza. "His name is Lewis Rede, or at least that's the one he's using this year." She took a bite and sat back chewing, her eyes on Evan. "He's a prick."

"Zero, you said you knew who might be killing people and making it seem like a Shade."

She shrugged. "I only know him as R. He's a guy who works for my father."

"Why do you think this R guy is the killer?" Evan asked.

Zero chewed and swallowed before looking up at him. "Because it's something my father would tell him to do, and he knows a lot about Shades." She rolled her eyes. "And he knows how to scare people."

"That's not a lot to go on," Evan responded, glancing at Raven.

"It worked for them in Utah, California, Oregon..." She shrugged as if it made no difference to her. "That got a little out of hand, so the old man is trying to go a little more subtly here."

Raven frowned. "What's his endgame?"

Zero finished her slice of pizza and grabbed for some napkins. "He's an egomaniacal sociopath with delusions of grandeur and a twisted idea that he can collect the powers of the five tribes and take over the country?"

Raven blinked at her, unable to tell if she was serious. Zero stood, shaking her head. "Like I said, he's a prick. Who knows why he does what he does." She pulled the wig off and rubbed a hand over her head. "I need to sleep. You still okay with me crashing here or should I go?"

"Of course, you can stay," Raven said.

Zero threw her dirty napkin in the tiny motel trash bin and crossed back to the bed where she dropped the wig on top of her bag. Raven watched her take off her boots and set them at the end of the bed. She slid into the far side of the bed, the furthest from the door and closed her eyes.

They stood there silent, watching her for a long moment before Raven sighed and turned back to Evan. "Sorry for springing this on you. I know you're not a fan of surprises."

Evan's face told her she wasn't wrong. He folded his arms and looked Zero over. "She's just a kid, so we can't just leave her on her own."

"Exactly," Raven concurred. "And if what she says is true... We need to know more."

"What are you thinking?" Evan asked, his eyes coming back to hers.

"Well, our mission was to discover who was killing, and she could be a witness. So, we keep her safe, see if we can find this R guy."

Evan nodded, picking up the keys to their SUV. "You stay here, get some sleep. I'm going to see if the police chief is more willing to talk now that Darvin's had time to work his magic."

"Be safe."

"You too."

She followed him to the door, locking it behind him. Raven sank onto the unoccupied bed, kicking her shoes off before laying down so she could look at Zero. She looked a lot younger with her face relaxed in sleep. There was something vulnerable about her that made Raven want to protect her.

Of course, she could already tell that protection was not something Zero was even interested in. Raven had seen the attitude before and she knew what it likely hid.

The problem they would face is that Zero was still a minor, and as such they couldn't legally take her across state lines without taking her into custody... which would not make the girl happy.

Putting Zero out of her mind, Raven closed her eyes. She needed sleep as much as Zero did. They had been running full tilt since they landed in Atlanta.

* * *

"In local news, Police Chief Al Brown has announced that the latest killings previously attributed to a Shade murderer, have in fact been the work of a non-Shade serial killer. They are keeping the details close to the chest for now, but we can confirm that they are no longer looking for

a Shade. Speculation is that the person responsible belongs to the anti-Shade organization known as the 8th Battalion."

Raven opened her eyes, somewhat surprised to see Zero sitting on the opposite bed with the television remote. She'd half expected to wake up to find her gone. As if sensing her surprise, Zero shrugged. "Looks like your friend got somewhere with the cops."

Raven sat up, rubbing her eyes. "He's good like that."

"He came back about an hour ago, said he was going to follow up on a lead and he'd call if he found anything."

"Did he say what the lead was?" Raven asked as she stood and headed for the bathroom.

"No, just that he'd be late."

Raven closed the bathroom door and relieved herself, then started some water running in the tub. "I'm just going to soak for a bit," Raven said, opening the door enough to see Zero.

"Whatever."

Raven smirked. If nothing else, Zero was clearly a teenage girl. She pulled off her clothes, dropping them on the floor. She settled into the tub, relishing the cool touch of the water, even if it was chemically treated and not free flowing. She'd gotten a good amount of water time in the last forty-eight hours, so it wasn't that she needed the soaking time, at least not physically.

Her fingers pulled the elastic band from the bottom of the braid that held her hair tightly out of the way, walking their way up to loosen it before she slid as much of her body into the water as she could and tried to relax. They had new information with Zero's revelation about her father. The idea had occurred to her before, that there might be someone outside the spotlight that was orchestrating things. Of course, she wasn't entirely certain how much she trusted what Zero said. There was obviously some bad blood there.

Submerging her head, Raven considered what she did know. The 8th Battalion was deep into the army's command structure, of that she was certain. If they weren't, troops would have been sent in to clear out the traitors on the west coast. It looked like they were determined to over-run the liberal west coast with their faith and fear driven campaign.

Her mind turned to Mason Jerah, and whether or not to believe he had survived the attack on his caravan. He was so green, it was difficult to believe he would have, but if the rumors she'd been hearing were true, and the 8th Battalion was determined to capture Shades and Shifters alive, it was possible.

Which would mean he was likely a prisoner somewhere, and she could only guess what they were doing to him. He was only a few years older than Zero. But then, she'd only been a year or two older when Darvin recruited her.

Unlike Mason or Zero, she'd been at least partially prepared for it though. Her parents had taught her to use her skills in inventive ways, put her through survival training from a young age. They'd known that life for a Shade could be dangerous.

Her first op had involved reining in a Shade with a mental disorder that made him forget what he was and left him vulnerable in odd ways. It made him dangerous. Back then that was the bulk of the agency's domain. They were tasked with keeping the nation safe from those with unusual gifts. Then came the task to keep knowledge of those others from the nation. The agency was beyond secret, most of the rest of the government didn't even know they existed, and Darvin always borrowed the authority of other agencies when they needed backup, using his influence to bring in the FBI or CIA when they needed a larger response.

Raven surfaced, rubbing water from her eyes. Many had come and gone since then. She'd worked with other Shades, a low-level Shadow or two, even a Sage that she'd considered a good friend. Evan was the first Shifter she was aware of, but if he was any indication, there could be more that she would never even suspect.

She could hear the TV as she pulled the plug and stepped out, wrap-ping a towel around herself, even as her skin absorbed most of the water. Zero looked up as she opened the bathroom door, gray eyes scanning her and then looking away.

Raven pulled clean clothes from her suitcase and dressed, turning away from Zero as she did. She could still feel the teenager's eyes on her as she pulled a shirt over her head. "What?"

Zero shook her head. "I... was just checking."

"Checking what?"

She huffed and sort of laughed. "I heard that Shades had tails."

Raven chuckled and sat on the bed to pull her socks on. "I'd heard that too, once. But no, no tail."

"Too bad. It might be kind of cool."

Raven scrubbed her fingers through her wet hair. "No horns either, see?"

Zero laughed, rolling her eyes. "Well, that will teach me to believe everything I hear."

Raven's cell phone rang and she crossed to grab it from the table. "Evan. Where are you?"

"Need you." He cursed, and she could hear him walking on gravel.

"Where are you?"

"Parking lot."

"On my way." Raven shoved the phone into the pocket of her jeans and shoved her feet into her shoes. "Stay put. I'll be right back."

"What's wrong?" Zero asked, her eyes wide.

"I'm not sure. Just sit tight." Raven grabbed her room key and opened the door, her eyes already scanning the area. She spotted their SUV and headed toward it to find Evan nearly unconscious leaning against the driver's side. "Hey, I'm here. What's wrong?"

He didn't respond, but as she touched him she understood why. Normally Evan was a tightly shuttered house of self-control. At that moment, he was in intense pain and his self-control was nonexistent. He gritted his teeth when her hand touched his arm, and she could hear him screaming in her head.

"Okay, where are you hurt?" Raven asked, her eyes scouring him for blood or other signs of injury while she scanned him internally as well.

"Can't...." His eyes closed and he struggled to push himself upright. "Not me."

"Can you move?" Raven asked when her scan of his body confirmed his statement. "Let's get you inside."

He didn't so much walk as he stumbled and clung to her, letting her just about drag him over the pavement. Zero had the door open as they reached it, her hands reaching out to help Raven get Evan into the room.

"Is he hurt?" Zero asked. Her face paled as her hands found skin and Raven could just about see the echo of Evan's pain in her face.

"He says it's not him," Raven responded, nodding toward the bed. It took doing, but they got Evan to the bed and laying down. Raven climbed up beside him, her hands moving to his face. "Evan, I need you to let me in."

His pain and fear might be full blown beyond his shielding, but that didn't mean he wasn't fully shielded. She was barely getting an accurate reading through all of the noise. "Can you hear me Evan?"

"I can help." Zero offered, moving to her bag and coming back with a jet-black stone. She sat opposite Raven and held the stone between her two palms for a long moment before she settled it on Evan's forehead, between his eyes. Raven could feel her presence, blanketing over Evan, pressing into him. It felt like a lifetime, but eventually Raven could feel the difference. Evan began to separate from whatever was causing the pain, pulling himself back inside. Zero looked up, her gray eyes dark. "Whatever you can do to calm his reaction to this, do it now. I won't be able to keep him like this for long. The strain is intense."

Raven nodded, immediately focusing her attention on the physical things she could actually affect. She sent warm energy into his rigid muscles, willing them to relax and encouraged his heart to a more efficient rhythm to get his blood moving more quickly. His back was screaming, though there was no obvious injury, so she poured energy into easing that pain as well. It was hard to heal something that wasn't real. When she had done all that she could, Raven pulled out, nodding to Zero who touched the black stone, sending a wave of something through Evan who shuddered. Zero lifted the stone and Evan's eyes fluttered before he mercifully passed out.

Zero was shaking as she pulled away, and Raven turned her attention to Zero. "You okay?"

She shook her head no. "He's...." She closed her eyes and exhaled slowly. "I'm not positive, but I think he was experiencing whatever was happening with his twin."

"Twin?" Raven frowned and slid across the bed to stand up.

"That's what it seemed like. Once I clamped down on the overflow, I kept seeing two of them, and one of them...." She hugged herself tightly and turned away. "If he isn't dead yet, he will be soon."

"Okay, but what about you?" Raven responded, reaching a hand for her.

"I'm okay." Zero turned away, then back. "I wasn't really ready. The initiation took more out of me than I let on."

"Let me help." Raven said.

Zero shook her head. "It's part of the process. If I can't handle the work, I can't handle the power." She moved to sit on the bed. "I probably shouldn't have done it all at once, but I was in a hurry."

"Do what all at once?"

Zero looked up at her, looking younger than she had a moment before. "All five clans at once."

Raven frowned at her. "I didn't even know that was possible."

"Most people only choose one or two." Zero said with a shrug. "I was planning on initiating in Fire and Water, because they're my strongest...but, my father is obsessed with this idea of his." Zero rubbed her hands over her arms.

"What idea?" Raven prompted.

Zero looked up as if she'd forgotten she wasn't alone. "He wants to combine the gifts, like all of them. All five clans from all five tribes. Like I said, he's crazy."

"How?" Raven asked, sinking to sit beside her. "That can't be possible."

Zero shook her head. "That's what I kept saying. He's got some geneticist working with him. She has the whole thing planned out. They just need to get their hands on the right people. I was supposed to be his Sage, but he was convinced I wasn't strong enough after the treatments didn't immediately make my earth and air skills better."

"Treatments. What kind of treatments?"

Zero hugged herself and stood. "I don't want to talk about it."

Raven could tell the girl would bolt if she pushed and turned her attention back to Evan. He seemed to be sleeping peacefully. For now. Because she wasn't really sure what had happened, she wasn't sure it wasn't going to get bad again.

Chapter Nine

Alaric shivered, his wet lower half making the night air feel a good ten degrees colder. It was already November, he reminded himself. His mother would skin him alive if she saw him in nothing but his underwear with the winter's first snow due any day.

Mason had chuckled and dropped backward in the water when Alaric had stepped out to put the pendant back in his pocket. Alaric watched the surface as the ripples that marked his passing settled and soothed. For the longest time, nothing moved. Alaric shivered again before he moved back toward the water, easing in until it was up to his waist. He could feel Mason's energy in the water, washing downstream, swirling around him.

When Mason rose, he tugged Alaric deeper, turning him. "Water's cold." Alaric murmured.

Mason nodded, keeping them moving, almost as if they were dancing. "I could warm it up."

Alaric's smile tugged at the corners of his mouth. "Yeah, you could."

Mason blushed again and rolled his eyes. "Not what I meant." He stopped their movement and closed his eyes, seeming to focus on his hands just under the surface of the water. The water between them warmed slowly until they were surrounded by water that was nearly body temperature. Mason looked up, his green eyes sparkling. "Better?"

Alaric nodded, leaning in to whisper, "Better."

"I wanted to… I should… say something." Mason said, his hands on Alaric's arms now. He was nervous, and his heart was speeding up. Alaric's heart quickened to keep the rhythm. "I mean, I like you," his face flushed pink and he looked up at Alaric, "like, I can feel… this thing between us… but…" His voice trailed off and he looked away.

For a split second, Alaric held his breath, then realized that he'd never considered the idea that Mason might already have someone, that one of the obligations he kept alluding to could be to a lover, or partner.

"No, not like that," Mason said, startling him.

"Did I say something?" Alaric asked, genuinely uncertain if he had voiced his concern out loud. He was still buzzing from the experience with the stone.

Mason let go of him, frowning. "I heard you." He shook his head. "Well, there was this girl… Shade. But it isn't like we made any commitments."

Alaric started to understand. He hadn't considered that either. "A girl. So, this is the part that's the problem?" Not only was he young and inexperienced, but straight, or maybe bi-sexual without realizing it. Until now. Alaric clearly knew how to stick his foot into a mess. Mason looked back at him, still frowning. "The part where I'm not a girl?" Alaric amended.

Mason shrugged and ducked himself into the water. "I never really thought about it I guess. But yeah, it's… different." He came back, tugging Alaric closer.

"Different?" Alaric asked, carefully keeping his hands away from Mason until he could figure out what Mason wanted this to be.

He huffed and licked his lips. "I've never… I mean… It's never…" He closed his eyes *"You know what I mean."*

Alaric did. He'd suspected, of course. Mason was young. Maybe younger than Alaric had assumed. "I don't want to pressure you," Alaric said softly. "I can back off."

Mason caught his hand as he pulled away, drawing him back. "No, not… I don't want that." Mason's eyes were dark, his pupils swallowing the green. "I just wanted you to know that whatever this is, I don't want to fuck it up. I'm not really good with people."

"I don't think that's true," Alaric murmured. "I think you're fine with people. I think you just need time to get used to the idea."

They moved slowly through the water, lips a breath apart. "Idea?" Mason murmured.

"That you're not alone," Alaric responded, letting their lips touch. "That you don't have to be alone." He licked along Mason's lower lip and when he opened his mouth in invitation, Alaric didn't hesitate, his arms sliding around Mason and pulling him closer as his tongue delved into his mouth. Their bodies rubbed together, the wet cotton of their underwear doing little to hide what the closeness did to Alaric.

Mason didn't move as Alaric broke the kiss, leaning into him, eyes closed. The water swirled around them, stirred by the energy Alaric could feel pouring off of Mason. His heart raced against Alaric's chest and Alaric could feel his body tighten, his hardness pressing into Alaric's leg.

Alaric slipped his lips from Mason's, onto his skin, kissing in tiny movements up his jaw, under his ear. "I want to touch you," Alaric whispered. His hands slid across wet skin, down to hips and the wet cotton that clung to them. *"May I touch you?"*

Mason tilted his head, offering his neck for Alaric's lips and his hands moved to cover Alaric's. *"Please."* He moved their hands down, over his ass, letting Alaric press in and pull him closer. Their groins rubbed together, kept apart by two layers of wet cloth.

Alaric nuzzled into his neck, licking and nipping lightly before closing his lips over a spot and sucking, making Mason surge forward and knock them both into the water. Mason clung to him, yet somehow managed to turn them and move them toward shore until he was lying on his back on the rocks, only his legs still in the water and Alaric straddled over him.

It was cold and wet, and Alaric wouldn't have stopped what he was doing even if he was freezing. He kissed his way down Mason's chest, pausing to trace over wet nipples with his tongue until Mason made a needy groan that shot through Alaric and into his stomach, making him want to hear that sound again.

He took the nipple in his teeth and bit just enough to feel Mason's body tense under him. "Damn," Mason grabbed his arm, lifting his head to look at Alaric. His green eyes were nearly glowing, and the water under them was going past warm.

"I've barely touched you," Alaric murmured, letting his hand slide down his torso to the waistband of his boxers. "What are you going do when I do this?" He tugged the wet fabric down, circling his hand around him and stroking up once, twice. Mason moaned, his hips lifting up to meet Alaric's hand.

Mason's grip tightened on his arm and Alaric shifted a little, bringing his groin closer. Alaric let go of Mason long enough to pull his own underwear down, pressing his skin to Mason's and stretching his fingers around them both.

The water was hotter now and heat flushed Mason's skin red as they moved. "Oh…" Mason closed his eyes, his hips rocking up as his orgasm began. All around them the water was steaming as Mason's orgasm coated Alaric's hand, hot and slick.

Alaric's own climax rocked through him and he moved his knees off the rocks, groaning. There was no way that wasn't going to hurt later. He slipped back into the water, washing his hands in the current and easing himself back into his underwear.

Mason was still lying unmoving on the rocks. "You okay?" Alaric asked, moving back toward him.

Slowly Mason sat up, his eyes still strangely glowing and he nodded. "Yeah… just… gimme a sec."

Alaric grinned and nodded, wading out of the water and heading for his clothes. He heard Mason moving around, sliding deeper into the water. When it was quiet, Alaric turned. Mason was nowhere to be seen, the water still. In the dark Alaric couldn't tell if he was under the water or gone, but he figured Mason would want his clothes, so he waited.

It took a while, but slowly Mason emerged from the water, breathing deep before shaking the water from his face and dark hair. He stepped out of the creek, smiling a little sheepishly at Alaric. "I... That was..." He shook his head. "Fuck, you must think I'm some sort of freak." He grabbed at his shirt, but Alaric stopped him with a touch.

"No, I don't."

Mason huffed and was clearly searching for words. "I don't know how to talk about things like this. But, when I'm with you, when you touched me like that... I've never felt that."

Alaric contemplated the connection between them, the signs he'd read from the first time he'd seen Mason, a face that came to him in a vision. He didn't know how honest to be. "Among my people, it is said that when two people are mates, there is a connection that makes everything they do together more intense, more powerful." He opted for truth, but not all of it.

"Mates?" Mason raised an eyebrow as he started to pull his clothes on.

"We mate... There are stages actually. There are strings of energy that bind us all together. Most can't see them, but they're there. They are different colors and thicknesses, some easily broken, some impossible to sever."

"Alaric!" They both turned to find a young man waving at them from the trees. "Got company."

Alaric frowned and lifted his hand. "I'll be right there." He started to get dressed.

"What kind of company?" Mason asked as he sat to put on his shoes.

"Hell if I know," Alaric responded. Chances were pretty good that it wasn't company they wanted. He pulled on his jeans and shoved his feet into his boots. Mason was at his side as he turned to head back toward the fire pit at the center of camp.

There was a crowd gathered as they approached, but they moved to let them through. A man knelt on the ground, hands bound behind his back, his eyes covered with a bandana. He lifted his head and turned unerringly toward Mason.

Alaric looked at the two men flanking him, nodding to the closer of the two. "We found him crossing the southern perimeter. He was not armed."

Mason crossed to look at him, his eyes narrow. "He doesn't need to be armed. He's a Shade." Mason was suddenly tightly shuttered, all the openness from a few minutes before gone and locked away.

Both of the men took a subconscious step away.

"I mean no harm." The man's voice was ragged and even around the blindfold, Alaric could read his distress.

Alaric looked to Mason. "You know him?"

"We know our own." Mason said, his voice tight. He turned his attention to the man, stepping closer. His face softened and he squatted beside him, one hand hovering over his left shoulder. "Are you hurt?"

The stranger shrugged, wincing in pain. "I should live."

"Who are you?" Mason asked, pulling his hand back.

"Just a Shade trying to survive. I lived south of here, but the army came..."

Mason stood and looked at Alaric. "I don't think he's a threat to you."

Alaric nodded and Mason moved to untie his hands. He eased the blindfold off and dark brown eyes swept over the gathered group. "Thank you."

Mason helped him stand. He had a slight build, his slender shoulder sagged and Alaric could see blood seeping through his clothing in a number of places. His dark hair was starting to gray and thin. "I am in need of sanctuary. Once my clan sheltered yours. Will you in return shelter me?"

More people had gathered and a murmur swept around them at the request. Alaric stepped forward. "What is your name?" he asked gently.

"I am Damon Estos."

Alaric reached out to read him lightly, getting a sense of the man's exhaustion and pain. He'd been running for more than a week, sleeping in caves and under piles of leaves. Beyond him, Alaric could feel the current of discontent among his own people.

He inhaled deeply and looked at Mason who met his eyes and sent reassurances. *"Don't turn him away."*

Alaric nodded slightly. "Mason, why don't you take Mr. Estos down to the water and do what you can to help him. I'll see about getting some clothes for him and find him a bed."

Mason thanked him with a nod, and reached a hand to Damon, moving in to support him as they started back toward the creek.

When they were out of sight, Alaric beckoned the two men who had escorted him in. "Tell me."

"Not much to tell," the younger of the two said. Alaric couldn't remember the kid's name.

"He triggered one of the outside warning wards and we left our post at the inner wards to investigate. We found him slumped against a tree near the triggered ward." Carter McDaniel was the second of the two men. "He said he needed sanctuary and asked to see the Shade."

"Did you read him?"

Carter shrugged. "Enough to know he didn't mean any harm and he was hurt. He's got good shields, so he'd know if I tried more than that."

Alaric nodded. "Okay, get back to your posts." He pulled a hand through his hair and let his eyes wander up the trail down to the water.

"So now we have two of those freaks," Bryan said, suddenly beside him. Alaric looked up at him, and Sahara who had appeared with him.

"He's hurt." Alaric said. "I wasn't about to turn him away."

"I'm not saying we shouldn't let the Shade help him, I'm saying is he really someone we want here?" Bryan said. "Might think about shoring up those outer wards too, if anyone can just wander through them."

Alaric clapped a hand to Bryan's shoulder. "Probably a good idea. We need to be vigilant. Can you and Jacob take care of that?"

"And what about him?" Sahara asked, her eyes on the dark trail where Mason had disappeared with the new comer.

"I'll take care of him." Alaric promised. "Don't worry about it."

"It's my job to worry," Bryan countered.

"I get it Bryan, you don't like Mason. You don't have to keep reminding me."

"It isn't so much that I don't like him. He ain't kin is all."

Alaric turned to look at him. "Neither is Sahara, but you seem to have adapted to having her around."

"I think what Bryan is trying to say is that some of us have good reasons not to trust Shades. One is bad enough, two is too many," Sahara offered, though her words didn't have the angry edge they had when he'd first brought Mason to the camp.

"I know the history," Alaric conceded. "Bryan, I haven't forgotten what happened to your great-grandparents. And Sahara, you were on board with this once, what's changed?"

She smiled, her teeth sharp. "I am on board with it, in theory. It's entirely another matter when there are actual people involved."

Alaric sighed. "I'm not even sure that Mason is staying much longer, if that makes you happy."

"I don't know about happy, but I'll certainly sleep better once they're gone," Bryan replied.

"And if he stays?" Alaric asked, looking away.

"Then he stays, and maybe he earns a pass like Sahara did."

Alaric glanced at him, wondering exactly when and how Sahara had earned anything. Maybe he'd been too caught up in Mason and not paying enough attention to his own people. "I expect you to be civil. Both of you."

Sahara's smile was something short of civil. "And I expect you'll keep the two of them on a leash as short as you're keeping ours." She stalked away.

"I wasn't aware I was keeping them on any leash." Alaric muttered, turning toward Bryan.

"She doesn't like rules." Bryan responded. "Like the one about keeping their human forms until they're outside the wards." Bryan looked at Alaric, then at Sahara's retreating back. "For what it's worth, I don't think she plans to rip the Shade apart," Bryan offered. "But she is capable."

Alaric sighed. "I know what she's capable of. I watched her hunting the other day." Bryan's shields were tight, but his amusement at Sahara and his concern over the Shades were easy enough to read. "Be careful, Bryan."

He nodded slowly. "You too, Alaric."

Bryan left him, following Sahara's trail. "Unite the tribes," Alaric muttered under his breath. "Because that's a simple thing to do."

"It will happen."

Alaric looked up, surprised to find Keisha still there, sitting on one of the logs around the fire pit. She stood, her eyes still on Bryan's retreating back. "Just takes some folk longer than others." She smiled tightly. "I take it they have family history with Shades?"

"Bryan does, I have no idea what Sahara's issues are."

Keisha's hand was warm on his. "The old stories tell us that in the beginning we were all one tribe, Shadows and Shades, Shifters and Sages, and man. Before our differences drove us apart, it was our common blood that kept us together. We can get back there."

"I hope so." Alaric said. "We need to if we're going to survive."

Chapter Ten

Raven left Zero with Evan, stepping outside with her phone. She'd scanned through him after Zero stopped talking, marveling at the extent of his reaction to injuries that didn't exist. Whatever his connection with this twin brother, it had to be intense.

It was late, but she dialed the number, biting her lip and pacing as it rang. "Raven?" Darvin asked in way of greeting.

"Yeah. We've got a problem." She paced outside the room while she tried to figure out what exactly the problem was. "Evan… he had a… I don't even know what, but he's down. Out cold."

"What happened?"

"He called me for help. I got to him and he was reacting like he was in extreme pain, but there were no wounds. I did my best to help, but I can't find a cause and I don't know how to actually help him."

Darvin was silent for a minute. "You can't. Can you get him home?"

"Theoretically, yes. We'll have to drive."

"Probably safer that way anyway."

"Are you going to tell me what's going on?" Raven asked a little more tersely than she meant to.

"Evan's twin brother, Sawyer. They're linked psychically somehow. Remember the personal business he was on before he met you in Atlanta? Well, it was his brother. His unit was sent to scout out the situation in Utah. He was undercover."

"And he was caught," Raven said softly. "So, what Evan was going through…"

"Sawyer was probably being tortured," Darvin confirmed. "What about this girl he was telling me about?"

"She's fine. Helped me with him actually."

"He said she's a Sage?"

Raven nodded and moved away from the door. "Yeah, a Sage with some Shadow mixed in. She's young and thinks her father might be caught up in this killing."

"Are you sure you can trust her?"

Raven really wasn't sure. "I saved her life; she saved mine. I think we have to operate as if she's on our side."

She could almost picture Adam rubbing his face. "Okay, bring her along."

"You're not recruiting her," Raven said. "She's sixteen, maybe seventeen."

"Is she safe there?" Adam asked, his voice soft.

Raven sighed, shaking her head. "Honestly, I don't know. Probably not."

"Bring her along. Be safe."

Raven listened as he hung up, dropping her head. It would be a long drive. She looked up at the sky. If they could get Evan into the SUV, they could at the very least get out of the city before daylight forced her to pull off and find a hotel. She pocketed her phone and let herself back into the room.

"Okay, do you think you can help me get him into the SUV?"

Zero looked a little stunned. "Now?"

"Even with tinted windows, I'd rather not drive during the day." Raven moved around the room, gathering their things and shoving them into suitcases. "If you need anything, now's the time to say so."

Zero stood, and crossed to her boots. "I need to make a quick stop if I'm coming with you."

"I won't force you to," Raven said, even if that was what Adam wanted. "But I think it's in your best interest to get out of Atlanta."

"Where are we going?"

"D.C. We have friends there."

Raven finished packing and grabbed the keys. "I'll get this stuff loaded up, then we'll get him up." She wasn't sure why, but she was feeling a sense of urgency now that it came down to it.

Ten minutes later, they had Evan in the back seat, and Raven climbed behind the wheel. "Where to?"

"It's easiest if I show you." Zero said as she pulled her door shut. Her hand touched Raven's and her voice filled Raven's head. "*Just relax.*"

Images followed her words, streets and turns and ultimately a building that looked abandoned. Raven nodded when she'd absorbed the information. "Buckle up."

It didn't take long to reach the building. "I won't be long," Zero said as she opened the door, leaving her messenger bag on the floor by her feet. She hesitated, looking up at Raven. "Keep your eyes open. If the tracker found the waterfall, he probably found this too."

"What exactly is this place?"

Zero shrugged. "Just a place I keep things. I'll be right back."

Raven watched Zero move through the shadows, around to the alley, where the dark swallowed her. It was nearly midnight. Streetlamps cast pools of light on the street, and long fingers of shadows that could hide any manner of danger.

Behind her, Evan stirred, and she turned to look at him. His eyes opened, but she wasn't sure he actually saw her. "Go back to sleep, Evan," Raven said softly.

She scanned the world outside the SUV, freezing when she thought she saw movement. She watched the spot for a long time before she was convinced it was her imagination. "Hurry up, Zero."

Raven was contemplating going in after the girl, but she didn't want to leave Evan alone. "*We aren't alone.*" Raven suddenly heard the words in her head, pulling her attention to the alley where Zero had disappeared.

She put the SUV in drive with her foot on the brake, ready to take off as soon as Zero was in. She could feel them now, three heartbeats that didn't belong, steady, strong. One was behind them, the others were nearby, on either side of the SUV.

Zero's face peeked around the corner of the building, then she was running, a big duffle swinging at her side as she sprinted the distance. Voices yelled, and Zero yanked the door open. "Go."

Raven took her foot off the brake and moved it to the gas before Zero had even shut the door. "Hold on."

One of the men watching them stepped out in front of her and Raven swerved around him, gunning the engine.

"Take the next right, we can lose them if we go through downtown," Zero said, buckling her seatbelt.

"You think they're following us?" Raven asked.

"One way or another, yes, but if we swing through downtown and up 85, we'll pass a bunch of nightclubs, lots of people, lots of un-guarded minds just leaking out extraneous thought and detail. It'll muck up the tracker and we can get a good head start."

Raven nodded and followed her direction. She didn't see any pur-suit, but she knew better than to believe that meant it wasn't there.

A couple of turns and several streets later, Raven saw the first neon signs indicating they had reached the start of the clubs. They spread out around and in front of them. She was forced to slow down as they hit traffic, but she could see the freeway sign.

Zero was quiet beside her, eyes closed. Raven could tell she was doing *something*, but couldn't tell what it was. Zero didn't look up until Raven had them on the freeway and headed north.

"I think we're clear for now," Zero said. "But we're going to want to change vehicles when we can. It's a good bet they'll be looking for us."

Raven nodded. "We can do that. Let's get to Charlotte at least before morning. We can return the car and get something else."

Zero shook her head. "Return the car, but we can't rent another one. They're probably already digging into who rented this. They'll have a whole history on you and your friend there before we reach Charlotte."

"What do you suggest?" Raven asked.

Zero smiled. "Mostly that you don't ask too many questions."

"I don't like the sound of that." Raven found herself checking the rearview mirror repeatedly for anyone following them, even as the traffic around them drifted away and there were only a few cars on the road as they left Atlanta. When she was sure they weren't being tailed, she relaxed a little, glancing over at Zero who had the duffle bag on her lap and was checking through the contents. "So, what's in the bag?"

Zero didn't look up. "Personal stuff, mostly. A little cash, some books, some tools of the trade." She held up a bright red wig. "Hair."

Raven chuckled. "I bet that's a good look on you."

"You'd be surprised. When I lost my hair, I was really upset, but my mom got me my first wig. It was this ridiculous purple thing with silver strands of tinsel."

"Sounds like she was a pretty great mom."

Zero pulled the wig onto her head. "She was."

"How old were you?" Raven asked as Zero's hands delved back into the bag.

"When? When she died or when I lost my hair?"

Raven blinked a little. "Either? Whatever you're comfortable with."

Zero actually snorted. "I left comfortable a long time ago. Before you pulled me out of that circle. That initiation was way out of my comfort zone." She was quiet for a long moment before she took a deep breath. "I was nine when I lost my hair. It was... well, it was a very good lesson in being very specific when working with magic."

Raven nodded, even though Zero wasn't looking at her. "What kind of magic were you playing with at nine?"

Zero moved her seat back a little, glancing behind her to make sure she wasn't impacting Evan, then put her feet up on the dash. "I started manifesting ability to work with various elements early, and a girl at school made fun of my hair... I wasn't overly specific when I tried to change it. I woke up the next morning surrounded by the hair from all over my body."

"So you have no hair? None?"

"Not a lick." Zero laughed. "As traumatized as I was at the time, it comes in handy now. Glamors are a lot easier when you can start with some quick real changes."

They fell into a comfortable silence and after a few miles, Raven glanced over to find Zero was asleep, or faking it pretty well. She sighed and settled in for the long drive.

* * *

Raven pulled the car to a stop in the rental returns at the Charlotte airport with a sigh. Turning the engine off, she looked behind her to find Evan alert and watching her.

"Where are we?" Evan asked, his voice heavy with sleep.

"Charlotte. We're changing vehicles, then finding a room. Sun will be up in an hour or so."

Beside her, Zero put her feet down and looked around them. "We still seem clear. You two get your stuff, meet me in arrivals."

She opened her door and started to get out, but Raven caught her arm. "Where are you going?"

"To get us another ride."

"We aren't stealing a car," Evan groused, sitting up and rubbing his head. "And what the hell did you do to me?"

"It isn't stealing... exactly." Zero said. She climbed out of the SUV, then leaned in through the door. "And I did you a favor. Give me fifteen minutes."

"Nice new friend you found," Evan said, leaning into the front seat. His eyes were shot with red, like he'd been drinking for days, and the tender skin under them was smudged with black. "What's the story? What are we doing?"

Raven turned to get a better look at him. "Apparently, we're getting our things and going to arrivals. How are you doing?"

He rubbed a hand over his face and groaned. "I'm still living."

"I was worried there for a bit that you wouldn't be."

"I'll be fine."

"Evan—"

He sort of growled at her and she let it drop, holding up her hands in surrender. "Fine. But I'm here if you need to talk."

"I don't." He opened the back door and got out of the SUV, moving to the back of it as Raven popped the back door open. He seemed a little wobbly on his feet, and she could still feel waves of pain rolling off of him, but he was upright and moving under his own power.

Raven took the car keys to the after-hours return drop, then came back to get her suitcase. Neither of them spoke as they made their way into the airport and past baggage claim. The air was cool but humid as they stepped out to wait for Zero.

"I don't like this." Evan said after a few minutes. He looked like he was ready to fall down as he leaned up against the wall, his eyes half closed.

"Neither do I, but you didn't really leave us a lot of choice."

"I don't trust her."

"Who do you trust?"

He doubled over, one hand holding his stomach, the other trying to reach his back. Pain was spiking through him and she reached a hand for him, sending a general wave of healing into him. "Evan?"

He grabbed her hand. "Fuck, he's cutting his wings."

His knees buckled and they were starting to draw attention. Raven squatted beside him. "Tell me how to help."

Evans eyes squeezed shut and he huffed, pushing her hand to his back. "Here."

She closed her eyes and focused energy through her hand at the places that seemed to be screaming out the loudest, all too aware that if someone saw them and realized what she was doing, what she was, they would be in a worse situation than they were already.

Fortunately, there weren't a lot of people milling about at four-thirty in the morning. Out of the corner of her eye, Raven saw a van pull up, and Zero was out and rushing toward them. "What happened?" Zero asked.

Raven shook her head. "Let's just get him into the van and get out of here." She supported Evan on his left and Zero got an arm around him from the right. He did his best to help but by the time they got him to the van he was screaming in agony, his body rigged. Zero got the door open and they shoved him inside.

"Do what you can." Raven climbed through to the driver's seat.

"I got the van so we could keep moving in daylight," Zero said, throwing the van's door closed.

"Later. Too many people just saw that." Raven pulled out and pointed them in the right direction. "Can you put him under again?"

"I don't want to hurt him."

"Trust me, he's in so much pain right now, he'll welcome the relief."

Raven *felt* the push that knocked Evan out again. A few seconds later, Zero climbed into the passenger seat. "He's not going to like the headache he's going to wake up with."

"It's better than the heart attack the stress could have caused," Raven countered. "I'm changing our route. It'll take longer, but maybe it will help keep them off our asses."

"Just get us somewhere that we can switch drivers. You can get in the back with him and I'll drive."

"Do you even have a driver's license?" Raven asked.

"Oh yeah," Zero responded with a grin. "Several."

Chapter Eleven

Mason could feel Alaric's concern as he led the new Shade away from the central fire, down the trail that led to the deepest point of the creek. The man's pain and exhaustion filled his senses though as they neared the water.

"Let's see if we can get you healed up," Mason said softly, helping him peel off his bloody clothes. There were several wounds that looked like bullet holes and a deep bruising that could indicate internal bleeding.

Mason helped him down into the water to sit on the rocks where not to long before he and Alaric had been more intimate than he'd ever been with anyone. He pushed the thought aside and stripped back down to his boxers before stepping in around Damon and helping him move deeper into the water.

Damon's eyes closed as he sank into the cold embrace. Mason helped him float on his back before he started assessing the wounds. The shoulder wound was the worst, so he started there, shifting through the energy patterns he had learned from Paul and Dr. Anthony until he found one that seemed to be working.

Mason felt the tissues begin to heal and moved his attention to the bullet wound on Damon's side. He felt his way past the surface bruising, running energy through the bullet's path. It seemed to have knocked around inside the man for a time before it was removed.

He was uncomfortable with the idea that another Shade had felt him from as far away as the ward line. It didn't help that this man was likely fleeing the same enemies that were probably still looking for him.

Mason shifted his attention to a more general energy pattern, one that would help right the body's systems and enable Damon to take care of the finishing details himself after a good meal and some sleep.

He let Damon float in the water, keeping him from floating with the current with one hand. The air was cold, but the water was better medicine for a Shade than anything they had on hand.

Damon's eyes opened just before his feet pushed down. "Thank you."

"I didn't do much." Mason countered, feeling awkward. "You should be able to finish up what I couldn't once you've had some sleep."

"You didn't need to do that much," Damon said. "The last Shade I encountered didn't." He turned his face to show the shadow of some bruising along his jaw. "I only asked for water."

Mason lifted a hand to feel into the healing bruise. "Another Shade did this?"

"He was afraid." Damon said. "And I showed up on his doorstep bleeding and running from an army."

"Still." Mason made a face as he moved toward shore. He was starting to feel the cold, and his stomach reminded him that he hadn't eaten yet. "Are you hungry?"

Damon's eyes followed him to where he'd left his clothes. "I haven't had food in days."

"Do you need to soak longer first?"

"I can soak later. I think food and sleep are more important, now that you've stopped the blood loss."

Damon moved toward the shore, the water absorbing into his skin as he reached for his clothes. He pulled his pants on, lifting his shirt and shaking his head, one finger poking through the bullet hole in the shoulder.

Mason chuckled a little. "Alaric said he'd find you something to wear." He reached out to Alaric mentally. He was too far away for words to form, but he got the image of Alaric with a handful of cloth, headed their way. Mason sent the image of the bunkhouse instead and gestured for Damon.

"Let's get some food. Alaric will meet us there."

Mason led Damon up the trail and to the bunk house. The fire in the fireplace was burning low, so he paused to feed it a couple of logs before he went into the kitchen, only partially surprised to find Emily already there.

"Shouldn't you be sleeping?" Mason asked as she smiled at him.

"I heard we have a guest who is hungry." Emily responded. "I'm warming up the chili we had for dinner, and there's a bit of cornbread left, if you want to heat it up too."

Mason smiled and moved to the counter where the cornbread was sitting. "You know, I could have managed this by myself."

"And deprive me of getting to meet our new arrival?" She stirred the chili with a big wooden spoon while Mason put the pan of cornbread into the oven to warm.

"I should know better by now," Mason said. Alaric was nearly to the bunk house; Mason could feel him. "I should go make him feel more comfortable."

"I'll bring this out when it's ready."

Mason found Damon standing by the fire, warming his hands. The door opened behind him, and Alaric entered, holding out a pile of clothes. "These should fit, or be close anyway," Alaric said, putting the pile down on the table. "And we have a cabin for you. I've got Riley getting it set up."

Damon sifted through the clothes for a shirt, pulling it on before nodding his thanks. "I appreciate the help."

"You're looking better," Alaric observed.

"Thanks to your friend here." Damon sat on the bench closest to the fire. "I already feel better than I have in a long time."

Mason could almost hear the questions Alaric had spinning around in his head. He sat across the table from Damon. "We don't mean to pry…" Mason glanced up at Alaric who was moving closer. "…but we need to know what happened. We have a lot of people here we need to protect."

Damon nodded. "That's fair. For what it's worth, I don't think I was followed after the last run in. And your wards are good. I would have kept going if I hadn't felt the presence of a Shade."

Emily appeared with a tray filled with steaming bowls of chili and a plate of cornbread, along with glasses of water. Alaric helped her empty the tray.

"Emily, this is Damon Estos," Mason said. "He will be staying with us, at least for now. Damon, this is Emily Lambrecht."

"I'm grateful you found us," Emily said with a soft smile, slipping an arm around Alaric. "I hope you continue to heal."

"Thank you, ma'am," Damon said with a nod.

Emily kissed Alaric's cheek and left them to talk. Alaric sat beside Mason. "So, you said the army came for you?"

Damon nodded as he chewed and swallowed. "My daughter and I lived in a small house near Oroville. One day this army unit in blue uniforms comes into town and starts blocking streets, takes over the police department, starts questioning people for no reason." He paused to take a drink. "They grabbed my daughter Arianna as she was leaving the movie theater one night, pulled her in and questioned her. Came for me the next day."

There was more to it than that, Mason sensed, but he didn't push. "What happened?"

"Arianna managed to warn me." He tapped his temple to indicate the psychic connection between Shades. "I got out just as they came in. That's when I got shot here." He held his hand to the spot on his side. "But I got away. Ran. They followed. I got hit the second time just before I felt a Shade nearby. Tried to get help, but he wasn't very friendly."

"What happened to your daughter?" Alaric asked gently.

Damon ate for a few minutes before answering. "I don't know. I lost contact with her. Not sure if it was the distance between us or..." He trailed off, keeping his focus on his food. "I don't know if she's even alive still."

Alaric's hand was warm on Mason's back, rubbing comfort into him. They were all quiet then, letting Damon eat. Mason's thoughts wandered to Paul, living alone up in the mountains, and how he'd react if the 8th Battalion came for him.

"She was pregnant," Alaric said suddenly, making Damon look up sharply. "Sorry, I wasn't... you're not very shielded right now."

"Yes, she was. Six months or so. The father is a Shade who lives in Arizona. She went there to learn from a teacher, was there almost a year. Came back just before this whole mess started." He pushed his bowl away and drained his glass of water.

There really wasn't much to say to that, so Mason finished his water as well. Alaric was the first to stand. "Let me show you where you can sleep."

Mason trailed after them as Alaric led them to a small cabin pretty well removed from most of the others. "It isn't much, but the windows are blacked out and it's close to the water." Alaric said, opening the door.

"I'm sure it will be fine. I appreciate the hospitality." Damon stepped inside, nodding. "I'll do my best to stay out of the way. I got the impression that not all of your people will want me here."

"It's time we unite or find ourselves extinct," Alaric said. "Don't hide too much."

Mason stood a few steps away, in the light of a nearly full moon, closing his eyes and turning his face up to the light.

He let the peace settle over him. It seemed such a long time since he had properly sat with the full moon and let it fill him up. He cleared his mind of questions and worry and let the moonlight wash through him, cleaning out the corners and washing away the remnants of his torture and the terror that had come with it.

So much had changed since that day when he had stepped off that train in D.C. He was a different person now. He wasn't just his Nana's grandson, or Darvin's spy. As he examined what he was feeling, he was surprised to realize that he was happier here than he'd been since before his father had died.

If he was honest with himself, Alaric was the only thing holding him here. He was healed, in many ways stronger than he'd been in a long time. He didn't understand why he felt so connected to the man, or exactly what had been going on earlier when they were together. His body had heated up in a way he'd never felt before.

He didn't have a lot to compare it to, but that was an experience like nothing he'd ever even heard of before. His body had vibrated, pulling energy from Alaric, from the water, from the air, and sending it out twice as hard, and when he'd orgasmed, it was enough to turn the world inside out for a couple of seconds.

Alaric was moving toward him. Mason could feel him, his heart beating to the rhythm that pounded in Mason's chest.

"You look like you're a million miles away," Alaric said.

"No. I was just soaking up some moonlight." Mason replied, turning to look at him.

Alaric nodded and slipped a hand into his, starting them moving back toward the central part of the camp. "Are you alright?"

Mason smiled and leaned closer, stopping to kiss him a little more surely than he had before in the water. "I'm fine."

Alaric's tongue slipped into his mouth, caressing lightly over his tongue. "*Yes, you are.*"

He could feel himself blushing, could feel the warmth rising inside him. Already he was half hard and wanting when Alaric broke the kiss. "I was worried. I don't want you to leave." Alaric murmured.

"I'm still here," Mason whispered back. "Need to know..." He opened his eyes, searching Alaric's face for... something.

"What do you need to know?" Alaric asked.

Mason tipped his face up to the moon, his hands rising up Alaric's back. "What this is," he responded after a moment, looking back at Alaric. "What it is I feel when you touch me."

"Then I should touch you more." Alaric replied, his lips moving over his chin and up his jaw. "I should touch you everywhere."

"Didn't we already do that?" Mason asked.

Alaric's chuckle was warm in his ear. "That was just an introduction." Alaric's hands slipped under his shirt, pushing up before he leaned in to let his lips ghost over Mason's skin.

"You realize we're out in the open," Mason said softly.

Alaric blinked a little and pulled back. They resumed walking, stopping again when they reached the fire pit. Alaric tugged Mason in, kissing him deeply while his hands went back to exploring Mason's chest.

His lips followed his hands, and when he pulled the shirt up off Mason, he captured his mouth, kissing him as he pressed Mason down to straddle over a log.

The touch of the moon was cool against his chest, which was flushed and heated. Alaric kissed down his neck, sucking lightly at skin over his collarbone.

"Alaric, we should—"

He cut Mason off by kissing him, slowly pressing him to lay back on the log. "Shh..." He went back to kissing down his chest, pausing to lick Mason's right nipple with the flat of his tongue, then he flicked it with the tip. Mason's skin tightened all around the spot, his breath catching as Alaric swung a leg up and over, settling over Mason's thighs.

Alaric straddled over his lap, licking in tiny movements across his chest to his other nipple and when he sucked, Mason grabbed his head, as his body started to tremble. Fire raced through his veins, the heat of it rising up to his skin as his heart beat against his ribs in a rapid rhythm.

Alaric's teeth grazed over the hard tip of his nipple and Mason gasped, making him chuckle. "I'm thinking you like that," Alaric said, glancing up at him.

"It would seem," Mason agreed, trying to steady his breathing.

Alaric went back to his chest, kissing and licking, then blowing cool air over the dampness. Mason slid his fingers through Alaric's hair, holding on to him as he slipped slowly lower. Alaric's tongue delved into Mason's naval and Mason could feel it in his groin.

He tried reaching for himself, but Alaric stopped him, sitting up and catching both of his hands.

"Maybe we should take this inside," Alaric said breathlessly. As if to emphasize his point, a cold wind blew over them with the promise of dropping temperatures and the possibility of snow.

Mason was trembling as he sat up, kissing Alaric frantically. "Yeah, okay."

Alaric's fingers twined through his as they hurried toward the trail. They nearly ran as they started up the path to the cabin, slowing only as they opened the door, scanning about for their cabin-mates before charging up the stairs to the small bedroom that they shared.

The door closed behind them, and Alaric pulled Mason in, pressing him to the wall as his lips covered Mason's, his tongue gliding over Mason's lip. His hands cupped Mason's face as he stepped back, turning them and walking Mason back until he could feel the bed behind him.

"Now then, where were we?" Alaric asked softly as Mason sat. He guided Mason to lay back, sideways across the small bed and he straddled over Mason's legs again. Mason reached up for him, but Alaric caught his hands. "Let me." Alaric pressed kisses into his knuckles before guiding his hands out and to the side.

Mason surged upward when Alaric's hands touched his zipper, sitting up and reaching for him, but Alaric just waited until he settled back to the bed. His heart hammered loud enough to hear in the still air, and his skin was hot. His breathing sped up as Alaric's fingers tugged on his zipper. Mason's eyes closed as Alaric leaned in, his lips moving over the bare skin of his stomach. When Alaric's tongue moved lower, Mason had to bite off a yell, lifting up off the bed.

Alaric licked and kissed over him as he eased Mason's jeans down past his ass, letting gravity pull them down toward his feet on the floor as he focused his attention on Mason. He ran his tongue over him, teasing with the tip of his tongue. "*What does this touch do?*" Alaric's voice in his head accompanied his mouth closing over Mason's erection and he sucked all the way up before taking the whole thing into his mouth again.

"Damn!" Mason reached for him, getting a hand into his hair. Every nerve ending in his body was alive with need, and the bed under him felt cold compared to his skin. He could barely keep from thrusting up already, and he was starting to pant with the effort.

Alaric's right hand was splayed out on his stomach, and the skin under it burned, tingled. Mason's senses were blown open, the smell of wood burning in the fireplace downstairs and trees and sweat combined with the sound of his heart and the buzz of noise in his head and the sound of Alaric's lips sliding over his skin.

His orgasm started before he was fully aware that he was even close, and Mason was still shaking when Alaric lifted his head. "*Come here.*" Mason held up his hand and Alaric took it, letting Mason draw him in to kiss. Mason opened himself up, inviting Alaric to do more than a surface read of his swirling thoughts and emotions.

Alaric looked him in the eye, his thoughts brushing over Mason's to make sure he meant it before Mason felt Alaric surging across and into him. It was overwhelming at first, the full presence filling him briefly before Alaric adjusted and found a comfort level. Images filled his mind, needs, desires, and his body reacted, filling him with an ache for more.

Mason shook his left leg free of his jeans and pulled it from between Alaric's legs, spreading himself open, inviting Alaric to touch more of him. He quivered as Alaric's hand passed over his thigh, an echo of it playing in his head as Alaric leaned in to kiss him. "*Are you sure?*" Alaric asked, his hand gentle as it massaged over his skin, down under him.

"*No,*" Mason responded before he could stop himself, his fear of what he was about to do urging him to stop. "*But yes… want to feel you.*" He tipped his head back, fighting the urge to clench himself tight as Alaric's finger circled around his opening.

"You don't have to." Alaric's spoken voice seemed so out of place, harsh and gravelly like he hadn't spoken in days.

"*Want to,*" Mason growled back, opening himself up more, breathing out and relaxing as Alaric pushed inward.

Alaric nodded, and Mason could actually feel him focus on carefully working him open. Alaric shifted, reaching for the nightstand. He pulled a bottle out, and spread some liquid onto his fingers before coming back, his hand returning to slide back under Mason. His other hand splayed out across Mason's stomach like an anchor to keep him from jumping out of his skin.

Mason closed his eyes, one hand holding Alaric's wrist as Alaric's hand lay on his stomach, while the finger of Alaric's other hand moved inside him. "*Easy.*" Alaric's voice whispered to him, calming as his presence filled Mason again. "*Here.*"

It took him a moment to realize what Alaric was showing him, then Alaric brushed over a control center in his brain and Mason felt the tightness in his muscles relax. Alaric kissed him then, distracting him. Mason did his best not to tighten up again as those fingers moved inside him. "Breathe," Alaric murmured, kissing him again, slow and easy as he kept his fingers moving.

Mason opened his eyes as Alaric shifted, the sound of his zipper pulling Mason up out of his head. Alaric's eyes met his, their minds intertwined, the whole world gone but for the two of them.

Mason opened his mouth to yell as Alaric pressed into him, but no sound came, only the echo inside them of the sound. Alaric moved slow, leaning in as Mason opened to take him in, his eyes locked on Mason's.

Mason panted through the pain of the stretching, unable to look away. Alaric's blue eyes were silvery in the light that came through the window, but the cool kiss of the moon did little to ease the fire burning through Mason. He opened his mouth to drink in the light as Alaric eased back. It was too much and he felt as though he were drowning in the sensation as Alaric pushed in again, a little faster this time.

Alaric lifted Mason's leg and settled it against his shoulder, and tilting Mason's hips a little, sending sparks dancing through his veins.

"A…ric," Mason gasped an approximation of his name, lifting his head off the bed beneath him. "Fuck."

Alaric's voice in his head was a groan and a whisper, his whole presence glowing and silver, and as he increased speed, Mason felt himself opening, felt Alaric inside him in places no one had ever been. Their bodies and minds melted together, intimate and intricate, and as Mason came for a second time he wasn't sure they would ever be able to sort out which pieces belonged where.

Alaric's orgasm began as Mason's ended, running together as one, both of them shaking with the force of it until finally Alaric eased back and out, panting as he fell beside Mason on the bed.

For a long moment neither of them moved, breathing in the moment and the cool night air. "*You okay?*" Alaric's voice stirred ripples around inside him, aftershocks of pleasure that made him groan and grab his cock to cradle it.

"*Yeah…*" He wanted to say more, but Alaric turned to him, kissing him lightly, and he knew he had no need.

Chapter Twelve

Raven felt the van slowing, pulling her up from a restless sleep. Evan lay still, his head on her lap. The pain from earlier seemed to have left him and all that remained was the headache that resulted from forcibly knocking him out. She put a hand on his head and urged healing energy into him.

He stirred and after a minute his eyes opened, meeting hers before he sat up, groaning a little. "Where are we?" Evan asked.

The van came to a stop and Zero leaned out of the driver's seat. "Just outside of Richmond. I need a break." She came back to them and squatted beside them. "It's about three in the afternoon. I've got us parked in some shade at a truck stop. I'm running inside."

She opened the side door of the van and then pulled it shut behind her.

"You let her drive?" Evan asked after a few minutes.

"It was that or get a room, which could leave us sitting ducks if those men found us," Raven replied. She rubbed over her face and up over her hair. "I need a shower."

Evan's eyes were dark as he opened the side door and got out to stretch. "Have you called in?"

Raven shook her head. "Not since just after you called me."

He nodded tightly. "I'll drive the rest of the way."

"Are you sure?" Raven asked, sliding closer to the door so she could get out too, her eyes darting around them to figure out how much room she had to move around. "I mean, considering... are you sure it's safe? What if it happens again?"

He didn't look at her. "It won't."

"Evan, how—"

His head snapped up, his face nearly a snarl. "My brother is dead. It won't happen again."

He walked away from her then, out into the bright afternoon sun. Raven couldn't have gone after him if she wanted to. She paced the shaded area, stretching and rolling her neck. Sleeping sitting up in the back of a van had done a number on her back and shoulders.

A few minutes later, Evan was sitting behind the wheel as Zero emerged from the store, her arms loaded down with snacks and drinks. She got into the passenger's seat and passed the keys over without a question before she passed a bottle of water back to Raven. She opened another and settled into the cup holder between the seats. "I figured water was a good bet. I don't know much about your people and what they need."

"Water is fine, thank you." Evan started the van and started them moving again. "Do I want to know how you got this van?"

Zero shrugged. "I asked a guy if I could use it. He didn't say no."

Evan sighed heavily but didn't respond.

"How's your head?" Zero asked.

"I'm fine," Evan said. "Thank you."

"No sweat. All I did was knock you out. She's the one with the healing mojo."

The van fell silent as Evan pulled them onto the highway. Raven zoned out, letting the rhythm of the road pull her out of her head and into a quasi-sleep that wouldn't necessarily help make her feel rested, but could at least take some of the dullness of time.

* * *

Zero paced nervously around the small room. They'd reached their destination hours before, and she'd panicked a little as the Shade and the Shifter walked her into a facility that wasn't unlike the one she'd escaped from days before.

At least, she thought it was days. Time tended to blur together sometimes. Zero had nearly run when they told her she needed to undergo a medical exam.

She'd gotten through it though without hurting anyone. It wasn't as bad as she'd been expecting, nothing like what she would undergo after her father's treatments. She shuddered, pausing in her pacing as scattered bits of memory danced around the walls in her mind.

The experiment had her exhausted, her body was covered in hives, her muscles trembling. Flashes of the exam room with it's cold metal table and instruments she couldn't name. Measurements and tests and Zero screaming until she was hoarse. What came next was worse. Instead of activating the gifts he'd been trying to push into her, the pain pushed her to her most powerful gift, the one that came to her completely naturally.

No one died, but the room was left a scorched-out shell, and the nurse who had been assisting ended up with second and third-degree burns. Zero had spent the next week confined to a cage of a room with glass walls that hid nothing, a cot, and nothing else to occupy her.

Zero shook the memory off. It didn't serve a purpose here. Raven told her she was safe here, but Zero wasn't sure she believed it.

These feds had given her a room, and she'd had a chance to shower off the last few days and change her clothes. Not that the choices they offered were all that flattering. The olive green of the standard uniform was boring and she couldn't resist putting on the bright red wig with it. At least her boots went well, though they had seen better days.

"Zero, sit down," Raven said, rubbing her forehead. "You're making me nervous."

She rolled her eyes and dropped into one of the chairs around the conference table. "What's taking so long?" Zero asked, jumping as the door opened behind her.

The man Raven had introduced to her as the boss was all business in an expensive suit with his hair slicked back. He had a file folder and a tablet in his hand as he took a seat at the other end of the table. He opened the file folder and she could see a picture of herself paperclipped to the top page.

Darvin looked up at her, his smile not putting her at ease at all. "Well, Miss Zero, you are a mystery, aren't you?"

She narrowed her eyes at him, trying to determine what he meant. "I'm not all that." She almost dared to try to read him, but she wasn't sure he wouldn't be able to tell.

He dragged his finger across the tablet and the screens on the wall filled with information about her life. "Born Alexis Chen Lewis, daughter of Chunhua and Thomas Lewis in Atlanta in 1999. Good student until her mother died, and then she disappeared from public records along with her father."

Zero stared at the screen, then dragged her eyes back to Darvin. "Chances are pretty good he knows where I am now. Thanks for that."

"He probably already figured that out anyway, if he's as good as you say he is," Raven countered.

"Agent Ivany tells me that he's using the name Lewis Rede?" He poked the tablet and new images filled the screen. "Is this him?"

The image was grainy and low resolution, and was not very close, but it was her father. She rose slowly and moved closer. "Where did you get this?"

Darvin sat back in his seat. She could feel his eyes on her. "It was taken outside a facility we had under surveillance in Salt Lake City just before we finally caught William Darchel."

"Darchel?" Something about the name and location bugged her. "The Shade who killed those women, right?" She turned to look at Darvin who nodded.

"Do you know something about him?"

She shrugged, digging through her memory, but nothing was surfacing. "Hard to tell." She returned to her seat and dropped into it, leaning back to kick her feet up onto the table. "He's messed with my head enough that I could have the secrets to cure cancer and end world hunger in here, and I wouldn't know it."

"And yet, you think he's involved in inciting violence?" Darvin asked.

"Yes. He is," Zero responded. "He's powerful. He has money and influence, and he's strong."

"He doesn't show up on any of our watch lists. If he's so powerful, shouldn't we have heard his name?"

"He doesn't like attention. He hides behind aliases and dummy corporations." She shook her head. "Why am I trying to convince you? You're the government. You figure it out."

"Zero, we're working on it. And Adam isn't saying we don't believe you. He's saying that there's work to do to confirm it." Raven soothed.

"And what do I do while you confirm it?" Zero asked. "Why exactly did I come all the way up here with you?"

"We can protect you." Raven said. "There's no way his men can get at you here."

Zero rolled her eyes. "Yeah, I'll believe that when they haven't kidnapped me out of here in a week."

"I promise you, they won't." Darvin said. He seemed sincere enough; he believed what he was saying. "And in the meantime, while we work on confirming your background, we could use your help figuring out who this man you call R is and how to stop him."

Zero inhaled and held it, considering the idea. The blocks and memory modifications that had been forced on her made it difficult. She had hoped that the initiation ceremony would break through them, but so far, she was struggling to articulate things she knew, let alone getting past those walls. She put her feet down and leaned on the table, her eyes finding Darvin's. "I'll tell you what, Mr. Darvin, I will do what I can and be as honest as I can be. If I can tell you, I will tell you. But I expect some compensation."

Darvin smiled, but Raven didn't seem as happy. "I'm sure we can come to some mutually beneficial arrangement."

"Good." She stood, stretching as she did. "We can start with food. I'm starving."

"Of course. Raven can show you to the cafeteria. I will set up a schedule for you, get you sitting down with the right people to give us what information you can. You can start tomorrow." Darvin gathered his things and left the room.

Raven sighed, shaking her head. "Come on. I'm hungry too." She led the way out of the room and through the corridors to the elevator. She was tightly shuttered, though Zero could tell she was annoyed just from her facial expression.

"What?" Zero asked as they stepped off the elevator.

Raven looked at her and shook her head. "I didn't want... that."

Zero frowned, trying to read her but just hitting a wall. "Didn't want what?"

She huffed and stopped walking. "Him. He sees everyone as someone to recruit. I brought you here so you'd be safe, not so you could go to work for him." Raven took her arm and drew her into a side corridor, lowering her voice. "Look. Adam is a good man, but he uses people, pushes them, and sometimes, a lot of times in fact, they don't come back."

"I can handle myself," Zero said reflexively.

"I know you think that," Raven said. "So did Lieutenant Chayton's brother. And he's dead now."

"So, what is it you do want?" Zero asked, crossing her arms.

"I want you to be careful what you agree to," Raven said. "And don't let him convince you to go into the field."

Zero could see Raven's concern, feel it in a wave. "Yeah, okay. I don't have a death wish." It wasn't like she had planned anything beyond getting free of the facility where she'd been kept for the last five years and getting out from under her father's control. Now that she had, Zero wasn't exactly sure what to do next.

* * *

Evan Chayton stood in front of the screens detailing everything they had on his brother's last mission, his eyes scanning over images and words as he tried to recreate what happened.

Sawyer's mission had been to get in close to Norman Douglas and his inner circle after intelligence had connected the senator and the 8th Battalion. He had gone in as security, working his way closer to the senator over a period of months.

None of the reports indicated any suspicion that he had been discovered. Evan manipulated controls, and brought up a series of pictures from recent Douglas rallies, searching for the images from the last rally before Sawyer's disappearance.

The last rally had been in Douglas' native Salt Lake City. Evan spread the pictures out across the screens, various images taken by the press from differing angles. Sawyer stood off to the side of the stage with other staff.

Beside him was a man in uniform, an army major. Nothing looked out of place. Evan sighed and cycled through other articles and images taken around the same time, stopping when he spotted a picture taken outside the rally as the senator and his staff were leaving. There were protesters, although there were fewer than they'd seen in rally stops on the east coast, and separating them from the senator was a line of men in uniforms that could easily be mistaken as private security.

Evan could tell the difference.

"Son of a bitch." The patches on their shoulders depicted an emblem he was starting to see in greater numbers. A navy blue field with a white cross engulfed in red flames.

Evan turned from the screens and sat down, turning his attention to the bond he'd shared with Sawyer. As identical twins, they had always shared a special bond, an intimate connection that let them share thoughts, even across miles.

It was how Sawyer turned in reports once he'd gotten in deep enough that he didn't want to risk getting caught contacting a federal agency. It confirmed that the security was actually 8th Battalion, and that Douglas was well aware of that fact.

Steeling himself for the onslaught of emotion and pain, Evan turned to the moments just after Sawyer reached out for help. They came in the middle of the night, breaking down the door of his hotel room and dragging him out. His hands were cuffed and a hood put over his head. He fought them, pulling and yelling and trying to get free, but they were strong and he was outnumbered.

There was a helicopter, and Sawyer tried to shift to get free, but before he could there was a needle and everything went sideways. Evan couldn't tell what kind of drug was used, and the memory ended shortly after as Sawyer lost control and couldn't reach Evan anymore.

Everything after that carried the wobbly nature that came from being under the influence of drugs designed to loosen his tongue and keep him sedated. Mostly, Sawyer could reach past them to send coherent thought only when the pain pushed him.

They started with questions about his work, who he was reporting to, what he'd told them. But then they turned to asking about his shifting ability.

The accompanying torture when Sawyer wouldn't answer was what Evan had experienced in Atlanta. At the time, it had been too overwhelming to fully understand what was happening. Now, though, he could turn the memory over and examine the faces that Sawyer had seen, the room he'd been kept in.

The men who had grabbed him and questioned who he worked for were different from the ones who came later. The first men were dressed in the 8th Battalion navy blue. The later ones wore more familiar uniforms.

One face in particular stuck out – an army colonel with a long face and short cropped dark hair. The name on his chest was Shallon. His was the last face Sawyer had seen as they pulled his wings back and cut them off.

Evan shuddered and pushed the memory away, looking up when the door to the room opened. "Am I interrupting?" Darvin asked as he stepped in.

"Not really." Evan turned back to the screens, his fingers moving over the keyboard to bring up a picture that matched the face in his brother's memory.

Darvin came to stand beside him, hands in his pockets as he looked at the picture. "Colonel James Shallon. Recently promoted for his performance in getting several cities on the west coast under control during the recent riots."

"You know him?" Evan asked.

Darvin nodded slowly. "I know of him, is more accurate. I've had my eye on him since an operative brought him to my attention."

Evan stood slowly. "This is the man who killed my brother." His voice was cold and dark, and it made Darvin turn to look at him. "I will kill him."

"I have no doubt," Darvin responded, his hand coming to land on Evan's shoulder. "Your day will come. I promise you."

Chapter Thirteen

Mason woke to the sound of fighting, gunfire echoing through the room, and he felt the bite as if it were his own skin it tore through. He was up on his feet before he was fully awake, charging out of the bedroom and down the stairs. He ripped the door open, blinking in the bright sunlight, squinting and holding his hand up to shield his eyes as he tried to find the source of the gunfire and the pain.

Alaric's mother was at his side a moment later, grabbing his arm. "Alaric's hurt," she said softly, her voice trembling with fear.

Mason nodded. "I know. Gunshot, left shoulder." He shook his head. "What's happening?"

"I don't know." She seemed to be listening to something.

Mason pulled out of her hand and started into the sunlight, but she grabbed him again and pulled him back. "You can't go out there."

"I have to. Alaric's hurt."

"He isn't the only one. You'll only get hurt yourself."

Mason looked at her, but her face was pointed out toward the sounds that were coming closer. "They'll bring the wounded to the bunkhouse," she said, gesturing. She handed him a coat and pointed at his feet. "Get some shoes on."

He looked down at his feet and out at the light dusting of snow on the ground, nodding. "Right."

"I'll go down and see if I can help organize."

Emily slipped out the door, and Mason sat on the couch to pull on his boots. He shoved his arms into the coat and pulled the hood up to shield his face from the sun, moving as quickly as he could toward the bunkhouse.

As he reached the doors, Riley appeared, his face angry and smeared with blood. Bryan followed, shoving an injured man in 8th Battalion blue to his knees outside the building.

Alaric came behind them, holding his shoulder, his face pale. He looked to Mason, then to the man on his knees. "Make sure the other three get dealt with." Alaric said to Riley. "We don't want them found."

Mason wanted to go to him, but Alaric clearly wasn't ready for him, so he stood there, watching as Alaric circled to the man on his knees. Other men were filtering into the clearing now with guns in their hands. Several of them were wounded. Mason could feel them.

Emily was suddenly beside him, handing him a canteen of water. "Step back out of the sun. We'll set up a triage line," she said to him, holding the door open for him and guiding him inside.

"Alaric—"

"He'll come in when he's ready."

Mason stepped back toward the fireplace where a fire had just been started. He drained half the canteen and looked up as Emily guided two men in carrying a stretcher. The woman on it was shot through the stomach and bleeding excessively.

Mason put Alaric out of his thoughts, guiding them to put her down on the floor and moving closer. He pulled aside her shirt to get a look, and she moaned.

He exhaled and centered himself, remembering his lessons from the doctor in Washington and what he'd learned from Paul. He'd never really dealt with trauma before, not like this. He licked his lips and settled a hand over the wound. It was bad, the kind that would kill if it wasn't cleaned up and dealt with. "Bullet went through," he murmured. He could feel the damage, but couldn't quite tell what he needed to do. "I need water." He didn't open his eyes, but he felt someone beside him and he could smell the water. "Pour it over her wound."

He connected with the water, followed it inside her, let it guide him and offer him energy to start the process of knitting her back together. He was sweating when he had done what he could. "Bandage her up. I've done what I can for now." Emily nodded to him and moved in as he went to the next person.

He worked on two more before he felt someone pressing a canteen into his hands. "Drink." He looked up at the midwife, who was also setting down a bucket of water beside him. "I've worked with a Shade before. I know you need it."

He nodded his thanks and drank deep of the cool water in the canteen before looking up at the three new patients. "I've handled the ones that weren't bleeding. You can see to them later."

"Thanks." Mason wiped his face and drank more of the water. "You know, I don't think I even know your name."

She smiled. "Keisha."

"Could you help Emily with the bandages?" She nodded and he moved on to the next wound, a young man with a gash in his arm and another on his forehead.

Three wounded people later, Mason was done with the serious traumas, all but Alaric's. He drank the last of the water and went to the door, squinting into the sun, looking for Alaric. As if on cue, Alaric came up the steps, his eyes seeking out Mason. He was hiding the pain from everyone else, but Mason could feel it.

"Sit down before you fall down." Mason guided him to the open bench, already feeling inside his shoulder. "Keisha, can we get some water and bandages over here please." Mason focused his attention on ripping Alaric's shirt open, wincing when Alaric hissed.

Alaric's head was a jumble of images and words and thoughts that came at Mason fast and furious as he tried to assess the damage. Keisha handed him warm water to wash over the wound. "You're exhausted. Let me triage him, you get some rest."

Mason wrinkled his nose. "I can stop the bleeding at least." His hand covered the wound and he exhaled slowly, and reaching inside Alaric.

He recoiled almost instantly, falling backward. "Shit. Fuck." His head buzzed with the contact against the bullet.

"What?" Keisha asked, holding Alaric upright.

Mason panted and shook it off. "Gold. The bullet is still in his shoulder and they laced the metal with gold." He moved closer, a little more cautious, and a little shaky. It wasn't just gold though. He frowned and lifted his hand to the wound again, feeling inside a little more cautiously. The metal was stuck in bone, designed with Shades in mind. Other than the gold, it was leaching salt and trace amounts of other chemicals into the tissue around it.

"I thought that was an old wives' tale," Alaric muttered.

To be fair, Mason had too, another old wives-tale blown out of proportion by Hollywood. "Apparently not," Mason responded. "I can't do anything until you get the bullet out."

"Yes, you can." Emily said, suddenly behind him and helping him off the floor. "You can rest."

"I should check—"

"No." Emily pointed toward the door.

"Emily, I'm fine—"

"Do not make me drag you to your bed, young man."

"She will too," Alaric said, chuckling a little.

"Keisha and I will see to Alaric until you're feeling better. You've done enough."

Mason wanted to argue, but he could tell the argument was lost, and so he nodded and headed toward the cabin, certain he wouldn't sleep. To his surprise, Emily followed him, and his perception of anything beyond her was muted. "Are you..."

She smiled and caressed his cheek. "I'm helping you. Don't worry. We'll wake you in a couple of hours." She walked him to the cabin and up to the darkened bedroom he shared with Alaric. Her presence pressed closer and closer until it covered him like a blanket as he lay down, making it easier for the exhaustion to pull him under.

* * *

Alaric waited until he felt his mother's wall go up between him and Mason before he reached out for Bryan. He winced as Keisha pulled the bullet from his shoulder, but let her continue her work. Bryan came in the door that faced the trail down to the parking lot, his face grim. Behind him Riley brought the prisoner. "Office." Alaric said, gesturing with his chin. "I'll be there in a minute."

"You should be going to bed, once I'm done with you," Keisha said softly as she worked on bandaging his wound.

He didn't argue, and she didn't say anything more about that. She stood back and stripped off her gloves, looking him in the eye. "I would stitch that mess up, but something tells me that it the Shade will take care of that soon enough."

"Thank you, Keisha," Alaric said, standing slowly. "I'll call you if we need any more medical care."

While she gathered up the medical supplies scattered over several tables, Alaric walked toward the small office. Riley was waiting by the door and lifted his chin in greeting. "You okay?"

Alaric nodded. "For now. See that we aren't interrupted." He moved into the office where Bryan stood behind the man, hands on his shoulders. He wasn't restrained to the chair, but Alaric could tell that Bryan's mental hold on him was more than enough. He nodded to Bryan and felt his rigid control pull back enough to give the man some ability to move and talk. "By now, you can tell that we aren't playing games."

"Where are the others?" the man asked.

Alaric licked his lips and had to fight to keep the memory from coloring his voice. "Dead. They gave us no choice."

The first of them had died before Alaric had even managed to respond to the sentry's call, killed in self-defense when the sentry had no choice. The second man died as Alaric and Bryan closed in, brought down by the weight of a half dozen minds pressing in on his. The third had fallen, his leg mangled, and had been offered his life in return for information. Instead, he'd pulled a second gun, and Sahara had claimed his life before he could kill them.

"Now, we can do this the easy way, where you tell me everything you know while my friend here is reading your mind to know that you're being truthful." Alaric paused for effect, glancing up to Bryan before meeting the prisoner's eyes once more. "Or, I let him rip the answers out of your brain."

The man fidgeted, trying to turn to see Bryan. Alaric could feel him trying to weight how serious they were. "The first way, you get to keep most of your personality and history intact. There will be a few holes, however. For safety's sake. The second way..." He shook his head. "Well, it hasn't been done in a while, so we aren't sure. It could kill you... or just leave you a vegetable." He shrugged. "So, what's it going to be?"

Bryan's fingers dug into the man's shoulders and his eyes widened. "I don't know anything." He swallowed hard. "I just go where they tell me to."

"Why all the way out here?" Alaric asked.

"Just scouting the area." There was fear in his voice as Bryan exerted a little more pressure.

"*He's telling the truth,*" Bryan sent. "*But there's a whole lot in here he won't say out loud.*"

Alaric nodded. He knew what they had to do, but he didn't have the stomach to watch it happen. "*Go ahead. Try not to kill him.*"

"*No promises.*"

Alaric cradled his injured arm. "Do what you have to. I'll be in my cabin." He left the room, closing the door. The prisoner was begging them not to, but then a blanket went up around the office, muffling the sound. He stopped where Riley was leaning against the wall. "If he needs medical attention when Bryan's done with him, get the new Shade to treat him. I don't want Mason bothered."

Riley nodded, but Alaric was already walking away, fatigue pulling on him. He needed to rest and try to process what had happened.

* * *

The air was still when Mason woke several hours later, and he could tell without sitting up that the sun was well on its way to being down. He sat up and found Emily had left him a pitcher of water and a meal on the table between the beds. He drank down nearly the whole pitcher and picked up the sandwich before standing and stretching.

The violence of earlier had interrupted his normal sleeping patterns, and the expenditure of energy dealing with the wounded had wiped him out. His head was still pounding with the aftereffects as he made his way downstairs.

Mason could sense Alaric before he reached the bottom. He was leaning against the mantle, poking at the fire.

"Shouldn't you be in bed?" Mason asked as Alaric turned toward him.

"Probably. I was waiting for you."

"You were shot," Mason reminded him. "And I couldn't help you."

Alaric rubbed at his bandaged shoulder, scowling. "I'll be fine. Keisha did a good job."

"Keisha is a midwife, not a Shade," Mason said. He perched on the arm of the couch. "I'm sure she's great with a bandage, but your shoulder is a mess. Just let me finish eating. I'll see what I can do."

"My mother said you pushed yourself today," Alaric said. Mason could sense his concern, and it was more than just about pushing himself.

"People were hurt." Mason took another bite. It made him uneasy, somehow. He'd only done what he was able to. Anyone else would have done the same. "I was fine. She's over protective."

"I'll give you that," Alaric agreed. He poked at the small fire in front of him with an iron poker. "It was 8th Battalion."

"So I gathered," Mason answered, watching him closely. He was hiding something behind a wall, something he didn't want Mason to know.

"Four of them. Scouts." Alaric turned back to the fire.

"Looking for me." Mason didn't have to see beyond that wall to know that truth, and Alaric knew it would push him away. It had been nearly a week since Damon's arrival, a week he'd spent telling himself he should go, a week he spent not leaving, intent on exploring this relationship with Alaric and how it changed his future. Consequently, it had been a week of not doing anything, and the last thing he'd considered was that the 8th Battalion would find them so soon. "Did you... Are they..."

"Advance scouts. We've doubled patrols, sent out our own men to make sure none of them got away to report back. We have no indication that there are any more of them in the area."

What he wasn't saying, of course, was what they had done with the men. Mason assumed the three he never saw were dead. The last one had been alive though.

Alaric sighed. "He's alive." He looked up at Mason, concern darkening his face. "He's given us a lot of information."

"You've read him?" Mason asked, trying to keep his voice neutral.

"Bryan has. It's more his gift than mine. We know that they're still looking for you, but blindly. Your name and picture were distributed widely. We know that there's a rift starting between the 8th Battalion and whoever it is who's been pulling the strings. They seem to have different end goals." He rubbed a hand over the thick bandages on his shoulder and sighed.

Mason nodded and tossed the remains of his sandwich into the fire before taking Alaric's hand and drawing him to the couch so he could get a look at Alaric's shoulder.

Mason kissed over the bandages, let the emotion roll over him, Alaric's pain, his fear that Mason would leave him, his devotion to his family, to his people. When all of that had stilled, Mason eased even closer, his arms slipping around to pull Alaric in, to hold him and let their minds bleed together, let the healing energy flow into more than just Alaric's body.

"I don't want you to leave," Alaric said in the silence that followed.

Mason lifted his head to look at Alaric. "I don't want to leave either." He kissed Alaric's cheek and went back to his shoulder, urging energy into the wound, restoring muscles and easing the pain. "This is going to take a while," Mason murmured as he finished what he was able to do. "I'll have to work at it a little at a time."

The skin under the thick bandages began to knit back together, the wash of pain receding, and Alaric sighed, his arms circling around Mason to hold him, draw him closer. His touch was soft, but Mason could feel the restraint, the way he guarded the parts of himself that he wasn't ready to open to Mason's touch.

"You're going to leave anyway," Alaric whispered. "I've known for days."

"That gift of yours can be a bit annoying," Mason murmured, turning Alaric's face toward his. "I don't want to go. But this just proves I'm going to bring them here."

"They're going to come here anyway, Mason. Eventually. We've known that since before we came here. This was always meant to be a temporary home."

Mason shook his head and tried to kiss him, but Alaric pulled away. He stood, moving back toward the fireplace. "I meant what I said, Mason. I need you if I'm going to save these people."

Mason stood to follow him. "But even you don't know what that means, or when. I have to go to Washington, if nothing else to get my Book of Line and my other personal things. I need to inform Darvin about what I know." He had so much left to learn from those other Shades, so he could do more.

"You don't need to be some super hero, Mason. I love you, not your gifts."

Mason froze in place, everything inside him stopped as the words replayed in his head over and over. "You... you what?"

Alaric scratched at his head and exhaled. "You heard me. I love you."

Mason wasn't sure how to respond. He had just adjusted to the idea of the physical aspect of this relationship. Neither of them had ever put words to this, and now that Alaric had, Mason found himself floundering just a little. "I... Alaric..."

Alaric smiled softly. "Relax, I don't need you to say it back. I just needed to say it. I need you to know." He wobbled a little, his face draining of color.

"Okay, now I know and what you need next is rest. Let's get you into bed." Mason slipped an arm around Alaric and supported him to the stairs. Alaric leaned on the railing, but Mason didn't let go. He eased Alaric down onto the bed and started to turn to leave, but Alaric caught his hand.

"Lay with me a while?"

The twin bed really was too small, but Alaric made room and Mason nodded. He lay down beside him, letting Alaric spoon up against him. Alaric sighed and Mason slipped an arm over his hip, closing his own eyes as Alaric's body stilled and his mind with it. It was easy to let himself be lulled by Alaric's steady breathing and the warmth of his body. He knew he should leave, but it could wait one more night.

And once he'd done what he needed to, he would come back. Because whether he was ready to admit it to Alaric or not, he was beginning to think that just maybe what he felt when Alaric touched him was love too.

Chapter Fourteen

Zero wasn't interested in the reasons Raven had brought her out; she was just grateful to escape the sterile environment where she had been hiding.

It had been five days since the Fed had searched her background, and there hadn't been even a blip that indicated her father or his people had come looking. Still, when Raven asked her to come along on her outing, Zero took precautions. The wig on her head was a sedate brown, and Raven had loaned her some clothes, so she mostly blended in with the people around them.

Zero sat at the table outside a café, her feet on the chair beside her as she cradled a mocha in her hands. To the casual observer, she was just another teenager hanging out, but unlike other teens, she was very aware of everything around her.

She knew Raven was behind her, in the coffee shop talking to someone. She knew the mother at the next table was exhausted and needed sleep, but the little boy in her lap was her entire world. She knew exactly how many people were close enough to cause her harm.

Raven emerged from the coffee shop and came to sit beside her, well hidden under a hat and gloves. There wasn't much sun to speak of, but the only skin showing was her face. Zero let her eyes skip over the area before looking at her.

"You okay?" Raven asked, sipping at her drink.

Zero nodded. "Just watching."

Raven nodded. "Good. See anything I should know about?"

"There's a kid over there with no coat on." Zero said, tipping her head in the direction she meant. "He's maybe fifteen."

Raven turned her head to look. "I see him."

"Probably a runaway."

"Is he a problem?" Raven asked.

"It's going to snow tonight," Zero responded, lifting her cup to her lips.

They were quiet for a long moment. Raven's fingers drummed against the table. Zero really didn't expect Raven to respond. It was an observance, more of a way to tell who Raven really was. Zero was inclined to trust the older woman; she had, after all, likely saved Zero's life.

She was surprised, then, when Raven stood, her eyes scanning the area before she started to cross the plaza toward the boy. Zero got up to follow.

He was shivering, and he didn't look up as he muttered a well-rehearsed, "Spare change?"

Raven slipped out of her jacket and held it out to him, getting his attention. He looked up, startled. "Ma'am."

She smiled. "It's a little feminine, but you're freezing. Take it."

"Thank you." He struggled to his feet and took the jacket, shrugging it on.

"Do you have somewhere warm to sleep tonight?" Raven asked.

"Warm enough, ma'am," the kid responded.

"Good. My friend and I are going to bring you something to eat. You going to be here when we come back?"

His eyes sparkled as he nodded. "I'll be here."

Raven's hand on Zero's arm was enough to turn them away from the boy, and Zero pointed to the pizza place at the end of the strip of shops. Raven nodded, and they headed in that direction, but half way there, Raven stopped, one hand sliding over her stomach as her head turned.

"What?" Zero asked in a hushed tone, instinctively aware that something wasn't right.

"Shade." Raven breathed, her eyes scanning over the faces around them. She turned back toward the boy. There was an older man approaching him.

Raven yelled and started running back. Zero followed, not sure what was happening. Raven flew at the man, knocking him down, but not before he had put something into the boy's hand.

The man struggled, trying to get his hands on Raven's bare skin, but she wasn't having it. Zero kicked him hard enough to loosen teeth and he went limp. Zero turned to the boy who was staring at them wide eyed. "He just gave me a sandwich."

Raven turned to him. "He was trying to hurt you." She was panting lightly as she turned to him. "Did he touch you?"

"What?"

Zero started to move closer, but Raven held her back. "I need to know. It's important."

"Y-yeah, he touched my hand. Why?"

"Okay, stay calm. Zero, make sure he stays out." She pointed to the Shade now on the ground. Raven moved beside the boy and held a hand over the hand he held the sandwich in. "I just need to check something, okay? I'm not going to hurt you."

"Raven?" Zero asked as Raven pulled her hand away like it had been burned.

"What's going on?" the boy asked, starting to panic.

"That man is a Shade," Raven said softly so her voice wouldn't carry.

The boy jumped, pulling away as Raven tried to stop him. "It's okay, but I need to deal with your hand." Raven said, standing from where she'd been squatting. "He did something—"

"Don't touch me."

"Let me help you." Raven said, reaching a hand for him. Instead, he grabbed his bag and took off running. Raven sighed and shook her head. "Damnit. Zero, stay with him, I'll call and get us a pick up. Don't let him touch you."

"Where are you going?" Zero asked, though she knew the answer.

"After him. Whatever this guy gave him, you can bet is made to spread." Raven pulled out her phone and dialed, even as she took off running.

Zero looked up and around, uncomfortable with the attention that was starting to be focused her way. She squatted down to check on the Shade, hoping whoever Raven was calling would show up soon.

"Is everything all right here ma'am? We got reports of an assault."

Zero stood to face the young police man. "Yeah, sir. This man tried to hurt a young man and my friend intervened." She looked the way Raven had run, but they were gone.

"And, where are they?"

She pointed. "He went running that way. She followed to be sure he was okay."

The officer squatted down beside the man who was starting to come around. "I wouldn't touch him." Zero said. "I think he's a Shade."

The man backed off, his look at her sharp. "Why do you say that?"

Zero shook her head. "Something my friend said."

Another officer joined them, a notepad in his hands. She was older, but not by much. "According to witnesses, this one knocked this guy out after another woman knocked him down."

"She says he's a Shade."

The woman's hand was on her gun as the Shade moaned and shifted. Zero stepped out of the reach of his hand and looked up. There were other cops in the plaza now and an ambulance was pulling up.

Zero was starting to feel trapped. "I need to go find my friend."

"You're not going anywhere." The officer moved to block her. "Not until we have some answers."

* * *

Raven turned a corner, grabbing the wall to keep from over-balancing. She'd followed the boy at least five blocks before he started darting into alleys, leading her through the dark underbelly of the city.

Now, she wasn't sure exactly where she was, but the boy was nowhere to be seen.

Which meant he was out there, carrying some form of contagious disease that he was going to spread. She caught her breath on the street corner, scanning the curious faces as she tried to decide between continuing to look for the boy or going back to Zero and mounting a proper search.

Leaving Zero alone probably wasn't a good idea. Witnesses to the incident would likely have called the police, and she had no idea how Zero would react to police. Raven looked around to get her bearings before raising her arm to hail a cab. It was the easiest, and likely the fastest, way back to the shopping center.

She gave the driver her destination and pulled out her phone, dialing Adam's cell phone. "We're on our way." Darvin said in lieu of hello.

"Good. The kid got away. We need to find him. He's in torn jeans and a black t-shirt, navy blue jacket, carrying an orange backpack. I lost him around 4th and Harrison. I'm on my way back."

"Best hurry, police radio is buzzing about your young friend and the Shade."

"I'm pulling up now. Get here quick." Raven paid the driver and sprinted toward where she could see Zero in cuffs, and the Shade held at gunpoint. Raven pulled her ID out of her pocket and calmed her breathing as she approached. "Federal Agent." She held up the badge and made eye contact with Zero. She was livid. "Who's in charge here?"

A police lieutenant stepped up from out of the crowd of at least fifteen cops. "Lieutenant Rogers, ma'am."

"Agent Ivany, why is my witness in handcuffs, Lieutenant?"

"She was being belligerent to my officers, ma'am."

"And yet my prisoner is not in handcuffs?"

The lieutenant looked at the man, then back at Raven. "No one wants to touch him ma'am. The girl said he might be a Shade."

"Yes, he is." She held out her hand. "I was off duty when I saw him attack a boy. I don't have any cuffs on me."

The lieutenant put a pair of cuffs in her hand and she moved around the crowd of police to the Shade who was sitting and fuming. She could almost feel him trying to think of a way out of the situation.

"*Keep your mouth shut and cooperate and I won't let these jumpy trigger fingers kill you today,*" Raven said to him in thought as she grabbed his arm and pulled it behind him. "My witness, Lieutenant?" Raven looked up at Zero and nodded.

At the far end of the plaza, she could see Adam and his men, including a prisoner van, pulling up. "That would be our ride."

By the time Adam was there barking orders, Raven had the Shade up on his feet, though listing a bit to the left and Zero was beside her, rubbing at her wrists. Several other agents moved in around them and escorted them toward the prisoner van.

Raven couldn't hear what Adam was telling the police, and she didn't really care. She focused on getting her prisoner into the van and securing him. "No one goes near him, understood?"

The Shade didn't fight as she pushed him into the van and into a seat. Raven secured him, switching the handcuffs for a set of manacles built for a Shade. Thick leather mitts covered his hands and locked above the wrist, and then they locked in to a bar that settled across his lap, connected to the floor with a reinforced pole. Once locked in place, he wouldn't be able to move much. When she was done, she locked the door and turned to find Adam approaching.

"All set?"

"We're secure." Raven affirmed. "Zero and I will meet you at home. Don't pull him out of the van until you have one of us on hand."

"Is he combative?" Adam asked, glancing at the door.

"No, quite docile actually, but he infected that kid and would have kept going if we hadn't stopped him. No one but a Shade touches him."

Adam nodded. "Got it. I've got Dr. Anthony coordinating with the men searching for your missing kid. If he's as infectious as the one in Chicago, we could be looking at an epidemic."

Raven nodded. "Good. If we're lucky, we can stop it before it gets to that point." She gestured toward the parking area where she and

Zero had left the government car they had borrowed for the day. Dark clouds were rolling in, bringing with them the freezing rain and possible snow that the forecast had promised.

"You okay?" Raven asked as they got settled into the car.

Zero nodded. "Fine."

"You're pissed I left you there to handle them."

"No," Zero responded, but she wouldn't look at Raven. "Okay, a little. What if they had arrested me?"

"We would have come for you." Raven said, starting the car.

"Before my father found me?"

Raven sighed. "Hopefully." She glanced at Zero as they pulled out into traffic. "I'm sorry, but I couldn't let him run off without trying to catch him."

"How bad is it?"

"I'm not sure. There was a similar issue in Chicago a month ago. By the time we got ahead of it and found the Shade responsible, there were ten dead and more than fifty hospitalized with a jacked-up version of the measles."

"So this isn't the same Shade?"

Raven shook her head. "No, he's not. That guy made us kill him. This guy... he's different." She couldn't place what was bugging her about him. Her contact with him had been brief, but she'd gotten no response from the man. There was no struggle, no declarations of his hatred or agenda. Nothing.

It was almost like he wasn't even aware of what was going on. They were quiet as Raven navigated through the busy pre-Christmas streets of Washington. They were nearly back at the facility before Zero cleared her throat. "I should... there's something I should say."

Raven glanced at her. "Go ahead."

"One of the things my father has been trying to do is to... brainwash people to... I don't know, do stuff for him. He hasn't really had a lot of success. At least I don't think so."

"What do you mean?"

"There was a Shifter in California, but she resisted. And my mother... he was kind of successful there. I know he had a Shade or two that he was tracking. Maybe more." She shifted uncomfortably in her seat. "My memory is so frustrating." She growled, seemingly at herself. "I can see these... things... and I can't..." She pulled her wig off and shook her head. "I can't tell you."

"I can see about getting one of the agency's Shadows to see if they can help," Raven offered. "But I'll warn you, none of them are particularly skilled."

Zero shook her head. "I don't want more people mucking in my head." She paused, staring out the window for a long moment. "But there may be another way."

Raven waited for her to expound, but Zero pulled her attention into herself and was silent. Raven turned her own thoughts to the captured Shade. Maybe Zero was right, and the man was under the control of another, some powerful Shadow, in which case they might not ever get information out of him.

There was also the boy, and whatever disease he'd been infected with. He was probably already spreading it. She knew Adam had teams out looking, but they were down to just a handful of Shades who could handle it. Dr. Anthony would be ready to jump in as soon as they found the kid, and he had that nurse who could help, but that was it other than her. Even if Jerah was still in the picture, he didn't have the skills.

Raven sighed and drove them the rest of the way in silence, parking near the doors in the garage. "So, what is this other way?"

Zero looked up, blinking. "I'd have to show you."

"Okay, show me."

Zero led her into the residential wing and into her room. Wigs hung on various corners and books covered the bed. Zero crossed to the small desk and lifted her large duffle bag from the floor. She rummaged around inside of the bag, then lifted her hands, holding them out. Four vials of an amber liquid filled her trembling hands.

"What are these?" Raven asked, reaching for them.

"Drugs, designed for specific things." She growled and shook her head. "Before treatments." She held up one vial. Raven took it from her and held it up so she could read the label.

From what she could tell, the liquid inside was a powerful psychotropic, possible more. "You were given this before your father subjected you to...." Raven looked up at Zero's frustrated face. She had never actually said what was involved in those experiments.

Zero pointed at the vial in her hand. "Sage." She held up each of the others in turn. "Shadow. Shifter. Shade."

"Did you steal these on your way out?"

Zero shrugged. "I thought I might find a use for them. Maybe unlock whatever he locked away."

"He used this on others?"

Zero nodded and dropped onto the end of the bed. "Always tinkering with the formulas. It..." She gestured at her head. "It puts me down. I have no control."

Raven nodded slowly. "Okay, let me get these to Dr. Anthony for analysis. I'm not injecting you with some drug without knowing what all is in it."

"You can try," Zero said. "But I'm betting it isn't just the mix of drugs."

Raven believed her. If Zero's father was as connected as he seemed to be, he had scientists and occultists at his disposal. Which meant that conventional analysis might not yield them anything.

In her pocket, her phone buzzed and she pulled it out to glance at the screen. "They're pulling in now. Try to relax, I will get back to you when I can."

Chapter Fifteen

Alaric slipped up behind Mason as he stared out the window at the snow accumulating in the canyon. It had been snowing for days and it showed no signs of stopping. He let his hands slide around Mason's waist, walking closer rather than pulling him back. Mason responded by rubbing his hands over Alaric's and guiding them around to embrace him fully.

"What's going on in that head?" Alaric asked, leaning in to rest his chin on Mason's shoulder. "You've been quiet all day."

Mason nodded slightly, drawing in a deep breath and letting it go slowly. "Not thinking. Just watching the snow."

Alaric kissed his cheek. He could tell Mason was worrying, and the tumble of thoughts covered far too many things for someone as young as Mason to be thinking. He was burdened with the need to get back to the people who had left him for dead, though Mason didn't see them that way. Alaric knew he was the only thing keeping Mason from leaving.

It was wrong to hold on to him the way he was, but Alaric couldn't seem to help himself. He turned his eyes to the snow outside, silently thankful for it dampening Mason's desire to leave the same way it muffled the sounds around them.

"You hungry?" Alaric asked softly, letting himself fall back into the comfortable.

Mason nodded. "Yeah, I could eat."

Alaric stepped back and reached for the coat rack, grabbing the coat they'd given Mason first and holding it for him. Mason shrugged into it, and Alaric grabbed his before sliding it on and taking Mason's hand.

The walk down to the bunk house was cold, but beautiful. Snow covered everything but the path that wound through the cabins and down to the showers and bunkhouse. They walked slowly and silently, and Alaric did his best not to eavesdrop on Mason's thoughts. Since they'd come together it was difficult not to. He could feel Mason's every breath.

It was easier when there were other people around. Alaric opened the door to the bunkhouse, and warm air spilled over them along with the smell of pine and smoke from the fire.

There was a pine tree in the corner near the stairs, decorated with homemade ornaments that the camp residents had been making. One table in the hall was still covered with craft materials, there for anyone to use to make their own mark on the tree. The ornaments ranged from simple paper chains and popcorn strings to various representations of the many different holidays celebrated by those in camp. Even the Muslim and Jewish families had added symbols of their faiths to the mix.

Christmas was still a week or so away. They hadn't heard from the outside world since the snow had started. The mile-long drive in from the state road was impassable, and the state road likely hadn't been paved, making driving on it a gamble at best.

For the time being they were cut off from the outside world. It meant that they were safer than they had been since their escape.

Mason pulled him closer, grinning. "Now who's gone quiet?"

Alaric stole a kiss, letting go of Mason's hand to caress the back of his neck. "Just thinking about Christmas."

Mason made a face and moved away, heading toward the buffet table that had been set up near the kitchen. It was more efficient when trying to feed the large group that came and went on each individual's own schedule.

"What?" Alaric asked, following.

Mason frowned at him and shook his head. "What what?"

"That face. You don't like Christmas?"

Mason took a plate and started to fill it. "I don't dislike it. I just... it was never a big thing in my family. We didn't do Christmas."

"Like, ever?" Alaric asked, following him along the table.

Mason headed toward a bench, shrugging once he put his plate down. "Nana was not religious. My mother followed the traditions of her clan, which I gather were similar to Native American traditions of one kind or another."

"Huh." Alaric sat across from him, and they ate in silence for a few minutes. "We've never been religious either." Their Christmases had always been filled with family and laughter. It was a day they could all be together and enjoy the company.

"To be honest, most of what I know about Christmas is what I saw on television." Mason said. "It seemed like a waste of money."

Alaric chuckled, nodding. "Well, the way some people do it, yeah, it is."

The door behind Alaric opened, and Bryan came in with Sahara in tow, both of them stomping their feet and brushing snow from their shoulders and head.

"Storm rolling in," Bryan said in way of greeting on his way to get a plate.

Alaric watched them get plates and come to join them. Bryan had been spending a lot of time in Sahara's company in the last weeks; it was something Alaric thought curious, considering Bryan's previous stance on the Shifter. He let himself reach out to read the surface of Bryan's presence, not surprised when he hit a brick wall, and Bryan pushed him back.

"So, more snow?" Alaric asked as if nothing had happened.

Bryan nodded. "Looks like. Otto says it's going to get bad tonight and stay bad for a few days. We'll be lucky if we don't lose access to the cabins at the higher elevations. We're moving people down now."

"The girls are out hunting, should be back soon. Hopefully with enough meat to last us awhile," Sahara said without looking up.

"Good. And how are we set for wood?" Alaric asked.

"I think we'll be okay. The shed is full, and we delivered to the eastern shed this morning. Each cabin got as much as we could manage too."

Alaric glanced at Mason who had gone quiet, his attention on his plate. He felt Alaric's eyes and glanced up. "I should probably get down to the water, since it might be a while before I can again." Mason said.

"It's awfully cold," Alaric countered. "And it isn't dark yet."

"I'll be fine," Mason said, standing. He picked up his plate and nodded to them before he headed into the kitchen to clean his plate.

Alaric watched him go and sighed.

"Everything all right?" Bryan asked.

"He's feeling a bit caged in," Alaric responded. "He's worried about getting back to Washington and thinks maybe he should have left before the snow started."

"He should have," Bryan agreed. Alaric raised an eyebrow and Bryan shrugged. "He doesn't belong here."

"That's what you said about Sahara, in case you've forgotten. You seem to have accepted her."

"Sahara can't kill me by touching my skin."

"Could kill you with the right touch," Sahara countered, her skin shimmering gold and her hand shifting toward claw as she reached for him.

Bryan covered her hand with his, pushing it down to the table. "You know what I mean."

"Do I?" Sahara countered, pulling her hand back.

Bryan frowned at her. "I thought you agreed with me."

Sahara pushed back from the table and stood. "Which proves to me that you haven't been paying attention."

She stormed away, leaving Bryan clearly puzzled at her reaction as she disappeared out the door. Alaric could feel the confusion rolling off of him, even as he shook his head and turned back to his food.

After a long silence, Alaric finished eating and pushed his plate away. "So, Sahara?"

Bryan rolled his eyes. "What of it?"

"Nothing. Not what I expected," Alaric said.

"Me either." Bryan inhaled deeply. "But yeah. I always did like the wild ones. She's just wilder than most."

"Just be careful," Alaric cautioned. "We need her, as much as we need Mason, Damon and Keisha."

"So you keep saying," Bryan said. "And yet, you haven't done anything to figure out why or how."

Alaric turned to look at him. "What, exactly, do you think I should be doing?"

Bryan looked him in the eye. "Have you even been to see the orb since we got back?"

Of course, he hadn't, and they both knew that. He had been busy with other things, he told himself. He also didn't want to admit that he was scared of it too. Letting the orb embrace him would mean that he accepted his father's death, accepted the role that he had fallen into. He pinched the bridge of his nose. "No, I haven't."

Bryan nodded. "Have you talked to Riley in the last few days?"

Alaric shook his head. Riley had moved into one of the small cabins on the other side of the creek to afford Alaric and Mason a little privacy. Alaric had only seen him once since the move. He and Mason had moved into the downstairs bedroom where they could share a double bed. If he was honest with himself, Alaric had shirked a good share of his responsibility to spend time with Mason.

"Maybe you should," Bryan said. "It's time you stop playing house with the Shade. Your people need you."

Alaric stood. "I'm not playing house." His face burned and he didn't like the feeling welling inside him. He knew Bryan had a point. "And I never asked to be in this position."

"Well, you are, so suck it up and put your big boy panties on. Go talk to Riley. Go do your thing with the orb. Vacation is over." Bryan turned back to his meal, his shields tightly shuttered.

Alaric grabbed his plate and headed to the kitchen to wash it. He left the plate in the drying rack and headed out into the snowfall without another word. It irritated him that Bryan wasn't wrong. He had been pointedly ignoring his responsibilities except when forced to them. He could tell his mother was worried, but not enough to have said anything yet.

He pulled his coat closer around him and picked his way down the slippery trail to the bridge. He resisted the urge to walk down along the creek to the bend where Mason went to soak. It would only entice him to put things off even more, and worse, he usually ended up in the water with Mason, and without a Shade's constitution, he'd end up with pneumonia.

Instead, he crossed the bridge and headed toward Riley's cabin. The snow was coming down harder than before, a stiff wind driving it down the canyon. It pulled the smoke from Riley's chimney along with it, and the smoke disappeared in the frenzy. Alaric knocked on the door, shifting his weight back and forth waiting for the door to open. The wind seemed colder, and he shivered.

Riley opened the door, looking rumpled and sleep deprived. His hair had gotten longer, the bleached tips no longer close to his scalp and the natural growth starting to look like dreadlocks. His eyes were bleary and dark circles told Alaric stories without having to try to read him.

"You look like shit," Alaric said as Riley stepped aside to let him in. "What's wrong?"

Riley closed the door, rubbing his hands along his arms as he moved back toward the fire and sat. He gestured to the only other chair and Alaric sat, looking Riley over.

"I haven't been sleeping," Riley said, rubbing his eyes. His voice was thick and slow, and he moved with a deliberate slowness that concerned Alaric.

"Bryan seemed worried." He understood it now that he'd seen Riley. "And now I am."

For a long moment, Alaric wasn't sure that Riley was going to even respond, then he drew in a shaking breath. "I've been... seeing." He shook his head. "It isn't good." He hugged himself and Alaric risked reaching out to get a better understanding of his friend's state.

Riley's heartbeat was sluggish, his breathing slow and deep. It was almost like he was in trance, despite the fact that he wasn't. "Riley, how long has it been since you slept?"

He shook his head. "Don't remember. Every time I close my eyes…" He trailed off and looked away.

"Can you show me?" Alaric asked, moving off the chair to kneel by Riley's feet, his hand sliding under Riley's. His skin was cold to the touch and it didn't take much for his shields to collapse and let Alaric in.

Images rolled out uncontrolled around him almost before Alaric was in deep enough for it to happen. Like before, they were fractured and in no comprehensive order, snippets of things that could happen, maybe would happen. Riley's hand tightened on his and Alaric gasped as the intensity grew until he was being slammed.

Burning bodies surrounded by screaming crowds, adulation at some rally, uniforms marching through empty streets, Mason's face bloody and marked, rows of dead in a parking lot, people huddling in abandoned buildings, barbed wire around government buildings.

It raced through Riley and into Alaric's mind at breakneck speed. He let it roll through him until he was seeing the same images and scenes for a second and third time. Then he disengaged enough to get a look at Riley's internal controls. Riley was frayed and it felt as though he hadn't fully disconnected from the visions in days, which would be why he couldn't sleep.

Alaric filed the visions away to examine later, on his own, and reached beyond them for the controls that would let him put Riley down. Riley didn't fight him until he was already pressing inward, and by then it was too late, Alaric had control and pushed Riley down past the point where the visions could hold on to his conscious thought.

Riley slumped in the chair, and Alaric moved to get him up, dragging him the few steps to the bed and easing him down. Alaric covered his friend with a worn quilt and sat beside him, keeping his control until he was sure Riley wouldn't waken. Then he took stock of Riley's physical condition, confirming his worry that the lack of sleep and uncontrolled altered state had taken a toll.

Briefly, Alaric considered asking Mason to come work on him, but Mason had done his share of the work. Instead, he reached out to his mother, asking her to bring Damon, along with a meal for when Riley woke.

With a sigh, Alaric retreated to the chair by the fire, keeping one eye on Riley while he turned his thoughts to the visions that had been plaguing Riley's mind. It wasn't unusual for someone with the gift of prophecy to become overwhelmed in times of turmoil. Especially if they were alone.

And that was on him. Alaric hadn't seen the signs that it was happening when he should have been there to help. But he was there now. The least he could do was to make sure his friend slept, ate, and took care of himself.

He started by focusing his attention on the vision that had been pulling Riley under. Like most of his premonitions, it needed interpretation. Alaric pulled apart the pieces, shifting them around until they seemed to be in a more linear sequence and let them play. Some of it was repetitive, similar to what they had already seen, but the new scenes were not encouraging.

Alaric paused the vision on a scene that reminded him of the information they had gotten off the 8th Battalion patrolman. There was a building surrounded by fencing and prisoners being pulled off a truck.

It reminded him that there was another duty he'd been ignoring. Bryan had pulled all the information he could from the young soldier, but his touch was less than gentle, and it had left the man with little knowledge of himself. Damon had done as he could to heal the body, but there was nothing to be done for the man's mind.

He was little more than a drone now, needing to be told to do the most basic of tasks to care for himself. It would have been more merciful to have taken his life.

Alaric let his eyes lift to Riley, watching him sleep. He rubbed a hand over his face. Riley needed more than just sleep. He would need to spend time with the orb to help him gain control of his gift, which seemed to be growing. But in order for that to be helpful, Alaric needed to accept his role and perform the ceremony that would confer on him the gifts of his tribe.

Alaric closed his eyes, remembering when it was his father's ceremony, remembering the changes that happened in his father. If his father were still alive, he'd have helped Riley manage before now.

He'd told himself he wasn't ready, that they had time yet. It wasn't true, but he told himself that anyway. Bryan knew. It was time to stop hiding.

Alaric scrubbed his hands over his face. There was a knock at the door and he crossed to let Damon in. Behind him came the slack face and almost empty presence of the soldier.

"Your mother said you needed my services?" Damon asked, his eyes narrowing as they found Riley's inert form. "I see."

"Do what you can for him," Alaric said.

Damon nodded and moved to the bed. Alaric stepped out into the frigid evening air, rubbing his arms. The snow was coming down thickly, already erasing the footsteps made by the two inside.

There was a peace that came with the snow, a feeling like the world outside their canyon was far, far way. But Alaric knew it wasn't peace, and soon enough the outside world would find them.

Chapter Sixteen

"How many?" Darvin asked as Raven and Dr. Anthony came in from the van.

"At least twenty. But we found the kid." Raven responded wearily. "It's hard to know if we contained it."

"You didn't. We have hospitals all over the city with patients, and at least two in Virginia."

"Damn it." She rubbed her eyes. "Give me a half hour, and I'll be ready to go out."

"You need to rest," Adam countered. "Both of you. The bulk of the victims are responding to antibiotics."

That surprised her. "I would have expected him to mutate it enough to be drug resistant."

"Yes, in my experience that has always been true," Dr. Anthony agreed. "Perhaps our new friend isn't as fully under the control of his handler as we thought."

Raven nodded. "Has he said anything yet?"

"Nothing coherent," Adam said, falling into step beside her as she headed toward her room to change. "He keeps repeating that nonsense string of words like a mantra."

"Maybe it's time we ask him a different way," Raven said. "I'm going to shower and change. I'll come down to detention after. I have an idea."

Raven turned down the corridor to her room and grabbed her shower kit before proceeding to the women's showers. She had been up most of the night and out on the streets with Dr. Anthony and a team in the attempt to locate the homeless teenager who had escaped her. They had reports of several locations where kids like him tended to gather in groups for protection.

Eventually they had found him at a small shelter, the disease in full effect as he lay shivering and drenched in sweat on a cot. All around him there were others in various stages of infection. It was a bastardization of a bacterial infection, hyped up to be ten times more contagious and sped up to go from contact to nearing death in under twenty-four hours.

It had taken the two of them working in concert to nullify the infections in the homeless they had found in the shelter.

Raven stripped down and turned on the water, welcoming the feeling of imagined contamination washing from her skin. She tilted her head back, pulling the elastic out of her tightly braided hair and combing her fingers through it to loosen it.

She'd always worn it long and kept it braided so that it was out of her way. Her father had loved her hair, she could remember him lovingly brushing it every night before bed. He told her how beautiful it was, and how it reminded him of his mother. Raven kept it long to keep that part of him with her.

Pushing away the sentimental thoughts, Raven washed her hair and body, opening her mouth to drink her fill of water as the soap rinsed from her skin. She turned the water off and stepped out of the shower stall, her skin absorbing most of the water before she could reach for her towel. It told her how dehydrated she was. She made a note to get some soaking time in before she went to bed, then wrapped the towel around herself and headed back to her room.

She dressed quickly in the plain olive uniform most people wore in the facility, though she preferred the black, and combed through her hair, pausing to braid it tightly. Getting the sickness contained was only part of the job.

What they needed to do is determine who this Shade was and why he was spreading the infection. The man had been locked in isolation since they brought him in, with interrogators questioning him via intercoms so that he couldn't infect them as well.

Raven headed for the detention level and let herself into the observation room overlooking the interrogation room where the Shade was held. He still wore his street clothes, and he was sitting in a metal chair, his hands cuffed behind him. He seemed quiet, dejected almost.

He was older than she had first assumed, his hair starting to turn gray, and the laugh lines around his eyes were deep. There was a deep furrow on his forehead as well. His clothes told her he was middle class; in fact he looked like he might be a teacher or librarian or something equally innocuous.

His was a face most people would instinctively trust. Raven sighed and resigned herself to what had to be done. "Hand me the fingerprint scanner. I'll see if I can get us something to go on."

The interrogator handed the device to her. "So far all he will say is that nonsense." He nodded to the window and thumbed on the speakers.

"Numbers. Fell. Door. Play. Wind. Stay."

Raven nodded and went to the door into the room. The man didn't look up right away, not until she knew he could feel her. He blinked and stuttered to a stop. "My name is Raven Ivany. I'd like to ask you a few questions."

She put the scanner on the table and sat across from him. "*Can you hear me?*" She waited for him to respond. When he didn't after a long moment, she went back to speaking. "I'm going to start by taking your fingerprints with this scanner, see if we can figure out who you are. Unless you feel like telling me."

"Numbers. Fell. Door. Play. Wind. Stay."

"Okay then, the hard way it is." She stood again, taking the scanner and moving behind him. She steeled herself for attack and squatted behind him, taking his thumb first and pressing it to the scanner's glass.

"*Help.*"

The word echoed in her head and startled her enough that she almost ended up falling and she let go of his hand. She had expected him to try to infect her, not finally respond with something other than the random words he'd been spouting.

Cautiously, Raven adjusted her position, putting one knee to the floor for balance and made contact again. *"How can I help you?"*

His thoughts were slow, like he was pushing each word through wet clay. *"Stuck. Can't break."*

Raven glanced at the window, aware that Adam had joined them and exhaled heavily. It was risky, trying to get inside a poisoned mind. Slowly, she stood, letting her hands move to either side of his neck. She hesitated before she made contact. "You better be recording…and have medical on standby."

She touched her hands to his face, closing her eyes and reaching inside of him. Everything was fire, and his voice was drowning in the flames. He grabbed hold of her consciousness, screaming into her. She let the words fly past her, attempting to calm the flames, bring some relief. She was shaking with the effort, burning as she tried to make sense of any of it.

There was water pouring over her and hands attempting to pull her away. She shrugged them off and fought harder, but the fire was stronger, and it singed her hands, ate into her skin.

"Mine."

A man's face filled her mind as she was pushed forcibly out of the Shade's thoughts. Raven fell backward into a black abyss surrounded by flames.

* * *

Raven fought her way back to consciousness, her eyes opening to find Dr. Anthony kneeling beside her. Beyond him, the Shade was held in the corner, pinned with UV light that she imagined she could feel. "I'm okay," she slurred, her words feeling almost foreign in her mouth.

"Let your doctor decide that. You got a good blast of something, and you cracked your head when you fell."

She pushed his hand away and sat up, leaning back against the wall. She could feel the bump on the back of her head, and the trail of Dr. Anthony's work to revive her. "He's got a trap set in his head."

"A trap?"

She nodded, reaching up a hand to rub over the sore spot where she hit the floor. "He's been programmed or something. He's still in there, but whoever did it managed to bypass his conscious thought, his moral center... He had no choice but infect whoever he came in contact with."

"So, a Shadow?" Adam asked, squatting down beside the doctor.

She nodded. "Yeah. It isn't something anyone other than a pretty powerful Shadow can fix either. That trap kicked me pretty hard."

"Okay, let's get you up and down to the pool," Dr. Anthony said. "Then we can secure the prisoner until a solution can be found."

She let them help her to her feet. Her head was starting to pound, and the words and images the other Shade had pushed at her rolled around randomly, mixing with her own thoughts and experiences in a dizzying sort of dance. Raven clung to Dr. Anthony's arm as they moved out into the hall where one of his associates was waiting with a wheelchair.

She balked at the idea of it, but Dr. Anthony patted her hand, pushing energy into her. "It's a long walk for someone in your condition. I want you to let her take you to the pools. I'll come see you after."

Raven acquiesced and sat in the chair. He was right, it was a long walk, and the more upright she was, the more her head hurt. With a sigh, she put her feet on the fold-down footrests and gestured for the woman to go. It would feel good to soak for a while and give her a chance to try to make sense of everything she had learned from the man.

She thanked her escort as they reached the pool. "I can manage from here. Thank you."

When she was gone, Raven stripped down to her underwear and bra before moving to the side of the pool. She had taken to wearing underclothing that was made for wear in the water when she started working for Adam. Naked wasn't generally something she wanted to be when she found herself in unfriendly waters.

Raven eased herself down into the shallow soaking pool, closing her eyes to relish the embrace as she sank down. For the first few minutes, she floated near the surface of the water, before she drew in a deep breath and sank down. It was only three feet deep, but it was enough. She focused on healing her physical body first directing energy to her head and the knot that had started to form. Once the knot dissolved, she let the energy move down her stiff neck and into the hard muscles of her back.

She surfaced when her lungs needed air and sank back down, charging the water and letting her body absorb what it needed. When she no longer felt the effects of the psychic booby trap, she floated up and relaxed so she could turn her thoughts to what she had seen and heard.

The Shade was a man in his mid-thirties, and she thought he had told her his name was Jeff. He had been a teacher at a night school of some kind before he had been turned into a weapon. The details around how he'd been taken were sketchy, murky with the quality of memories from a drunk night out or the feeling of drugs in the system. What she did know was that he fought.

He did not want to do the things he had done, and he had fought the only way he could, keeping the diseases he doled out from being lethal. At worst, he had started epidemics of various normally minor ailments, ramped up to cause high fevers and intense symptoms. If the infected individuals didn't seek medical help, the diseases could kill, but they did not approach the level of damage a Shade could inflict.

If they could find someone with the skill to undo what was done, there was a good chance the man would return to normal. The problem was, full blooded Shadows with those kinds of skills were not as easy to find as one might think. She'd heard rumors of some of the clans trying to reconnect, but for the most part they had scattered and intermarried with normal folk, their gifts diluted and slowly vanishing.

Raven opened her eyes and pushed her feet down to the bottom of the pool, starting a little when she spotted Zero leaning against the wall. She walked toward the steps, frowning a little. "What are you doing here?"

Zero shrugged a little, fussing with the bright red wig. "Was bored."

"And it's better to come watch me soak?"

She shrugged again. "I think my father is in town."

Raven could see the concern beyond Zero's casual tone. "What makes you think so?"

Zero pointed at her head. "I can hear him. Sort of." She stood up straight and crossed her arms. "I mean, it's like this… whisper, in the back of my head. I can't really hear it, but I know what it wants."

Raven pulled a towel from the rack to dry off the water that didn't absorb into her skin before she dressed again. "Okay, so what does it want?"

"For me to go back to him." Zero's face showed her feelings about that very clearly. "He has to be nearby for me to hear it. Within a few miles."

"Can you use it to actually find him?" Raven asked as she pulled her pants back on.

Zero looked startled by the question. "I don't know? Maybe? I've never tried. Usually I'm running in the other direction."

Raven nodded. She wasn't going to push the girl. From what she could tell, her father had put her through hell. To be honest, Raven wasn't entirely sure that they could capture and contain the man, if he was as powerful as their current knowledge suggested. "I hope you know that you're safe here, with us."

"Am I?" Zero fell into step beside her when Raven headed for the door. "I feel pretty useless."

Raven could understand that feeling well. "What is it you want to be doing?"

She shrugged and shook her head. "I don't know." Zero was nervous, jittery. "I heard what happened... With the Shade."

"Word gets around fast."

"No." Zero stopped her, a hand on her arm. "*I heard it happen.*"

"Oh." Raven nodded slowly. "I'm sorry."

"It's my father's work."

"How can you be sure?" Raven asked, resuming her walk back toward her room.

Zero rolled her eyes. "I just know." The image of the man she had seen in the Shade's head popped into her head, and Zero seemed to poke it.

"Is that him?" Raven asked.

"The one and only. He likes to sign his work." She bit her lip. "I might be able to help."

"No." Raven wasn't about to allow that. "It's a very powerful trap. No one but a full-blooded Shadow should even try."

Zero stopped her again. "I am. At least theoretically. It's where his experiments started."

"I don't follow."

Zero huffed. "I don't advertise what a freak I am." She rolled her shoulders and wouldn't look Raven in the eye. "I'm half Shadow, half Sage. Except he did genetic stuff, experiments, on me. It was supposed to make me fully both. Except it wasn't instantaneous the way he wanted."

She crossed her arms and took a step back. "If we use the Shade and the Shadow drugs on him, I might be able to get behind the wall and break it down."

"What about the wall in your own head?" Raven asked.

"Maybe if this works, we'll be able to break it, too."

Raven considered it while she resumed walking. "Let's talk to the doctor, see what his take is before we go jumping into something so dangerous."

Chapter Seventeen

Mason sat on the bluff overlooking the valley, watching lazy curls of smoke rise on the still air. Most of the people there below him were sleeping. The air was cold, but warmer than it had been. Christmas was behind them, and New Year's was only a day away.

The time had passed faster than he'd expected. He knew he needed to leave. He needed to get back to D.C., and he knew that if he didn't leave soon, he wouldn't leave at all. He was comfortable here, even though not everyone accepted him.

Then there was Alaric. Being with him was different than anything he'd known. In some ways it was overwhelming. He was attentive in ways Mason had never experienced, and there was no denying that the sex was mind blowing.

Mason huddled down into his coat and put his hands in his pocket. Riley had told him that the roads still weren't passable, but that he might be able to get to Brettles, where they were more likely to have plowed a route out to roads that were.

He smiled as he felt the familiar brush of Alaric's mind against his. It was warm and easy to melt into. Mason stood, turning as Alaric reached the head of the trail that led up from the valley below. "It's almost midnight, shouldn't you be in bed?"

"I was working with Bryan on some plans to defend the camp, and then I checked in on Riley."

"How's he doing?" Mason asked, letting Alaric pull him in. When he'd last seen Riley, he was still recovering from what Alaric had called psychic shock. He'd offered what he could to ease the physical pain of it, though Damon had clearly done his share as well, and Riley had accepted gratefully. He'd been through the worst of it by then, but Mason had diligently worked through his body, easing strained muscles and infusing his major organs with energy to help him along.

"Better," Alaric said before kissing him lightly. "He said you stopped by."

Mason nodded. "You should have told me he needed a hand. It didn't have to take this long to get him on his feet."

Alaric sighed and nodded. "I know. I was… being cautious. Besides, Damon was great."

"It's been over a week," Mason chided. "Next time…" He stopped as he realized what he'd been about to say.

"There isn't going to be a next time, is there?" Alaric asked softly. "You're going to leave."

Mason pulled away to hide the part of him that wanted to cling to Alaric and whatever this was between them. "I have to. If nothing else, I have to get my things, and quit my job."

To his surprise, Alaric didn't argue, he just sat on the boulder and nodded. "I've known since Christmas."

Mason licked his lips and sat beside him. "I'll come back."

Alaric glanced at him, then turned his gaze out over the valley. "No, I think we'll come to you." He sighed. "We can't stay here forever. There's a war coming."

"We don't have to be part of it," Mason said softly.

Alaric's smile was sad. "I think we already are." He lifted a hand to brush over Mason's face. "But we won't be alone."

"*Unite the tribes.*"

Mason heard the words as if they were spoken and he sat back a little bit. "What?"

Alaric's face flushed pink. "I'm sorry. I didn't mean for that to slip through." He stood and walked to the edge of the bluff.

Mason followed. "What does it mean?"

Alaric shook his head. "I haven't fully figured it out. I thought maybe I'd understand once I had you here. We have at least one of every tribe here. I thought I'd be able to figure it out."

"And now I'm leaving," Mason said.

He nodded and slipped his arm around Mason, tugging him in closer. "We'll find each other again."

It was a promise that hung on the air, something neither of them could be certain of, and yet, it was soothing to believe.

* * *

Mason came down the stairs just before sunset, a backpack over one shoulder. Emily was waiting for him, a canvas bag in her hands.

"You were going to leave without saying goodbye," she said.

"Sometimes it's easier that way," Mason responded, not even trying to deny it.

"Come here." She gave him the bag, then pulled him in to hug him, holding him tight. "You come back to us when you can, you hear me?"

"Yes ma'am."

She let go of him and brushed her hands down his arms. "Now, listen to me. Keep your head down, don't trust water in pools or small ponds. Keep moving until you know you're safe. There's food in the bag. And an extra canteen of water."

He smiled. "You trying to mother me, Emily?"

"It's what I do, darling." The door opened behind him, and her eyes skipped to it and back. "You best get moving if you're going to make shelter before daylight."

"I was hoping to see Alaric."

"He left you this." Emily lifted a manila envelope from the table and held it out to him. "He said your boss would know what to do with it." She kissed his cheek. "He'll meet you on your way out."

Mason nodded, tucking the canvas bag and the envelope into his backpack before he shouldered it. "I'll see you soon."

"You better."

Riley smiled at him from the door and held out a pair of snowshoes. "These should help. You ready?"

"Yeah, I'm good. Let's go." The sky was heavy with clouds, and the dark was deep in the valley. Riley took him up the ridge and away from the camp. There were footprints in the snow, a path of sorts stamped out by guards who were tasked with watching the camp's borders. Near the barrier Mason could feel, Riley stopped and handed him a map.

"I mapped you out a couple of routes so you can alter as you need to." He stopped and pointed to a couple of places. "Your best bet is probably to head toward Vegas."

Mason nodded. "Thanks."

"Be safe." He pointed. "You're just going to follow this ridge to that hollow tree, then head east and south. Follow that until you get to Brettles. You can shelter there for the day. Old Man Keller at the tavern will barter with you for a ride, not sure he can take you all the way to Vegas though."

"I just need to get somewhere that I can contact my people," Mason said, scanning the map.

Riley nodded, his eyes squinting as he looked the map over. "Just be careful. Phone lines are probably being monitored, even up here."

"It's okay, I'm pretty sure I can manage." One of the first things drilled into him in Darvin's "spy school" was how to communicate without giving away who or where he was.

Mason shook his hand and pocketed the map. His eyes scanned the trees. He could feel Alaric but not see him. He left Riley and started walking, sighing when Alaric fell into step beside him. "I was beginning to think you were just going to follow me and not say goodbye."

Alaric's hand slipped into his, fingers threading together. "I won't say goodbye. But I'll walk with you awhile."

They walked in silence until they got to the hollow tree. Mason stopped them then and turned to Alaric. Before he could say anything,

Alaric kissed him, pressing him into the tree. Sadness and resignation rolled off of Alaric along with a surge of barely repressed desire. "*Stay.*"

"You know I can't," Mason whispered back.

"I know." Alaric closed his eyes and sighed. "I would come with you..."

"You're needed here," Mason answered.

"You have to cross desert." Alaric sounded almost petulant.

"I'll be fine." Mason caressed his cheek, his eyes skimming over his face. "I want you to have something." He fumbled with the layers of shirts, finally getting under them and pulling out the talisman he'd carried since his grandmother's death. He pulled it off, coiling up the rolled leather that he wore it on and putting it into Alaric's hand.

"This was your grandmother's," Alaric whispered.

"*From when she was still a small child. Her grandfather made it.*" Mason closed Alaric's fingers around it. "I want you to hold on to it, until we can be together."

"Mason... I can't..."

He kissed Alaric then. "You have to, so I know you're safe. Keep it close to you and think of me." He kissed him again, then slipped from between him and the tree, walking without looking back, because if he did, if he looked back and saw Alaric, he'd stay, and he knew that he needed to go.

* * *

Mason stopped to strap on the snowshoes once he was far enough away that it didn't feel like Alaric was within reach. The snow was thick and deep, even with the tree cover that surrounded the trail.

He stopped once to rest, giving himself a half hour to drink some water and eat a sandwich before he set out again. He was making better time than he expected, which showed exactly how much he'd recovered in his time with Alaric. It had only been a few weeks, but in some ways, it felt like a lifetime. It was still an hour or more before dawn when he reached Brettles, but to his surprise, the old Shade that ran the bar was sitting on the covered sidewalk like he was waiting for him.

"Bed's made. You hungry?"

Mason shook his head. "No, could use a phone and maybe a ride east." He bent to unstrap the snow shoes, setting them on the wooden sidewalk.

"Phone's inside. We leave at sunset."

Mason frowned at him a little. "Just like that?"

The old man grinned, showing off a mouth low on teeth. "Well, I'll ask a favor of ya, 'for I see ya off. Come on, phone's in here."

Mason followed him through the tavern and into a back office where an old rotary phone sat on a desk that didn't look like it should still be standing. The old man put a key in his hand and shuffled off, leaving Mason alone.

He stared at the phone, thinking through what he wanted to say to make sure he was understood, but not give away his location or plans. He picked up the phone and dialed the number he'd committed to memory early on in his training.

"Operator."

"This is 4532."

"One moment please."

There was a click followed by silence and a few minutes later a familiar voice sounded in his ear. "You okay?"

"Fine. I thought I would go to the meadow this week."

"You should see the river." There was relief in Adam's voice. "How long will you stay?"

"A few days." Mason responded, indicating that it would take him time to get there.

"Look for the bird."

Mason hung up the phone and exhaled. Raven would meet him in Vegas at the Rio. Sure, it wasn't complicated code, but it was enough to slide under the radar of casual listeners. Mason glanced at the key and the number one in faded gold lettering on the tag. He made his way into the bar and up the stairs to the room he and Alaric had stayed in just a few weeks before with the matching number one on the door.

He had no idea what favor the old man would ask, but he supposed it didn't really matter. Short of asking him to do something against his sense of morality, Mason knew he'd do what he needed to in order to get back to DC.

Mason sat on the bed and pulled open his bag. He smiled as he pulled out the food Emily had packed for him, a couple of sandwiches and fruit. He pulled out the canteen as well, then stopped, his hand finding something unexpected.

He pulled out a photograph that he knew he hadn't packed. Alaric smiled out of it at him, his arm around Riley's neck, his eyes sparkling. Clearly it had been taken before they had run, back when life was easier and more carefree.

His thumb rubbed over Alaric's face, remembering the taste of their first kiss, the rush of their first touch. He closed his eyes, and it was almost as if Alaric was there with him.

Mason exhaled and tucked the picture back into the bag. He'd have to remember to thank Emily when he saw her again. He saved the food for later in the journey, not knowing what to expect between Brettles and his destination. He drank from the canteen though and set the bag by the nightstand, turning his attention to the envelope. He dumped the contents out and sorted through it. There was a map marked with blue dots and a folder with information.

They'd pulled that information from the mind of a captured 8th Battalion soldier. Mason remembered the last time he'd seen the man. He was an empty shell. Damon had said he was helping as much as he could, but there wasn't much of his mind left.

He knew Alaric was ashamed of letting it happen, but was determined to put the knowledge they'd gleaned to good use. Mason gathered the papers and stuffed them back in the envelope before stretching out on the bed to sleep.

It was fitful, bothered by dreams of being chased and tormented, images of Alaric in pain and his Nana's voice, though he never figured out what she was telling him. He woke barely rested long before sunset.

He filled the bathtub and soaked for a while, trying to still the restless churning of his mind. His hand kept rising to play with the talisman that wasn't there anymore, sighing in frustration. When even the water wasn't helping, he got out and dried off, dressing before pacing until he figured it had to be close to sunset.

He refilled the canteen and shoved it into his bag before heading down the stairs. A younger man was at the bar, and the old man was waiting for him out front, leaning against a beat up old blue pickup.

"Get yerself in. Don't got all night."

Mason climbed in and the old man got behind the wheel. "Damn 8th Battalion is watching everything, but if we get past Reno, we'll be okay."

Mason pulled the map from his pocket, tracing the line Riley had marked. It was back roads until they got on 95 headed south, provided they didn't run into any 8th Battalion forces along the way.

* * *

The drive was mostly uneventful until they were past Lake Tahoe. The old man cursed as they spotted barricades blocking them from the back-road route he'd been planning to take.

He cut them back to the west, veering off paved roads at one point to get them headed south again. "Not the most comfortable ride," he grumbled as they bounced over rutted dirt roads until they found themselves back on pavement. "Was hoping we'd get further south before trying a state highway."

Mason didn't say anything. He was too busy scanning around them for 8th Battalion. The night was more than half gone, and the morning would come quickly. He didn't want to be stranded anywhere near the 8th Battalion waiting for the day to pass.

"Schultz." Keller pointed out the window. "Not much to speak of, half the place has already get gone out of here when the mine went flat. Rest are staying, one reason or another."

"Doesn't sound very friendly." Mason said.

"Imagine not." They pulled into town in the early morning hours before the town was awake. Keller drove them to the southern end of the town and into a sleepy rest stop. The only other vehicles there were a pair of eighteen wheelers. "Reckon you can find a ride south from here."

Mason looked at the old man, trying to size him up. "So, what's this favor you want me to do for you?"

The old man nodded slowly. "I lived a long life, saw lots of shit. But this?" He waved his hand at the window. "Figured I'd die and take the last of my line with me 'til I felt you coming." He fumbled at his neck and drew a talisman up out from under his shirt. He held it for a long time. "Got no one to take what I got to give."

He turned to look at Mason, and before Mason could respond beyond blinking at him, the old man grabbed him and pressed their mouths together, breathing forcefully into his mouth.

Mason's throat closed and he tried to pull back, but a last breath was not going to be denied, and almost against his will, he gasped inward, pulling the ball of memory and energy into himself. It was bigger than the gift his Nana had given him, the collected line not his own, sinking into him as the old man pressed the talisman into his hands and slumped over, dead before Mason had finished swallowing.

He sat back and closed his eyes, his fingers closing around the talisman. The ball of memory and power sank slowly into him, and it was going to take him time to let it settle, but he knew he couldn't do it there. Soon it would be daylight and the roads would get busy again.

He stumbled toward the bathroom, fighting the urge to throw up. He sat in the cold bathroom for a long time, wishing he could hide in the dark and sleep. He couldn't though – he needed to find a ride.

His eyes strayed to the old man's truck as he emerged from the bathroom, wondering if he dared try to drive. The windows were tinted dark enough, but Mason hadn't ever driven before. He shook his head. No, he needed to leave the old man some peace. He lifted his eyes instead to one of the rigs and the man getting out of it.

Mason hefted his backpack and waited for the driver to head into the bathroom. He lifted a hand in greeting. "Morning."

The man looked up at the sky and smirked. "Not quite. You looking for a ride?"

"Headed to Vegas to meet a friend," Mason said. "If you've got room."

"You look like you've been up all night."

"Just about."

"Let me see to business first. I'm headed to Vegas myself."

Mason sighed in relief. It almost felt like he could relax, except for the burning ball of foreign memories unspooling inside him. *One thing at a time,* he told himself. *Get to Vegas.*

Chapter Eighteen

Zero watched as Dr. Anthony finished attaching the leads to various monitors he'd insisted on before he would agree to let her try to free the trapped mind of the prisoner Shade.

He was on the bed beside her, likewise strapped to monitors, a mild UV light sapping his strength. He'd already been given mild doses of the drugs she'd stolen.

Zero rolled her head to loosen up, pulling her chair closer to the bed. "Okay, I'm going to start easy. You ready?"

Raven answered by putting her hand on Zero's shoulder. Zero nodded, lifting her hand to hover over the man's arm. She moved with deliberation, stealing her mind for the first onslaught, which they expected to come in the form of attempting to foist his illness onto her.

She met no resistance as her hand touched skin, however, and used the contact as a bridge between her mind and his. Where she'd expected an ordered mind and rigid walls, the space she encountered was empty, an expanse of mind that showed no response to her presence.

"So far, so good." Zero breathed as she moved further in. "No outside defenses. Going deeper." The imagery shifted, the landscape focusing into long dark corridors. Normally, she would expect for those corridors to lead backwards in time, from the most recent back to childhood. There was a big jump in time though, back to the night he was taken.

Zero followed the memory through to its end in abrupt darkness. She shook her head, finding herself at a dead end.

"*What's wrong?*" Raven asked.

"*It just... stops.*" Zero responded, turning slowing in the dark. "*There should be more here.*" She pressed into the space. The black spot should have been a continuation of memory, but instead it just seemed to push back at her.

Zero frowned, scanning her own memory from the times she'd been under the drug's effect. Tentatively, she pressed harder against the resistance of the dark space. It pushed back, then gave, and a wall fell, dropping Zero into the very ordered controls her father had put in place. "*This is it. You can come in now.*" Zero said.

Raven's presence followed Zero's trail as she examined the walls and partitions that had been erected, blocking the man from his own body. "*I was right,*" Zero said. "*Using the Shadow formula temporarily disabled the trap.*" She pointed to what looked like a panel of controls like one might find in a control room at a television studio.

"*This isn't what I expected,*" Raven said.

"*I think it's just showing me something I can understand,*" Zero responded. She studied the panel's readouts. "*We need to take down the walls that keep him from controlling his body, and disable the trap.*"

Zero reached for a dial she thought controlled the wall she had broken through, glancing back at it as she turned the dial. When it responded predictably, she turned it off. A series of levers looked like they would control the walls that kept the man's mind at bay. She reached for it, then hesitated. She needed to find the trap first, she wasn't sure that would be completely suppressed by the drugs.

She turned and looked around her. "*What were you doing when it triggered?*"

Raven was likewise scanning the space. "*Just trying to reach him.*" Raven was suddenly beside a small door, her hands flat against it. "*Here. This isn't natural.*"

Zero snorted. "*None of this is.*"

Raven shook her head, but Zero crossed to her. The wall was a natural construct, a partition between memories, but the door was not. She squatted beside it, touching it tentatively. *"If you've got shields, now is a good time to use them."* She tugged the door open.

Her father's voice screamed out at her, a projection meant to protect the trigger. Zero reached into the small space and grabbed a knot of what felt like bone and yanked. Almost immediately they were both shoved out of the Shade's mind and crashing back into themselves.

Zero's entire body was thrumming, and the pain in her head was growing. Behind her, Raven had stumbled back into the wall. Zero opened her eyes slowly.

The UV light was gone and Dr. Anthony was working on the man. Zero looked down at her hand, half expecting to find it grasping the trigger.

"Did you get it?" Raven asked, her voice harsh.

Zero nodded. "I think so." She was shaking as she tried to stand. "We probably won't know until one of us tries to go back in, or he wakes up." Pain lanced through her head and she staggered until she could grab the bed to steady herself.

Distantly, she could register concern from both Raven and the doctor, but her senses were shutting down, unseen hands moving to crush her mind. Zero reached out a hand as she started to fall, but the pain was too much and she curled into herself to escape it.

* * *

Raven sat beside the bed where Zero lay, and both Raven and Dr. Anthony had expended a good amount of energy to help counteract the reaction that had followed their attempt to read their prisoner.

It was the first time Raven had gotten more than a cursory look into the girl, and she didn't want to admit that what she had seen had scared her. She had physical scars aplenty, but the landscape of Zero's mind was like a minefield of scabs and scars and walls that were not of her own making.

Raven was more convinced than ever that Zero needed their protection.

"How's she doing?"

Raven glanced up at Adam in the doorway. "She's going to be okay. I think."

"Good. I hate to pull you away, but I need you in Vegas."

She frowned and stood. "What's in Vegas?"

"Jerah."

"What?" She moved away from the bed, pushing past him into the hallway to give Zero some quiet.

"He made contact early this morning. He's headed for Vegas and he needs you to get him home."

"Is he okay? Where has he been?"

Adam held up a hand. "It was just a pickup request in code. I don't know anything. Get yourself ready, I've got you on a commercial flight out in a few hours. I have people getting his documents ready so you can fly him home."

"Do we have a read on the situation in Vegas?" Raven asked as they headed toward the elevator.

"It's back and forth. They have a loud anti-Shade movement, but it's small and not gaining much traction. Keep your head down, and you should be fine."

She left him at the elevator, headed down to her small room. Jerah had been missing in action for months. She had just about given him up for dead.

Raven slammed through packing up what she would need into a bag, checking her urge to pack a weapon. She had no idea what she was walking into, but a weapon would mean declaring her status as an agent, and she decided that flying under the radar would be a better way to go. They didn't need any added scrutiny.

She paused in her packing as something Zero had said came back to her. Jerah had been gone a long time. If he'd been caught, he could have been broken, like the Shade they had in custody.

They were the last of the Shade operatives Adam had recruited, her and Jerah. If Jerah was lost to them, no matter whether that meant dead or turned, it made her life a whole lot harder. She pushed the thought away and headed for Adam's office. One thing at a time. She'd know soon enough if he had been turned.

Adam met her in the doorway of his office with a manila envelope that had a boarding pass paper-clipped to it. "Jerah's ID is in here, along with your tickets back from Vegas."

She took the envelope and nodded. "And if we run into trouble?"

Adam met her eyes. "Whatever it takes, bring him home."

"What if he's the trouble?" Raven asked.

Adam's expression softened a little and he sighed. "I had considered that. Still, do whatever you need to do to bring him home."

"Got it."

"And be careful."

She nodded. "I will be."

"I have a car waiting to take you to the airport, and a room in your name at the Rio. He'll find you there."

* * *

"The field of Republican candidates for the presidency continues to thin as today two more of the original twelve dropped out of the race, leaving the Senator from Utah, Norman Douglas, a televangelist from Nashville, Andrew Lloyd, and the former Marine general who left the military for the judicial bench, Larry Buchanan, as the only men still standing as we head into primary season. The contentious contest is expected to get even more lively now that the first debate is scheduled to happen in two weeks. Subjects expected to be discussed are the proposed round up of Shades and other quote 'non-human beings' that's currently being discussed in the House, as well as immigration and marriage equality."

Raven turned away from the television and crossed to the doorway. She hadn't heard from Adam since just after she had checked into the room. They didn't know for certain when to expect Jerah.

She paced back toward the television, rubbing her hands together. She was more nervous than she cared to admit. The whole flight out she had gone through scenarios for getting them out of Vegas if things went sideways. She'd planned at least five escape routes from the Rio to the airport, and another five to the nearest car rental. But those only worked if Jerah wasn't compromised. She had no idea how she'd extricate them both if he turned on her.

It was nearly sundown. She could tell from the angle of the light under the curtains that covered the windows. The newscaster on the television was prattling about some protest happening in Minnesota, and Raven turned the TV off in frustration. She grabbed her room key and shoved it in her pocket, deciding that she needed to get out of the room.

The casino floor was a busy place. The noise almost drove her back to her room. She paused near some slot machines and inhaled deep and slow, pushing her irritation down and letting her breath clear out some of the extra energy.

Her eyes scanned the room before she moved herself toward the front doors, sitting herself at a slot machine that let her watch people coming in. Raven smiled at the waitress as she approached, ordering a mineral water. She'd rather have whiskey, but she didn't dare until they were safely on their way back to Washington.

She sipped at her mineral water, slowly feeding coins into the machine as she watched the people around her. Las Vegas had the advantage of being a night time town, which made being a Shade somewhat less obvious, but it was still the desert, which always made her nervous.

Twenty-four hours had passed since she'd arrived and checked in. Their flight home was forty-two hours away.

Raven watched an older man and woman come in, wearing wedding clothes. He held the door for her and took her arm as they passed Raven's perch, smiling at each other as if no one else existed. Two stools down from where she sat was a tired looking woman chain smoking as she pushed the buttons in front of her. In the distance, somewhere behind her, she could hear announcements being made about a poker tournament that was due to start.

She finished her drink and handed off the glass to the waitress, her eye catching on movement near the doors. She turned, watching several men in suits spread out. She hid her face as one passed her, not certain who they were, but it seemed that they were looking for someone. She didn't want to take any chances.

The men circled back to the doors, then escorted someone inside. She was well dressed and petite, and she stayed hidden inside the phalanx of men moving like a single unit around her, with photographers trailing after them. Raven looked away as they reached the elevator, convinced it was just some celebrity or politician on her way to her room.

In the uproar left behind, Raven almost missed Jerah all together. He slipped in behind them, blending into the crowd of onlookers almost seamlessly. His hair was longer than the last time she'd seen him, and his face was dusty with the signs that he hadn't shaved in a few days.

She stood, shifting toward the group of people until she could catch his eye. When he saw her, relief flooded his eyes, and he nodded tightly. She turned and headed toward the elevators, knowing he would follow.

They said nothing as they stepped into the elevator, or as they rode up to the floor of her room. Raven led him to the door, opening it and leading him inside. Once the door was closed, Jerah seemed to deflate. "Man, am I glad to see you."

Raven kept herself a full arm's reach away. "You okay?"

He nodded and pulled a hand through his hair. "Yeah, I think so. A little dry, and I really need some time to incorporate this last breath I was forced to take."

She frowned and stepped a little closer. "Last breath?"

He nodded, packing to the windows. He was jittery, his hands shaking. "Long story." He pulled his backpack off and dropped it by the window. "I haven't had time… had to function enough to hitch a ride."

"From where?" Raven asked, watching him for signs that he wasn't the same man he had been. Of course, she didn't really know him before his disappearance, so she wasn't even sure what to look for.

"Um... some rest stop, north of here."

Raven wanted to grab him, force him to give up the details, but she didn't need another psychic slap-down like what happened before. "So, what happened? The caravan was ambushed; everyone was dead. Everyone but you."

He sank into the chair nearest the window. "Right, I feel like it's been forever. I got grabbed by these men, the ones that hit us. They knew I was a Shade. Took me to some compound in the desert." The shadow of pain crossed his face before he looked up at her. "They questioned me, tortured me." He shook his head. "I expected to die there."

"Obviously, you didn't."

"There were other prisoners who had an escape planned. They took me with them."

"Who were they?"

"Shadows," Jerah said, standing again. "They helped me get back on my feet. As soon as I was strong enough, I did what I could to get somewhere for a pickup."

"Shadows." Raven didn't like the way that made her stomach churn. "We have a Shade in custody that was compromised by a Shadow, turned into a killer against his will."

Jerah's face paled a little. "You think... no, Alaric and his people didn't..." He stood, holding out his hand. "Let me show you."

She hesitated, but knew that eventually someone was going to need to do it. With a deep breath, she put her hand on his and opened just enough that he could make contact.

"*I promise you, I'm not going to hurt you.*"

Raven followed his invitation, as he dropped all pretense of self-preservation. Almost instantly she was aware of the angry ball of memory that wanted to expand inside him, then she could see beyond it, where he showed her his capture, torture, escape. There was a little blur over pieces of memory with the one he called Alaric, but she recognized it for intimacy he didn't want to expose.

She pulled back first, satisfied that the men who had captured him hadn't been the men who had brainwashed the Shade they had caught in D.C. "You should soak and rest. Let that last breath out before it explodes." She gestured toward the bathroom. "I'll get some food sent up."

Raven waited for the bathroom door to shut before she pulled out her cell phone and dialed Adam. "I've got him. He's clean. Needs sleep, but otherwise okay."

"I'm getting reports of anti-Shade activity in your area, are you secure?"

"I haven't seen anything, but I haven't been outside the casino since I got here." She went to the window and pulled the heavy curtain aside, but they were too high up to see much on the ground below. "We should be fine. I'll call you if we need anything."

Chapter Nineteen

Alaric rubbed over his face, listening as the argument raged around him. He was tired of the politics, of the arguing, and the weight that it all put on his shoulders. He had never wished he could just run away more than he had since Mason left.

"The snow is already melting. The state road is mostly clear. It isn't going to be long before we're at risk." Riley said, crossing his arms. "We have to do something before the 8th Battalion finds us again."

"Let them come," Bryan said. "Every patrol we make disappear means fewer men from them to attack us with."

"I don't like the idea of killing," Marcy said, cradling her infant son. "We never agreed to killing."

Alaric sighed and lifted his head, sympathetic with the feeling. "We might not have a choice. We can't risk any scouts reporting back to their command about us." He didn't mention that they had already killed most of one patrol. "And we can't trust that any reprogramming we do to men we capture will hold."

He stood and moved toward the fireplace, leaning against the mantle. "Riley is right. Out best move is to start heading east. Together we're too big a target."

"Anywhere we go, we're going to have the same trouble," Bryan said, standing to pace around the table. "I say we stand and fight."

"What are we going to do, declare ourselves our own country?" Joseph asked, his hands on Marcy's shoulders. "You know where that would lead."

"Do I?" Bryan asked. He crossed his arms as he moved closer to Alaric. "Do any of us? For all we know they don't care about us."

"Because we don't have any intel hiding up here in the mountains," Emily said, joining the conversation for the first time. "Even Anson knew this was a temporary solution. It got us out of immediate danger. We weren't meant to be here long term."

Alaric looked at his mother, sensing her discomfort. She had been the one to bring up the idea of breaking the group up. "If we stay here and they do come, we're trapped." Alaric said. "We don't have the manpower to hold our borders, not against any force bigger than the scouting party we've already seen."

"We would if we gathered the tribes." Sahara moved away from the window, her eyes glowing gold in the light of the fire. "Legend says we were once one people, coexisting until they put us out into the wilds, turned us against one another."

"Right." Bryan shook his head at her. "What we need is a valley full of freaks. Like that will keep the 8th Battalion off our backs."

She growled at him. "They haven't seen what a pack of us can do. Let us off our leash, and we'll show you."

"It's thinking like that that got you landed in that truck we took you out of," Bryan responded.

Her nails were out and nearly to his throat when Alaric slammed his hand down on the mantle. "Stop. Enough. Clearly nothing will be decided tonight." He sighed and turned to look over the council. "Go back to your families, discuss the options presented. We'll meet again tomorrow."

He sank down to poke at the fire with the iron poker, not watching as they left the bunkhouse. He knew without looking up that Bryan and Riley had both stayed. He sighed. "I don't want to talk any more guys." He stood, putting the poker back in its stand before pulling his hands back through his hair.

"Actually, we were hoping you would listen," Riley said, leaning back against the nearest table. "And not about all this crap, not directly."

Bryan came to stand on his other side. "You look like shit."

"Gee, thanks." Alaric crossed his arms and looked up at them. "What is it you want?"

"Well, we figured you didn't use the globe when Mason was here because Mason was here. But he's been gone almost a week now." Riley started.

Alaric wrinkled his nose. "And?"

"And still you haven't even been in to look at it since you got back to camp." Bryan said.

Alaric sighed. "I'm not ready."

"We risked our lives to go back to Sacramento to get that for you." Bryan frowned at him, and Alaric didn't need to be able to read him to feel the frustration rolling off of him. "We sat in that makeshift gulag for more than a week."

"I know. I know." Alaric walked to the table, sitting slowly. "Do you really think now is the time for me to do that?" He had reasons beyond the fact that it would incapacitate him for days, reasons he wasn't ready to articulate to them.

"If not now, when?" Riley asked. "You see how the people are floundering without a real leader."

"I won't use the globe to make them do what I want Riley. I'm not that guy." Alaric shook his head.

"No one is saying that. But it will give them a sense of belonging again. We haven't had that since your father died."

Alaric turned to look at them. "Let me think about it."

"Don't think too long," Bryan said, clapping him on the shoulder. "Another patrol could find us any day."

He watched them walk away. He knew they wanted what was good for the people. He just wasn't sure that him taking on the actual burden of leading the clan was going to do them any better than just bearing the relative burden.

He sighed and left the bunkhouse, but he paused at the fork in the trail that led down to the water. The orb was in a cave on the other side, hidden, still in the crate they'd used to hide it to get it out of the city. He had to do it sooner or later, he knew it. Dragging his feet would do nothing to help them.

Alaric ducked into the cave, trying to center his thoughts as he moved into the dark, guided only by the pull of the orb that he could always feel. It was stronger now as he got closer. He opened the crate, and the globe glowed softly. It had been in the dark a long time and would need to be charged before he could undergo the ritual that would confer on him the gifts of his clan.

He sat on the floor beside it and closed his eyes, though for a long time he didn't let the energy past his barriers. Everything would change if he did this. He wouldn't just be leader because they expected him to be. He would be taking up the mantle left to him by his father. The globe would unite them, give him the ability to communicate with them. With all of them, anywhere. It would open him up to his fullest potential, take down the blocks and barriers that kept him safe from himself.

Alaric fumbled to pull Mason's talisman out from under his shirt. His fingers rubbed over the stone, feeling out each line and dip in its design. He breathed in deep, holding an image of Mason in his mind.

It took a long time, but he felt something stir, a vague sense of conscious thought. "*Mason.*"

"*Okay?*"

Alaric sent a wave of reassurance and affection. "*Miss you.*"

He got a sense that Mason was shifting, moving, water. "*Miss you too.*"

Mason couldn't maintain the connection for long over such distance; he was already slipping away. Alaric caressed against him and pulled away, dropping the talisman to his chest. If he did this, he would need to appoint at least two people as Keepers, preferably three.

He held up a hand, pressing it to the outer barrier of the globe's energy field. He had been one of his father's Keepers, so the energy recognized him, connected to him quickly. Immediately, memories began to flood his mind: his father's oath taking, the flurry of violence, Abigail's gruesome death, the separation as he and his mother ran, leaving his father behind. He pulled back then, tears already running down his face.

He knew what would follow. He was going to have to relive it all – his failure to keep his father safe, to protect the globe, the darkness… the pain, and not just his own. When he took on his father's role, his father's memories would be a part of him too, along with each leader before them. They would continue to reside in the globe, but only once he had experienced them so he would know the joys and sufferings of their people, the heartbreak of loss and the triumph of finding their place in the world.

But Bryan was right. They couldn't continue like this. Already it had been too long. The lines were fraying.

He stood and gathered himself, wiping his eyes. He needed time to prepare. The ritual itself was relatively simple, but when it was over he would be left in a pseudo-unconscious state, and he would need to be tended by his Keepers while his powers were unlocked, amplified. When it was done, he would be a new man with the burdens of a leader and the gifts of his entire clan.

He left the cave and went to Bryan's cabin. Bryan answered the door with a grunt, gesturing him in. Alaric shook his head and stood on the porch, uncomfortable and awkward. "I'm going to need men I can trust."

Bryan crossed his arms. "Yeah, you are."

Alaric exhaled. "Will you stand with me?"

Bryan stared at him a long time. "That's a big responsibility."

"You don't have to tell me."

"Who else you asking?"

"Riley, I think."

Bryan nodded slowly. "You should ask Sahara."

Alaric frowned, and Bryan held up a hand. "She's got the gift for it, and a hell-cat in your corner is never a bad thing."

"You've tested her?"

Bryan shrugged some. "Let's just say it had reason to come up. When?"

"Get the globe ready. It's going to need to be charged, and I want around the clock guards on it. No one gets close but you and Riley. And for fuck's sake, don't do something stupid, like touch it."

Bryan held up both hands. "I know better."

"I'll talk to Riley before I head in. I'll start prepping for it tomorrow."

"And Sahara?"

"I'll think about it."

"It's about damn time."

Alaric waved him off and headed to find Riley. He hadn't been in his cabin when Alaric passed it. He found Sahara and the other two Shifters instead, laying out on rocks near the river. It was easy to forget that like Mason, they were more inclined to the moon than the sun.

"You're out late," Sahara observed, her eyes tracking him.

He nodded, turning his face up to the half-moon. "Can I talk to you?"

"Sure." She slid off the rock with the grace of the cat. "What about?"

Alaric wiped his hands on his pants and drew her away from the others. "Well. Ah, Bryan suggested that you might be… able… and willing…" He shook his head. This should not be as difficult as it seemed to be. It wasn't unheard of to have ungifted Keepers or Keepers from other clans, but it hadn't happened in recent memory. "There's a ritual I need to perform soon, and when it's over I won't be as capable of defending myself completely, so part of the ritual creates guardians of a sort for me. Keepers. Bryan seems to think you would be a good choice."

"Why won't you be able to keep yourself?"

Alaric inhaled. "Well, as part of the ritual, my mind is linked to my entire clan, it creates certain… distractions. I become a better leader, but everything that happens to me can be radiated out to the entire clan."

"So, like a bodyguard."

Alaric nodded. "Yeah, something like that."

"Can I think about it?"

"Yes, of course. I didn't mean you had to decide right away. We need a few days to be ready for the ritual anyway."

"Okay, I'll let you know."

"Actually, let Bryan know. I'm going to be unavailable until we're ready. I have… things to do to get ready."

She nodded. "Alright then. I'll let Bryan know."

"Good. You ladies have a good night."

He left them there on the rocks and headed toward the bridge, where Riley was standing as if he was waiting for him. "You make a decision?"

"Boy, cut right to it, why don't you," Alaric said, crossing his arms.

"Why else would you come looking for me after dismissing us the way you did?"

Alaric looked him in the eye. "Yeah, okay. We'll do it. I put Bryan in charge of getting it ready. He's going to stand with me. Will you?"

"Bold move, picking two keepers who see things so differently."

"Three," Alaric countered. "I asked Sahara too."

Riley stepped back. "Wow, didn't see that coming."

"Things have changed Riley, we can't let go of traditions completely, but we need to adjust or we'll die out here."

Riley nodded. "Yeah, I'll stand with you, Alaric, but that don't mean we won't die out here."

"I know." Alaric left him standing there. "I know."

* * *

Bryan oversaw the moving of the orb from its safety in the cave, up the trail to a clearing at the top of the highest point above the valley. Once it was placed roughly in the center of the clearing, he approached the crate cautiously.

He could feel it even before he began uncrating it. The warmth of it caressed his face as he freed it from the wood that housed it, a familiar touch. Like Alaric, he had been one of Anson's Keepers. He hadn't really understood what that meant before the ceremony, but he did now.

He'd considered saying no. It was a big responsibility, one he wasn't sure he wanted again. Bryan cleared the last of the wood and set it by the trail to be taken away before the ritual. The orb pulsed and he could almost feel it pulling energy from the sun.

Bryan approached slowly, holding a hand in front of him, letting it brush against the outermost barrier of energy. It served as a warning, keeping away those who were unprepared for the full power of it.

Memory washed over him of that first ceremony nearly seven years before, the fire as they were all connected, pulled together. From that moment on they were a team, connected on levels it was difficult to articulate.

There was a footstep behind him and he withdrew from the orb's energy, turning to see Riley at the start of the trail down to camp. His eyes were on the globe though, wide and awed as he took a hesitant step closer.

"I felt you open it," Riley said, his eyes darting to Bryan, then back to the globe. "I've been able to feel it since Jordan and I pulled it out of that storage place, but this is different."

"You can come closer, just don't touch it. It doesn't know you well yet."

Riley took a few steps, then started to walk in a circle. "When I was little, my mother told me stories." He licked his lips. "I always thought they were just stories. She never showed me..." He shook his head. "And Dad wanted nothing to do with the history. His people..."

Bryan knew a fair bit about the people of Riley's father, even though he had never met the man. They were from a distant clan, and like all people of color, they had been treated badly. Some managed to hide in Voodoo and Santeria, but others had been slaughtered as the white people feared their gifts.

Their traditions were different, but there was no denying that they shared the same gifts.

Riley shook his head as he finished his circuit around the globe. "Sorry. I didn't mean to get so caught up. I came to see if you needed help with anything."

Bryan nodded and pulled his attention from the orb. "We need to set up guards to keep people away while it charges. I want two we can trust not to get sucked in to wanting to touch it up here, two more on the trail."

"I can set that up," Riley said, moving back toward the trail. "What about Sahara, did she agree to do this?"

Bryan nodded. "I'm going to need time with you and Sahara to go over the ritual, and explain what your jobs will be after. It's a lot of information." Bryan left the orb to cross to Riley. "Get the guard set up and bring Sahara in the cave where the orb has been. Best to do this away from others."

Riley nodded and headed down the trail. Bryan picked up the pieces of wood that had been the crate and started down the trail too. He waited at the bottom until two men called hellos as they approached. Bryan approved of the choices. Both had minimal gifts, and thus would be less tempted by the pull of the globe.

"No one gets close," Bryan told them as they headed past him. "And don't touch it."

He dropped the crate pieces near the trail and followed it down to the cave they had just taken the globe from. Some of its energy still bounced off the walls as he entered. Bryan sat where the globe had been, closing his eyes and reaching into himself for the memory of that day all those years before when he and Alaric had stood with Victoria to witness and guard the leader of their clan as he took on the gifts of the orb.

He felt Riley's approach, then the gold fire that was Sahara's psychic signature, and he drew them to him, keeping his eyes closed. "Sit, get comfortable."

When they had joined him – Riley to his right, Sahara to his left – he held out his hands to them. "Take a deep breath and center. The easiest way to do this is to show you. It's going to be powerful."

He felt Riley's controlled breath and his shields opening for him. Sahara was only slightly behind him, her mind strong and ordered. He whispered his thanks into their minds and let the memory play.

When it finished, he pressed the knowledge of their roles into each of them, the words they would need, the power that would come to them and the responsibility that came with that power. He was sweating when he was done, and tired. He eased back from the link he'd created, opening his eyes and stretching.

"Go slow," he said out loud as both of them opened their eyes. "You've been sitting longer than you think. It's nearly suppertime."

Sahara's eyes were bright as she looked at him. "When will we begin?"

"The globe needs to charge in the sun all day tomorrow. We will begin at dawn the day after. Until then, I suggest you both sleep well and eat hearty. This will be unlike anything you've ever done, and when it's over, our job will be to keep Alaric safe while he recovers."

He led them out of the cave and into the slanted light of the setting sun. He too needed to sleep, but first he would stop to let Emily know that they were nearly ready.

As ready as they could be this far removed from their past anyway.

Chapter Twenty

Foreign memories unspooled into him, filled with passionate anger and furious fears, lives lived secretly behind rigid rules. Mason let them come, sinking into the tub as it filled with cold water.

The old man's people were cautious and painfully closed off. He lost himself in the wash of other lives, holding himself under water as the memories sorted themselves, shifting into place among those of his mother and grandmother. The water siphoned off the heat from his skin as he worked through the bulk of the collected life of a man he barely knew and all of his ancestors.

He was nearly done enough to deal with his other physical needs when he felt a tickle in the back of his mind. It was warm and familiar, then Alaric's presence filled him, pushing aside everything else. "*Mason.*"

Mason caressed against the feeling of him, wanting to touch him, but it was strain just to make words form. "*Okay?*"

"*Miss you,*" Alaric responded and Mason felt a wave of affection and reassurance flood him.

Mason sat up, holding the edges of the tub. "*Miss you too.*" He wanted to hold onto Alaric's presence, but the distance between them and his exhaustion made it impossible. Alaric drifted away, leaving Mason alone in the rapidly warming water.

He got out of the tub and wrapped a towel around himself. Most of the water on his skin absorbed quickly. He pulled the plug on the tub and opened the bathroom door. Raven was just setting up the table in the corner of the room with the food from room service.

"Oh, I brought you a change of clothes. All you had in your room was the uniforms, so I borrowed from Chris down in intelligence. He's about your size." Raven said, reaching for a duffle bag on the floor by the bed closest to her.

Mason padded across the floor, his stomach rumbling as the smell of the burgers and fries hit him. He sat at the table and pulled a plate closer. "This smells good."

"Better be for the price," Raven said, dropping a pile of black on the end of the bed.

He took a bite of the burger and sat back in the chair to chew. It seemed strange to be back in civilization again. His eyes scanned the room, coming to stop on the television. "This may seem like a strange question," Mason said, "but I've been so cut off… what's going on?"

Raven looked at him for a second, then seemed to grasp what he was asking. "Well, it isn't good." She sighed and crossed her arms. "There are attacks of one kind or another every day it seems. Killings that are made to look like Shades did it, bombings at Jewish community centers and mosques, KKK style cross burnings and lynchings, retaliatory strikes by Shades and at least one by a Shifter. Most of the west coast is locked down by the military, big chunks of the south are as well."

Mason swallowed and reached for the glass of water she had set beside his plate. "And politically?"

She sighed. "Not much better. The president won't commit to any protections for Shades and the 'others' and Congress is debating a bill that would force all citizens with extra abilities to register." She made a face. "And then there's the whole Republican mess. We're down to three men fighting for the nomination, and every one of them is championing even stricter sanctions on us."

They ate quietly for a few minutes while Mason processed the information. "Just before we got ambushed, I heard that the UN was considering stepping in, at least to observe the military actions against civilians."

Raven nodded. "Yeah. So far all they've done is send a few observers to the west coast. Canada is limiting border crossings after originally opening the borders for anyone who felt they were being targeted. Our allies are all watching, but no one has taken action."

Mason finished off his burger and sat back. "So where do we stand in all of this?"

Raven shrugged. "Adam doesn't say much. I suspect he's operating on the assumption that we'll be okay until we make waves, and considering that we're down to a pretty small crew of agents that would actually qualify as 'others,' I suspect he's probably right."

"How small?" Mason asked, not sure he wanted to know the answer.

"You, me, a Shifter, though technically, he's military. A couple of low level Shadows in intelligence." Her face scrunched up a little. "And there's Zero. Though she isn't an agent."

"Zero?" Mason asked.

"Part Sage, part Shadow. I found her on a mission in Atlanta." Raven paced a little. "I'm going to see if I can get us on an earlier flight out. Now that you're here, I'm ready to get back to whatever safety Washington provides."

"Not going to argue," Mason offered, stifling a yawn.

Raven lifted her phone and gestured at the bed. "Get some sleep. We're okay for now."

Mason didn't need more of an invitation. He abandoned the rest of his fries and crawled into the bed. The weariness was deep, and it would take little to convince his body to sleep.

His dreams were restless, from quiet moments with Alaric in a cabin as the snow fell to frantic running from faceless men through abandoned cities and rough desert terrain. He woke breathlessly, blinking in the half light of the room.

Raven stood silently at the window, looking out at the city. She turned her head. "You okay?"

Mason grabbed the glass of water she had set on the nightstand beside him and swallowed it down before nodding. "Dreams."

"I was just getting ready to wake you. Our flight is in three hours. We should get moving."

Mason pulled a hand back through his hair. "Yeah." She went back to staring out the window. "Something going on out there?"

She shrugged and moved away. "Can't tell. I'm just restless I think."

Mason pulled the clothes she'd brought him from the end of the bed, shaking out the pants and sliding them on. They were a little snug, but they did the job.

Raven tossed an envelope on the bed. "Adam had a new passport made for you."

Mason opened the envelope and dumped the passport and new agency credentials onto the bed beside him. Standing, he slipped the passport into his back pocket, before he retrieved his backpack from where he'd dropped it earlier to tuck his credentials into.

He finished getting dressed, watching Raven pace. "Is there something you're not telling me?"

She crossed back to the window. "I'm just nervous. Adam said that there might be local trouble."

"What kind of trouble?" Mason asked, joining her at the window and pulling the heavy drapes aside. Below him the lights of the city where bright, casting a hazy glow that ate into the darkness of the desert.

"Protests maybe." She shook her head and sighed. "The whole world has gone crazy."

"You'd think that in Vegas, of all places, the people would be a little more open minded," Mason said, his eyes transfixed on the lights spread out below them.

"Yeah, I sure as hell don't want to be the one to test that theory," Raven said, turning. "You ready? We can get a cab to the airport, grab some food there."

"Let me get my shoes on." Mason sat and shoved his feet into the boots Alaric had given him. He closed his eyes against a sudden flood of images and flush of affection. He could feel the color rising in his cheeks as he finished tying the boots. Raven was smirking at him when he stood. "What?"

She shook her head. "You're blushing."

"I thought we were leaving?" Mason lifted his backpack and went to the door.

Raven was close behind him and together they moved down the hall to the elevator. Mason nodded in greeting to the older couple already in the car as they stepped in. It stopped twice more, picking up a tall man in a cowboy hat and two girls dressed for a night on the town. By the time the car stopped on the first floor, Mason was feeling claustrophobic, and he moved quickly to find some free space. Raven's hand found his elbow while he was still trying to catch his breath. It was steadying. She nodded toward the door and they headed out to grab a cab.

The air was warm and uncomfortable as they climbed into the back of a cab. He'd expected to relax once he'd made contact, but he was nearly as on edge as he'd been climbing into the old man's truck.

Maybe he was just reacting to Raven's nervousness. Maybe they'd both calm down once they were on the plane. He watched the city whiz by as the cab headed toward the airport, longing for landscape that wasn't filled with neon lights and air that smelled of pine trees. Or maybe it wasn't the landscape or air that he was missing.

* * *

Alaric could feel the pull of the globe, pulsing in the clearing up on the top of the cliff behind him. It beckoned him, and soon he would heed its call, climb up the trail and perform a ritual as old as time itself to take on the role his father left him.

It wasn't quite daylight and the valley stretched out quiet below him. His mother moved behind him, readying the small cabin far from most of the camp. He would need time to recover once the ritual was done, days to rest undisturbed while the gifts of those that came before him integrated and his connections to those within his clan were strengthened.

The ritual would awaken any dormant powers within him, but would also grant him the ability to borrow the power of anyone in the clan. It would probably take him weeks to fully adjust.

His hand slid up to the talisman Mason had given him before leaving. It still felt like Mason, that slight vibration that told Alaric where the talisman belonged, reminded him that he was merely holding on to it.

Under that another pendant lay and Alaric let himself hold that a moment too. The moonstone was cool to the touch, despite the fact that he had not removed it in days. He intended to wear it through the ritual too, imbuing it with more than just his blood.

He could feel the first kiss of the sun as the golden light caressed his face. His stomach grumbled, angry at the days with little more than water as he prepared himself.

It was nearly time.

He stepped down the three steps away from the cabin, turning his face into the rising sun. Behind him, his mother stepped out as well, shading her eyes. He smiled in her direction. "All will be well."

She nodded. "Be safe, Alaric."

It was his destiny to lead his people, to take up the mantle and the burden that came with it. Only with a leader who was tuned in to the clan could they survive. Only with the knowledge of the ancestors would he understand what needed to be done.

Somewhere above him, a horn sounded – his call. He nodded to himself and walked toward the trail that would lead him up to the clearing, to the globe, to the sacred space where Bryan, Riley and Sahara awaited him.

At the top of the trail he was met by two young women, one carrying a smoldering bundle of sage. She softly blew the smoke toward him, over his face and down to his chest, over both legs and around to his back. The other held up a circle of gold, set with a crystal.

Alaric bowed his head and she settled it on him, the crystal sitting on his forehead. He could already feel it opening him up, the power of the globe pulsing at him, the thoughts of those around him racing into him.

He took a deep breath and focused on the crystal, on the globe, carefully blocking out the others for the moment. Once he was in control, he lifted his head. Everything vibrated with color as he stepped away from the women.

The space had been cleared of snow, a circle marked out in black. Four guardians stood at the cardinal points, facing outward. A second circle was marked in white. The globe was in the center, the white energy of it filling the space. To its right, Bryan stood, his head circled with a similar gold band, though the crystal was much smaller. The traditional robes they had worn when both he and Bryan had become keepers were somewhere back in Sacramento, but Bryan had tried to honor the ritual, dressed in the dark green of his position as Alaric's first keeper.

Alaric went to him first, as the primary of his Keepers. Without touching him, Alaric leaned his head forward and Bryan did the same, until the two crystals touched.

Like a light electrical current, Alaric felt his body tingle with the contact. He stepped back and Bryan turned to face the orb. Alaric moved clockwise and stopped where Riley stood, his clothes in shades of blue and wearing the gold band as well. Alaric leaned in, let their bands connect.

He was already thrumming with energy when he moved to Sahara. Her eyes were amber fire, and her skin rippled with golden hair that she normally kept hidden. The gold gave way to the red of her shirt and the combination reminded him of fire. He could feel her in a way he never had, the power she contained, the animal within. He touched their bands together and felt it flow into him.

He pulled back and inhaled slowly, then let it out just as slowly, taking his position in the empty spot between Sahara and Bryan. This was it, the point of no return. Once he began, there was no turning back. He nodded to Bryan, then closed his eyes.

The chant was so old no one really knew the exact translation anymore. Riley picked up the chant, then Sahara. The globe's light grew, reaching toward Alaric. He breathed it in, welcoming the surge of energy as he likewise reached for it, both hands making contact with the surface. His body shook, heat flooding him as he panted and the globe assessed his ability to fulfill his role. Once it accepted him, they could continue.

Fire laced through his veins, licking at his organs, burning through any barriers that might have been. For a long moment, he knew nothing but the fire, then slowly it receded until he was once more separate from it.

Alaric didn't need to open his eyes to see everything around him. The globe pulsed in time with his heartbeat as he turned to Bryan, who bowed his head and went to both knees, offering up his hands. The ceremonial blade lay across one, waiting for Alaric to take it up.

"As I take up this burden I am reminded that I am mortal, flesh and blood." His voice sounded odd to his ears, a vague accent making it seem formal and older somehow.

Alaric lifted the blade and set the point against the palm of his left hand. He traced it over his skin, slicing a shallow cut into the flesh before lifting the blade again.

"I will take the keeping of your flesh and your blood, that you might lift this burden with ease," Bryan said, looking up at him.

Alaric set the point of the blade over Bryan's heart, pressing just enough to break the skin. He pressed his bleeding palm over the hole. "My blood binds us; my body is in your keeping."

Bryan's eyes closed as the bond was made, and his thoughts opened to Alaric in ways they had never before. His body felt lighter, even as Bryan seemed heavier and stronger. His eyes opened, and they glowed with the energy passing between them. He stood, his hand taking the knife back as he stepped to Alaric's right hand side. Together they moved to Riley, who knelt as they approached.

"As my mind is opened, my body is without defense."

Riley lifted his eyes. "I will defend your body, that your mind might be free to serve."

Bryan set the point over his heart, piercing the skin. Alaric covered the wound with his hand, and shivered a little as their minds touched and merged. He'd long known that Riley had untapped reserves, abilities that he'd never used, but now that was made manifest, opening to Alaric. Riley shuddered as Alaric pulled his hand away and was a little shaky as he stood to take Alaric's left side as they moved to Sahara.

She met his eyes before going to her knees and lifting her hands.

"As I offer refuge to our people I stand alone in the path of danger."

"I will stand with you, and join our people as one."

Bryan pierced her with the dagger and Alaric set his hand on the wound, steeling himself for the anticipated onslaught of an untrained mind. Instead, what he found was order and ferocity, walls of fire that fell for him easily, and a hint of laughter tracing the pathways as he pulled back.

Sahara stood, stepping aside for the three of them to pass her and falling in behind them. Alaric led them then, around the circle, around the globe, three times. On the final pass, they each took their places once more and Alaric came to stand at his place. He checked on his timing, making sure the sun was where he needed it to be.

"I am one with my people. I am one with those who passed before me. I am one with those who have not yet come." The globe pulsed a little faster as Alaric lifted his bloody hand. "I offer myself to the service of the clan, and these, my Keepers, as guardians. If it be pleasing, take me within that I might know the story I carry forward."

Fire circled his wrist as it penetrated the energy barrier of the globe and he spared a glance at Bryan before he took a deep breath and stepped closer. The fire burned up his arm, pulling him into the light. He closed his eyes and let it take him, let it pull him into the light completely.

He was buoyed up on the energy, carried into a place that existed outside of the physical. Some part of him knew that it was only his spirit that was within the globe, but it felt physical enough.

Voices moved around him, the sounds of his ancestors, moving him, readying him. Slowly, one voice transcended the others and Alaric opened his eyes to his father's face. "About damn time, Son."

"It's good to see you." Alaric let himself be pulled into the embrace, relishing the gift of having his father back in his life, however briefly.

"Are you ready?"

Alaric nodded.

"Close your eyes." His hand covered Alaric's face, fingers pressing lightly to his eyelids. "Trust me and open yourself to me."

Alaric's mind lay open, the familiar touch of his father's mind caressing his before everything was wrenched to the side and he was falling through time, flailing even though he knew he was safe. Memories rushed at him, and faces, voices surrounded him, swirling together in a kaleidoscope of history that had been known to drive some insane.

Chapter Twenty-One

Zero sat up, her nose crinkling as something stirred in the back of her mind. It was familiar, and yet not. Someone, somewhere was waking, and she could feel him stretching. She shook her head and put her feet on the ground.

For a moment, it all felt wrong, like she was meant to be somewhere else, then there was a knock on the door and it opened to reveal Dr. Anthony.

"I see you're feeling better."

"Good as new, Doc. How's your other patient?"

"Well, he's able to communicate more." Dr. Anthony took a couple steps into the room. "His name is Jeffrey Moore. He's a teacher at a night school in Baltimore."

She'd gathered that much information during her foray into his mind. "Does he remember anything?"

He shrugged. "Not that he's said. He knows what he did, however."

"Is Raven back yet?" Zero knew that Darvin had sent Raven on some mission while she was still recovering from her attempt to break the psychic hold on the Shade, but Zero had no idea what the mission was.

"She arrived very early this morning, actually." Dr. Anthony said. "Why don't you lay back and let me make sure everything is in working order?"

Zero stood instead. "I'm good to go, Doc. Thanks." She reached for the robe that was draped over the chair, pulling it on over the hospital gown.

"Young lady— "

She held up her hand. "Don't. I'm fine. You've had enough time to do your thing. Save it for someone who needs it."

Zero dodged around him, padding on bare feet over the cold tile. The pale blue hallways of the medical floor were stark contrast to the dark concrete floors and walls of the rest of the facility. She felt around her for the way out, finding the elevator and moving quickly for it. There was an urgency building, and she wasn't sure what was causing it.

She needed to find Raven.

Zero exited the elevator on the residential floor, heading for her own room where she shed the hospital gown in favor of the black uniform pants and her boots, along with a black t-shirt. She paused long enough to pull the red wig off the corner of her mirror and slide it on. She found that the people there looked at her less suspiciously when she had hair.

Once she had it on straight, she left her room, casting about for Raven's presence. Zero followed the feeling until she found Raven in one of the common rooms.

Raven turned as Zero entered the room, but her smile was fleeting, her eyes distant. "Everything okay?" Zero asked.

Raven sighed. "I'm okay. Everything else…" She gestured at one of the televisions. "There was another attack in New York city. Fifty dead, hundreds injured."

Zero nodded and moved closer. "Your mission went okay?"

Again, Raven sighed, sinking into one of the chairs. "Yeah. Fine. I just can't shake this feeling that something is coming."

"Like what?" Zero asked, leaning back against the pool table.

Raven shook her head. "I'm not sure. It's been bugging me since Vegas." She inhaled deeply and exhaled slowly. Almost physically, Zero could feel her shift her attention. "What about you? How are you doing?"

"I'm good. Dr. Anthony says our Shade is better."

Raven nodded. "Yes, I had some time with him when I got back. He's not a hundred percent, but I think we're past him hurting anyone."

"So, we're ready to work on me." Zero said.

Raven held up a hand. "I don't know that we're there yet. I'm not ready to go messing around with things we don't understand."

"And I don't want to keep waiting for my father to pull some trigger he's buried in here" She gestured toward her head, even as she looked away. She hadn't meant to say that. It was a fear she preferred to keep to herself.

It made Raven sit up though. "Are you afraid he might have programmed you too?"

Zero rolled her eyes. She opened her mouth, but the words wouldn't come. She growled instead. "It's exhausting, figuring out how to say things. I *know* things... stuff..." It was her turn to sigh in frustration. "There's...." She could see the knowledge. She could open the door and look into the room, but when she tried to explain any of it, she could *feel* her father suppressing her ability to communicate.

Raven's hand touched hers and a soothing wave of comfort followed. "Take it easy, before you hurt yourself."

Zero stopped pushing and opened her eyes. "I just want him out of my head."

Raven offered her a tight smile. "I know. And I promise we'll get there. I got a pretty good look inside your head after you passed out. I'm not sure either I or Dr. Anthony can help you, even with the drugs."

"So, I'm stuck like this." Zero's heart sped up as she considered living with a minefield in her head.

"I didn't say that. We just need to find someone with more experience."

"What if I hurt someone?" Zero asked softly.

Raven squeezed her hand. "I won't let you."

"Promise?" Zero asked, looking her in the eye. "Promise me you'll put me down anyway you have to if I'm going to hurt someone, if I lose control."

"It won't come to— "

"Promise me," Zero insisted, holding Raven's gaze until she nodded. "I promise."

Zero nodded and sank into a chair. Out of the corner of her eye, movement on the television caught her attention and she squinted at the screen. The volume was off, but the news was covering politics. Norman Douglas was in town, judging by the video of him getting out of a car. He waved to the people crowding in to see him, and as he moved, Zero froze.

"What is it?" Raven asked.

Zero pointed at the man beside Douglas. "My father." She grabbed the remote and paused the TV. "He's here. With Douglas."

Raven was at her side instantly. "Do you think he knows where you are?"

"He knows I'm in the city," Zero said, her hand starting to shake. "He'll be looking for me." Raven's hand rubbed Zero's back, and she could feel the warm comfort Raven was trying to send, but it wasn't enough to thaw the icy fear in her veins.

Raven took the remote from her hands, turning the volume up and letting the video play.

"*...and entourage are in town for a rally to bolster the Senator's pres-idential campaign. Here in the capital, sentiment has turned against the senator as his competition uses his congressional voting record against him.*" The camera switched views to a line of people with protest signs lining the street. "*Meanwhile, across the street protestors are gathered with signs that call out the Senator's stance on faith-based initiatives, abortion, religious freedom, Shades and more. I think it's safe to say that Washington D.C. will not be an easy win for Norman Douglas.*"

Zero imagined she could feel her father's mental hand on her neck, though she knew it was only in her head. He was focused on getting his pet Senator into the white house. She breathed in slowly, trying to push the anxiety back.

"What is he doing with Douglas?" Raven asked.

Zero blinked and exhaled, looking up at her. "What?"

"What is your father doing with Douglas?"

Zero shrugged. "Same thing he's been doing with other politicians for years, I'd guess."

"Controlling him?"

Zero nodded. "One way or another. You should expect an uptick in violence. He'll set people off, pit them against each other. If R is with him, expect Shade related deaths."

"Like the ones in Atlanta?" Raven asked.

Zero shrugged. "Maybe, or actual Shades, like our friend Mr. Moore."

"I don't like this." Raven murmured.

Zero didn't voice her agreement. There was no point. Her father had always been the one in control, and despite escaping, despite Raven's help, Zero felt just as helpless to stop him as she ever had. The only difference now was that she was on the outside of whatever he was planning with no way to listen in.

* * *

Sahara paced outside the cabin where Alaric was resting. Since the end of the ritual, she had been restless, filled with energy she couldn't seem to disperse. She was more aware of the world around her, and it felt like she could feel Alaric inside her.

Not just Alaric... She knew without thinking about it that Bryan was headed to relieve her, and Riley was just settling in to sleep. She was hyper aware of the sounds around her, of the movement in the trees, the heartbeat of the people and animals within reach.

Glancing down, she was surprised to see her skin covered in fur, her hands nearly to claws. She needed to run, to let go of herself and hunt. With deep breaths, she pushed the cat back inside her, exhaling slowly as Bryan came into view.

"He's asleep," Sahara said.

Bryan nodded. "I know." He held out a plate. "Brought you something to eat."

She shook her head. "Thanks, but I need... more."

He shrugged and pulled the plate back. "When was the last time you went in?"

"About an hour ago. Added wood to the fire. I got some broth into him."

"Good. I'm ready to take watch. Riley will relieve me in six hours."

"I'm going to hunt." Sahara stepped away from him, headed down the creek, past the last few cabins on that end of the camp. She pulled her coat off as she cleared the wards, stopping by a large boulder. She put her coat on the rock, then proceeded to strip down, shivering a little in the cold.

Sahara stretched out, rolling her neck and preparing herself for the change. It had been almost a week since she'd felt free enough of her obligations to enjoy the freedom the cat provided her.

She let the change come, reveling in the feeling of strength that flowed through her. Dropping to all fours as the process neared complete, Sahara lifted her head, smelling the air. Her stomach rumbled, demanding hot, fresh meat.

Abandoning her clothing, she set off into the dark of the woods. Somewhere nearby there was a rabbit that would be a good start. She ran, following the scent and taking the rabbit with ease. It did little to appease her appetite, however, and she ran off in search of bigger prey. The night passed as she hunted, and close to morning she was sated enough that she began working her way back toward the camp with the notion that she would find a deer to bring back.

She paused at a stream, bending to drink until her senses told her she wasn't alone. She lifted her head slowly, smelling the still air and turning to see the dark world around her.

Upstream from her she saw movement and she froze, watching the spot. A bear crossed the stream, moving slowly. She crouched low to the ground. It was odd to see a bear out before the first thaw.

It turned her way and something in its body language told her it wasn't any ordinary bear. It lumbered up the bank of the creek and stood on its hind legs, roaring out a warning.

Sahara heeded it, keeping her body low as she crossed to the other side of the creek and slunk through the foliage. The bear didn't follow.

She kept her senses tuned and worked her way back toward the camp, at least until she smelled deer. Letting thoughts of the bear fade, Sahara stalked the deer, a young buck with wide antlers. He was easy to take down, meaty enough to feed the camp for a few days.

She dragged the kill inside the wards, but left it by the boulder where she'd left her clothes. She was suddenly drained and the effort to get it all the way to the bunkhouse seemed enormous.

Sahara shifted back to her human form and paused to use handfuls of snow to clean the blood off her face and hands before she dressed again. She was shivering by the time she pushed her feet into boots and headed toward her cabin.

Mila and Maddie were in the living area as Sahara opened the door, and they looked up expectantly. She nodded a greeting and crossed to the fire to warm the chill that had settled in while she was getting dressed.

"I brought down a deer, but I couldn't get it in by myself. It's down by the boulder at the far end of camp."

"You okay?" Mila asked, her eyes filled with concern.

Sahara nodded. "I will be. I need to sleep."

"You look worried." Maddie said.

"I saw a bear," Sahara said. "I think it was a Shifter."

They looked at each other quickly, then her. "Do we need to be worried?" Mila asked.

Sahara shook her head. "I don't know. It didn't get close, so, I couldn't say."

"I thought the bears were all gone," Maddie said. "Didn't Dad say something about the bear tribe?"

Mila nodded. "Yeah, I remember. I guess we're all so spread out, no one really knows."

Sahara yawned. "Get someone to go with you to bring the deer in, and I want you two to stay close to camp for now. We don't know if it's alone or what it wants." She rubbed her eyes. "I'm going to bed. I need to be back out on watch in a few hours."

She left the girls and headed to bed, stripping down to her underwear before sliding in under the blankets. As her eyes closed, she could sense the movement around her. Riley was on watch. Bryan was eating breakfast. Alaric was… aware.

Not awake, but she recognized his mind and the way it was analyzing what she had seen, pulling the memory out and watching it play several times. It was a strange sensation. She was about to get up and go to his cabin when he pulled back, comforting her and whispering for her to sleep.

Even if she'd been inclined to disobey, his touch seemed to blanket over her, and she fell quickly past her ability to try.

* * *

Bryan was concerned. The sun was setting. His mother was pacing in the cabin they used to share. The perimeter patrol was changing. Riley was in the room with him. Sahara was eating dinner at the bunkhouse.

Alaric knew all of this before he was fully aware he had returned to his body. He was stiff, and it would be difficult to move without help. When he had been one of his father's Keepers, they had needed to carry him for most of his first day after waking up.

He opened his eyes slowly, knowing that his vision would be altered forever now. He lay on the bed, his limbs cold, his mind still full of visions and words and memories. He breathed in deep and before he could figure out how to ask, Riley was there, helping him to sit up.

He smiled as he sat beside Alaric and offered him water. Alaric nodded gratefully, his ability to make words work seemingly vacant for the moment. His father hadn't spoken for days.

He didn't remember them moving him from the clearing, but he knew that it had been several days.

Conscious thought was slipping away even as Riley lifted a cup. The smell of the broth made him salivate. Riley lifted it to his lips, and Alaric took several long sips, his thoughts already turning back to the abundance of knowledge inside him. There was so much information to process: the thoughts and movements of his people around him, the feeling of the earth as it turned.

The broth was hot and it warmed him as he swallowed, comforting and grounding. It helped.

Riley's hands helped him lay back down and he heard Riley's voice telling him to sleep. Alaric needed little encouragement for that, letting Riley guide him down and cover him with a blanket. He closed his eyes, the exhaustion dragging on him until it dragged him into sleep.

Chapter Twenty-Two

The ground shakes and people scream as gunfire echoes. He stands in the midst, untouched, watching as swarms of blue uniforms sweep through town after town, and in their wake leave only the dead and dying. Down through California and Nevada, all the way to the Mexican border, until the blue covers the land, and the storm front turns east. Black smoke rises from funeral pyres and worse as the new borders are lined with a horrific display of death. Shades and those branded witches burn on platforms, their screams tearing holes in the sky.

He came awake with a start, sitting up and gasping as Mason's face filled his mind. Mason dying. Alaric grabbed at the talisman on his chest and closed his eyes, willing his heart rate to slow and his mind to ease.

The dream was fed by experience, and not his alone. The memories of his forefathers and the thoughts of his clan filled him and mixed with his own gifts, bringing him a glimpse of a possible future. He breathed out and reached within, felt for the clinging sense of *Mason* on the talisman and used it to reach out.

There was confusion and concern, and Alaric pulled back instantly, aware of Mason's surroundings and duty in that single touch. He was okay for now. Alaric stood and reached for his clothes, dressing quickly. He was unsure how much time had passed since the ritual, and he felt the need to make connection with his people soon.

Riley jumped to his feet as he emerged from the cabin.

"*Easy.*"

Riley grinned at him. "Didn't expect to have you up and around for another day or two. You were pretty gone."

Alaric nodded, rubbing at his grumbling stomach. He had vague memories of Riley rousing him enough to eat a few times, or maybe it was just once and repeated through his jumbled memory. "How long?"

"Just about three days."

"Food?"

Riley nodded, moving to the table on the porch. "Boys brought in a mess of rabbits this morning. Got some stew."

"I need some sun."

"I'll bet. Here." Riley handed him a bowl of thick stew from the small table on the front porch and together they walked down the steps. It was late afternoon, and the touch of the sun felt like the kiss of a lover as he stepped out into it. He closed his eyes and savored the feeling.

The valley breathed below him, every heart softly echoing his. With a thought, he could beckon any of them to him, and they would come without question. It was a heady thought. He walked toward the central fire and sat on one of the logs that they used for benches, cradling the bowl close and tasting the stew before looking up.

Sahara and Bryan had joined them. "What news?" Alaric asked softly.

"We've had a number of sightings of people getting close to the wards. No one has seen through them." Sahara responded.

"Jordan came in last night. He's still sleeping," Bryan added.

Alaric set his stew aside half eaten. "We should gather our heads of family; I should speak with them. I need to go to the map. Have them join me at the bunkhouse."

"You could just call them." Bryan said.

Alaric offered a soft smile. "I don't want to start out by showing off." Bryan and Riley turned to leave, but Alaric drew Sahara to him when she started to follow. "Have you seen the Shifter again?"

She looked surprised, one eyebrow lifting. "No. I think the wards are still distracting him. But, he will eventually see through them."

Alaric nodded. "Okay. I think we should shore up those wards, just in case."

"Already done," Sahara responded.

Alaric stood, grabbing his stew bowl and heading up the path to the bunkhouse. Sahara came with him, stopping in the main hall while he went to the office to pull the map from the wall. Pulling an array of pens from the desk, Alaric took the map out into the hall and laid it across a table. He chose a red pen and drew a deep breath, digging into his mind for the dream. His hand drew the lines, including their valley in the zone that would burn.

"How soon?" His mother's voice. He opened his eyes and scanned the map.

"Soon, but we have time yet." He inhaled and reached out beyond the valley, tracing the route Jordan most likely took to get back to them, marking out places where travelers could hide, highlighting people who would help those trying to get out. His hands moved over the map in echo. By the time he opened his eyes, the room had filled with the people who would make decisions for their families.

Alaric nodded to himself and met each eye one by one. "We've reached the point where we can't wait anymore. We have to leave, and we have to do it within the week." He looked specifically at Bryan, expecting an argument, but he'd obviously picked up enough of the thought process that he just nodded.

"What you see here are best chances at getting out of 8th Battalion territory. We need to move while they're distracted with the fight to take the last of California. They've called nearly all of their people west. These areas," Alaric's fingers splayed out to touch the routes he'd plotted, "will have fewer patrols."

He let it sink in before licking his lips and looking up at all of them. "I'm not saying this is safe. I'm saying it's safer than staying here. We'll leave in small groups, and we'll start tomorrow. Bryan and Riley will relay a schedule and routes. Go let your people know and get ready.

You're traveling light. We have eleven vehicles, and we need to fill them with bodies, not things." Not that most of them had much.

He turned away as they filed out, his mind drifting, taking stock of the mood of his people. Most of them seemed resigned to his decision, but some were afraid. Images flashed through him, faces contorted in pain as fire scorched their bodies.

They had reason to fear.

* * *

"What do you mean, you can't reach them?" Darvin yelled, his voice tightly pitched and louder than Mason had ever heard.

He obviously didn't like the response. "What do I want? I want you to do your fucking job, that's what I want. Get me someone in California above the rank of Lieutenant." Darvin slammed the phone down and stalked toward the wall of screens, his face red as he pulled his hands through his disheveled hair.

"What the hell is going on?" Darvin muttered as he stared at the screens.

"Darvin?" Mason asked. Darvin turned, nodding as he spotted Mason near the door. "Problem?"

Darvin made a face and moved back to the table. "Apparently, some general in California ordered a bunch of troops to relocate, and no one seems to know why. The intel you provided tells me we may have already lost the west coast…and that give me a really bad feeling."

Mason moved away from the door, his eyes scanning the screens. "What's all this?" He gestured at a screen with a list of deaths up and down the eastern coast.

Darvin sighed. "That's my other headache. We seem to have yet another rash of Shade killings."

"Raven said something about a killer trying to make deaths look like Shades did it."

Darvin nodded tightly. "Yeah, we've seen that too. These though…"
He came to stand beside Mason. "These are real. No drained blood.

This was straight up manipulated diseases. Measles, cancer, and here in D.C., the flu."

"That isn't good."

"No, it isn't." Darvin agreed.

"Is it one Shade, or several?"

"We don't know." Darvin sat in one of the chairs and sighed. "And we don't have the manpower to find out. Our funding has been frozen."

"What does that mean?" Mason asked, glancing aside as an aide came into the conference room to hand a file to Darvin.

Darvin took the file with a nod, flipping it open and scanning it quickly. He handed it back. "Yes, that will do. Get it started. I don't know how long we have before we get shut down. I need everything moved out of here before then."

"We going somewhere?" Mason asked, his concern warring with his desire to leave himself.

"I'm relocating our resources." Darvin answered. "Most of these murders were political in nature. The last one was that televangelist who was the closest competition to Senator Douglas for the republican nomination. Before that it was an aide to Senator Goldsmith. All of them very vocally anti-Shade. I'm expecting blowback."

Mason turned his eyes back to the screens. In the far-left corner was a list of names that drew his attention. "Is this a list of Shades?"

Darvin sighed and turned. "Suspected Shades. And a few Shifters. We haven't confirmed most of them. We've been trying to contact as many as possible. We can't protect them if we don't know where they are."

"You can't protect them at all," Mason countered. "If you're worried about getting shut down, I would destroy that list. In the wrong hands…"

"Trust me, I know."

All around them, screens started flashing warnings and the phone was ringing. Darvin jumped for the phone, and Raven came running into the room. Mason turned to her, feeling her anxiety before she had even come to a stop. "What— "

She took a deep breath. "The President has just been killed on national television," she said. "It looks like it was a Shade."

Darvin was obviously getting the same news over the phone, and he manipulated controls to turn the center four screens on to the news. People were screaming and running in the video replay as the President crumpled at the podium where he'd been speaking. The Vice President, who had been sitting off to the side with his wife was dragged to the ground by a secret service agent.

"*Several people are dead. We are getting conflicting counts right now. Some say five, and another report indicates it could be as many as ten. We don't know the cause yet. There were no shots, no evidence of any violence. Many are speculating that the President was brought down by a Shade operative, possibly several working in concert.*"

"Right. Thank you." Darvin hung up the phone. "You two need to get out of D.C. Now."

Mason didn't understand at first.

"How long?" Raven asked, pulling on Mason's arm.

"I don't know," Darvin said. "My contact in the White House said that it would take them a while to sort it out, but eventually someone is going to remember that we have Shades on the payroll."

"Do we know who it was?" Raven asked as she tugged Mason toward the door.

"We think so. There is video of a man touching a secret service agent who then touched another. We have five secret service agents dead, plus the president and his wife. Two other agents are circling the drain. It seems to be an accelerated form of cancer, based on the evident tumors on those who died first."

Darvin waved them to the door. "Go on and pack up. I'll get you an untraceable car and phones. Jerah, your Book of Line, probably not something you want to lug around on the run. Get it to me and I'll ship it with the rest of our library. We'll keep it safe."

Mason's stomach twisted a little at the idea of leaving his book of Line in the hands of the same government that might now be looking to kill him. Raven's hand slid down his arm, making skin contact as it reached his hand.

"He'll keep it safe, but we have to move."

He nodded, swallowing the knot of fear and pushing himself past it. "Yeah, okay. Where are we going?"

She shook her head and got them moving again. *"Not here. When we get on the road."* That made sense. He shook off the confusion and followed her to the elevator. "Pack light," Raven said as she jogged away from him toward her quarters.

He opened the door to his quarters, his eyes skipping over the room. He hadn't even been back a week and here he was leaving again. He thought briefly about Alaric, but California was a long way away, and he couldn't even be sure they would still be there if he made it back.

Mason started with his Book of Line. It lay on his desk alongside the ancestral one. He stacked them together and shoved them into a canvas bag. Raven had told him that Darvin had a library of books from various clans. He had books from the other tribes too. She said he could keep the books safe.

That was something he couldn't guarantee if he kept them. He had no idea where they were going or what was going to happen along the way. He shook off the uneasy feeling that gave him and set about packing his backpack with the essentials.

A knock on the door interrupted him just as he was finishing and he opened it to find Raven and the red-headed teenager she called Zero.

"Adam said he'd meet us in the garage with what we need."

The hallways were bustling with activity as Raven guided them toward the garage doors. Darvin was standing inside them, barking orders at an array of aides around him. Mason swung his bag onto his back as they approached, holding out the canvas bag with his books, trading them for the envelope Darvin was handing them. An aide handed a bag to Zero, and a second gave Raven a set of keys and a couple of cell phones.

"Food to hold you over for a bit, some cash, identification, information you might need," Adam said, pointing to Zero, then Mason. "Only number in those phones comes to me. Don't use it for at least two weeks. Then I will be able to give you instructions."

"You better not get yourself killed," Raven said, suddenly embracing Darvin. "I won't be there to bring you back this time."

"Hey, what about Dr. Anthony and Liza?" Mason asked, suddenly remembering that he and Raven weren't the only Shades on the payroll.

"Already gone," Darvin said. "You better get moving. They've called in the national guard to close down the city."

Raven took off into the garage, and up to a black SUV with tinted windows. "Everybody in."

Mason took the passenger seat while Zero climbed into the back. Raven pulled out of the garage at speed before Mason had even buckled his seatbelt.

No one spoke as Raven drove them through the city, avoiding any area near a government building. It wasn't until they were on the freeway that Raven glanced aside at him. "You okay?"

"Honestly?" Mason asked. "I'm not sure."

"They caught the Shade." Zero said suddenly from the back seat. She leaned forward and tapped her temple. "I'm getting a lot of interference, but he's being reported as either caught or dead."

Mason frowned. "I thought you were a Sage?"

Zero shrugged. "Yeah, that too."

"Anything we need to worry about?" Raven asked, looking in the rearview mirror at Zero.

"Nothing I've picked up. We should be in the clear."

"What about your father and Douglas?"

Zero sat back. "I think they'll take advantage of the situation to push their anti-Shade agenda, probably."

"This is going to give the nomination to Douglas, probably the presidency," Raven murmured.

Mason couldn't argue with that. His Nana's worst fears were coming true around him, and he'd seen enough of the common man of the country to know that fear overwhelmed reason. "So, where are we going?" Mason asked when the silence had grown long.

Raven sighed and bit her lip for a second. "There's a place I know. It's in Arizona."

"Arizona?" Mason asked, frowning. "Deserts aren't the most Shade friendly."

She smiled a little. "Forest, actually. I spent time there as a kid. It should be safe. Very few people know about it. We can regroup and figure out our next step."

Chapter Twenty-Three

Sahara was helping one of the remaining children with their suitcase when she sensed something wasn't right. She stopped and looked around them. The family had been in one of the cabins closest to the wards, and therefore closest to the wildlife around the camp.

She turned her head slowly, lifting her nose to the air. Bryan stopped beside her, his hand warm on her shoulder. "Everything alright?"

Sahara met his eyes and pressed the feeling, and its likely cause, across to him. "Get them out of here." She was already starting to shift, pulling at the restraint of her clothing. Bryan scooped up the girl Sahara had been walking with and gestured with his head to the rest of the family to follow him.

The air was thick with the scent of bear and blood that had already been spilled. She could hear it now too as she dropped to all fours and let her animal out.

She charged toward the smell, picking out Mila's scent as she got closer. One on one, Mila didn't stand a chance against a regular bear, let alone one who was a shifter. Sahara didn't have to go far to find them. Mila's hackles were up, her muzzle stained with red. She must have gotten a good bite in. The bear stood on his hind legs, towering over them, his roar shaking the ground under them.

Sahara took up position near Mila. The bear turned his attention to Sahara, roaring his displeasure at her. Sahara responded with a warning growl of her own. It pawed the air before dropping to all fours and charging at them. Mila split left so Sahara dodged to the right, drawing the bear with her.

Somewhere behind her, Sahara was aware of people moving closer. They had to keep the bear from them. She jumped, claws extended and raked them over the bear's muzzle. He shook his head, and she only barely got clear of his answering paw. Mila had used the distraction for her own attack, getting a claw through the thick bristled hair to open a gash in his stomach.

Shouts pulled her attention, and she wished she could vocalize words in her cat form so she could warn them off. The bear lifted his head, snorting as the scent of fresh meat filled the air. He used his shoulder to shove her to the side and she reached for his leg with her mouth. She came away with a mouthful of hair instead.

The bear was picking up speed, charging past the trail toward the cabins. Sahara and Mila chased after him, gaining ground even as the bear's mammoth claw connected with one of the men who had come running to help. Blood sprayed across her face as Sahara leaped and dug her claws into the back of the bear's neck, throwing her weight in the same direction as her momentum in an effort to pull the bear away. His mass resisted and she was forced to let go and roll off, nearly landing on Mila who was trying to get around in front.

The bear was ignoring them, his focus on attacking the people who were now running. She ran after, leaping up again to his back, her claws raking through fur until they found purchase in skin. The bear roared his fury and reared back as she opened gashes on either side of his neck. Sahara slipped down his back, landing on all fours, ready to pounce again, but before she could Maddie joined the fray, moving in a blur under him as he was dropping back down, her claw digging through his stomach.

He turned toward Maddie and Mila jumped between them, leaping.03

at him and swatting both front claws at his face, her voice a guttural growl.

The bear swiped his paw at her, and she tumbled away, down the hill that led toward the creek. The bear charged after her. Maddie and Sahara took off behind him, catching him before he could reach Mila, who was slow in getting to her feet.

Behind her people were yelling and she could sense Bryan herding people away. Riley was suddenly too close and the bear took a swipe at him, missing, but not by much. Sahara circled around so that she was between Riley and the bear, which was when she could see why Riley was there. Cassandra was huddled behind him, her face white, her eyes filled with fear. Sahara nodded to Riley and turned her attention back to the bear.

Mila was up, but moving slowly. Maddie was holding the ground between her sister and the bear. Sahara was aware of the arrival of more people, and a swell of energy flowed into her. She recognized the touch as Alaric's.

"*Keep him distracted, we have guns.*" Alaric's words filled her head and she spared enough thought to acknowledge it before she was leaping back into the fray. Sahara kept herself between the bear and the people, moving to draw his attention. He snorted and bellowed loudly, lashing out with powerful paws. Sahara felt the blood before the pain, falling and rolling away as he continued to come at her.

Shots rang out, and suddenly the bear was towering over her. Several more shots and she felt hands pulling her away. The bear toppled over backward, and by the splash it sounded as though he had landed in the creek.

Hands pressed to her bleeding side, and she could feel Alaric and Bryan and Riley all trying to assess her injuries. She shifted to her human form, yelling as her insides shifted under the wound and the adrenaline of the fight began to wear off. Riley was the one squatting beside her, his hands covered in blood as he pressed his own shirt against her torn skin.

"The girls…" Sahara lifted her head, but she couldn't see past Riley, and he touched her chin with his free hand to pull her attention back to his face.

"The girls are being seen to, focus on me."

There was movement and the feeling of Alaric's presence got stronger. "How is she?"

"Losing a lot of blood." Riley said as Alaric went to one knee beside her. "Sahara, where else are you hurt?"

"Let me in." Alaric was suddenly gone and the Shade took his place. There was a smear of blood on his face and his expression was grim. He pulled away the bloody shirt Riley had been using to hold her insides in. "Shit. Okay, this might hurt."

Sahara felt him do something she couldn't trace, and she felt as though he had reached through from her back to pull her stomach back inside her body. She could hear someone screaming, and distantly realized it was her own voice she heard.

"I've stopped the bleeding." Damon said. "But it won't hold for long, we're going to need to do some old fashioned doctoring here."

"I'm here." Sahara didn't recognize the voice at first, but slowly the dark skin of the midwife came into view.

Her attention drifted as people moved around her. The bear was gone and in his place was a large man covered in bites and gouged flesh. She could see Bryan near him, squatting beside...

"No." Sahara struggled to lift her head to see better. Mila's eyes were cold, her body crushed beneath the weight of the bear.

"Stay still."

Hands pushed her down, but she needed to know if Maddie was still alive. "Maddie?" Her voice was too quiet, even though it rang in her head. Riley moved so that he was blocking her view, his hands stroking over her face. "Shh. You need to focus on you right now, Sahara."

He was soothing her in more ways than just his voice or fingers on her face she realized just as his presence dropped over her like a muffling blanket. Between him and the Shade, she found herself dropping into the dark.

* * *

217

Three dead, four if he counted the bear Shifter. Alaric stood out of the way as they were brought in, one by one, and laid out on tables draped in sheets. The first was a young man who had been out with Matthew, shoring up the wards before they left. Alaric didn't even remember his name.

Half his face was missing. Alaric turned away from him, only to be confronted with Mila's broken body. They didn't have the whole story, but Mila had fought like hell, and she had paid a horrible price for it.

Beside her lay what was left of the man who had been an enemy soldier before Bryan took most of him out in his search for information. In the first spontaneous action he had made since that day, he'd jumped in front of Damon when the bear barreled after Mila.

Alaric moved away from her to the table where four men were putting the dead bear Shifter. He set a hand on the man's temple and closed his own eyes, bringing his focus down to what remained of the man's mind. There hadn't been a true necromancer in his clan for many generations. All that remained was a semblance of the gifts that he could call on.

There wasn't much left that he could access, flashes of faces the man had known, remnants of the fight. Then there was a flash of a face, a man Alaric had seen before... in one of Riley's premonitions.

Alaric pulled back, shaking his head lightly at Riley's unasked question. "Go on, get cleaned up. Let's organize everyone, and empty this place out." Alaric said softly to Riley and those who had gathered. "Leave the van for us."

He left Riley to organize and headed up the steps into the dorm room where they had taken Sahara and Maddie. The room was quiet. Damon knelt beside one bed, his head bent over Sahara's body. Keisha and her oldest were at the next bed, working in tandem on Maddie. Bryan stood near the door watching, his face streaked with blood, holding his right shoulder. "*You okay?*" Alaric asked mentally to avoid disturbing the others.

He nodded tightly, his eyes never leaving Sahara's face. Alaric turned his inner eye to watch Damon work. He seemed to be mostly done with Sahara's internal injuries, at least from what Alaric could tell.

"I could use a hand," Keisha said suddenly, her voice controlled, but urgent.

Damon stood and moved to her side. "I've got her insides healing, close her up for me?" He sank down on his knees beside Maddie, his hands immediately moving to the open wound down the length of her back. His energy flow was starting to falter. Alaric ducked out of the room and hollered down the stair for a bucket of water. Keisha's younger son appeared a moment later with it. Alaric took it with a nod and brought it back to the bunk room, setting it down beside the Shade.

Damon nodded his thanks, almost immediately plunging bloody hands into the water, cupping them and bringing water up to the wound. They worked in silence, only the occasional murmur of instruction or rustle of hands on torn skin to mark the passage of time.

When Damon looked up, his eyes were circled in dark black and he looked ready to pass out. Alaric moved to his side as he tried to rise, easing him up and moving him to an empty bed. Bryan appeared a moment later with a pitcher of water which he handed to Alaric.

Alaric helped Damon hold the pitcher as he drained it, nodding his thanks as he finished. "I've done all I can for now. They should sleep a while, and so should I."

He looked down at his bloody hands and clothes. "We'll get you something clean to wear," Alaric said, nodding to Bryan. "Do you want to try to get down to the showers?"

Damon shook his head. "No, just… later." He gestured to the bucket of water, and Alaric brought it over, setting it on the floor beside the Shade. Damon pulled off his shirt before thrusting his hands into the already bloody water, then used his shirt to wipe his skin clean. He toed off his shoes and collapsed back onto the bed, his eyes already closed.

Alaric turned to Keisha and her son, who were cleaning up used supplies. "How are they?"

"They should live," Keisha said, with a nod toward Damon. "But only because he was here." She handed her son a pile of bloodied bandages. "Go on and burn these, no sense attracting any animals. Then get yourself cleaned up and check on your brother."

"Thank you, Keisha. You should go finish getting ready. I'm sending everyone out of here."

"What about them?"

Alaric looked at Sahara's pale face and reached out for her mind. Reassured that she was still there, he sighed. "Damon will stay with us. Riley, Bryan and I will take them with us when we leave."

"I'll put together some supplies for you," Keisha said.

Alaric watched her leave and sighed again. Bryan cleared his throat. "I'll sit with them for a while. Riley needs you downstairs."

He nodded and headed down the stairs into the main hall. The air seemed chill, even with a small fire on the hearth. The bodies lay still, accusing in their silence. Riley and Cassandra were busy cleaning them. They would need to bury their dead before they moved on.

Riley looked up, his face grim. Alaric could feel the questions and held up a hand as he crossed the room. "They're both holding their own, for now," Alaric said as he stopped by Mila's feet. He'd barely known the teenager. They seldom interacted, and she and her sister had largely kept to themselves.

She'd defended her sister fiercely though, and in her final act she had defended them all the same way. Her left shoulder and chest were crushed, her face gouged by the bear's vicious claws. Cassandra touched his arm, pulling his attention away from the corpse.

"I was just going to get her dressed."

"Good." Alaric turned from Mila's body to look at the other Shifter. No one had touched him, he was as dirty and bloody as when Alaric had last seen him. He bore the marks of the attack, claw marks that ran from superficial to deep and gaping. The back of his head was gone, courtesy of the shotgun that put him down.

"Matthew and a few others have started digging," Riley said softly. "I wasn't sure..." He trailed off, his eyes distant. "Damn." He sat heavily his hand grabbing Alaric's wrist. Alaric could feel the premonition crash over him, and Riley opened easily to his questing touch.

Flashes of familiar images started the barrage, then slowed to show a scene in Washington D.C., chaos as people dropped dead, martial law descending, the start of war.

Riley was breathing hard when it stopped. "That wasn't all future," he said as he caught his breath. "I think the president is dead."

"I think so too," Alaric confirmed, reaching out through his clan for confirmation. "By a Shade's hand."

"That's not good."

Alaric agreed. The future they had foreseen was coming faster than he'd imagined. Soon there would be nowhere safe. "Let's focus on getting our people buried and moving out of here."

"Yeah, but to where?" Riley asked.

Alaric wasn't completely sure. "Back east to start, we'll worry about the rest once we're out of the war zone."

"Pretty sure everywhere is going to be a war zone," Riley responded.

Alaric nodded. He knew that too, but he somehow knew that back east would be safer than staying here. In the back of his mind there was an idea about Canada, an enclave of the tribe that would welcome them, but he wasn't ready to leave his country. A voice inside him said that it wasn't his country anyway. He pushed all of that aside and clapped Riley on the shoulder before heading out into the gathering night.

The air was chill and he shivered with more than the cold. Alaric moved silently through the camp, across the bridge and up to the point. He stood there, staring out into the shadows, though he saw little of them. His hand closed around Mason's talisman and he turned his thoughts east, searching through the landscape of attuned minds for the one he sought.

Mason was moving, though he wasn't panicked, so he was safe enough for the moment. Alaric started to pull away, but to his surprise, Mason reached out for him. Alaric steadied the connection, and the feeling of Mason rushed into him. "*I was worried,*" Alaric said.

"*I'm okay,*" Mason responded, rubbing against him affectionately. "*We got out of D.C. pretty fast. What about you?*"

Alaric couldn't repress the smile on his face. "*I'm good. We're leaving camp soon.*"

He could feel Mason's frown. "*Where are you going?*"

"*Not sure yet.*" Alaric could feel that Mason wasn't alone. There was another Shade and... He stretched a little more and found a mind unlike any he had encountered before. She reacted not by throwing up shields as he expected, but turned to examine him the same way. She felt like one of his people, and yet not. It intrigued him. He could hear Mason chuckling.

"*That's Zero.*"

Mason was tiring, Alaric could tell. The distance was a strain without the extra benefit of Alaric's new-found power. "*Be safe,*" Alaric said, starting to pull back.

"*You too.*"

Alaric let him go, and let his mind drift over the distance between them. All of his people were distressed. Alaric sent a wave of comfort through his connection, bidding them to stay calm but alert.

Eventually they would need more of a plan, but for now, his plan was just to get them out of the immediate line of fire.

Chapter Twenty-Four

It was just after dawn when the SUV pulled to a stop outside a diner just west of Nashville. They'd managed to get out of D.C. before martial law was declared, and had been racing westward on back roads since. Raven yawned and stretched before turning off the engine. "I need coffee."

"You sure it's safe?" Mason asked, eyeing the place.

"Safe enough," Zero said from the backseat. "Only an old guy and the waitress, both too tired to care."

"We're going to need gas too," Raven said. "Just play it cool, and we'll be fine."

Zero was the first one out the door, the brown hair of her wig lifting a little on the breeze. Mason sighed and followed, angling for the men's room as they entered the place. He took care of business quickly and washed his hands. When he emerged, Raven handed him some cash. "I ordered us some sandwiches and coffees. Zero's gone to fill the gas tank. I'll be out in a minute."

Mason pocketed the money and moved to the counter to wait. His eye caught on a newspaper lying just out of reach. He sat slowly on the stool and pulled the paper toward him. "SHADE KILLER ON THE LOOSE" was the lurid headline, complete with a picture of the president dead on the floor of the stage.

He skimmed the article, pulling the pertinent information. They had at least two Shades in custody, though one was likely to die after being shot several times. No one was willing to touch him to try to save him. The death toll had climbed to include the vice-president, ten secret service agents, and a large number of civilians in the surrounding area.

Riots scattered across the city, and the number of deaths associated with them was still climbing. It was madness.

"Here you go, honey," the waitress said, putting a bag on the counter in front of him. "That will be twenty-five dollars and forty-three cents."

Mason peeled three tens off the money Raven had given him and smiled at her. "Keep the change."

Raven emerged from the ladies' room as he lifted the bag. The early morning sun was bright, and they waited just inside the diner's doors for Zero to return with the SUV.

"You've been quiet," Raven said softly.

"Not much to say," Mason responded.

"This whole thing is nuts." Raven was shaking her head. "To think, a year ago, I was working with troops overseas... Now..."

Zero pulled up before she could finish, waving at them with some urgency. "*Troops, headed this way.*" Zero pressed the thought into their minds, and they both headed for the vehicle quickly. "We should stay off the main roads. It looks like they're setting up checkpoints," Zero said aloud once they were both in with their doors shut.

Raven nodded, and Zero pulled them out onto the road. Mason settled into the back seat, pulling within himself where he felt a soft tickle of something... a presence. Alaric. He was already pulling away when Mason realized it was him.

Mason reached for him, earning a surprise that filled his head with the memory of Alaric's smile. Alaric's energy focused, steadying the connection, and Mason let himself surge across, reveling in the warm familiarity.

"*I was worried,*" Alaric said.

"*I'm okay.*" Mason responded, rubbing against him affectionately. "*We got out of D.C. pretty fast. What about you?*" He got little sense of where Alaric was, only the strong sense of him.

"*I'm good. We're leaving camp soon.*"

Alaric was worried; no, that wasn't quite right. He was sad. "*Where are you going?*"

"*Not sure yet.*" Mason could feel Alaric's curiosity, stretching out past Mason's mind to the others in the car. Raven glanced up at Mason, but didn't react otherwise. Zero, on the other hand… Mason laughed out loud as Zero seemed to turn her head, even though she was still driving and looking out the windshield, her own curious examination of Alaric clearly unexpected.

"*That's Zero,*" Mason said, by way of introduction. He yawned involuntarily, suddenly aware of the energy drain the connection was having. Alaric started to pull back, whispering, "*Be safe.*"

"*You too,*" Mason sent after him, yawning again.

Raven turned to him, her own exhaustion clear in her eyes. "Sleep. We have a long way to go."

* * *

Zero, and then Raven, drove them through back roads, zigzagging around small towns and long lines of fields that had not yet begun to be worked for the coming season. In a straight line, the drive would have been long. Taking back roads easily doubled the length of time it should have taken. Mason could feel the relief when they finally crossed over the Arizona border.

Raven relaxed visibly. "It won't be long now."

"You still haven't really told us where we're going," Mason said, leaning up between the two front seats.

Raven glanced at him before taking a turn off the two-lane road. It wasn't quite sunset, and tall pine trees began to surround them. "There's a small town up here." Raven said. "My grandfather brought me here when I was little. It was founded by Shades."

"A whole town of Shades?" Zero asked. "Isn't that a little bit risky?"

"It's never felt like a risk," Raven countered. "There were only ever a handful of people, and they aren't all Shades. Last time I was here there were maybe twenty Shades, half of them kids."

They continued up a gravel road, the trees growing thicker around them, casting long shadows as the sun edged down behind the horizon. The road wound through the woods and climbed higher until it eventually crested a ridge, then began to slope downward again. Mason could sense water, a good-sized body of water.

They found it a few minutes later, a pristine mountain lake that called to him. He wanted to strip down and soak in the icy waters. "Patience," Raven said, though he wasn't sure if it was meant for him or for herself.

The lake disappeared behind some trees as they followed the gravel road, and suddenly there was a small town in front of them. Small houses dotted the hillside that swept upward on the opposite side of a group of buildings that seemed to be much like the small town near his Nana's home.

He could see what he took to be a town hall or meeting place, and a couple of buildings that looked like stores. All of them were single story, low to the ground and painted in shades of brown and forest green. In a field to their left there were a number of parked vehicles. Raven maneuvered them to park beside a beat up pickup truck.

"I've never seen this many cars here." Raven said as she climbed out of the SUV. "Leave your stuff here for now. We should check in with the Elders."

Mason followed into the embrace of the town buildings with Zero behind him. Slowly, people emerged from doorways, watching the trio carefully. His stomach twisted, telling him that many of these people were Shades.

Raven looked bewildered as the number of people kept climbing, well past twenty when she finally found a face she seemed to recognize, and she jogged away. The older man had a thick head of purely white hair, and he held his arms open to receive Raven, picking her up as they connected and squeezing her tight.

Mason and Zero held back a little, not wanting to intrude on the reunion. When they finally separated, Raven waved them over. "Manny, this is Mason Jerah and Zero." The man quirked an eyebrow at Zero's name, but held out a hand. "Mason, Zero, this is a good friend of my grandfather, Manual Louis Laredo."

Mason shook the man's hand with a nod. "Pleasure to meet you, sir."

"Welcome." He shook Zero's hand before turning back to Raven. "We've been worried."

"How is he?" Raven asked as they started walking away. Mason wasn't sure if they were meant to follow, but Raven glanced back with a slight nod.

"He has his good days," Manny said, guiding them out past the town's buildings and up a dirt road to a small house. The siding was old and needed paint, but the porch looked welcoming, like a place where family could gather on a summer evening.

Manny took them inside and pointed Raven to a door, while he nodded toward a comfortable living room for Mason and Zero.

Mason took the hint, his eyes scanning the walls and shelves with pictures of a smiling little girl in long black braids that he assumed was Raven. In some of the pictures she was smiling beside a red-head who was a few inches taller.

"Sister," Zero said, her voice soft as she looked over his shoulder.

"Can I get you two a drink?" Manny asked from the entryway.

"Water would be nice," Mason responded with a smile. "Thank you."

Manny served them both a glass of water and they settled in to wait. It was nearly a half hour before Raven emerged, her eyes wet with tears. "Sorry about that," she said. "I should have said something. My grandfather... Well, he doesn't have long." She touched Manny's arm gently. "I was hoping we could stay here, at least for a little while."

Manny nodded. "If you girls don't mind sharing. It's gotten pretty tight around here lately. Lot of folks seeking shelter."

"We can share," Raven said, her eyes checking in with Zero. "And, Mason and I could use a good soaking after the last few days."

Manny smiled. "Go on down. Half the town will be down there before long."

Mason could almost feel the water on his skin as he and Raven left the house and headed toward the lake. "So, your grandfather?"

She nodded. "He moved up here permanently after my sister died. I try to come visit when I can, but..." She sighed. "I think he has been holding on waiting for me to come back. I won't be surprised if he passes in the next few days."

"I'm sorry."

She grabbed his hand and squeezed. "Thank you."

As they approached the lake, he could see there were already several people in the water. It made him a little nervous. Raven was pulling off her shirt, waving to someone she apparently knew. She noticed his hesitation. "You're safe here."

He nodded, watching her strip down and jog toward the water. He took his time, toeing off his shoes and pulling his jeans down. He set them on a picnic table and eyed the water. He chose a spot mostly away from the others, stepping into the icy blue water and closing his eyes to savor the feeling. It seemed like a lifetime had passed since he'd felt the embrace of cold, clean water.

Mason waded in up to his knees on the soft silty sand that was the bottom of the lake. He could almost imagine he could see the steam as his body cooled with the touch of the water. He let himself fall backward, dunking himself under and floating until he needed air.

He surfaced, surprised to find two boys staring at him. "You're new," the little blond one said. He had a wide, nearly toothless grin, his top and bottom front teeth missing.

His companion was a little older, his skin a dark brown and his eyes nearly black. "I'm Parker, this is Liam."

"Mason," he said, sinking back into the water so that he was nearly the same height as the boys. "I just got here."

"Liam and his father got here two days ago," Parker said. "I've been here my whole life."

"Where you from?" Liam asked.

"Around," Mason said.

"I'm sorry." Mason looked up to find an attractive woman with dark skin approaching. "Are they bothering you?"

"No, no bother, ma'am," Mason said, standing and offering his hand. "I'm Mason. The boys were just introducing themselves."

"The boys were told to get to their studies, not lay around in the water." She looked at them pointedly. Parker rolled his eyes, but tugged on Liam's shoulder, heading them toward shore. The woman turned back to Mason. "I'm Aliya, Parker's mother. Raven and I have been friends since we were six." Mason wasn't sure how to respond, so he didn't. "I see you're uncomfortable."

"Just not much accustomed to people, ma'am," Mason countered.

She smiled. "I'll leave you to soak then. I've invited Raven, and you, to dinner later. If you want."

She swam away, leaving Mason once more alone. He turned to find Raven, who was talking to a small group of Shades standing knee deep in the lake. As if she felt his eyes, she looked his way, meeting his gaze and seeming to ask if he was okay. He sort of nodded, then dropped under the water.

As he tried to relax, he could hear his Nana warning him away, that this could only lead to trouble. He pushed the thought away and instead tried to remember the exercises Paul had taught him.

As he surfaced, for air, he noticed Raven approaching with an older man. Mason put his feet down and stood, wiping water off his face.

"Mason, I wanted to introduce you to Charlie Magena. He's the last descendant of the founder of this town."

Mason reached a hand out to shake the man's hand, his eyes narrowing. "Magena? My mother was from the Magena clan."

Charlie smiled. "Yes, she was my cousin. It's a pleasure to meet you finally."

"Finally?"

Charlie nodded. "Your mother left home and never looked back. I don't blame her; she was right to get out. But I only heard from her sporadically after she left, and the last time it was right after you were born. We talked about her coming out here to visit with you, but it never happened."

"We kept to ourselves mostly. My grandmother was afraid we'd be found out."

Raven touched Mason's shoulder. "Charlie here is one of the town's teachers. I mentioned you might have some holes in your training, and he's offered to help."

"Yeah?" Mason looked from Raven to Charlie. "My grandmother didn't teach me much. Most of what I know comes from my Book of Line and what I've learned along the way, kind of crash course style."

"You aren't alone in that. A lot of Shades come to us with very little or piecemeal knowledge."

Mason felt himself relax just a little. "I'd be appreciative of any help."

Charlie smiled. "Great. Let's give you some time to settle in. Say, we start day after tomorrow?"

"That sounds good. Thanks," Mason agreed. He shook the man's hand again and Charlie waded toward shore.

Raven inhaled slowly and let it out. "I'd forgotten how much I like it here."

"And you're sure we're safe here?" Mason asked, still unsettled by the idea of so many Shades in one place.

She smiled. "Yes, we're safe. As safe as we can be anyway. You hungry? By now Manny will have a huge breakfast made."

Mason's stomach rumbled at the thought of food, and Raven laughed. "Come on. We can grab our bags from the SUV and head in.

* * *

Zero fidgeted at the window of the room she was sharing with Raven. The sun was just starting to come up in the distance, hidden behind trees and the ridge to the east. Something didn't feel right.

She shook her head. It was probably just the sudden proximity of so many minds with the ability to project their thoughts.

"Everything okay?" Raven asked as she returned from the bathroom.

Zero nodded. "I think so. I don't sense that we were followed."

"That's good, right?" Raven asked, coming to stand beside her.

"Yeah. I guess." Zero moved away from the window. She pulled the brown wig off and tossed it onto the dresser. "You know that if they figure out this place exists, they'll burn it down."

"I've heard that before." Raven said, closing the shade and curtains to protect her from the rising sun. "And we're still here."

Zero watched her crawl into the queen-sized bed. "For now. But things are different." She reached out for the slippery edge of a vision, but it stayed elusive. "We need to watch our backs."

"We're safe," Raven countered, pulling the sheets up to cover herself. "Let yourself rest. You've been on high alert since we met."

Zero didn't argue, just dropped her pants and climbed into the bed. Raven was probably right. She was projecting her own discomfort into some threat. It was clear that the people of this town welcomed them, and she sensed no threat from any of them. She closed her eyes and told herself to sleep.

Chapter Twenty-Five

Bryan stopped the van just outside the wards, and Alaric stepped out, exhaling and pushing past his fatigue to close the wards completely. They would hold against most trespassers, unless they were part of the tribe.

He climbed back in and nodded to Bryan. Alaric looked back at their passengers as he buckled himself into the seat. Sahara's eyes were open, but he wasn't sure how much she was aware. Riley sat between her and Maddie, his hand settling onto Sahara's shoulder. A few seconds later, Sahara's eyes closed.

"So, where are we going?" Bryan asked, once they were on the road.

Alaric rubbed his temples. He still hadn't actually decided. "Mom is at the estate in Virginia. We could head there."

Bryan looked at him. "You sure you want to be that close to Washington right now? If what you and Riley saw is true..."

"No, I know," Alaric responded.

Damon stuck his head between the seats from behind. "I know a place. We can get there in twelve hours or so. We can get help for the ladies."

Alaric got a vague impression of the place he was thinking of, a remote village where Shades gathered. He nodded slowly. "It's better than nothing." He put his hand out. "Show me."

Damon's surprise was followed by his hand on Alaric's and his mind opening tentatively. Damon showed him the route he was thinking of, east and then south and into Arizona. He then showed Alaric the lake, and the village that had grown up on the west side of the lake. Alaric thanked him with a nod, and reached out on his own to get an impression of the place. To his surprise, he found Mason. He couldn't suppress the smile as he brushed across Mason's thoughts. He was close to sleep, and responded slowly, warmly.

"*Okay?*" Mason murmured softly.

"*Sleep. I will see you soon.*" Alaric pulled away and sent the important information to Bryan.

"Got it," Bryan said, glancing aside at him. "Why don't you get some sleep? I'll wake you when it's your turn to drive."

"You sure you're okay to drive?' Alaric asked. "It isn't like any of us have gotten much sleep."

Bryan nodded. "I've got a few good hours in me."

"Riley?"

Alaric felt more than heard his answer and rather than arguing, he accepted the respite. He closed his eyes and leaned his seat back as far as it went. Sleep wasn't the first thing on his mind. Instead, he centered himself and opened himself up to his clan. He could trace them, a stuttering stream of movement east. Some went north. He stretched a little until he found the warm presence that was his mother. He relayed their plans to head to Arizona and promised to keep her updated before he reached behind them, out to the west, trying to locate any who hadn't gotten out. There were a good number of them scattered down the coast.

Most were people he had never met. Some responded to his check in; others ignored him. There was little he could do either way, but it helped him to know how many they left behind.

If they continued to lay low, they might survive what was coming.

Alaric pulled back into himself and made the attempt to sleep. They had a long drive ahead of them, and he needed to be ready to do his fair share of the driving.

* * *

Mason stretched as he stepped out of the small house just after sunset. All around him the village was coming to life, a big change from most places he'd lived. Daylight was for sleeping here, and by night work was done. For him and about ten others of various ages, that included lessons in things once learned in the home from parents and grandparents: the basic history of their race, and the basic skills required to utilize their gifts to the fullest of their potential.

He'd been welcomed like family, given a room in Raven's grandfather's house and food to eat. The water was clean and inviting. In only days, he felt as though he belonged there. Charlie had put him through some testing and had devised a learning plan that would fill the gaps in his knowledge. But really, every passing moment was a learning experience; living among Shades who lived the traditions, who embraced the entirety of their gifts was incredible.

The power of his line was stronger now than it had been when he'd taken his Nana's dying gift to him or even when Paul had helped him integrate it properly. Now he understood what it was to be the keeper of his line, and not just his, but the old man's as well.

The air was still warm from the long day, a steady wind rustling the leaves of the trees. From inside the village you wouldn't know that they were in the middle of a state known mostly for its desert. Shades had lived on that land for generations, and the natural forest had transformed because of it.

The trees here grew taller and thicker, their shelter allowing Shades to move about in daylight to a degree. The lake was deep and cold and teeming with the energy of the Shades who lived there. The symbiotic relationship was more intense than he had ever imagined it could be.

Mason stepped down off the porch headed toward the lake. Already there were two others soaking. Mason waved and slipped out of his shoes and jeans.

"You're up early," Charlie said, coming up behind Mason. "I figured after the workout I gave you yesterday, you'd be out until at least eight."

Mason chuckled and shook his head. "Bring it on. You haven't begun to wear me out."

"Oh, I hear a challenge. Tonight, your ass is mine."

"I've heard that before." Mason headed into the water, stopping as something caught his attention. It was echoed in the water. Something wasn't right.

Beside him Charlie had turned toward the northwest, his head lifted up, his eyes scanning the horizon. A few seconds later, Zero was running toward them. "That guy, the one who contacted you in the car..." She gulped air as Mason frowned at her.

"Who, Alaric?"

She nodded, her wig sliding a little on her head. "Not far, accident. People are hurt."

Charlie nodded, already headed toward the village meeting hall. "I'll round up our best trained who can handle trauma and get supplies loaded up." Mason picked up his jeans and shoes, following.

They were jogging now, and Charlie spared Mason a glance. "You're going to want to get dressed."

Mason looked down at himself and nodded. He stopped to pull his jeans on and shoved his feet into his shoes. He reached out, trying to find Alaric, but he couldn't sense him. Zero grabbed his hand, her mind bridging him over the distance. Alaric responded sluggishly, and his words were slurred even over the mental connection.

"Concussion," Mason murmured. "How far away?"

Zero let go of him and shook her head. "A couple miles." She adjusted her wig as they reached the road. Charlie called out from the back of a truck that was slowing beside them. Mason jumped up beside Charlie, reaching a hand for Zero, only to find that she was already beside him.

"I'm not sure of what I saw," Zero said as the truck started moving. "There was something about rage, and then a big cat, and then the van went off the road."

"A cat?" Charlie asked.

Mason nodded. "He was likely traveling with a Shifter. Possibly as many as three."

"That should make things interesting."

Mason couldn't tell if the Shifters were going to be a problem, but he figured they would cross that bridge after they dealt with the immediate trauma. He could smell burnt rubber as they rounded a corner, and skid marks led off the side of the road into the trees.

He was the off the truck before it had even fully stopped, his heart pounding as he ran toward the van. The back door was open and he spotted Riley first, his face bloody, his chest ripped open. He was alive, his eyes opened as Mason approached. Mason squatted beside Riley, a hand hovering over the wound. It was bad. He moved Riley so that he was laying on his back, already pressing healing energy into the bloody flesh.

The others were catching up. Charlie squatted opposite Mason, watching and offering guidance. There was a groan from inside the van, pulling Mason's attention. "Alaric."

"Go on. I've got him." Charlie said.

Mason jumped, climbing into the van. He found Sahara first, slumped against the wall. Her injuries seemed older though, partially healed. He touched her hand and closed his eyes, accessing her condition. He could sense another Shade's work.

There was a pile of shredded clothing beside her. That meant that it was one of the younger Shifters that had hurt Riley. A moan pulled him away from Sahara toward the front seat. Bryan was slumped against the wheel, a bloody gash down his arm, and points of blood on his thigh, spaced as if a large claw had held him down.

Mason reached for him, easing him back from the wheel. A large knot was forming on his forehead from impact with the wheel. He glanced out the front windshield and spotted a flash of blond hair.

Mason jumped out the passenger side and ran for Alaric. He was on the ground bleeding from a number of places, and his hand was clasped around a girl's wrist. Mason couldn't tell which of the younger

Shifters it was, but just past her, Mason could see Damon, the Shade he'd helped at Alaric's camp.

He too was injured, but starting to move. Mason yelled for more help, turning his attention to Alaric. He ripped what was left of Alaric's shirt off and set his hands to Alaric's chest, reaching inside for this heart. Once assured it would continue beating, he followed the blood flow to the worst of the wounds, focusing his attention on knitting together the vessels to staunch the flow of blood.

On the periphery of his thoughts, he could feel the approach of others, but he kept his focus on what he was doing. Someone poured water, first over his hands, then over his face. He opened his mouth to receive it, nodding his thanks before sinking deeper into Alaric's body.

He was tiring, but he kept going, feeding energy into Alaric's major organs before moving to explore the head injury. Alaric stirred beneath him, but Mason urged him back under, so that he could assess the damage.

"Mason."

He heard his name but ignored the voice. A hand touched his shoulder, but he didn't respond. *"Mason, let us finish the work."*

He was shaking, his whole body trembling as he flushed through with heat, and he couldn't seem to stop the energy from leaving his body for Alaric's. His sense of the world around him narrowed down to where his hands touched Alaric's skin, blackness creeping closer and closer, until hands yanked him backwards, and he fell headlong into the night.

* * *

Pain lanced through him, shaking him and making him curl up into a ball. "Mason, can you hear me?" The voice was too loud, too much, and Mason tried to pull away from it.

"Is this better?" Charlie. He recognized the voice. *"Don't fight me."*

At first Mason didn't understand what he meant, but then he felt Charlie inside him, helping him straighten out his cramped-up muscles and running through a series of exercises to get the energy flowing again.

Slowly Mason realized he was lying in a shallow pool of water and he cast about for the presence of the man he'd been bent over. "*Alaric?*"

"Let's worry about you for right now," Charlie responded. "Can you open your eyes?"

Mason opened his eyes, wincing, even though the room was fairly dark.

"Good. You over extended yourself." Charlie reached behind him and held up a bottle of water. "Drink."

"Is Alaric okay?" Mason asked, even as he took the water and sat up enough to drink it.

Charlie ran a hand over his drawn face and nodded. "He'll live. He's not going to be up to a lot for a while, but you saved his life." He stood and went to get more water to add to the bed-shaped pool. "It nearly killed you though. I had to fight to get you off him, and then it took two of us to keep you from dying. You can't sink all of your energy into someone like that."

Mason ducked his head. "I... I know.... But I couldn't let him die."

"Well, you're lucky we were there. And you are not to get out of that water until I tell you to." Charlie looked exhausted himself, his face drawn, the circles under his eyes dark smudges. Mason imagined all of the Shades looked the same.

"What about the others?"

"They will all recover. But I really do want you to focus on you for right now. There are plenty of Shades here seeing to your friends."

"I want to see Alaric."

"As soon as he's strong enough I'll have him moved in here with you." Charlie handed him a second bottle of water. "Finish both of those, then get some more sleep. I'll have Aliya come in and work on you in a little bit."

Charlie ducked out of the room and Mason drained the water he'd been given. His body was tight and hurt in strange places. He contemplated trying to get up and find Alaric, but he doubted he'd even be capable of standing upright.

He could feel the lingering effects of the work Charlie had done, and the water in the bed was helping. Mason lay back and closed his eyes, letting himself drift, feeling through his body inch by inch to carry on what Charlie had started.

It was only moments before he knew he couldn't continue, fatigue pushing him toward sleep. With a hope that sleep would finish restoring him, Mason surrendered.

* * *

The door of the room opened and Mason felt a brush of the familiar, pulling him up from his light doze. Two men he didn't know came in, supporting Alaric between them. Mason shifted, surprised to find a cot beside his bed. He hadn't heard anyone bring it in.

The men lowered Alaric to sitting on the cot, then helped him lay back before they left.

"Hey." Alaric reached a hand for Mason and Mason took it, smiling.

"Hey." Their fingers touched and Alaric seemed to surround him and draw him in, and suddenly it was as if they were standing on the rocks above Alaric's valley, the two of them, alone in the world. Mason looked around them, then up at Alaric. "Wow."

Alaric smiled at him. "I probably shouldn't, but I need to hold you."

He tugged on Mason until he could do just that, wrapping his arms around Mason and breathing in deep. "I've missed you," Alaric whispered.

"I was so worried," Mason responded, tilting his face to brush his mouth over Alaric's lips. "I'm glad you're okay."

Alaric opened his mouth, his tongue tingling along Mason's lips. There was a flicker, and then they were back in the tent, Alaric panting. "Sorry...don't have the strength to hold it for long."

"Don't be sorry. You're here and you're alive. We have time for other stuff," Mason countered, grinning at him.

"What about you?" Alaric asked, gesturing at the water.

"I'll live. Just over extended myself a little." In fact, he would probably be up and around in just a few hours, maybe less. He felt stronger than he had when he first woke up, and his muscles had all relaxed.

"Because of me," Alaric said, glancing away.

"No." Mason shook his head. "Because I haven't learned what I need to know to be who I want to be." He rubbed at his head.

"I'm told you saved Riley, and me," Alaric said softly.

"Charlie and the others did most of the work." Mason sighed. "You were lucky we were so close. What happened?"

Alaric sighed. "Maddie isn't fully through her change and can shift unpredictably. Sometimes it's brought on by stress or pain. She found out her sister was dead, and that, combined with her injuries..."

"She shifted?"

"Uncontrolled, she lashed out. Riley was keeping an eye on them. He took the worst of it." Alaric said. "Damon and I chased after her. I only caught her because of her injuries. She ripped me up before I could put her under."

"What happened? How did Mila die?"

Alaric closed his eyes and rubbed them. "There was a bear, a Shifter. He attacked the camp. Sahara, Mila and Maddie defended us. Mila and a number of others didn't make it."

"I'm sorry," Mason offered, turning to get a better look at Alaric. He was pale, but looked better than he had out in the woods. "You should rest."

"Look who's talking," Alaric said with a smile. "I'll sleep if you will."

"Deal." Mason rolled back and closed his eyes, content with the knowledge that Alaric was safe.

Chapter Twenty-Six

Sahara could feel eyes on her as she moved slowly toward the place where they had been treated for their injuries and were now using as an apartment of sorts. Her injuries were mostly healed, but she was kept to a slow pace by tense muscles that would only loosen up when she was able to shift. She probably was healed enough for it, but it didn't feel safe, not here.

She couldn't see the people behind those eyes, but she felt them all the same. The afternoon sun was still high in the sky, keeping them behind closed doors.

Putting the villagers out of her mind, she closed the door behind her. Alaric and Bryan were down by the lake, enjoying the late afternoon sun.

Sahara stopped by Riley's room first, knocking lightly on the door before she poked her head in. Riley was sitting up, his face pale above the white bandages that still covered part of his chest. He offered a smile.

"How are you feeling?" Sahara asked, stopping in the doorway.

"Bored out of my mind," Riley responded. "But better."

She nodded. "Good. Maddie is incredibly sorry." That was an understatement. The teenager was morose. Not that Sahara could blame her for it. She'd lost her last family member, and then nearly killed the only people who had shown her any kindness.

"It wasn't her fault," Riley said. "I should have realized… she just kept dreaming about her sister, asking for her. I shouldn't have told her."

"She was going to learn the truth eventually," Sahara said. She shifted to lean against the door frame. It had all happened so fast, and Sahara herself had been barely aware of what was happening as Maddie's distress pulled her out of the Shade-induced sleep. "She was never going to take it well."

"I suppose." He shook his head. She could almost see the moments replay across the connection they shared, sense the fury that took away what little control the teenager had of her shifting. He cleared his throat and changed the subject, pushing the memory aside. "So, a whole town of Shades?"

She accepted the transition and offered a smile. "Around thirty, as far as I can tell. And probably as many who aren't Shades."

"That won't be awkward," Riley said, scrunching up his face.

"Now you know how we felt," Sahara countered. "Alaric says it will be okay."

"Alaric always does, if you haven't noticed," Riley said. "Still, they did save our lives."

"Yes, they did." As uncomfortable as the whole thing made her, that was a simple truth. They had saved the lives of everyone involved.

"Who's the Shadow?" Riley asked, his eyes lifting to hers. "The one who Alaric reached out to during the accident."

Sahara crossed her arms. "She's someone who came here with Mason. She calls herself Zero. I don't have the whole story yet. She's… different."

"How did Alaric know she could help us?"

Sahara shrugged. "Not sure." She hadn't asked, and Alaric hadn't offered. For all that they were connected psychically since the ceremony, he could still keep secrets.

Riley yawned, and Sahara took that as her cue to bow out. "I'll let you rest. I should check on Maddie."

Sahara closed Riley's door and moved down the hall to the room she was sharing with Maddie. As she expected, Maddie was curled up tight, facing the wall. Her lunch lay untouched on the table between the two beds.

Sahara sighed and closed the door. "You need to eat." Maddie flinched, but didn't otherwise move. "Mila wouldn't want—"

"Stop." Maddie said, her voice muffled by her arms and blanket. She rolled onto her back and looked at Sahara, her eyes red and swollen. "Mila is dead. She doesn't get a say any more."

Sahara came to sit on the side of her bed. "Everyone is okay. No one blames you."

"I shouldn't be around people," Maddie said. "You should have left me out in the woods."

"No, I could never do that." Sahara took Maddie's hand in hers. "I promise you, it's almost over. You should be through the change soon."

"And then what?" Maddie pulled her hand away. "I get to live the rest of my life as a freak."

Sahara sighed and stood. She couldn't blame the girl for her pain. She remembered very well the day she realized she was alone. Well, maybe not in quite the same way. Sahara still had family in Mexico, and she supposed in India as well.

She felt Alaric alerting her that there would be food soon and acknowledged it. "We're being invited to eat."

"I'm not hungry," Maddie replied, rolling back toward the wall.

"I'll bring you back something," Sahara said from the door, listening for a long moment before she left, hoping Maddie would change her mind. She remained silent, and Sahara left her there, hoping it wouldn't take too long for the girl to come around. They weren't out of danger just yet.

Hell, she wasn't sure that they ever would be, at this point.

* * *

The village was quiet just before sunset. In a town filled with Shades that was to be expected. They were just starting to wake up to start their night. He could smell bacon cooking as he approached the house that Raven had been gracious enough to welcome him into.

Mason was awake, but not yet out of bed. Alaric stopped on the porch, turning to watch the sun sinking in the west. It was peaceful, but that peace wouldn't last. Already he could feel the approaching chaos.

He'd learned a lot in the day spent crossing the country, glutting on news to counteract the vacuum they had emerged from. He also had incoming information from his scattered clan, some from as far away as Canada, giving him a more rounded picture of what was really happening.

In the wake of the assassinations of the president and vice-president, the country was in turmoil. It was to be expected, he supposed. At least three Shades had been executed in D.C. since the event, supposedly killed while evading arrest, but the more he saw, the more he knew that no one had wanted them arrested.

The west was even worse off as the 8th Battalion moved to firm up borders and claimed everything on the coast. They cut a jagged line from the California/Arizona border up through Nevada and into Utah, and back along the Idaho border with Wyoming, straight up to the Canadian border. They had given up the pretense of being part of the United States military, and there were rumors that they were executing anyone stuck behind their lines still loyal to the federal government.

That left them far too close to the 8th Battalion for his tastes. Not that dealing with the federal government would be any better at this point. In fact, the only areas that he was reading safety at all was along the northern states in the middle of the country, and a few pockets of rationalism in the south.

"I wouldn't count on that."

Alaric turned to see Zero standing on the porch. He raised an eyebrow, and she rolled her eyes. "For someone who is supposed to be the head honcho of a group of Shadows, you sure don't keep your thoughts to yourself." Zero said.

He had to concede the point. He hadn't been very shielded. He adjusted and smiled. "Better?"

She nodded and moved to sit on the stairs. He joined her. "What do you mean?"

She shrugged. "Things in the south aren't like you think."

"No?"

Again, she rolled her eyes at him. "No. It's a false peace. It's being controlled."

Alaric nodded. "Mason told me about your father. But I have to say, I haven't sensed another Shadow with that kind of power."

"You wouldn't." Zero scuffed the sole of her boot against the step. "He's got shields like no one else I've ever met."

Alaric turned to really look at her. She was younger than he had first assumed, and she hid behind a projection of confidence that he could tell was largely bravado. Under it she was nervous, scared even. "Tell me about him."

She shrugged and pulled inward a little. "He's an asshole?" Her face scrunched up and he could feel her trying to say something, straining against some block. "I can't..."

Alaric lifted a hand and she cringed. "Easy," he said softly. "I'm not going to hurt you."

"He put all of these blocks in my head," Zero said. "I can't get around them."

Alaric nodded. "Will you show me?"

She hesitated, then moved down a step closer. "Can you tell me if he left any... like, triggers?"

"What do you mean?" Alaric asked.

"He... he controls people. That Shade that killed the president..."

Alaric nodded, offering his hand. "I can look."

Zero settled her hand on his, and he could feel her shields roll back. Her mind was colorful, the open space as he entered filled with surface thoughts leading back toward the walls that hid her memories and secrets. She led him toward a spot where the color bled away and there was a sense of dread surrounding it. Alaric reached into the black space tentatively.

Ice spread around him and he felt almost physically pushed away. The block was expansive, hiding a swath of memory that seemed vast for someone as young as Zero. It wasn't something he was going to fully understand with a simple reading. He pulled back slowly, opening his eyes to find her staring.

"So?" she asked.

"He's got skills. I haven't seen that kind of work before."

"Can you unblock it?" He could tell she was trying to hide the hope that he could.

He inhaled and considered it. "I think we can clear it out, but not just sitting here on the porch. I'm going to need my Keepers, and some guaranteed privacy. You should know it won't be easy, and it could cause damage."

She nodded. "I want him out of my head."

The door behind them opened and Mason stepped out onto the porch, a bottle of water in his hand. Alaric stood and climbed up the stairs to meet him. "Hey."

Zero stood, bouncing down the stairs. Alaric called her name, and she turned. "Give me a day or two to set it up." She nodded as Mason slipped an arm around Alaric's waist. Alaric turned to Mason, brushing a kiss along his cheek.

"Food's almost ready," Mason said, his eyes on Zero's retreating back. "She okay?"

Alaric took a deep breath, still examining what he'd seen in the girl's head. "She will be, I think."

Mason nodded. "I was going to go check on Riley."

Alaric tightened his arm around Mason's waist. "Riley is fine. Charlie was planning on giving him one last treatment before we start getting him up on his feet."

"And Damon?" Mason asked.

"They've got him isolated," Alaric responded. "Said he isn't responding well. I'm pretty sure they aren't telling me everything."

Mason nodded, but his thoughts were far away. Alaric turned his head, following the general direction back into the house. Behind closed doors, Raven sat with her dying grandfather. He could tell the man wouldn't make it through the night.

Sahara and Bryan were approaching as Manny appeared in the doorway. "Food's on the table. I'll be in with Raven."

They moved into the house quietly, respecting the delicate balance of life that was about to shift irreversibly. They sat at the table in silence, eating without looking at one another. Alaric let his thoughts drift back to Zero, to the complex blocks and locks in her brain. It was a wonder she could even function on any level. It spoke to the girl's power, and to the power of the Shadow who had locked her down that way.

Alaric could only imagine how powerful the girl would be once they stripped the blocks away. Sahara and Bryan moved to begin clearing the table, setting aside plates of food for those who hadn't joined them. Beside him, Mason inhaled sharply, taking Alaric's hand. Through him, Alaric felt the combined grief as Raven let the community know that her grandfather had passed.

The door to the room where the man had lingered his final days opened, and a visibly shaken Raven emerged, wiping at her tears. Mason stood and went to her, one hand rising to her shoulder. Something passed between them and he nodded, turning back to the others. Raven slipped away, out the front door before Mason spoke.

"Raven asks that you observe Shade tradition. She has taken her grandfather's final breath and will withdraw to the water to integrate it. She will return before the sunrise. No one is to enter his room nor speak his name. At sundown, the town will gather and she will take his body to be buried with those who came before."

Alaric lifted his eyes to Bryan, nodding at the thought that they would go back to his room to be out of the way. Mason reached out a hand and Alaric took it, letting Mason lead him out the back door of the house and down a dirt path that led them into the woods and up to a bluff overlooking the lake.

Mason turned his face up to the moon, which was nearing full again, leaning back against a tree. He seemed more content than Alaric expected. Alaric sat on the grass, stretching his legs out in front of him. The moon seemed to warm his chest, where Mason's talisman and the moonstone pendant tangled under his shirt. He pulled them out, rubbing a finger over the moonstone which had taken on a red tint since the accident, his blood seeping into it.

Mason's eyes caught on his, then traveled down to the two pendants. Alaric closed his eyes and covered the moonstone pendant with his hand, reaching in to feel the bubbling presence of those who had worn it before. It had been months now since that first touch, since he'd learned what the pendant meant. So much had changed in those months, and the cool touch of the stone brought that moment back in crystal detail, the words of Mason's ancestor filling his head. His heart raced as he stood, the pendant heavy in his hand.

Alaric crossed to Mason, moving so that Mason had to tilt his head back to look at him. "I have something for you."

Mason raised an eyebrow, his hand lifting to touch the pendant. Alaric leaned in to kiss him, lingering as their minds twined together. The talisman and the moonstone hung in the space between them, rubbing against Mason's chest, sending ripples of intent through them both.

"I've worn these since you left me." Alaric pulled them up and off, holding them above Mason. "This one you gave me so that I could keep you close." He lifted the talisman over his neck and settled it over Mason's. "And this..." Alaric caught the silver oval around the stone and held it between them. "Your ancestors told me that if I intended to bind my life to yours, I should bleed onto the stone, tie my life to it."

He reached for Mason's hand, pulling it up to kiss before sliding it over the stone and closing his eyes. Like that first time they both held it, the world around them shifted. Voices filled his head, impassioned words of love and devotion, promises and images that came to life until they were surrounded by those the stone had touched. *"I would offer it to you, as a token of my love."*

The silver band that had always connected them grew brighter, and Mason looked up at Alaric, his eyes glowing. He leaned forward and kissed Alaric passionately, catching Alaric by surprise. "Put it on me."

Alaric's hands were shaking as he lifted it, settling it over Mason's head. The silver band wound around them, then Mason was kissing him again, kissing him, and pulling him down, both of them ending up on the ground. His hands were frantic, pulling at their clothes as if he would die if he couldn't touch Alaric's skin.

"Easy," Alaric murmured, not entirely sure if the word stayed in his head or found vocalization. Either way, Mason slowed down, exhaling shakily as he moved between Alaric's legs.

"Want…"

Alaric nodded, even as he moved, reaching for him. There was an urgency between them as Mason opened him up quickly, and before he was really ready, Alaric was pulling his hands away and urging him closer.

"Want you, too." Alaric whispered. It burned as Mason pushed in, but Alaric didn't care, he couldn't get Mason close enough. They moved as one, bodies sliding together faster and faster. The moonstone swung in the air between them, then settled on sweat damp skin as Mason leaned in, deep inside Alaric.

Alaric shivered as his orgasm began, as Mason sucked the whimpering sounds of pleasure from his mouth and fed them back in the next breath, and that silver band pulled them tighter together, until Alaric wasn't sure where either of them ended anymore.

When Mason's orgasm flushed inside him, Alaric's own finished, and Mason fell against him, trembling. It was a long moment they both lay silently, then Mason lifted his head, smirking down at Alaric.

"What's funny?" Alaric asked, brushing hair out of Mason's face.

"Not exactly your typical traditional wedding ceremony," Mason replied.

Alaric pulled him in to kiss him. "Don't need tradition. Just you."

"Always," Mason responded solemnly. "Always, Alaric."

Chapter Twenty-Seven

Zero stood with the rest of the outsiders, well removed from the funeral gathering, watching as the town laid a beloved old man to rest. She hadn't seen Raven much since the death, and she felt even more like a freak standing there with the assortment of non-Shades.

Alaric hadn't said anything more about helping her, and she felt like she would be intruding to ask. He seemed all wrapped up with Mason anyway. She'd *known* about the two of them on some level, but it was odd to her for two people to be so demonstrative with their affection. Worse, she knew they were containing it for the sake of the others. She didn't want to imagine how they'd be if they didn't control themselves, like a couple of teenagers in heat.

She shook her head and turned her attention to the other pair that gave her pause. Unlike Alaric and Mason, Sahara and Maddie were all cool detachment. She couldn't get a good reading on either of them.

Of course, she knew that they were Shifters and that Sahara was one of Alaric's Keepers, but beyond that they had kept pretty much to themselves. Maddie turned to look at Zero as if she could feel the light prying. Her face was pale, but her eyes were dark with her exhaustion and grief.

Zero pulled her eyes away and looked back to Raven. The body of her grandfather was buried, and she stood by the headstone as the others came to offer her their respects. Even at this distance, Zero could feel the brief exchange of power as each Shade touched their forehead to hers. In silence, they filed out of the small cemetery until only Raven remained.

There would be a silent supper in the town hall. Once the sun rose, the town would return to life as normal, but for this one last night, no one would speak. It was their way of honoring the long life of one of their own.

Zero could respect that, even if she couldn't understand that kind of emotion. As Raven left her grandfather's grave, Zero turned to head back toward town. Alaric fell into step beside her, lifting a hand to her shoulder.

"*Tomorrow, just after sundown. I want at least one Shade on hand.*"

She nodded, not asking why. She knew why. There was a very real chance that what they were going to do would shred her mind, cause her body to shut down. As eager as she was to have her mind back, she had to be reasonable about what to expect.

Alaric stopped her as they reached the road into town. Beside him the others, his Keepers, gathered. His hand still on her shoulder, Alaric introduced him.

"*This is Bryan, Riley and Sahara. They're going to help me work out what's going on inside your head. Everyone, this is Zero.*"

She looked at each of them in turn, nodding in greeting. Now that it came down to it, she wasn't sure what to say to them. Alaric squeezed her shoulder, and they set off toward the town hall. Zero crossed her arms and pulled herself in tight, trying to find her center, the place inside her that wasn't tainted by her father's touch.

As usual, she couldn't find it, so she settled for the small corner she had built for herself when she first realized what he was doing to her. It was a space filled with her favorite colors, where she could pretend she was in control.

* * *

The wind that gusted through the village smelled to Mason like an omen, a warning. He was up early, driven from the bed by dreams that felt far too real. He'd barely waited for the sun to be far enough down to cast half the lake in shadow before he was in the water to soak.

Mason was uneasy. He didn't really understand everything Alaric was about to attempt, but he could read enough to know that both he and Zero were nervous about it. He nodded to Charlie who slipped from the shade of one tree to the next, making his way down to the water. He paused beside Mason under the shade of the pavilion.

"Everything okay?" Charlie asked, squinting at him.

"Not sure," Mason responded. Something didn't feel right.

"What is it?" Charlie leaned back against the table.

"Smells like trouble," Mason said softly, instinctively reaching for Alaric, who was prepping for the work they were going to do. Alaric's mind rubbed against him, acknowledging that he too felt uncomfortable.

Charlie nodded, his eyes narrowing. "I don't like it." He stood, and Mason could feel him tracking something.

They stood there, side by side as the sun slid down in the distance, neither of them moving, each of them closed up with their own thoughts.

The spell was broken as Riley returned from his regular evening walk, working on building up his stamina again. He raised a hand in greeting, his eyes meeting Mason's in question.

Mason shrugged it off, gesturing at Riley's leg, which had been the slowest of his injuries to heal. "How's the leg?"

Riley made a face and rubbed his thigh. "Still twinges, but it's good."

Mason dragged a hand back through his hair and turned to where Riley was pointedly not watching him. "Are you sure about this thing with Zero?"

Riley shrugged. "Alaric knows what he's doing."

Mason nodded. Beside him, Charlie stretched. "I should get down to the water if I'm still helping with that."

"Alaric says he'll be ready in about an hour," Riley offered. "We're set up in the clinic where you had me."

Charlie nodded and headed for the water. Mason watched him go, still feeling like something was off, almost like they were being watched. He didn't like the feeling.

"You're pretty high strung," Riley said softly, looking at Mason from under long lashes. His hair was freshly cut short, all the blond that had adorned the ends gone now.

"I can't shake the feeling that we aren't safe here," Mason said.

Riley stepped closer, shoving his hands in his pockets. "You're not alone."

It didn't help that the news from the world outside didn't offer them much in the way of hope. Add to that the nightmare that had pulled him out of a deep sleep, a nightmare that he recognized as not his own. It had spilled from Alaric into him, war, death... And it all had a ring of truth to it.

"Woah." Riley touched his arm. "You got all of that?"

"What?" Mason asked, frowning.

"Sorry, I just... I could see it, probably because it came from me."

"You aren't making any sense, Riley."

He licked his lips. "The dream you were just thinking about. I... It was mine, part of my rather annoying precognition. You must have gotten the overflow from Alaric. I'm sorry about that."

"So, that isn't just your subconscious making your fears seem real?" Mason asked, suddenly not really wanting to know, not with what he'd seen.

"No," Riley said. "But the future is never set in stone, Mason. It changes all the time."

Mason nodded, but didn't say anything. He was stuck on the way Alaric screamed his name, on the sight of a row of stakes set up for burning. After a long minute, Mason tugged his shirt on. "I'm going to grab some food. I'll meet you at the clinic."

* * *

Alaric looked up as Zero opened the door to the room. It served as the town's clinic, seldom used in a town full of Shades, but it would serve their purpose. It was stocked with first aid supplies, and they had made a few modifications of their own.

He smiled at the girl, but let her come at her own pace. Sahara stood closest to the door where she would play a guardian of sorts to make sure they weren't interrupted. Bryan stood near the end of the hospital bed, where he would be in charge of monitoring Zero's energy, and following Alaric inside her head, to protect them both from any potential traps. Riley and Mason stood against one wall, ready to move in to monitor Zero's body once they got started. Rounding out the crowded room, Charlie sat in a corner, to observe and step in if Mason needed his help.

"Little bit crowded," Zero said, her eyes skipping around the room, then up to Alaric.

He nodded. "I told you I needed them to keep you safe."

She crossed to the bed, one hand gliding over the sheet to finger the restraints. He could see fear in her eyes. "Those are to protect you too," Alaric said softly. "And me."

It took her a minute, but she eventually nodded and turned to sit on the bed. "Okay, so... How do we do this?" she asked as she moved to lay down.

"You just relax, for starters." Alaric nodded to Riley who moved closer as Alaric reached for the strap that would cross her chest. She was far from relaxed as they buckled the straps down. Her eyes flicked around the room and her hands clenched into fists. Alaric left Riley to finish and turned his attention to her. "It's okay, Zero. You're safe here."

She nodded tightly, but he could still sense her distress. "Let's start with a simple breathing exercise. Look at me, follow my breath."

He breathed in slowly, and she followed, though her eyes kept darting around then coming back to him. Slowly he extended his senses over her, drawing her in until she was focused. "Good. Now close your eyes." Zero blinked a few times before she closed them, and he shifted to thought.

"I'm going to help you relax, but I need you awake." He slipped slowly through her half-raised shields, flooding her with reassurance. Alaric caressed against her controls, reaching out for Mason. He felt Riley bridge Mason into the connection, and he relayed instructions for how deep Mason should let Zero go. Next, he pulled Bryan into the connection. *"Trust them, they're here to keep you safe."*

There was a snort of derision. *"You mean alive."* Zero said.

Alaric shored up their connections, then sent out tendrils to both Sahara and Charlie so that he could bring them in if necessary. When that was done, he moved a little deeper into the color strewn opening in Zero's mind. He swept through the area with quiet calm, then moved to the place he'd found when he'd initially read the girl. Whoever had segmented her mind had done a very thorough job, and he was going to need to break through the walls before he could fully understand the controls.

Zero took him to the blank wall that didn't belong there. *"He's in there."* She shivered a little.

"Do you know how he set it up? Is there anything I should look for?"

"I…" He could feel her straining. Then she seemed to take a breath. *"He likes order, control. Whatever you find, it will be clear that it isn't mine."* She sort of chuckled. *"I'm not as… neat."*

"Okay, let's see how we get in."

It wouldn't be pleasant. Alaric stood and contemplated the barrier. It was strong, and it was designed to deflect even Zero's attempt at knowing what was behind it. He pushed against it, monitoring the ripples as it reacted to his touch, slipping along its edge until he felt a slight weakness.

Alaric pushed harder, nodding his head and feeling his body do the same. The Shadow who had done this was extremely powerful, but there were flaws in his technique. He reached for Mason, directing the healing energy more physically into Zero's head, urging Mason to strengthen her own natural defenses.

Metaphorically, he took Zero's hand and then forced himself forward, pricking a hole into the wall and pressing into it, making it grow.

Zero stiffened and gasped, trying to pull away, but he tightened his grip and kept moving.

He could feel Mason warning him that her heart was racing, her adrenaline spiking. "*Stay calm.*" Alaric murmured to her, but her panic was making it more difficult to continue his progress.

Blackness surrounded them, hazy and fuzzy against his shields as he forced himself through the thick layers the Shadow had used to build the blockade. Zero was in distress beside him, and he was fighting both to keep going and to keep her with him. Mason's alarm surged toward them, and Alaric felt Charlie's energy joining Mason's. He was starting to think about abandoning the effort when he felt the thickness begin to thin. Another push and he was inside the compartment, pulling Zero with him.

He knew the wall would likely close behind him, cutting him off from the others, so he wasn't surprised when the hole he had made closed with a snap, strangling the line between him and his friends. It was still there, but it was strained, and everything feeding through it was muffled and slow.

Zero seemed dazed, or sedated, as she trembled. Alaric paused, anticipating there would be traps. He wasn't surprised, then, as the first of them sprung and fire raced through his psychic body, pushing them back against the artificial surface behind him. He widened his shields around them both, then scanned around him for the controls.

It took him a few minutes to be able to see past the blasting energy, but eventually he found what looked like a glass panel. He fought through the blasting energy to touch it, stumbling as the flow stopped. The panel was the work of a master at skills Alaric had never encountered other than in the combined memories of his clan.

He was tiring, and he could tell Zero was too. That was the design of the barrier and first trap, to cause an intruder to burn out before they could get any further. The first thing he needed to do was drop the outer barrier so that his connection to the others could feed him energy and input. "*Zero, help me.*" He had to reach back and pull her toward him, helping her focus on the panel.

It looked like something out of a science fiction movie, a touch screen with buttons and dials, any of which could cause catastrophic consequences. Some of the flashing lights and touch-screen buttons and dials would lead to traps. Some would be counter-intuitive. One might even kill the girl.

Alaric stilled himself and reached inside for memory, opening himself for the guidance and feeding energy into Zero's psyche. Her eyes fell to a button near the bottom of the panel. He reached for it, murmuring a prayer that he wasn't wrong before he touched the button. The barrier retreated slowly, and the sense of the others rushed into him once their connection had stabilized. The room around him lightened some, but was still mostly dark.

Zero was struggling, fading from beside him. The two Shades were working to keep her alive as her body tried to shut down. Bryan fed energy into Alaric, his urgency to resolve the situation clear. *"She won't take much more."*

He turned to the controls, reaching into them to understand what they did and he had to admit, it was impressive. If they had the orb, he'd be able to clean it all out… But they didn't, so he needed to improvise.

"I'm going to focus on keeping the barrier down and giving her back control to start."

It had risks. She could trip another trap inadvertently, or the control the barrier exhibited might also control something else he couldn't see. He would need to come back in to clean out the traps, make sure there wasn't any of the programming that terrified her. Alaric reached for the controls, making sure that the external barrier would stay down, and dismantling the first defensive trap. Then he scanned through what he could, pulling at the barriers that kept her from telling them what her father was up to, what he had done to her. He hesitated, watching a memory play out, the pain of her treatment rocking through him. She shuddered around him, and Mason urged him to hurry.

Alaric didn't like the mess he was going to leave behind, but he knew he couldn't continue. He erected a softer wall between Zero's conscious mind and the mess, one that would let her access the information, but absorb anything that might try to leak out or exert control.

He did his best to sooth the surfaces as he pulled back, sending waves of gentle comfort as he retreated back to his own body and opened his eyes.

Zero's face was pale, her eyes closed. Both Mason and Charlie were bent over her, and Alaric could visually see the energy they were circulating through her. The room was tensely quiet for a long drawn out moment before Mason lifted his head and nodded a little.

Charlie came up just behind Mason, his eyes sunken, exhaustion pulling his features into a frown. "She's going to need rest before you do any more."

Alaric nodded. "So will the rest of us. We'll go back in tomorrow. For now I need to make sure she'll stay under. I don't want her poking around in that landmine."

Charlie nodded. "She should stay down at least until morning. We can have someone stay with her."

Sahara moved from near the door. "I'll stay. I can reach out if I feel her coming around."

"Good. Bryan, Riley, get some sleep."

"What about you?" Mason asked, rubbing the back of their hands together.

Alaric smiled sleepily. "I need sleep too."

"I need the water," Mason countered. "But I'll walk with you."

Some part of him wanted to follow Mason down to the lake, but he knew better. He was going to need to be fully rested to tackle the next part of the work to give Zero back her mind. "Make sure you get some sleep too."

Mason kissed him lightly. "I will."

They walked wordlessly to the path that led down to the water, then parted ways silently. Alaric yawned as he climbed up to the house. The pull of his fatigue made his steps slow, his feet heavy. He stumbled a little as he reached the stairs, catching himself on the rail.

Something was wrong. He eased himself down, feeling that thick barrier descend over him nearly physically. He could hear Zero screaming, Sahara's mind pulling on his as he stumbled to his knees.

Chapter Twenty-Eight

Raven paused as she neared the clinic. She knew that the Shadows had gathered to try to help Zero, but she had kept her distance. She was very aware of her emotional state, and Zero needed stable minds around her while they worked.

Now though, she sensed something wasn't right. Zero's voice split the night and Raven wrenched open the door, racing inside.

The Shifter was holding Zero's face as the girl arched up on the bed, her body held in place by the leather restraints.

Raven touched the first body part she could reach, Zero's ankle, sending her senses through the skin to try to determine what was wrong. Raven gasped as the pain registered, every nerve ending in the girl's body was a live wire pulsing in time with her heart. Raven poured soothing energy into Zero as she tried to find the cause.

She felt the Shadow enter the room, felt him push past her and into Zero's mind. Raven kept her focus on Zero's body, doing what she could to ease the pain.

After several long moments, Zero's body eased down and settled. Raven lifted her head, blinking a little as she pulled back into herself. Alaric sank to the floor beside her, his exhaustion evident. Raven reached for him, but he caught her hand and shook his head.

"I'll be fine."

Sahara turned to him, helping him into a chair, the look on her face telling Raven she didn't believe Alaric any more than Raven did.

"You should let me take a look anyway," Raven said.

"I'm just tired."

She raised an eyebrow, but didn't want to argue the point. "What happened?"

He rubbed his hands over his face and sighed. "I'm not completely sure. Whoever did this to her made a mess." He pinched the bridge of his nose, and she could feel him pull his focus inward. "It looks like he was experimenting on her, but kept the results of his experiments locked down. I think I may have inadvertently unlocked them."

Raven frowned. Zero had hinted at what her father had done, but she had always indicated that the experiments had failed. Cautiously, Raven put a hand on Zero's hand, reading her lightly. Her nerves were still randomly firing, but with less punch than before. "Her energy is all over the place," Raven said softly.

"He... Actually, I don't know *exactly* what he was trying to do," Alaric said, his voice low and filled with exhaustion. "But, whatever it was, it changed her. Or is changing her now that it's loose."

"She always said his experiments were failures." Raven said. "She's never been able to say what they were exactly."

He nodded. "It wasn't just memory that he blocked. It feels like parts of her that were asleep, inaccessible, are waking up. Whatever he did, he didn't want her to be able to use that power." He pushed himself up to his feet, and Sahara slid an arm around him to help hold him up. "She's going to need time and rest. Which I also need. Sorry, but if I don't move now, I'll be asleep in the chair."

Raven nodded. "Go on. I'll stay with her."

She didn't watch them leave, just pulled a chair up close to the bed and sat with her hand still on Zero's so she could monitor her.

Raven wasn't sure how much time had passed when she felt eyes on her and turned. The younger Shifter stood in the doorway, her eyes on Zero's face. Raven hadn't seen much of the girl since they had arrived in the town. Mason had said she was grieving the loss of her sister.

"Is she okay?" the girl asked, her voice soft.

"I think so," Raven answered.

"I heard her earlier." The Shifter took a step closer. "She's young."

Raven wasn't sure how to respond to that. "She's been through a lot."

"Sahara told me a little. Her name's Zero?"

Raven smiled a little. "That's what she calls herself."

"I'm Maddie." Her eyes darted to Raven's, then back to Zero.

"Raven."

Maddie came to the end of the bed, her fingers caressing over the leather strap that crossed Zero's legs just above the ankle. "Why is she strapped down?"

Raven sighed. "So she doesn't hurt herself or someone else." She suppressed a yawn.

"I could sit with her," Maddie offered tentatively. "If you needed to sleep." She looked at Raven, her eyes sad, but Raven got the sense that Maddie needed the connection to someone her own age.

"That would be nice."

"Sun's up though." Maddie glanced back at the door. "Sahara is with Bryan, so our room is empty. You can sleep there."

Raven stood and nodded. "Thank you, Maddie. That's very kind. If she wakes or seems distressed, come get me?"

Maddie nodded, and Raven left the room, pausing in the lobby of the building. Morning light spilled in through the small window near the door. She considered braving the sun to go to her own bed, but decided that she should be close for Zero's sake and headed down the hall to the room they had made up for their guests.

* * *

It was quiet as Mason slipped from the shadows of the porch to the shadows of the trees. The sun was slipping down toward the mountain, casting long fingers of dark across the road that made it easy to get to the lake.

Mason pulled his shirt off as he got to the pavilion, dropping it on the table. It would be another hour before the lake was filled with Shades soaking up the water and natural minerals of the lake.

Mason preferred to be there when it was like this, just him and the water and the full moon rising over the trees. It reminded him of home somehow.

He finished stripping down and crossed to the edge of the water. The feeling that something wasn't right still niggled at the back of his brain, like a vague undercurrent. He paused and looked around him, examining the horizon for some sign of impending disaster, feeling around him. The familiar feeling of lives being lived, sleepy and waking up was all that came to him, no indication of impending doom.

Alaric and Bryan had gone down to work with Zero. Mason had felt Alaric leave the bed hours before without asking Mason to join him. Nothing seemed out of place, yet there was something he couldn't name bothering him.

He shook it off and moved to the rocks that jutted out into the deeper water, glad that this side of the lake was the first cast in shadow as the sun set. The rocks made a natural diving platform, letting him drop into the deepest, coldest, clearest spot in the lake.

Mason dove in and was nearly to the bottom before he recognized a problem.

Salt.

The whole lake was salted. He reached the bottom and kicked for the surface, fighting to keep the water out of his mouth and nose. He broke the surface, gasping. He could already feel the burning of the salt on his skin.

It wasn't just a light salting either. It was toxic levels.

And if it was in the lake…he swam hard for the shore, trembling as the pain rose to a crescendo and by the time he pulled himself out of the water he had open sores on his skin. He grabbed his shirt and started wiping himself down as he ran for the village in nothing but his soaked boxers.

He reached out for Alaric as he stumbled, sending the important part of the message – "*salt in the water... warn them.*" He needed to get the salt off his skin, but he knew that if the water in the lake was tainted, so was everything in their taps. A shower would only make it worse.

But they had bottles on the supply truck that had come the night before. He changed direction and headed for the supply truck, his steps slowing as the salt that had gotten into his system hit him hard. Then there were hands, helping him and supporting him, laying him out on the tailgate of the truck.

Water, pure and clean, poured over him, rinsing the salt away. Hands pulled his boxers down and away, then covered him with clean linen, pouring more water over it before handing him a bottle to drink. He had to dilute whatever had managed to get into him.

In the distance, he thought he heard gunfire and people screaming. All around him there was a scurry of activity and voices as people ran. Alaric was suddenly there with him, climbing up in the truck beside him. Riley was there too and together they pulled him further into the bed of the truck.

Mason struggled to sit up as the truck lurched forward, wanting to see what was happening, but Alaric pushed him back down, his presence covering over him like a blanket, dampening down all external input. There was an explosion, the truck rocking from the blast, but Alaric kept him down. The truck kept moving, and dark moved in around them as they left the village behind.

Alaric let him up after a while, though he kept something between Mason and the village. "What happened?" Mason asked, his voice ragged from the salt. Riley handed him another bottle of water.

"*The village was attacked.*" Alaric's eyes caught his, and he fed Mason the images of people screaming about the salt in their water, then the fire that started near the old stables and spread and shadows that looked like men in uniform descending on the town.

"How?" Mason shook his head. Images flashed between Riley and Alaric, but he couldn't be sure what he was seeing, and what was real or what was premonition.

"Someone had to have given us away," Riley said aloud.

There were others in the covered back of the truck with them, Shades that they'd managed to get out of the chaos. "Charlie?"

Alaric shook his head and looked away. "Don't know. Couldn't find him."

"We need to go back." Mason tried to pull the linen off him, but Alaric pushed him back to laying down.

"We can't go back, and you need to heal. Right now you can't even put clothes on."

"I'm fine." Mason struggled against him, but Alaric's face was hard set.

"*You have open sores on two thirds of your skin. You aren't fine. Stop fighting.*"

The truck swerved off the road stopped.

Alaric jumped down, but Riley kept a hand on Mason's shoulder, keeping him still. Mason could hear Bryan now, his voice gruff as they took inventory of what they had and who had made it out with them.

"I know another vehicle got out ahead of us." Bryan said. "We've got the SUV and the truck."

"Maddie?" Sahara asked.

"She was with Zero and Raven when I ran for Mason," Alaric said. "Raven will look after her."

"Who all is in the truck?" Bryan asked.

"I've got Mason, Riley, a handful of the Shades." Alaric said. "Sahara?"

"A few Shades, one is in bad shape. The others are working on her."

They moved away and Mason found his attention drawn by one of the Shades kneeling beside him. "Mason, remember me?"

"Aliyah." He lifted his head, looking for signs of her son.

"He's with Liam and his father. They're okay." She put a hand on his shoulder. "Let's worry about you though. Lay back and let me see to these burns."

He nodded and closed his eyes, letting her energy sooth the pain and drifting off as she worked.

Mason woke with a start, suddenly remembering the danger. He could taste the difference in the air, they had left the mountain and were barreling through the desert. It had to be close to morning, judging from the unease around him and the gray of the skies he could see out the back of the truck.

"We're going to need to get off the road," Aliyah said beside him as Mason pushed himself up.

She had done a good job, and he was a long way toward healed. He needed some clean water, and a soak, but he would survive.

"Alaric's working on it," Riley said beside him.

"Do we dare stop?" someone else asked. "If that was the 8th Battalion, won't they follow us?"

"We aren't sure it was the 8th Battalion," Riley countered. "It isn't clear what exactly happened."

"Maybe not to you."

Mason eyes darted to an older man he didn't know. "It was the 8th Battalion."

"You saw them?" Mason asked.

He nodded. "My place is at the northern edge. Saw them come sneaking through the woods."

"How'd you get past them?" Aliyah asked.

"Did what I had to." The man looked down at his hands, then away. "Two of those men won't be going home."

"What I want to know is how they managed to salt the lake." Mason said, sitting up. He was weak, but managed to slide back to rest his back against the wall of the truck.

"Good question," Riley said. "I don't think we'll answer that any time soon."

Mason nodded. He knew it meant they had a traitor among them, possibly sitting inches away.

* * *

Alaric nodded when Sahara pointed at the motel. It was risky, but they needed to get indoors before the sun came all the way up over the horizon. The truck pulled off, raising the dust around them. The SUV came to a stop beside them, Bryan stepping out and looking at Alaric.

They were going to have to bluff their way into rooms. Alaric pulled out his wallet and the forty dollars he'd kept tucked away in case they needed it. He handed the cash to Bryan. "Get us at least three rooms. More if you can."

Bryan nodded, his face grim as he headed into the office, and Alaric went to the back of the truck. "How is he?"

Green eyes met his. "He's fine," Mason said.

Beside him the woman nodded. "He'll live. Needs a nice ice bath once you get him inside. And more sleep. By nightfall though he should be back on his feet."

"Good. Stay with him until we get the rooms."

Alaric stepped away from the truck and breathed in deep. Almost instantly Riley and Sahara were with him, and he exhaled. "*How does someone sneak into a village of Shades, with the four of us there, salt the lake that strongly, and lay explosives without us knowing?*"

Riley shook his head, looking back the way they had come. Alaric could sense him scanning for anyone following them, but so far, they seemed to have gotten away clean in the chaos. "*Obviously, someone inside. Did you figure out who?*"

Alaric shook his head. "*No, whoever trained the bastard did a good job. I couldn't track him.*"

"It was likely someone with a family," Sahara said, turning to look at him. "Someone they could exploit."

Alaric nodded in agreement. "Or someone who met Zero's father and was being Shadowed." He'd seen what the girl was afraid of, and it was obvious that her father was a Shadow to be reckoned with. How he was operating at that level without Alaric being able to sense him had him worried. It meant they had to be extra cautious. "And until we're sure it isn't one of the ones we brought with us, we're all on guard."

He turned back to look at the ragtag bunch. Aside from Mason and Aliyah there were four others. He knew none of them well, and Aliyah hardly at all. They'd only met in the last few days.

As if she could feel Alaric, Aliyah's head lifted and her eyes met Alaric's. Bryan re-joined them and pulled Alaric's attention away. "I got us three rooms." He held up the keys.

Alaric took one of them. "I'll take Mason and the old man," he said, pointing at the oldest of the Shades. "Sahara, take the two women. Bryan and Riley, take the other guy. And, let's move the vehicles around back. We don't want them visible from the road in case someone comes looking." He stopped them before they could walk away. "It's time to stop being nice, I want you to read them. Deep reads, use whatever means you need to."

Chapter Twenty-Nine

The water surrounding him had warmed, but it had done its job. Mason inhaled deeply and stretched before pulling the plug and standing. He reached for the thin motel towel and gently dried himself, careful around the few spots left on his skin to mark the salt burns. He knew he'd been lucky to get away with as little damage as he did, and that there was fresh water so close at hand.

He could hear voices in the room, Alaric and someone else. He eased open the door. The room was gloomy, even with the bedside light on. Alaric looked up, his mind brushing along Mason affectionately. On the other bed was the Shade that had seen the 8th Battalion in town.

"We scrounged up some clothes." Alaric said, standing. He grabbed a pair of jeans and a t-shirt off the chair and brought them to where Mason stood in the bathroom door, the threadbare towel his only covering.

"Where are we?" Mason asked as he took the clothes.

"Not really sure, a motel in the middle of the desert."

Mason nodded, but was still frowning. Alaric leaned in to kiss along his forehead. "We're safe for the moment."

His eyes darted to the older Shade, then back at Alaric. "You going to tell me what's going on?" He didn't feel particularly safe. In fact, there was an undercurrent of danger that had Alaric's normal energy all jangled and tight.

Alaric sighed. "Get dressed. We'll talk."

The jeans were too big, but better than just the towel. Mason heard someone at the door and more talking, and when he emerged, the Shade was gone and Alaric had a collection of cookies and candy bars on the bed beside. "Breakfast." Alaric said, waving his hand at it. "Best we could do; the motel doesn't have a restaurant."

"Where's…"

Alaric looked to the door, then back at Mason. "Carl? He went next door to give us some privacy."

Mason snagged a bag of chocolate cookies and sat on the bed.

"You look better," Alaric said.

Mason reached for him mentally. "*Hey, talk to me.*"

Alaric inhaled and nodded. "Yeah, okay, so… we aren't sure what the casualties were, or who made it out other than those with us." Alaric stood and paced. "I got your distress loud and clear and was halfway to the lake when I got your message about the salt in the water, sent Riley to you and started pounding on doors, but by then people were already up and showering and drinking… chaos in the streets and then the fire… It engulfed one of the trucks down by the stables, and it exploded, and the fire kept spreading."

He turned to look at Mason and the images and sounds leaked across, even the smells. Mason nodded. "And…"

"We ran. I gathered up who I could as I ran back toward you. We piled into the truck and we ran."

"What about the 8th Battalion?" Mason asked.

Alaric shook his head. "I didn't see them myself, but yeah. It was 8th Battalion." He closed his eyes and turned away.

Mason put down the cookies and stood, crossing to him and running his hands up Alaric's tense back. "*What aren't you saying?*"

Alaric rubbed against him, turning to press their foreheads together, then kiss him lightly. When the kiss deepened, Mason recognized the distraction technique. Alaric had used it before. He stepped back. Alaric followed, his hands catching Mason by the waist.

"Stop." Mason put his hand on Alaric's chest. "I know you think you're protecting me from something, but I'm a big boy."

Alaric rubbed a hand over his face and looked away. "I don't know anything for sure."

"Someone betrayed us." Mason already knew that much. Mason stepped back from Alaric, rubbing his forehead. "Why would any of them... I mean... It doesn't make sense."

"I don't know for sure, Mason." Alaric said again, crossing to the bed to sit. Alaric pulled a hand through his hair. "We have to consider everyone. I'm convinced none of the Shades with us have been compromised."

Mason nodded, mulling over what he knew of the Shades that lived in the town and the ones who had recently arrived. His mind flashed on Zero, on her fear that she'd been programmed like the assassins who had killed the president.

"It wasn't her." Alaric said softly. "She hadn't been out of the bed since we put her down."

Another thought dawned on him slowly. "Damon."

"What?"

"Think about it. He said he had family. He came to us. He came with you."

Alaric shook his head. "I don't think so. He was the one who brought us here. If he'd been compromised, the town would have been hit months ago, before we even left California."

"Who then?" Mason paced a little, but Alaric intercepted him, taking his hand and tugging him back toward the bed furthest from the drape covered window.

"We won't solve it here." Alaric said. "You need some sleep. I'm going to go check on the others."

Mason yawned involuntarily before he could protest. Alaric pressed a kiss on his forehead, draping him with that mental blanket that pushed him toward sleep. Mason let it come, slipping into the relief of sleep.

* * *

It was still daylight when Mason left the other Shade sleeping and slipped from the room looking for Alaric.

"We can't," he heard Alaric say as he neared the shaded patio between the office building and the motel building. "It isn't safe anymore."

"So where are we going?" Riley asked.

"We're going back into hiding," Bryan supplied, his voice clearly expressing his distaste for the idea.

"Do you see another choice?" Alaric asked, moving as Mason shifted and made himself known. "We go east; we get undercover. At least there we'll be protected from the 8th Battalion."

"I'm not sure that's true," Mason said as he came around the corner. "If they're using Shades against Shades, they can use your own people against you too." He looked at Alaric. "Okay, maybe not you specifically, but you can't keep tabs on every single person at every moment."

"What do you know—" Bryan stood, but Alaric cut him off with a hand raised.

"No, he's right, Bryan." Alaric rubbed his forehead. "I can't tell you exactly what every person is doing at any given moment. We can be broken the same way the village was. Someone could betray us. I don't want that on my head."

"We have spent the last generation pulling our clan back together." Bryan argued. "Your father—"

Alaric cut him off. "No, my father was wrong. Together we attract too much attention."

"I'm going to have to side with Alaric on this." Riley said. "In one place, we're too easy a target. We need to separate, make it harder to find us."

"We're stronger together," Bryan argued.

"We're also a bigger target," Alaric responded. "We leave as soon as the sun's down. We head for Jordan's safe house."

They scattered, leaving Alaric and Mason alone. "You shouldn't be out here," Alaric said, gesturing at the sun.

"I'm fine in the shadows." He took Alaric's hand and drew him to the picnic table. "Are you sure Bryan isn't right? Shouldn't you be with your people?"

Alaric put his hands on Mason's hips and smirked as he leaned in closer. "I have you, I couldn't possibly need anyone else." Mason let Alaric kiss him, opening his lips and relishing the taste of Alaric's mouth on his.

"I don't have what it takes to keep you safe. They do," Mason murmured when Alaric pulled back. "If something happens..." He looked up at Alaric, into the deep blue of his eyes.

"Nothing is going to happen to me," Alaric whispered back, "as long as we're together."

Mason wasn't convinced of that, but he knew it was an argument he wasn't going to win. "Well then... we have a few hours to kill. Any idea what we can do?" Mason licked his way into Alaric's mouth, moaning as Alaric's hands tightened on his hips.

"I have a few ideas," Alaric responded, pressing him back until he was seated on the table. Alaric nudged Mason's legs open and moved between them so that their groins were flush against one another. "Lots of them really... mostly involving one or both of us having fewer clothes on."

"We are outside, and not on your private little mountain," Mason countered, sliding his hands around Alaric's belt and tugging him closer. "And there's the matter of Carl asleep in our room, not to mention the impending doom of the 8th Battalion."

Alaric's smile faded, and he nodded tightly, though he leaned in for a kiss. "Riley and Bryan did some work after we finished deep reading everyone. We think we have a working theory."

Mason looked at him, waiting and when he didn't continue, Mason, pulled him back to him. "Tell me."

Alaric blinked, like he was pulling himself back from chasing after some elusive thought and glanced at him. "It wasn't a full 8th Battalion attack. They couldn't get that many men into Arizona unnoticed. We're thinking it was a small strike force."

"Guided in by one of us," Mason supplied. He thought through what he remembered, trying to see past the pain of the salt burning his skin and his fear for the safety of the others.

"They wanted to disrupt the village, scatter the Shades, but they were specifically looking for you."

"Why me?" Mason asked, frowning at him.

Alaric shook his head. "When I pooled all of the memories, including ours, I kept hearing someone thinking, 'find Mason Jerah,' over and over again."

"But you're sure it isn't one of the people who made it out with us."

"Here." Alaric took his hands and closed his eyes. After a second of hesitation, Mason closed his as well. Almost immediately he was standing in the middle of the chaotic village, people running around him, yelling and the sounds of the fire. Then someone ran past him – "*Find Mason Jerah. Find Mason Jerah.*" He turned, trying to find the thought, but it slipped behind more running and screaming, and then he could hear Riley's voice, pulling his attention back to the truck.

There was a pop, and he was back in the shaded picnic area of the motel. "I can't hold it for long, sorry." Alaric said.

Mason kissed him lightly. "It's amazing you can do it at all." He squinted out at the late afternoon sunlight, back the way they had come. "So, are we expecting them to follow us?"

"I think we have to," Alaric said.

"Okay, then I say we chance the sun and get moving now," Mason said

Alaric's head popped up, his eyes going dark. "I think you may be right, we need to—"

There was a strange whistle in the air, and Mason identified it two seconds before it was too late, grabbing Alaric and shoving him, diving after him. The world around them exploded as they rolled. When they stopped, Alaric was bleeding, his eyes glazed over and flames danced around them, far too close for comfort. Mason scrambled up and pulled Alaric with him.

They moved away from the flames, toward the back of the motel where the truck was parked. Mason winced as the sun found his skin, but kept moving, his arm around Alaric who was starting to get his feet under him.

Mason didn't think the head injury was serious, but he would look at it once they were in the truck and moving.

"Bryan, Riley…" Alaric pulled him to a stop and tried to go back.

"You first," Mason said, tugging a little to pull Alaric's attention back.

They were nearly to the truck when Alaric stopped again, pointing. "I'm fine. Help them."

Mason looked up, spotting Riley through the smoke. He nodded and jogged back toward Riley. He and Sahara had one of the women supported between them. The Shade was burned, and Sahara was sporting bruises but seemed intact otherwise.

"You okay?" Mason asked as he reached them. He reached a hand to the Shade, trying to assess her injuries.

"Bryan's trying to get the others out." Riley said. "We're okay."

"How bad?" Mason asked, though he was pretty sure he knew the answer.

Riley shook his head. "Bryan and I were with Sahara or we wouldn't be standing."

"Okay, I'll go get Bryan. Get Alaric and go. We'll catch up." More of the building was burning now, and Mason fought through the dense smoke to what had once been their room. He could see movement in the shadows thrown by the flames.

"*Mason, hurry.*" Alaric's voice in his head startled him, pulling his eyes up and down the road they had come in on. Headlights were coming toward them, two, maybe three vehicles.

Mason stepped through the hole in the wall, ducking away from flames that flared as they found new fuel. "Bryan!"

"Here," Bryan called, raising a hand to show Mason where. Someone was trapped under debris, bleeding from more places than Mason could make out in the smoke. "Help me move this."

Mason leaned in, putting a hand on the man's face. There was no point. Even if they got him out, he wouldn't survive. "He's gone, Bryan. And we got company coming. We gotta go."

He pulled on Bryan's arm. He could feel Alaric's worry, but he pushed it aside to focus on getting them out. The headlights were closer now and he could hear shouting. Bryan pushed him back against the only wall not already burning as gunshots rang out.

They were cornered. "Search everything still standing."

Bryan elbowed him and gestured to the bathroom door. Mason nodded and they inched along the wall. He glanced into the small room. Flames licked the ceiling, but the fire hadn't started down the walls. "Window?"

More gunshots rang out and voices shouted from just outside the room. Bryan was wrapping his hand in a towel and stepping up on the toilet to break out the window.

"They're in here!"

Mason looked up as men appeared at the gaping hole in the wall and crowded in toward Bryan.

The bullet hit him as Bryan grabbed at him, and he fell backward into the sink. He could taste blood and salt and he could hear Alaric screaming in his head. But then the noise of his own pain drowned out everything but Bryan's fist in his shirt, hauling him up and shoving him out the window.

Riley was there to catch him and Bryan was through the window quickly. But even as they hefted him up, he knew they weren't going to make it. His vision swam as they carried him toward the truck.

His feet fumbled to find the ground, but no sooner had he connected to push himself up, then they were all falling, Riley going limp as shots rang out, and Bryan pulled him away.

Mason groaned as Bryan dragged him into the brush to give them some cover. "Get me up," Mason murmured, reaching up for his hand.

Bryan helped him to his feet and they made a few more feet before his legs went to jelly and he pulled Bryan down. "Hey, come on. Stay with me."

There was more blood in his mouth now. Mason fisted a hand in Bryan's shirt and pulled him close. "Run."

Bryan shook his head. "Alaric will kill me."

Mason opened his eyes, opened his mind, inviting Bryan in to make him understand. The bullet had ripped him up pretty good, but it was more than that. The little bit of sun exposure had done its job, and the flames had helped, and he'd already been a lot drier than normal after his bout with the salted lake. The bullet itself was lodged inside him somewhere, laced with gold, leaching salt and other chemicals into his blood.

It was a bullet made for a Shade. And it had found its target.

Mason let go of him to pull at his shirt frantically, finally pulling out the twined together leather strings that held his amulet and the moonstone Alaric had given him as a binding gift.

"Give... give this to Alaric." Mason turned away, spitting out blood. His eyes rolled, and he licked his lips. "Tell him I loved him. Go, I'll do what I can to keep them from following."

Bryan took the pendants with a shaking hand. "I can't—"

Mason shoved him. "Now."

For a moment, he didn't think Bryan would go, but then Bryan nodded and moved away, into the slowly growing darkness as the sun finally sank below the horizon.

Mason swallowed the taste of blood and lifted his head. He pressed both bloody hands to the sandy soil under him, grateful that he had learned some of the darker ways to use his gifts from Paul. He'd sworn not to use them, not to kill, but he wasn't about to let the 8th Battalion catch Alaric and the others.

He reached inside him for his pain, feeding it out into the ground under him. The first man to reach him got close enough to touch before the energy Mason was forcing out of himself dropped him. He felt another, then another fall, but his strength was failing.

His eyes closed, and he whispered Alaric's name before he let the darkness claim him.

Chapter Thirty

More than half his attention was with Riley, who he had sent back to help Bryan when it was taking too long and the approaching men were too close. Mason was hurt, but Alaric couldn't tell how badly. His stomach burned, like Mason's pain echoing through him. He opened his mouth to say something, but then there was an echoing bang and everything went black.

All of his senses shut down. He was blind and deaf. Pain ripped through his head, as if the bullet had struck him. He was screaming, but no sound was coming from him. Beside him he felt the flicker of Sahara behind the wheel of the truck. It lurched and Alaric grabbed the dashboard as the truck jostled them.

He wasn't sure Sahara was even on a road. He could make out very little detail but the emptiness where Riley was supposed to be and the movement of the truck.

"We have to go back." He thought he said the words out loud, but he couldn't be sure.

The truck wasn't turning though.

"Sahara!"

Riley was dead. Alaric couldn't escape the loss; his head was filled with buzzing noise and blackness. Everything was wrong and couldn't function. He was shaking.

Over the buzzing he could start to hear Bryan, but he couldn't make out words. He pushed to try to reach Mason, but all he got was pain lancing through his head and stomach until he couldn't take more and he passed out.

It was several hours later when he managed to pull himself up out of the blackness. He opened his eyes, his head rolling on the back of the seat to see Sahara still driving. She spared him a glance before turning her eyes back to the road. "I was worried," she said softly.

He touched her arm, but couldn't manage words. Everything inside him ached. Riley was dead. There was no question. The bullet had hit him at the base of the skull and severed his spine. He was dead before he hit the ground.

Mason and Bryan were a mystery. He couldn't feel them. He couldn't feel anything outside of the truck. He looked at Sahara again and she nodded. "I've learned a thing or two from Bryan."

She reached over and rubbed his head. "Go back to sleep. I'll wake you if I need you."

Alaric closed his eyes and tried to control the fear that was gripping him. Riley was dead. Mason had been shot. He was too affected by the shock to function. The bullet that took Riley had struck him in a way. He'd been too far into Riley's head when it happened. It could be days before he regained control.

Sahara's hand touched his. "We're safe for the moment. We're headed east. I'll get us where we need to go." He opened his eyes again. She seemed to understand even though he couldn't make the words to ask. "No, I haven't heard from Bryan. I don't do the long distance well."

He glanced behind him where the female Shade was sleeping. She didn't look well.

"Sleep." Sahara urged and Alaric nodded, closing his eyes. He let himself drift, hoping he would be closer to himself when he woke.

* * *

Alaric felt someone trying to reach through the still significant blocks his mind had thrown up to protect him from Riley's death. His hand slid across the seat to Sahara, letting her bolster his energy to reach out.

"*Alaric! Thank god you're okay.*" The connection was barely there, but there was no denying his mother's voice. "*Where are you?*"

"*Just outside San Antonio.*" Sahara provided. "*I need to get us off the road.*"

Alaric opened his eyes. It was almost dawn. He didn't know how long he'd been out. "I need some sleep," Sahara said aloud.

He nodded. They were probably safe from pursuit by the strike team now that they had crossed two state borders. They could afford to slow down.

He vaguely recalled stopping before the Texas border to drop the dead Shade. It felt wrong, but Sahara had pointed out the difficulty in driving around with a dead body.

Alaric inhaled deeply and focused himself, then reached out for anyone local that might shelter them.

It took far too long, but eventually he felt a response and fed directions to Sahara. A young woman and her elderly father living on the eastern edges of the city could provide them shelter, space to sleep, and food. Her skills were rudimentary, her power small, but she had responded.

A little while later, Sahara parked them outside a small house with a well-kept lawn and roses. The front door opened as they climbed wearily out of the truck. Sahara stayed a step back while Alaric approached the young woman.

He smiled, hoping his gratitude for her help was leaking through. He still wasn't fully in command of his senses, and his ability to form words hadn't returned yet. She gestured into the house, and he stepped past her. He stopped when he reached a living room.

There was an old man in a recliner, reading a newspaper. He looked up. "Always taking in strays," the old man murmured, putting the paper down. He pushed himself to standing and Alaric could feel him accessing the two of them as Sahara caught up. "Reckon you could do with some sleep. Come on."

He shuffled away, leading them down a hallway. "This here room is the guest room. Ma'am, my daughter's room." He pointed at a door across the hall, then he pointed to the next door. "Bathroom end of the hall. Towels in the closet."

The man was more gifted than his daughter, but he was subtle. He clearly knew who they were and when he followed Alaric into the bedroom, he realized the man had an inkling of what they'd been through.

"I'm going to have Barbara bring you some tea."

Alaric started to shake his head, but the old man grabbed his hand. "Medicine. It will help with... that." He waved a hand at Alaric's head. "You drink it. All of it. Then you sleep."

Alaric nodded with a little smile.

"Good." He disappeared out the door. Alaric sank down on the bed and looked around the room. It looked like it had once been a teenager's room, with posters and books and some sort of trophies on the dresser.

It seemed so odd, after the last weeks and months. It was normal. He'd almost forgotten what that was like. It was a few minutes before there was a knock on the door, and the young woman ducked her head as she came into the room with a coffee mug in her hands. "My father said you needed this. Chamomile, rosemary, golden root and water hyssop. My grandmother's recipe."

Alaric took the mug and smelled the concoction. There was more to it than the herbs in it. What she lacked in psychic power, she more than made up in other ways. He nodded appreciatively and she smiled, then left him.

He sipped at the tea, tasting the magic, the energy infused into the mix. It reminded him of a woman he'd only ever known as Aunt Lily. She wasn't his aunt in any relational sense, but she was a staple of his childhood. She too brewed special teas designed to cure whatever was wrong with you. That in turn reminded him of Victoria. It made him wonder how much the tribes had intermixed over the generations.

He settled in, shutting down external input, turning his thoughts and emotions inward as he drank the tea. He sorted through what he could of the detritus of the trauma of Riley's death. His mind had slammed up defenses to keep the damage to a minimum, and it wasn't going to relinquish those controls until he dealt with the damage. Had he not reacted the way he did, there was a very real chance that his mind would have splintered, and it wasn't likely that he would have survived.

Alaric finished the tea and set the mug aside before returning to the cleanup job. Fatigue pulled at him before he was done, but he was already making progress when he lay down on the bed. He hoped that by the time he woke, he'd be able to speak again.

* * *

Sahara was talking to their hostess. There was food ready and just waiting for him. Alaric could read them all as he came awake. He stretched stiff limbs and examined the repair work he had done.

He wasn't a hundred percent, couldn't really feel beyond the house without applying effort. He lay still a moment and tried, reaching out for any sign of Mason or Bryan. He sighed in frustration when all he got was static, but chances were good it wasn't just his limitation.

With Mason hurt, Bryan would keep his attention closed to the tasks at hand. With Mason hurt, he had no spare energy to respond to Alaric's questing.

A thought crept through him that he shoved aside. He'd know if they were dead. He repeated that over and over as he sat up. He would know.

He took the mug and headed out to the kitchen where Sahara and Barbara sat over coffee. Sahara smiled at him. "You look better."

"You too," Alaric said, his voice dry and gravel filled. "News?"

Sahara shook her head. "Nothing but what the papers and TV are saying."

He sat beside her. "What?" As long as he kept to small words he seemed to be doing okay, but he couldn't seem to string many together.

"Same as before. The 8th Battalion is bolstering its eastern border. The Feds are saber rattling. The Southern Coalition is telling both of them to leave them out of it."

Alaric nodded. "Atlanta?"

"I thought you'd want to eat first, maybe spend another day here?" Sahara countered, looking concerned.

"I'm better," Alaric responded.

"*But not healed.*" Sahara said. "*We're safe here.*"

"You are welcome to stay," Barbara said, her hand warm on his. "Y'all seem like you could use the time to recover."

Alaric considered it. "Jordan?"

Sahara nodded. "We've sent word."

He glanced into the living room at the old man. They were safe enough for the moment. He could continue healing, and when he was fully himself, he'd be able to tap into the full gifts of his people to find Mason and Bryan. "Okay. We stay."

Barbara smiled. "I'll get supper on the table."

"Let me help," Sahara said, standing with her.

Alaric sat back in his chair, remembering Mason's face as the mortar came roaring at them. They both would have been far more wounded if Mason hadn't shoved him down and away from the imminent blast. He'd come away with a minor head wound.

Mason, on the other hand… Alaric had felt the bullet, but Mason had pushed him away, distanced him so he had no idea how bad it was. Fear was creeping up on him, fear that was fed by the knowledge that the strike force had been actively looking for Mason, fear that they had finally found him.

"Fear ain't gonna bring them home, son," the old man said, startling him.

"No," Alaric agreed. It was all he had though, fear for Mason and the duty he had to his people.

Sahara put a bowl of potatoes on the table, checking in with him. He nodded for her. She was afraid, too, but she was hiding it better.

He pushed his fear back and focused himself on eating and getting himself back to one hundred percent. The old man was right, fear wasn't going to help him heal or get Mason and Bryan to him any faster.

* * *

It startled him out of a sound sleep, the sudden return of connection. Alaric sat up, throwing his senses out beyond himself, gathering information. He touched in with his mother, assured himself that he and Sahara were still safe.

He scoured through images and thoughts available to him, looking for any sign of Bryan or Mason. He latched onto it when he found it, though the connection was barely functional. It was an image, Bryan coming through a checkpoint.

Alone.

Alaric pulled back, suddenly and breathlessly. Bryan was thin and wearing some stolen suit, passing through the Texas border with a stolen ID.

Alone.

Mason.

Alaric tried to corral the panic that shot through him. He cast out wider, searching for some tremor of Mason's presence. He was sweating and starting to shake when he found Bryan instead. He was waking up, but Alaric broke the connection and climbed out of bed.

He could feel Bryan trying and threw up a wall between them. He didn't want to know anymore. He needed to cling to the idea that Mason was safe somewhere, that they would be reunited.

Bryan was close. He knew it now, and he would be coming. The closer he got, the harder it would be to keep him out, to block his mind.

Alaric paced the confines of the room. Mason was dead. They'd left him there to die.

No. Alaric shook his head and rubbed over his face. He'd known since he'd laid eyes on the Shade that Alaric needed him, not that he knew exactly what that meant.

An image formed in his mind with the taste of a vision: Mason lying in a pool of blood, his hands feeding death into the earth around him. Alaric raced for the bathroom, falling to his knees and vomiting into the toilet.

Sahara was in the doorway when he looked up. "Are you…" She didn't finish. It was obvious he wasn't okay. She helped him up and watched as he splashed water over his face and rinsed his mouth. "Bryan will be here soon," she said.

"I know." Alaric responded. "I…I can't…"

She gathered him in her arms and drew him back to the quiet of his borrowed bedroom. "How can I help?"

He shook his head. "I don't know."

She sat beside him, her arm sliding warmly over his back. For a long time they sat there like that, silent. Alaric focused on the feeling of her hand on his back. If he let it, it would be comforting.

He wasn't sure he wanted comfort.

He felt Bryan long before he was at the door. Sahara left him, went to Bryan in the hallway outside the room. For a long moment, Alaric sat in apprehensive silence, unmoving. The door creaked open and Bryan entered, his presence dripping with sadness.

He held his hand out toward Alaric wordlessly. Words weren't necessary. Alaric stood, turning to face him. Mason's talisman and pendant hung from his hand, blood staining them. Alaric reached for them slowly, his hand closing over them.

Bryan wasn't prepared for Alaric's next move, pulling Bryan in and entering his mind full force, ripping through to find the memory of what had happened that afternoon.

Mason's face, blood on his lips, the weight of his body as Bryan dragged him… The awful truth as Mason revealed how the bullet was killing him, how he was only holding on to give Bryan the cover to get away. The pendants... the final act, seen as Bryan looked back, expecting pursuit. Three, four men fell dead...Bryan running into the night.

Alaric stumbled backwards into the dresser and sliding down until he was on the floor, the tangled pendants in his hand.

Mason Jerah was dead.

He opened his mouth to scream, though there was no sound. The pain rippled out, amplified and burst across every connection he had.

Mason Jerah was dead and as one, Alaric's entire clan knew it.

Dear reader,

We hope you enjoyed reading *In Gathering Shade*. Please take a moment to leave a review, even if it's a short one. Your opinion is important to us.

Discover more books by Natalie J. Case at
https://www.nextchapter.pub/authors/natalie-j-case

Want to know when one of our books is free or discounted? Join the newsletter at http://eepurl.com/bqqB3H

Best regards,
Natalie J. Case and the Next Chapter Team

The story continues in:

Where Shadows Fall

To read the first chapter for free, please head to:
https://www.nextchapter.pub/books/where-shadows-fall

About the Author

Natalie Case was born telling stories, or so she says when asked. Words were her first love and she grew up finding new ways to put words together to tell stories. Known to occasionally commit random acts of poetry, Natalie primarily dabbles in worlds where magic exists, where vampires and shape-shifters share page time with gods and demons and the characters that are born inside her head find themselves struggling in a world made real through the magic of words.

Refusing to be confined to a single genre, Natalie's current works in progress span, and sometimes combine, horror, fantasy, sci-fi and more.

She currently calls the San Francisco Bay Area her home, splitting her time between her day job in the city and writing and photography in Walnut Creek.

In Gathering Shade
ISBN: 978-4-86752-861-7

Published by
Next Chapter
1-60-20 Minami-Otsuka
170-0005 Toshima-Ku, Tokyo
+818035793528
12th August 2021